THE
MORNING
RIVER

W. Michael Gear

FORGE®

A TOM DOHERTY ASSOCIATES BOOK
NEW YORK

This is a work of fiction. All the characters and events portrayed in this book are either products of the author's imagination or are used fictitiously.

THE MORNING RIVER

Copyright © 1996 by W. Michael Gear

Cover art by Karl Bodmer, courtesy of the Joslyn Art Museum, Omaha, Nebraska; gift of the Enron Art Foundation

Maps and interior illustrations by Ellisa Mitchell

A Forge Book
Published by Tom Doherty Associates, Inc.
175 Fifth Avenue
New York, NY 10010

Forge® is a registered trademark of Tom Doherty Associates, Inc.

ISBN: 0-812-55153-2
Library of Congress Card Catalog Number: 96-1409

First edition: July 1996
First mass market edition: May 1997

Printed in the United States of America

0 9 8 7 6 5 4 3 2

ACKNOWLEDGMENTS

The book you now hold would never have made it to your hands without Kathleen O'Neal Gear's constant encouragement. From its original draft in 1985, Kathy always believed in the story and characters. She kept the book alive despite countless rejection letters from all manner of publishers.

Harriet McDougal, our incomparable editor at Tor/Forge, dissected the manuscript with her usual competence. Harriet always pushes us further than we think we can go—but, then, she *is* the best in the business.

Linda Quinton, marketing director at Forge Books, deserves special thanks for her constant support and encouragement. She likes packrats and buffalo, too.

Special appreciation is given to Sierra Adare, our hyperefficient business manager, for all her hard work. Doug Nichols, our ranch manager, had to listen to bits and pieces of the story over coffee in the morning, and was very patient with a writer's odd proclivities. Thanks, Doug.

Finally, special thanks go to Jessie, Berdina, Pancho, and Firedancer for helping to remind me what is really real.

HISTORICAL FOREWORD

I accept as axiomatic that history is nothing more than the official version of the myth. As an anthropologist and historian, I've always been disappointed with historical novels written about the American frontier. Most such novels have consistently rewritten the old myths, and while occasional authors will research white history with great diligence, the Native peoples are usually stereotyped in one way or another.

The Morning River is set in 1825, at a time when white Americans were about to enter the tail end of a three-hundred-year-old North American industry: the fur trade. Lewis and Clark had explored the length of the Missouri River and crossed the Northwest. The Astorians had followed in their wake. Manuel Lisa had outfoxed his competition and placed ephemeral fur-trading posts up and down the Missouri until his death in 1820.

A wealth of goods were flowing along the Missouri, making chiefs rich, upsetting the old social order. Disease followed on the heels of the white traders, rolling up the river in waves, decimating entire villages, weakening established tribes. At this time, too, the Sioux swept westward like Mongols, murdering, stealing, looting, and pillaging all that lay before them.

In 1823, the desperate Arikara fired on William Ashley's expedition, killing several men and goading a military response. Hearing of the army's advance, the Sioux allied with the American military in hopes the joint effort would end in the extermination of the Rees. Instead, the Arikara withstood a bombardment that blew their village apart, and ghosted away in the middle of the night. The Rees were loose, and the Sioux were furious and scornful of anything American. As a consequence, the Missouri was closed to traders until 1825 when Congress sent the Atkinson–O'Fallon expedition to reopen the river.

This, then, is the story of the beginning of the end for the peoples of the Northern Plains.

One of the goals of *The Morning River* and its sequel, *Coyote Summer,* is to give the reader a glimpse of the incredible cultural diversity present in the Northern Plains prior to American acculturation in the mid-nineteenth century. While some traits were shared by most Plains people, each band or tribe had its own stories, social structure, and unique adaptation to the land. Some, like the Pawnee, had stratified, hereditary chieftainships, while others, like the Shoshoni, lived in fluid ethnic bands governed by community consent. The Omaha were patrilineal, the Crow fiercely matrilineal. The Arikara and Arapaho spoke languages more different than English from Persian. Many, like the Sioux and Cheyenne, were newcomers to the Plains, originally corn farmers from the East. This wealth of rich cultural detail has been largely ignored in American fiction.

We have created many myths about the Plains Indians since their final conquest. The truth, as usual, is a little less palatable to modern tastes. The people of the Plains took slaves, murdered women and children, committed genocide on their neighbors, and broke treaties. From archaeological sites, we know that scalping dates back at least five hundred years before the arrival of the Europeans—and the taking of trophy heads more than two thousand. Once the rose-colored glasses of the modern age are doffed, historic Native peoples become curiously *human* in retrospect.

The Morning River and *Coyote Summer* were originally

contained in one manuscript that grew too large to be published as a single volume. A Selected Bibliography is appended at the end of this volume for those who wish to learn more about Native American ethnology or the fur trade era.

CREE

BLACKFEET
(PA'KIANI)

ASSINIBOIN

HIDATSA

ATSINA

MANDAN

Arikara
Village

YANKTONAN S

MOUTH OF THE BIG HORN

CROW
(ANI)

GRAND
DETOUR

DUKURIKA

Willow Captured

TETON SIOUX

Ku Chendikani

Fort
Kiowa

Wah-
Menitus Village

YANKTON S

PONCA

Packrat Killea

OMAHA

Fort
At

PAWNEE

PLATTE
RIVER

KAWS

KANSAS R.

KANSAS

OSA

Morning River

Richard's Journey Westward

Willow's Journey Eastward

Miles 0   100   200   300

C. Mitchell
1992

COYOTE'S PENIS
MOUNTAIN
PA'GOSHOWENER
(Hot Springs)

Big River

SLIM
POLE'S
CAMP

WIND RIVER
MOUNTAINS

WILLOW'S HUSBAND
BURIED

POWDER RIVER
MOUNTAINS

DUKURIKA

WILLOW CAUGHT
BY PACKRAT

Hat River

North

THE
MORNING
RIVER

ONE

Boston—January 1825

A bitter wind drove an angry chop across the gray waters of Boston Harbor. Waves slapped the hoarfrosted hulls of ships snugged against ice-cloaked piers. The gale moaned through the furled rigging, sang in the taut lines, and whispered past the red-brick buildings facing the waterfront. It whipped down the cobblestone streets in eddying gusts that twirled faded bits of paper and soot-speckled snow across patches of dirty ice. The hanging signs swayed and creaked forlornly over firmly latched oaken doors.

Driven by the wind, the terrible chill ate through wraps and woolens until a man's bones ached, and a deep breath seared the lungs. The few courageous pedestrians shivered as they hurried along Boston's slick and winding streets. They scuttled forward, bent into the wind, coats hugged tightly about them, lost in thoughts of warm fireplaces and cheery stoves. Exposed flesh prickled as the relentless blow tore frosty breath from nose or mouth to hustle it away into the gray afternoon.

The freezing wind bulled across the Commons to rattle the paned windows of an imposing house. It surged against the firm brick walls, twisted at the gables, and wormed around the fretwork and trim; but the house stood as solidly as the stout man poised behind the quivering second-story windows.

Like a master at the wheel of his ship, Phillip Hamilton had his feet braced, hands clasped behind him. A black cummerbund graced his thickened waist and snugged the crisp white shirt. A full-cut coat hung from his shoulders. Once so broad, they had bowed with age.

His rough-hewn face looked bulldoggish. The stubby nose might have been mashed onto the thick cheeks. Lines strained the pale skin around his clamped mouth as though he were enduring pain, and hard gray eyes glared out at the world from under grizzled brows. His brown hair was shot through with silver now, and pulled back into a severe ponytail—archaic, given the fashions of the time.

Phillip Hamilton lifted his chin as he caught sight of the figure that rounded a far corner, glanced back and forth, and started irresolutely across the track-dimpled Commons. Against the powdery white background, the young man seemed to be a wavering apparition, hardly human in form. He progressed in halting, uncertain steps, peeking at the house as if he could sense Phillip's hard gaze.

Is there nothing of me in him?

Richard John Charles Hamilton—Phillip Hamilton's only son—shuffled his way through the drifted snow. From Phillip's window he looked as if he were taking an absurd pleasure in the agony of his cold feet and the needling sting on his half-frozen face.

Phillip rocked on his feet, frustration wrapping around his heart. Damn it, just once couldn't the boy act like a man? Walk with pride in his step, head back?

Not when he understands what is about to happen. Surely he must know why I've sent for him.

Phillip snorted, fortifying himself. Dealing with will-o'-the-wisp Richard always agitated him, set his stomach to churning. God's blood, if the boy didn't grovel so, maybe it wouldn't be so tempting to grind him down. A little backbone, that's all it would take.

My fault . . . all my fault.

Richard stamped snow from his feet as he stepped onto Beacon Street. He thrust balled fists deeper into his coat and kicked at a pile of frozen horse manure.

Come on, boy. Let's get it over. It's just as hard for me as it will be for you.

The trees on the Commons formed a black lace of branches, stark against the sullen gray-white sky. Occasional crystals of ice drifted down, dancing in the numbing wind. Richard raised his apprehensive gaze to his father's red-brick house.

Phillip instinctively stepped back into the shadows. To either side of the bulging bay windows hung the Belgian lace curtains Phillip's wife had once delighted in.

Thoughts of her touched that deep-seated callus of anxiety and grief. *I should have been there for Caroline.* His eyes narrowed as he watched the boy. *And for him.*

He'd been at sea when Caroline bore Richard. During the following weeks when her life ebbed slowly out of her body, Phillip had been in Paris, Madrid, and Amsterdam, negotiating the agreements that would make his fortune.

What God gives with one hand, He takes with the other. A triumphant Phillip Hamilton had returned to his house one week to the day after his wife's death. And, there, had encountered the end of his dreams—and an infant son lying in a wet nurse's arms.

Phillip craned his neck to see the street below.

Richard had slowed to a stop in the center of the street, and his thin body erupted in shivers. With a mittened hand, he reached up to brush a loose strand of honey brown hair from his sensitive brown eyes.

Caroline's eyes. You can see so much of her in him. But where is that spark of daring and courage? How could he have so many of her looks, but so little of her spirit?

Richard had received his father's summons that morning. Jeffry, Phillip's household servant, had described the young man crouched by the tiny tin stove in his rented room, co-

cooned in threadbare blankets, studying a new translation of Hegel's *Phenomenology of Mind.*

Phenomenology of mind? What kind of idiocy could *that* be?

Upon sight of Jeffry, the boy had gone pale, his hand trembling as he broke the wax seal and read the note. Phillip's perfectly formed letters stated: *Richard, I need to see you immediately to discuss your situation. A carriage is waiting for you downstairs.*

For long moments Richard had stared glumly through the panes of his little window, the sill delicately mantled with snow.

Jeffry had reported him as saying, "I can't come now. Not now. I—I'm feeling poorly."

In his preoccupation, he had accidentally kicked over the clutter of empty wine and ale bottles amassed along one wall. They had rolled across the slanted floor in a tinkling racket.

"Your father's carriage is downstairs." Jeffry had that cold, precise nature about him. Phillip could imagine him, standing tall, black face as graven as solid walnut.

"I have errands," Richard had stated, and Phillip could imagine the tremor in the young man's voice. "I'll be there as soon as I can. Tell him . . . tell him at one. I'll be there at one."

Jeffry had inclined his head, taken his leave, and reported back. Phillip needn't glance at the old ship's clock to tell that it now lacked fifteen minutes of two. And there the boy stood, shivering in the snow, trying to muster the guts to knock at his father's door.

So, where had the boy been? That student's hideout, no doubt: Fenno's Tavern on Washington Street. Was that it? Did young Richard need a stiff shot of whiskey just to face his father?

I've failed . . . failed miserably. From the shadows behind the lace curtains, Phillip watched his son close his eyes, breath puffing before his thin face. He'd be a handsome young man were there a little color to his cheeks, a little meat to his shoulders and arms. The high brow, the thin nose, both spoke of aristocracy and privilege—of everything

Phillip Hamilton could never have been or had were he not American.

Apparently, Richard nerved himself. One by one he climbed the steps and reached for the ornate knocker on the heavy door.

The hollow sound carried to Phillip's second-story study.

They had fought this same battle many times before. Richard, for all his talk of philosophy, freedom, and natural law, clung desperately to the umbilical cord of Phillip's purse. It seemed that one could not be a philosopher unless one had a wealthy father to support the luxury.

Today, however, Richard's luxury was coming to an end.

Rousseau . . . yes, Rousseau. Richard liked to imagine himself as a man in the state of nature, possessed only of virtue and happiness. What had the boy said that day? Yes . . . "Father, you have embraced all the curses of civilization: property, money, power, greed, and the corruption of the soul that led one man to place another in bondage."

And he'd had the audacity to say that at the very instant that Jeffry was ladling soup into Richard's silver bowl!

"Father, you find no study more fascinating than a ledger page. All you do is hunch at your cherrywood desk, peering at your books by the light of an oil lamp. You call that life? Balancing figures over and over again?"

Yes, boy. Those figures keep your belly full, and buy your books. Or, at least, they have up until now.

The younger Hamilton claimed that civilization had fallen from God's natural grace.

Well, boy, you may have God's grace. Unfortunately, today you'll have to deal with mine.

The heavy door downstairs closed with finality.

Phillip sighed, hitched around on his good leg, and stumped across the ornate parlor. After the death of his wife, Phillip had practically lived here, behind the cherrywood desk, surrounded by his fortress of ledgers. Here he'd made war on the markets with tobacco, rum, slaves, lace, tinware, porcelain, muskets, glassware, tea, and all the other things that ebbed and flowed in the international trade. He'd lost ships and crews to hurricanes, icebergs, pirates, disease, and impressment. He'd battled tariffs, interest, and insurance with the same fiery spirit that he'd once shown the British. Just over there, across the bay at Breed's Hill.

He stepped into the gracious hallway, bracing himself on the handrail as he walked to the head of the stairs. Plush carpets lay underfoot, carried here from the Ottoman Empire. Walnut wainscoting rose to white-plastered walls. The giant brass-mounted ship's clock tick-a-tocked monotonously where it hung next to the oak-banistered stairway that led downstairs. Phillip stopped at the head of the stairs, looking down at the first-floor landing. To the left, a double doorway led into the office where he met with his agents and factors. To the right sat the hall chair with its tall mirrored back, and beyond that the French doors which led into the dining room.

Jeffry stood between Richard and the door, a hand extended as he asked, "May I take your hat and coat, Master Richard?"

Richard pulled off his frost-crusted hat, baring his light brown hair. His shabby black coat hung loosely on his skinny frame. The boy wasn't eating right again; his normally pale complexion looked death-pasty in the dim light.

Jeffry stepped away, bearing his tattered prizes to the cloakroom with stately grace.

"Richard? You're late." Phillip struggled to keep his voice from turning gruff. "I suppose philosophers don't pay much attention to time. One o'clock is just about as good as two, wouldn't you say?"

"Yes, sir. I—I mean . . . no, sir." Richard lowered his eyes.

Damn it, did the boy always have to look like a whipped puppy? "Join me in the study, Richard."

Resigned, Richard climbed, eyes focused on his wet boots. They left droplets on the walnut steps. At the head of the stairs, he sought to muster a smile that died stillborn.

Phillip could hear Richard's nervous breath rasping in his throat as he gestured the boy through the doorway. Phillip hesitated, fingers on the cool oaken door. Richard jumped when the door closed solidly behind them.

Phillip sighed and limped toward his ornately carved desk and its neat piles of papers. The fireplace popped and crack-

led, the brass wood bin beside it half-full. Books covered one wall from floor to ceiling. From the bulging bay window behind Phillip, the Charles River could be seen, ice-choked now, the water pewter in the afternoon light. Two whale-oil-filled glass lamps, one to either side, illuminated the desk. A crimson Persian carpet cushioned the floor. In one corner sat a globe, and behind it, the Charleville musket, powder horn, and bullet pouch Phillip had carried in the Revolution.

Phillip reached the overstuffed French chair and, with effort, lowered himself behind the huge desk. Here he was in his element, everything in place: the quills in their stand; the ink in its well; a solitary copper button he'd ripped from the scarlet jacket of a British officer he'd killed at Breed's Hill; and beside the left-hand lamp, his ledgers. Finally, his wife's heavy leather-bound Bible lay just at the extent of his reach to the right. He sighed before pulling some papers from a stack. Thick fingers pinched his glasses onto his nose.

Richard remained standing. From the way his long fingers crumpled his stained black trousers, panic was fraying the last of his composure.

"Now then," Phillip began. "I have here a list of expenditures accumulated for the last four months at the university. If I do say so, you have already spent more than enough time at Harvard." He glanced up over the rims of his spectacles. "Not to mention money."

Richard wet his lips. "Father, I have more studies. I *must* continue my education!"

"Why, Richard?" Phillip asked woodenly. "I see no progress in your work. I pointedly refer to progress in useful studies . . . those which will prepare you to deal with our modern world. At this point you have all the education required of a gentleman. You know the Classics, speak Latin and Greek as well as French, German, and a smattering of Portuguese. What more does a gentleman need?" Phillip spread his hands. "To what earthly use will you put this 'philosophy' of yours?"

"To become a professor, Father." He knotted his thin white fingers into bony fists.

"A *professor*? When I sent you to the university, it was to learn about the world so that you could take a position here, with me. I can't run the company forever, Richard. You have responsibilities to me, to society. And by that, I mean *American* society. I refuse to treat you like a child any longer." Phillip paused as he picked up a quill and rolled it between his fingers. "Nevertheless, I shan't be accused of denying you a defense. Tell me . . . what have you learned?"

"I—I've learned a lot. I just . . . just don't think you would . . . well . . . understand, sir. That's all."

Phillip tightened the corners of his mouth. "I see. A matter of understanding. Very well, I confess to be a man of open mind. Tell me something of the nature of man. I've heard you use that term. Let me hear it . . . and how it will put bread and meat on your table. Let me hear how it will keep a roof over your head."

Richard took a deep breath and locked his knees to keep from trembling. Did he act this way standing before Professor Ames? Were that the case, they should have thrown him out long ago.

"From . . . from what idea, if any, does the idea of . . . of chains . . . I mean . . ." Richard winced.

"Chains?"

"Rousseau, Father. I—I'm sure you've heard of him. Man was born free and everywhere he is in chains. It's . . . It's because man has fallen from the natural grace and virtue of his creation." The words began to flow. "Once we were all happy, living in a state of innocence. Unlike the scriptures, which blame the downfall of man on an apple, Rousseau blames the first man who enclosed a piece of ground and called it his. From there it was only a matter of time until inequality riddled society. Possessions, property, they are the root of envy and struggle. They condemn us . . . the foundation of tyranny."

Phillip's heart warmed. "You would tell me of tyranny? Your father, who stood at the foot of Breed's Hill?" He thrust a finger toward the old Charleville in the corner. "There, boy, is the only counter to tyranny—and you'll notice it's a 'possession,' the kind you so easily spurn."

"But don't you see? Possessions have separated us from our natural instincts. In the beginning we were concerned with existence. The products of the earth fulfilled our needs—not the products of factories, or . . . or of suppressed labor. To realize our true selves we must return to the land, recover our freedom by rediscovering our natural state. This drive for *things* has corrupted our souls, made us slaves of our society!"

"And I take it you don't approve of our society."

"No, Father, I don't." Richard shifted uneasily. "What have we become? Possessed by the demons of gold, silver, silk, and luxuries! What about your soul, Father? You're as bad as the rest. What about the uplifting investigation of higher ideals?"

"I go to church three times a week."

"I'm not talking about corrupted Anglican values. I mean *true* inquiry into the soul! The discovery of who you really are!"

"And you think philosophy does this?"

"Yes, Father!"

"Boy, I happen to *like* this society we've begun to build. I began as a loyal subject of the Crown. I grumbled about the taxes and the—"

"That has nothing to do with what I'm—"

"Don't you *dare* interrupt an elder!"

Richard winced and swallowed hard.

"I can't believe I'm hearing this from you. By condemning American society—which I have struggled, fought, and bled to build—you're indicting every ideal I hold dear." Phillip threw his quill across the desk and rubbed his forehead. "This civilization you rail against has given you everything, Richard; your philosophy, your music and art. As for your scorn of possessions, I would remind you that you've eaten off the finest china, slept warm in the worst of storms, and enjoyed leisure to pursue your . . . *studies.* Assuming that you really despise such a life, the door is open. You may step out into the street and pursue nature and its benefits to your heart's content."

There, the gauntlet had been cast. Phillip raised an eyebrow. *Come on, boy, show me some backbone. Turn on your heel and stomp out of here.*

"I told you that you wouldn't understand." Richard's expression betrayed a growing panic.

Phillip smacked his desk. "Tarnation! Very well, enlighten me. Where is the flaw in my argument? Hasn't civilization given you everything you now have? If life is so bad—and yes, I've heard about your Rousseau—you can bloody well go live with the savages beyond the frontier! Go, boy, nothing is stopping you!"

"That's nothing more than the Socratic argument, Father. There's more to . . ."

But Phillip had lost the boy's words. *The savages beyond the frontier?* He glanced from the corner of his eye at the carpet bag that sat just to the side of his old musket.

Richard raised his hands, the gesture that of desperation. "We owe something to ourselves, Father. Not just the state. Surely, if you've studied Rousseau, his arguments must have made you think, caused you to reconsider your own role in our hypocritical society. And what about the savages? What right do we have to inflict our society upon theirs? We're ruining them! Turning them into little copies of ourselves in an obscene foundry of civilized ideas. The ones that don't form just right, we break and toss in the rubbish! How can you call *that* morality!"

Phillip's attention had fixed on the heavy grip. He muttered, "Rousseau was a fool, primarily because no one ever shot at him."

Thirty thousand dollars. Enough to outfit an entire brigade for the Santa Fe trade. New Mexico was starved for goods, and they paid in silver. William Becknell had turned a two thousand percent profit. A man could still build a solid foundation in the far Western trade. A fortune could be made with the right Yankee mind at the helm.

"What, sir?"

"Hmm? Oh, nothing." Phillip took a deep breath and nodded to himself. "My son, I can see now that I've made a terrible error."

"Then I can go back to my studies?" Relief began to shine in Richard's large eyes.

"Absolutely not. No, Richard, I've had enough." *The time has come, boy, to correct some of the mistakes.*

Richard blinked hard, then shook his head in disbelief.

Phillip leaned back in his chair, plucked off his spectacles, and rubbed the bridge of his nose. "As of this moment you may either leave this house . . . or take up your duties, and be productive for once in your meaningless life."

"But, I . . . You *can't* do this to me!"

"Why not?"

"Because I'm your *son*! It's your duty! You *owe* it to me!"

"As long as you live out of *my* purse, I can make you do any damn thing I like!"

A choked sound escaped from Richard's throat.

Phillip sighed wearily. "I've made a lot of mistakes in my life, Richard. Many of them in raising you. I had no idea that your studies would take you so far from productive reality. Nevertheless, I shall make amends . . . late though it may be. Boy, the world out there is not an abstraction, not as Messer Rousseau's fanciful treatise would have you believe. It's a very calculating place. One from which I have sheltered you. I'll not have any son of mine while away his life as a professor of philosophy. Your mind has been ruined by these quacks and charlatans."

"They're neither quacks nor—"

"I will not have you perpetuate such absurdities on other susceptible young minds. Instead, Richard, you will assume the responsibilities that I have too long allowed you to avoid. That is all! The final word! So long as you live on my money, you are not going back to the university. Is that clear?''

In a futile attempt to save himself some dignity, Richard looked up. ''You don't understand.''

''I'll send Jeffry over to Cambridge for your things. What's this? I'll not brook that pouting face. You look like a scolded little boy. You're twenty-two years old, for God's sake, and you can damned well act it! We'll talk more tonight at dinner. I have some arrangements to see to . . . some friends I must discuss this with.'' Phillip cocked his eyebrow again. ''Or, you could just walk out that door downstairs and take responsibility for yourself.''

Richard gaped in stunned disbelief. ''Responsibility . . . for myself?''

Phillip's heart sank. ''You may go. You'll find your room the way you left it. Jeffry will call you to supper. Please, make yourself presentable for the table.''

Richard slipped through the doorway as quietly as possible. Phillip slumped in the overstuffed chair. Was this the right thing? He reached behind him and pulled the bell cord.

Within moments, Jeffry answered the tinkling summons, opened the door, and crossed the carpet to stand before the desk. Jeffry stood over six feet, whip-thin, posture as unforgiving as a ramrod's. His cropped hair had silvered, adding to his distinguished look. The white silk scarf at his throat contrasted with his dark-hued skin.

Phillip stared at the desktop. ''I've cut off his money. I would like you to go over to that hovel he's been living in and clean it out. He won't be going back.''

''Yes, sir.'' Jeffry studied him neutrally.

''Can you believe it? Twenty-two years old, and I sent him to his room! I've failed him, Jeffry. I'm not sure how, or what I could have done differently, but I failed him.''

''He's young, sir.''

Phillip glanced up wearily. ''At his age, I was lying in a hospital, biting on a bullet while the surgeon tried to make up his mind whether or not to cut off my leg. Fortunately, they were so busy with dying men I lay forgotten for a couple of days. Jeffry, I'm thinking, thinking of sending him west . . . to Saint Louis.''

"With the banknotes, sir?"

Phillip stared into the past, seeing his wife's face, strong, beautiful. He could almost feel her cool hand against his cheek as she told him it was all right to leave, to take a year and sail to the major markets to set up accounts. That risks could be taken, that she'd be waiting when he returned . . .

"Yes, Jeffry. He's got to learn to be a man. We didn't fight and die to make a nation of children. Imagine. He's twenty-two . . . and doesn't even own a rifle! A Massachusetts man without a rifle!"

Phillip reached over and laid his hand on the leather-bound Bible that rested on his desk like a silent guardian. *Isn't there* anything *of me in him?*

TWO

◊

Mankind are so much the same, in all times and places, that history informs us of nothing new or strange in this particular. Its chief use is only to discover the constant and universal principles of human nature, by showing men in all varieties of circumstances and situations, and furnishing us with materials from which we may form our observations and become acquainted with the regular springs of human action and behavior.

—David Hume, *Of Liberty and Necessity*

Her name was Heals Like A Willow. She stood shivering, rubbing her half-frozen hands while the wind blew snow down over the cracked sandstone caprock. Misty white flakes swirled around her in a mocking dance. The tiny crystals pattered on her cold face and dusted the buffalo robe wrapped tightly around her.

Her true people were the *Dukurika,* the Sheepeaters of the high mountains. The husband she was in the process of burying had been a man of the *Ku'chendikani,* the Buffalo-eaters who traveled from basin to basin on horseback, hunting bison, fishing the rivers, and ambushing the elk. She had fallen prey to his flashing smile and warm humor. In the years since leaving her father's lodge, she had lived like the red-tailed hawk, rising high during times of plenty, only to plummet during those of hunger and warfare. Even in the direst of days, her husband had kept her happy with his reassuring smile and the twinkle in his dark eyes.

With the birth of their son, their souls had grown together like tangled vines of nightshade. How much of herself had been torn away by death?

You can't afford to feel. Not yet. Soon, she would. Life, by its very nature, would force her to find out how deeply that wound ran.

Save that for the eternity stretching before her. *Just live now. Finish this last responsibility.*

She braced herself awkwardly on the steep slope. Here, just under the rimrock, the footing was treacherous. Above her the red sandstone rose in a sheer face, the surface rounded by eons of wind and storm. Each step had to be placed with care. Snow had drifted in around the angular rocks that had tumbled down the slope. Old drifts, newly mantled, had crusted hard, broken here and there by branches of sage and bitterbrush, and chunky red stone. When she found a rock the right size, she kicked at it to break the frost's stubborn hold. When it finally broke free, she picked it up with mittened hands and stared upward at the long crack in the caprock. Most of the crevice had been carefully rocked in. Only one last hole remained, black and gaping—like the wound in her souls.

She retraced her steps back through the wind-driven snow and studied the rocked-up crevice. Stretching, straining, she grunted as the stone wavered in her grip. As if for once *Tam Apo* favored her, she slipped it into place, arms trembling from the effort. She teetered for a moment, caught her balance, and sighed as she rubbed her stained mittens on the heavy buffalo robe she wore.

"That is the last. Rest well, my loved ones."

The numbness lay heavily upon her souls, unbreachable even by tears. As she stared at the dull red cliff, small flakes of snow chased angrily past her and the wind ripped at tendrils of hair pulled loose from the hood of her buffalo coat. Above the red cliff the sky brooded with heavy clouds and the continued threat of snow.

How did I have the strength to do this? Images, dreamlike, spun through her head.

She had needed a juniper branch to wedge her husband's frozen body into the narrow crevice. Her son, so much smaller, had been laid in the packrat-tracked dust at his feet. She'd sung the prayers then, calling on *Tam Apo,* "Our Father," the Creator, then upon Wolf, who had helped to fashion the world after the Creation. She'd pleaded that they would receive and cherish her loved ones, and that they would show them the trail to the Milky Way, the Backbone of the World, and hence to the Land of the Dead.

Such prayers had to be sung to ensure that her loved ones would not lose their way on the journey across the sky. Should they do so, they might return to *Tam Sogobia,* "Our Mother," the earth. *Mugwa,* ghosts who lost their way, no matter what their nature in life, harassed the living by appearing as whirlwinds and shooting sickness into people.

She raised her eyes to the bitter sky, masked by sullen gray clouds. Snow blew down upon her, but she sang the mourning song again, fingers knotting in the thick leather of her mittens. The dead could find their way through clouds, couldn't they? *Storms don't matter,* she reassured herself.

Willow closed her eyes against the sting of the wind. Enough trouble was loose on the land.

They stared at her from the hollows of her memory: her husband's face, so strong and serious, trusting her to cure him; her little son, his round face sunken, his black eyes bright with fever.

I failed you . . . both of you. Traitorous muscles sent shivers through her. She opened her eyes as the wind battered her robe, and studied the patterns of rock where she'd walled their corpses in. Her soul's eye could see into the darkness where they lay. Her husband's face had looked unnaturally pale, a juniper-bark mat covering his eyes and a leather band around his mouth. To meet the gaze of the dead was to summon one's own death at best, and to court possession by evil at worst. Terrible things could issue from a dead man's mouth: corruption, disease, or soul loss.

The injustice of it goaded her, and for a moment she glared upward into the stormy sky, angered that *Tam Apo* could have created a world where such a loving and kind man as her husband could become so threatening after death.

It's not him. He's gone. His souls are searching the way to the afterlife and its rewards. She turned her attention back to the rocked-up crevice; snow had begun to settle in the niches and hollows. They had planned so many things together. His eyes had sparkled as he played with their son. She had imagined them together, snug in warm winter lodges, walking arm in arm through green high-country meadows in summer, slicing hot meat from his kill on a frosty fall morning.

Together, they would have watched their son take his first step. Hand in hand, they would have seen him earn his boyhood name. She would have smiled to herself as her husband taught the boy the intricacies of stoneworking, arrow making, and the rituals all hunters must know. And later, she would have marveled at her boy's first kill, that critical step toward manhood.

Gone now, all of it.

There, behind that stack of wedged rock, lay the empty death of dreams.

I didn't have the puha *to save them. I couldn't send my soul into the Land of the Dead to bring them back.* But then, such things were *omaihen,* forbidden to a woman. Only the greatest of *puhagan,* the most powerful of medicine men, had that kind of *puha.* Such power was never granted to a woman.

She lowered herself, back braced against the cold stone, and stared off across the valley. White wraiths of snow danced like capering ghosts, twirled by the wind as they settled onto the rounded junipers and the rangy limber pine dotting the slopes below. Sagebrush stippled the snow-choked canyon bottom, barely visible in the haze of flakes.

Willow closed her eyes, bowing her head into her hands, while the storm blew down around her.

Richard dreamed . . .

He sat with his friends in Fenno's Tavern. Soft candlelight and sounds of revelry surrounded them as they leaned eagerly across the scarred table. Over foaming mugs of ale, they had been discussing morality, Professor Ames smiling benevolently as his students dissected the intricacies of proscribed behavior.

But something wasn't quite right. Professor Ames kept looking at Richard, a sadness behind his smile. "You do understand, don't you, Richard?"

I do, sir. I really do.

A soft rapping intruded, and finally brought Richard back from his dreams. He blinked awake, stared around the dimly lit room, and sat up. The knock came again as he unwrapped the twisted blanket. Home, his father's house . . .

"Yes?"

The door opened wide enough to admit Jeffry's dark face. "Master Richard, dinner is served."

"I . . . I'll be right there." His breath could be seen against the slit of light cast by the door.

"Very well, sir."

Richard rubbed his eyes. The door closed with a click. He groped about in the dark until he found the washstand. Jeffry, efficient as God Himself when it came to Phillip's business, had filled the white porcelain pitcher. Richard poured the washbowl full, gasping at the water's biting cold.

Unwilling to face himself in the mirror, he stared at the whitewashed wall as he combed his hair.

Philosopher, he thought. *Some Socrates I am.*

On rubbery knees he went down the stairs, and bit his lip to nerve himself before opening the double doors. His appetite dissolved as he quietly entered the dining room.

Phillip sat at the head of the big table. Oil lamps cast a warm yellow light over the high-ceilinged room. The portrait of Richard's mother stared beneficently down from one wall, her brown eyes doe-soft, the faintest of smiles on her innocent face.

He considered the painting for a moment, briefly imagining Laura Templeton's face superimposed on the image, then chastised himself for blasphemy.

The table had been set with white linens and lustrous silver. Lamplight gleamed on the fine china, and reflected from the salt-glazed mugs. A single high-backed chair had been placed at the far end of the table for Richard. The other chairs stood in a forlorn line against the white-plastered wall. Behind Phillip's seat the sideboard squatted on stubby, curved legs, basking in mahogany glory, displaying ceramic ware.

Sally, the family cook, promptly appeared through the kitchen door, aproned for duty as she carried a porcelain tureen. She was in her late fifties, broad of hip, with her hair wrapped in white cloth. Her black face remained expressionless while she went about her duties. Though a free woman, she kept a room in the cellar as did Jeffry and Bit, the household tweeny.

"Richard, you're late." Phillip's gruff voice echoed in the room.

Late! Late! Late! It's always something, isn't it? Richard took his chair and unfolded the napkin, eyes on his plate.

"For God's sake, Richard, look at me." Phillip shook his bulldog head and muttered, "Lord God, I've raised a rabbit." Then, louder, "It is unbecoming of a man to pout. You're acting like a child."

"If you say so, sir."

"You are not a prisoner here, Richard. I just want you to begin to manage your life as an adult. A whole world lies

beyond the door—beyond Boston. You've got to live in it
. . . deal with it. You can't spend your entire life isolated
behind a redoubt of philosophy books. Reality has a nasty
habit of creeping into a man's affairs. When that happens,
you're going to have to know how to deal with it . . . and,
I dare say, your philosophy hasn't given you those skills."

Silence.

"Do you hear me?"

"Yes, sir."

"I'm not punishing you." Phillip ignored Jeffry, who began ladling soup while Sally returned to the kitchen for another dish.

"Then why won't you let me go back to my studies?"

Phillip filled his spoon. "I have other business for you
now."

Images of moldy ledger books formed in the depths of
Richard's mind. He could picture himself bent over the
pages, squinting in the candlelight as he entered endless columns of debits and credits with a dripping quill.

Phillip waggled his spoon. "I've given thought to our
earlier conversation. It has become startlingly clear to me
that you have no understanding of the world. Therefore,
travel is to be recommended."

Richard straightened. Europe? Oxford, or the Sorbonne,
or Salamanca perhaps! Europe literally burst at the seams
with cultured people. If only he could get to Königsberg!
He imagined himself in the German states, walking in the
steps of Immanuel Kant, or even studying with Georg Wilhelm Friedrich Hegel himself.

With a slow smile, his father said, "I thought you'd understand the advantages. You see, Richard, your universe
has been limited to this house, this city, and the university.
A wide continent stretches out to the west of us. That untamed land is your future. There you should be able to see
for yourself how this nonsensical philosophy of yours stands
up against the travails of life."

Wide continent? Untamed land? *The frontier?* "Oh, my
God," Richard whispered. He stared at Phillip in disbelief.
"Father, you can't mean . . ."

"Oh come now, son. It will be the best thing that could

happen to you. Think of the excitement! To see new lands—virgin country! If only I were younger—and hadn't stopped that damned English ball. How I wish I could step into your shoes.''

He longs for it! Crazy old fool. "You may step into my shoes any time, Father. I'd never try and dissuade you from seeing the wilderness." *And God willing, a bear will eat you and I can live happily ever after.*

Phillip sipped the last of his soup and patted his lips with his napkin. "Were I a philosopher, I would look forward to it. The frontier should be a proving ground for that philosophy of yours, hmm? I don't see enthusiasm in your eyes. Very well, I'll make you a bargain. If you still hold with your ideals after another couple of years, well and fine, you may return to that ridiculous university and study whatever you like."

"I'm *not* going to the frontier."

"I need a package delivered to a man in Saint Louis. You'll be carrying a substantial amount of money—and I have no one else to entrust it to. Let us call it a gamble, Richard. You are my son . . . and you must have something of your mother and myself in you."

Mother, yes. You . . . never.

Sally had delivered the main course, steaming carved turkey on a platter. Jeffry held it efficiently at Phillip's side as he served himself.

Phillip's sober gaze didn't waver. "I'm making the gamble that when push comes to shove, you'll not denigrate a serious responsibility. Isn't that one of your precious philosophical concepts? Responsibility? Morality? The fulfillment of obligations? Or did I miss something in my reading of Plato?"

Richard glared hotly down the table.

Phillip took a turkey leg from the platter Jeffry offered, adding, "On the other hand, if you succeed, you shall have learned something about yourself and, I hope, the world in which you live. Perhaps you'll come home acting like a man."

"I *am* a man."

"I'd phrase it thus: You've reached your majority, Richard.'' Phillip smiled wearily. ''You can walk out of this house and do any damn thing you wish, whenever you wish. Patrick Bonnisen needs dockhands at this very moment.''

Richard helped himself silently to some breast meat.

''Ah, I see. You would call yourself a man—and assume the privileges—but only as long as I hand you the money.''

''You are a monster, Father.''

''No, my son. Not a monster . . . only a failure as a father. Would that your mother had lived. Perhaps she could have foreseen this. I never had any intention of raising a weakling.''

''What do you know of strength?'' Richard gestured with his fork. ''I have strengths of conviction. A morality of right and wrong. A morality grounded in being a *free* man!''

''As free as the dollars in your father's purse, eh, Richard?'' Phillip sank his teeth into the juicy meat. ''Today is Friday. You'll leave on Monday for Saint Louis. You are to carry my package and partnership papers. They are to be delivered to a Mr. James Blackman of Saint Louis. Mr. Blackman will sign and seal the documents, which you will then return to me along with a receipt. Blackman will buy up silver from the Santa Fe trade, and ship it to my agents in Philadelphia.''

''You don't really expect me to—''

''I *don't* think I must belabor the value of thirty thousand dollars. Or does that sum mean anything to a philosopher?''

Richard's teeth ground angrily. His father planned to invest thirty thousand dollars on some mad fur-trading expedition; yet he begrudged his only son a few hundred a year for his education?

''How do you know that I won't just run off with it?'' Richard asked suddenly.

''Oh, I'm quite sure, Richard. You claim to be a moral man.'' Phillip looked positively predatory as he smiled. ''Given your penchant for what you regard as moral, I offer you a challenge. Go ahead. *Take it!* I dare you.'' He paused. ''Or have all those long hours you've spent lecturing me on morality been for naught?''

Richard lifted a skeptical eyebrow.

''You don't have the slightest idea, do you?'' The old

man's eyes gleamed. "You see, Richard, you would prove
my point that your love of philosophy is so much rhetoric.
True, I'd be out most of the year's profit—but you'd never
close your eyes again without seeing my smirking, triumphant smile."

Richard's fork clattered on his plate as he threw it down.
He kicked his chair back so violently it tottered, before settling on all four legs again.

"I'm not hungry." He turned, stalking from the room.

Phillip dropped the last bone onto his plate and dabbed
at his lips with a napkin. "What do you think?"

Jeffry, face thoughtful, stared at the doorway through
which Richard had bolted.

"He will attempt to deliver the package to Saint Louis,
sir."

Phillip hung his head, exhaling wearily. "You think I'm
wrong, don't you?"

"It's a dangerous trip, sir."

Phillip nodded, staring dismally at the scraps in his plate.
"Sometimes risks must be taken. God gives us no guaran-
tees, Jeffry. We both know that, don't we?"

"Yes, sir."

"But if anything happens to that boy . . ."

"He'll make it."

Phillip raised his tired eyes to meet Jeffry's masked gaze.
"What makes you so sure?"

"He's your son, sir."

Phillip chuckled. It sounded like hollow bones rattling in
a desiccated barrel.

THREE

Cold this numbing was unusual in Saint Louis. Travis Hartman had survived worse—but that had been up in the mountains, far to the west, at the birthing place of the rivers, where the peaks rose in ragged white majesty against skies of crystalline blue. The cold felt different up there in the Shining Mountains—a crispness that bit at the skin. This wet flatland cold in Saint Louis sucked at a man's heat like swarms of hungry flies.

Hartman led his horse along the frozen street. Snow twirled out of the night sky in endless masses of fluffy flakes and crunched under his tripled moccasins. The footing was uneven, ruts had cut the now-frozen mud, and the snow hid treacherous ice. Even the brick-hard piles of horse manure could turn a foot and sprain an ankle.

To either side, squat buildings hunched against the storm. Here and there yellow squares of windows shone with candle or lamplight that gave the swirling snow a golden glow. Odors of smoke, manure, and refuse mingled in the biting air. Despite the cold, dogs trotted past in packs, shivering, snow-backed, pausing only to sniff distrustfully at him and the horse before vanishing into the night. No one else seemed to have any desire to brave the cold and snow.

Main Street, so the joke went, was the only navigable watercourse in town for larger craft, while streets like Walnut and Olive would serve for pirogues and bateaux. To accent the point, Hartman's foot slipped on snow-covered ice and he caught himself at the last instant, startling his horse.

"Easy there, Shelt. Whoa, old hoss." A mittened pat on the neck reassured the sorrel gelding. "Weather like this, I otta be ridin' a mule." He paused. " 'Course, no mule would be silly enough ter be out hyar, neither."

He wore a heavy buffalo coat, snow-caked now, with a soft beaver-hide cap covering his long gray-white hair. A ragged woolen scarf was wrapped about his neck under the frozen beard. Once the scarf might have been red; years of grime had turned it a shiny gray. In one mittened hand he carried a heavy half-stocked Hawken rifle. His powder horn, possible sack, and bullet pouch hung over his shoulder. What looked like black leather pants had begun life as honey brown buckskin—the finest Crow workmanship, smoked to pungent perfection. Over the months, soot, grease, blood, mud, sweat, and all manner of things had stained the leather to its dark sheen.

Hartman looked up into the dark snowfall. He'd had enough of cold and snow during the last two months, while Saint Louis had been his destination. Well, tired and hungry, he'd finally arrived.

He didn't like cities much, although Saint Louis was better than most he'd set foot in. Too many strangers. People who didn't know him always stared. Sometimes the ones who knew the story stared, too. It bothered a man, seeing them start, then flinch at the sight of his face. Even Saint Louis was wearing thin; each time he came here, the city had changed. New buildings had been raised. More people, dressed like Easterners, flocked the streets. Some damn jackass in the legislature would have proposed a batch of new laws—and the other jackasses would have passed them. Hell, who knew, it might be that a man would get his arse arrested for spitting in the same streets he'd been spitting in for years. Cities always brought him trouble. Yet here he was plodding down the morass of Main Street.

He puffed out a frosty breath and squinted through the falling flakes.

Then he saw his destination. It stood proudly on the corner of Oak and Main, rising like a telltale castle of old. The Missouri Hotel, built of stone, four stories tall, with high gabled windows. Six years old now, it hadn't changed. The first state legislature had sat there in 1820. Made a man feel right important just to see it. And, of course, Travis had special memories of the place. Three years back he'd been thrown out the back door after trying to gut some Yankee son of a bitch who dared to refer to Manuel Lisa as a greasy cheating Spaniard.

Now he walked up to the double doors under their sunburst fanlight and tied his snow-dusted horse off on the hitching post. He reached for the door, then remembered that he'd reentered civilization and batted the white crust of snow from his head and shoulders. The ice in his beard would just have to take care of itself.

In reassuring tones, he said, "You mind yerself, Shelt. Won't be long. Injuns won't be trying ter sneak ye off."

Hartman stomped the snow off his feet, climbed the steps, and opened the door to the small lobby. The warm air carried scents of tobacco, oil lamps, and fabric. A flowery carpet didn't hide the squeak in the wooden floor as he strode to face the primly dressed man who sat behind the wooden fortification of a desk. The fellow looked up, one eyebrow raising. Then came the familiar reaction: startled horror. From the expression on his smooth-shaved face, Travis could guess him for a newcomer to the city. A Yankee Doodle, certain sure.

"Might . . . might I help you, sir?"

"Reckon ye might." Travis pinned the man with his hard blue eyes. "I'm a-looking fer Dave Green. Got word he wanted ter see me. Name's Hartman. Travis Hartman."

The clerk nodded slowly. "I'll inform him of your arrival, sir. A moment please."

Hartman waited while the Doodle slipped from his warren and paced hurriedly for the tavern. A soft chuckle escaped

Hartman's thin lips. *What does that little dandy think? I'm here to scalp him?*

As he waited, Travis inspected the lamps on their high shelves, the upholstered chairs, and the porcelain spittoons. He craned his neck to see the big ledger book resting on the counter, and mentally growled at the senseless black scratchings. Water had begun to drip from his beard, and he pulled back before he made a mess on the paper.

"I'll be damned!" the bluff voice called. Dave Green, smile splitting his wide face, walked forward with a hand outstretched. Familiar blue eyes took in Hartman's soaked garb and mud-stained moccasins. "You just arrived?"

Hartman pulled his mitten off and took Green's hand, engaging in the old game of testing his grip. "Been nigh on four years? Five?"

"Five." Green said, the warmth of the smile growing. "Been missing you, old coon."

Hartman fingered Green's heavy cloth coat and poked a callused finger at the ruffled white silk scarf. "What's all this foofawraw? They done made a Doodle out of ye?"

Green chuckled. "Price of success."

As Hartman took in Green's shiny black boots, the slim trousers and white shirt, the clerk slipped into his warren, still eyeing Hartman nervously.

Green cocked his head, the angle making his broad face seem broader. "Had anything to eat?"

"Not since noon."

"Come on. I think the kitchen can produce something that will fill your hole."

Following Green down the hallway, Hartman found himself in the dining room, the white-plastered walls supporting a wooden ceiling. Long tables and chairs of various shapes and styles—all of local manufacture—crowded the floor. Travis leaned his rifle in a corner before shucking his coat and scarf. He took a seat self-consciously, relieved that the lamps cast only dim light.

Green spoke to one of the servants and then took a chair opposite Hartman's. He grinned and rubbed the end of his thick nose. The light glinted in his blond hair. "You don't look much better than the last time I saw you."

Travis fingered the scars crisscrossing his face. "I'd look a sight worse if'n ye'd not taken care of me, Dave. Ye were a damned fool risking yer scalp that way." Hartman smiled, aware of what the action did to his face. "But this child's plumb grateful ye did."

Hartman didn't look up as the plate slid in front of him. The server retreated rapidly. Hartman glanced up to see the woman wincing. At that, he became aware of his sweat-stained buckskins. "Reckon I'm a hair ripe. Winter's not the time fer bathing. Not in cold like this."

Green waved it away. "Get yourself a bath tomorrow."

Travis reached for the hot roast pork on his plate, caught himself halfway there, and picked up the fork, grinning. "Reckon it's been a while since I had the hang of a God-honest eating tool a'sides me knife."

"How have you been?" Green asked, dropping his voice. "You still got hair under that hat, or have the Blackfeet taken your topknot?"

"Still got hair." Hartman attacked the steaming meat, washing it down with strong ale from a tin mug. As the plate emptied, Green motioned for more. They sat in easy silence as only old friends can do.

Three plates later, Hartman pushed the dish back and belched long and loud. "Good fixings, I dare say." He glanced at Green over the rim of his mug. "I was settling down ter a pleasant winter by the fire, doing a mite of hunting, and swapping lies at Pratte's post. Got word there that you wanted ter see me in Saint Louis. Cal Cummings run me down."

"How is old Cal?"

"Notional. Like always."

Green tapped his blunt chin with a finger. "I thought about him. Thought about old John Tyler, too. Both good men. But I think I need you, Travis."

Hartman waited, watching the little muscles around Green's mouth tighten.

Green took a swallow of ale. "I did well in the Santa Fe trade. Made enough to outfit a boat. I took a big chance and bought a pile of trade goods. Invested everything I had."

"And just where are ye planning on doing this trade, Dave?"

Green rocked his tilted mug on the dark wood of the table top. "Mouth of the Big Horn. Remember Lisa's old Fort Raymond? The same place. I want to corner the Crow trade."

Hartman leaned forward. "Pilcher tried that. Built Fort Benton. Remember what happened to Immel and Jones? Bug's Boys—the Blackfoot—done shut that country off to Americans."

"I think we can handle the Blackfeet." Green grinned. "The Crow are mostly cut off since Lisa's death. They'd have a stake in helping us keep shy of Blackfeet."

Hartman stared into the frothy head on his ale. "I'll be plumb damned. Just how much did ye make off'n Santy Fee?"

"Between you and me . . . about eighteen thousand dollars. That's in silver, too. Not banknotes. If I play this right, Travis, I can control the Crow trade." Green pointed his finger. "Time's going to run out on the Blackfeet. Everyone on earth hates them."

"'Cept the British."

"Who in hell are the British? No, you listen, old friend. The country's changing. I know the Crow. Good people. We get them the guns, give them a fair price for their furs, and they'll help us whip the Blackfeet. Name a tribe up the Missouri that would ally with the Blackfeet when they—"

"Atsinas."

"—could take an opportunity to . . . Atsinas? They're not that tight with Bug's Boys, are they? Myself, I just think the Atsina ally with the Blackfeet because no one else likes them. The Arapaho are related—and *they* don't even like them. Besides, I think a little influence in the right place with the Arapaho could split 'em away."

Hartman twisted callused fingers into his beard and tugged thoughtfully.

Green waved his hand. "Travis, twenty years ago folks thought Tecumseh and his Shawnee couldn't be whipped. Twenty years from now, people will look back on the Blackfeet the same way. As the Blackfeet are whittled away, I can help my Crow move right into those prime beaver lands. And that's just the beginning. We can expand our posts. Place one at the bend of the Yellowstone where it runs out of the mountains. Another up the Big Horn at the Hot Springs. And still another at the Three Forks. In thirty years I expect to control all the trade in the upper Yellowstone.''

Hartman chuckled. ''If you don't take all Hob.''

''Manuel Lisa taught me well. Reach for those things most men think lie just beyond their grasp. Act while they're still trying to make up their minds. Be there by the time they finally get started.''

''Don't have ter remind ye that Manuel Lisa died young, do I?''

Green ran a hand over his hair. ''I've promised myself that I'm going to die sitting by a big roaring fire smack dab in the middle of my post. And when that day finally comes, I'm going to be the *only* trader on the upper rivers.''

Hartman slapped the table. ''By God, ye just might at that. Is that why ye sent fer me?''

''I want you with me, Travis. I'm going to need a strong right hand, a hunter and scout. You know the river as well as any man alive. You lived with the Crow—married that girl. You can talk Mandan, Crow, and some Sioux, Ree, and Pawnee. You can sign-talk as if you were a born Injun. They respect you, Travis. You got yourself special medicine, grizzly medicine.'' Green stared soberly into Travis's eyes. ''I've staked everything I've got on this. I'm calling in my debt.''

Hartman sucked at his lips for a moment and grunted. ''Ye don't have ter call in no debt. I reckon I'll throw my stick in with yers just ter see how it all plays out.'' He paused. ''I'll be stitched. Young Davey Green, a rich booshway. Got hisself a boat cram full of trade goods, a title, and government permit all set ter—''

''That's the other thing.''

''What other thing?''

''The other reason I need you.''

Hartman raised an eyebrow.

Green shrugged. ''You see . . . well, it's the permit. Clark won't issue me a trading permit. I'm still working on it but it's Ashley, Pratte, Chouteau, and the others. You know the politics, the wealth that can be made. I intend on having a share, seeing this thing through. I may have to get my boat, cargo, and men upriver—illegally.''

"Now that, old hoss, is going ter take a mite of doing.''

Green smiled grimly. "That's why I need you. I think I know how we can do it . . . but I must have someone I can trust with me.''

The bitter night air bit into Richard's bones as he walked past darkened shops. Countless feet had packed the snow on the walk into a treacherous ice. His breath puffed around him like a personal fog.

The invitation from Will Templeton had come that afternoon; a reception, in his honor, was being held that evening. All of his friends would be there, and he couldn't stand the thought of facing them. Better to take to the streets and avoid such an inquisition.

Yes, much better this way, he assured himself. He was leaving Boston on Monday. By the time he returned from distant Saint Louis, it would be late summer, and everyone would have forgotten the reception—and the fact that the guest of honor hadn't been there.

"Richard!" a voice cried from a carriage clattering down Union Street. He turned to see the cab slow to a stop and Will Templeton lean out, gesturing. "Come on! I've been searching high and low for you. You didn't forget our party, did you?''

With a sinking sensation, Richard swallowed his pride and climbed up to sit on the cold leather seat next to Templeton. Templeton wore a dapper silk cloak, a heavy black wool coat, a muffler, and black felt hat. His face had that elongated, half-starved look of English nobility. The nose was long and straight, slightly rounded on the tip. Black hair curled out from beneath the hat to accent the dancing gleam of charming eyes.

"Everyone is waiting for you. Where have you been?''

"Last-minute errands. You understand, I'm sure." He smiled wanly. "I was just on my way—"

"Splendid!"

"—and dreadfully sorry to be late."

"Oh, Richard, it should be an exciting evening. Professor Ames arrived at the last minute. We just couldn't let you charge off to the wilderness without an appropriate send-off." Templeton tipped his new beaver hat and knocked on the wall to signal the driver. The carriage rocked and began rattling along the icy streets. They proceeded down Hanover to Tremont, then south on Common Street toward the Templeton home.

Dear Lord God, how am I going to stand this? They all know. Richard shot a glance at his companion. Of all his friends, Templeton consistently proved the most reliable—despite being the son of a ship's captain who'd reportedly had mixed allegiances during the Revolution.

Will glanced at him. "There is something I don't understand. Why is he sending you, Richard? I thought you and your father didn't agree."

"Oh, but we do! We agree that we don't like each other. But . . . well, you see, there's no one else he can trust on this matter. I'm surprised he trusts me." As if he did—but the lie eased Richard's soul.

"From the tone in your voice, Richard, I dare say there's more to it."

Damn you, Will. You always see through things, don't you? Richard forced a smile. "He doesn't believe that my philosophical tenets will allow me to deal with the real world. So, it's a sort of, well, challenge between us."

Templeton exhaled, watching his frosty breath swirl about the interior of the coach. "After having met your father, that really doesn't surprise me. Tell me more of this challenge . . . and how your superior mind will rise above it."

"I have to deliver a package to a Santa Fe trader and his illiterate associates—clear out there in the wilderness."

"Smashing!" Templeton laughed. "Just like the prophets of old. How splendid! I almost wish I could go with you. Richard, it will be an adventure. Think, man, you will have the ability to prove yourself superior to the elements and the ruffians. Why, it wouldn't surprise me if you owned the West after having been there for three weeks. Daniel Boone, Meriwether Lewis, and *Richard Hamilton!*''

Hardly the analogy Richard would have chosen. To be ranked with frontiersmen? Men little better than the savages they consorted with? He laughed bitterly, watching the passing lights as the coach bumped over the ruts and swayed on its leather suspenders.

''Perhaps.'' Richard gestured with his pipe. ''Instead of dealing with the world of perception, I will deal with the world of observation. Keeping Kant's beliefs in mind, of course, I shall investigate Rousseau's hypotheses of man in nature. I shall be able to observe man in his true state. Unsullied by the corruptions of our civilization. Wild Indians walk the streets in Saint Louis. Think of the comparisons that a trained mind can draw between the savages and the vanguards of our civilization.''

Will held up a hand in warning. ''Beware, my friend, that you yourself do not fall victim to the primitives.''

''I shall be a fortress!'' Richard clenched his gloved fist. ''Give me your barbarian masses, Will. Let's see what they can do to a man of character and education.''

''Bravo!'' Will applauded. ''Here I sit—with a warrior! Hail, conqueror of ignorance, savagery, and darkness! But ho, we have arrived at our destination.''

Will tossed a coin up to the driver before slapping Richard on the back.

The Templeton house was a huge three-story affair, built of brick, with a high-pitched slate roof. Elaborate white lintels graced the windows, each charmingly illuminated by a candle on the sill. The steps were of Vermont granite, the giant front door imported from Paris.

Once inside, a black servant took Richard's hat, coat, and scarf. The hallway was warm, lit by glowing lamps. A stairway of polished walnut rose to the upper stories. To the right, voices carried from the parlor. Will placed a hand on Richard's shoulder and gestured for him to proceed.

The parlor was tastefully done, white walls with maple wainscoting, and a broad-planked floor covered with thick Persian rugs. A warm fire crackled in the hearth, and above it, small porcelain sculptures and silver knickknacks were displayed on the mantel. The couches and chairs were French, upholstered in white with blue flower patterns. A polished harpsichord stood in one corner, and an ornately carved buffet in the other.

Richard nerved himself and walked forward to greet his friends. It was a small gathering, but then, he'd never really had many friends. They looked up as he entered, questions in their eyes.

Professor Ames nodded and lifted a cup of tea. He was short of stature, barely five feet tall, thin-boned, and white-haired. He weighed little more than one hundred pounds— even after Christmas dinner. Age had lined the pensive face. Those gentle blue eyes belied his vigor when at the lectern, but outside of the classroom, he was a mild man, fatherly in his actions. Ames always dressed conservatively in black.

"Richard! How grand that you finally made it!" George Peterson said.

Richard shook his hand while the others, Thomas Hanson and James Sonnet, patted him on the back.

"Richard!" Professor Ames clasped his hands. "We have heard from your father that you shall be going to the interior. As a result, we have gathered here to pay you our respects and wish you well."

"I, for one, am happy that you have." Richard accepted the goblet Sonnet handed him, and toasted them. The brandy ran warmly down his throat and he savored the mellow flavor.

Will gestured for attention. "Most of you don't know what Richard is about to endure. He is headed to Saint Louis, on the far frontier. He enters a land of darkness and ignorance. Richard's father has offered him a challenge of philosophy, and Richard has courageously accepted. Mr. Hamilton believes that the real world is different from that perceived by the mentors we study. Richard disagrees, and will prove by his venture into the unknown that his convictions are stronger than ignorance and brutality."

Tom could barely suppress a smirk.

"Further," Will cried, "he will take the opportunity to make observations on man in his natural state of savagery—

which we all know cannot be done in Boston, center of light and knowledge. Let us all raise our glasses in the hopes that the real is the rational!''

Cheers burst out.

Professor Ames rubbed the side of his cup with a delicate thumb. ''What will you do if Hobbes is correct and life is little more than conflict? Where shall you go to find defense? The state, with its laws and institutions, will not be there to protect your liberties.''

Richard swirled his brandy. ''I sincerely believe that the mind of the individual, when strong enough, can overcome the lack of social contract, Professor. I believe in perception and moral strength. As a free man, no one can force me to become that which I am not. What I perceive, will be.''

''You seem very sure of that.'' Ames raised an eyebrow. ''This will not be a lecture, Richard, but life.''

''When I return, I'll be the same man who leaves Boston on Monday. That I assure you, for I have found truth by noting that the real is spiritual and not material—a grievous fault my father has fallen heir to.''

''And his son never will?'' Tom asked as he studied Richard through half-lidded eyes. Thomas Hanson had settled into one of the chairs. For some reason beyond Richard's understanding, God had given Tom a ruggedly attractive face, bold and blocky, with a mobile mouth and dancing blue eyes that hinted of deviltry. He walked with an athletic grace, broad-shouldered and sure of himself. Even Tom's sandy hair curled insolently. Worse yet, Tom attracted women the way a lodestone drew iron filings.

You've already scratched me from your ledger of associates, haven't you, Tom? You wouldn't be here if Ames hadn't come. Look at the derision in your eyes. God's plague upon you. ''I believe that logic functions in the world. If I believe and act rationally, what I desire will occur. If I can understand what happens to me, I can overcome. Let's call it a rational extension of perception.''

''And if your assumption is flawed?'' Tom shifted. ''After all, you would have perceived yourself to be attending classes next week, wouldn't you?''

Richard's gut churned with humiliation. ''We agree, don't

we, that the human mind is endowed with certain qualities: logic, reason, and spirituality, among others? Would it not follow, then, that even a brute can be prevailed upon by reason? If this be the case, any man's behavior can be modified by a superior mind which points out advantages to be gained by reasonable action.''

Tom raised an eyebrow. "If you really think creatures like Indians are human. Are they, Richard?''

Ames shot a sympathetic glance at Richard and asked, "Tom, do you disregard every aspect of Rousseau's argument? Aren't the Iroquois and Shawnee already tainted by our civilization?''

Tom said flatly, "Rousseau was an idiot. Indians—and all the primitive races, for that matter—are beasts. They can't be tamed. Just like wolves and foxes can't be domesticated into dogs. They can only make way for civilization with its nobler institutions.''

"We're getting away from the argument," Will interrupted uneasily. "Go on, Richard. You were making a point.''

"Ah, I know what Richard is getting at," George Peterson said as he wiped his mouth. "A synthesis of enlightenment and romanticism with just a dash of rationalism. Exquisite, Richard! I shall be impatiently waiting to hear how your wild frontiersmen receive that.''

"On the end of an Indian war lance, no doubt," Tom gave Richard a dour look.

Richard waved them all down. "I shall be in no danger. I should be more than well enough prepared for any eventuality of the frontier. As I perceive it, my greatest problem will be communicating with men who have no understanding of proper English. I'm not sure I can translate the concepts while speaking in grunts and moans.''

Chuckles erupted.

"That could be a problem," Peterson agreed. "How do you attempt to elevate an ignorant clod to the finer things in life? I doubt that they can pronounce metaphysics, let alone comprehend it.''

"Richard will probably be eaten by a bear," Tom said.

"I've heard they feast on people without regard to education or social standing."

"Is it true that bears prefer to treat their palates with men who read Greek?" Sonnet asked. "Or is it Latin speakers they cherish?"

"He won't be eaten by a bear!" Will insisted. "It's the human beasts I'd worry about."

"Consider me a beast trainer," Richard said with mock seriousness. "Like Caesar of old, I shall no doubt return to Boston with several frontiersmen snarling at the ends of their chains."

Ames leaned over. "Keep in mind, Richard, that moral frameworks vary among different peoples. Logic is wonderful, and rational action provides a basis from which we can understand and interact with others, but you must always realize that not everyone shares your perspective. If morality were perceived universally, we should all embrace the same ethics."

Richard shrugged. "Sir, I cannot help but believe that there is a supreme morality based upon rational action. Truth is either absolute, or it is nothing. The result is that anyone can be trained to accept a rational morality if they are indeed human. Do you see a flaw in that?"

"In the grand sense of the human condition, no, I do not," Ames said with a slight smile. "That is exactly what I have attempted to teach you in my lectures. But the grand sense of the human condition, and the perceptions of the individual, are two different things." He paused, a kindly look in his eyes. "Be careful out there, Richard. Not all of the world is Boston."

At that moment, Laura Templeton entered the room with a swish of her long dress. She smiled radiantly, a delicate girl with long blond hair, the curls gathered within a turtle-shell hair clasp.

Richard stood, transfixed. She had to be the most beautiful girl in the world. The first thing a man noticed about Laura was her large blue eyes. Set in her alabaster face, they never failed to betray her animation and enjoyment of life. Now they sparkled in the lamplight. From her smooth forehead to her delicate nose and high cheeks, she looked regal. Full red lips made for smiling, and a pert chin, were framed by her heart-shaped face. A ruffled blue taffeta dress accented her slim waist and full bosom. The pleated lace on her cuffs almost obscured her slender hands and thin fingers. As she walked forward, her grace took Richard's breath away.

Tom immediately stepped forward and bowed. "What have we here? Can it be? Has an angel truly blessed us with her company?"

Laura offered her hand and tilted her head. "A good evening to you, Mr. Hanson, and thank you for your fine compliments."

She greeted each individually, and stopped before Richard. "It is good to see you, Mr. Hamilton." Richard's heart skipped at her smile. "I hear that you are off on a great adventure."

"Yes," Tom called. "He's going off to the wilderness to be scalped and eaten by a bear—though we've yet to decide if bears prefer to dine on men who speak Latin or Greek."

"Greek, I'm sure," Laura supplied as she charmed Richard with her dimpled smile.

Richard's breath had gone short, his face hot and flushed. He'd never known what to do with women, and here, for the first time, the most beautiful one in the world was staring up at him with those incredible sapphire eyes.

"Yes," he forced the words, "I'm off . . . on business, you understand. I'll be back, of course."

Her smile brightened. "But think of the adventure, Mr. Hamilton. You'll see so many marvelous things."

"I will."

"Come," Tom said, slipping in beside Laura and taking her arm. He gave Richard a deprecating glance as he guided her away. "Sit, and let us entertain you."

Richard sipped his brandy, unable to do more than stand like a ramrod, as the others clustered around Laura. The talk turned to the lighter things, jokes and anecdotes, stories of rowing and parties, things he'd never had much to do with.

Will came up to take Richard's arm, leading him to one

side. Richard couldn't take his eyes off Laura. She sat at ease, laughing, surrounded by a knot of her admirers.

"Quite a beauty, isn't she?" Will watched him from the corner of his eye.

"Indeed."

Will poured another brandy, lowering his voice. "You know, she's always liked you. Asks me innumerable questions about you."

"Oh?"

Will pursed his lips, frowning thoughtfully into his glass. "It wouldn't be a bad thing—you and her. Have you given it any thought?"

"She's the most beautiful woman to grace God's great Creation." Richard took a deep breath to settle himself. "But . . . why me?"

Will shrugged. "You'd make an admirable catch, Richard. You could provide for her in the manner she deserves. And, well, not that I'm a prejudiced brother, but I think she's the most charming girl in the world."

"She is that."

Will placed a hand on Richard's shoulder. "Think about it. A union between our families might benefit all concerned." He paused. "She'd be a great help to you, especially now that you're taking over some of your father's responsibilities."

"I suppose."

Will shook his head. "I'd hate to see her spend her life with a rake like Hanson."

Richard turned, staring at Laura as if at a sudden revelation. A girl like her? Married to him? A giddy excitement rushed in his veins.

"Ah," Will said as he read Richard's expression, "so, you can be heart-struck. I was afraid you'd never come down from the clouds."

"Clouds?"

"Your endless obsession with philosophy, Richard. You have a keen mind, my friend. With the right application, there's nothing you can't do. If you turn that acute mind of yours to business as you have to philosophy, you'll be one of the most powerful men in Boston. You know that, don't you?'' Will paused. "Stay a while after the others leave."

Richard nodded, dazed. He almost had to shake himself as Professor Ames walked up and clasped his hand. "Richard, I'm taking my leave. I'll miss you in my classes. You've been one of the brightest students I've ever had the pleasure to debate." He placed a hand on Richard's shoulder. "Be prudent in your travels, Richard. Come and see me upon your return."

"It's only for a short time, sir. You'll find me in the front row of your lectures again. I promise." Were it not for the whirlwind of sudden hope conjured by Will, Ames's departure would have saddened him to the core.

Tom Hanson, of course, was among the last to leave, dominating Laura's time until the very end. He took the final opportunity to kiss the back of her hand.

"Quite the ladies' man, our Thomas Hanson," Will noted after Hanson had finally retrieved his hat and coat and gone out into the night.

"He's most interesting," Laura said evenly, casting a demure glance at Richard. "But I think there is more to life than parties and clever stories, don't you, Mr. Hamilton?"

"Yes, of course."

Laura smiled coquettishly. "Tell me about your trip, Mr. Hamilton. Oh, I so envy you. How wonderful to set out on a dangerous adventure! I want to hear all about it."

Encouraged by the look in her eyes, Richard explained about his trip, and the philosophical challenge between him and his father. As he talked, the words seemed to come with greater ease. She hung on his every word, nodding, delicate hands clasped in her lap. What would it be like to hold hands like those?

At last, when the clock struck one, he forced himself to take his leave. Will clapped him on the back and went to fetch Richard's hat and coat.

For the moment, he was alone with Laura.

"Thank you, Mr. Hamilton," she told him, her voice intimate. "You've made this a most pleasant evening."

Richard mustered all of his courage. "Will said that . . . that is, that I might hope to—"

She cocked her head. "That you might come courting?"

"Yes, that is, if you and your family—"

"I would like that, Mr. Hamilton." Her laughter was musical. "I would like that a great deal. I can't wait to hear about all of your adventures."

"Might I take the liberty of writing you while I'm gone? I'll send you a letter a day, I promise."

"I would appreciate that, sir. And I'll write you, too."

"I'd like that." Richard shrugged awkwardly. "But where will you send them? I'll be traveling, on coaches and steamboats and such."

"Oh, yes, I see. Then, I'll just read your letters and wait until you've returned. But I do want you to know I'd write if I could."

He could hear Will's footsteps in the hall. She offered her hand. Trembling, Richard took it. His body thrilled at the touch. She seemed softer than down, and his lips tingled as they brushed the back of her hand.

"Have a safe trip, Mr. Hamilton. I'll be waiting for you when you return." For long moments their eyes held, until reluctantly, she withdrew her hand.

That smile had been for him, alone. He walked from the parlor like a drunken man, his heart pounding fit to break his ribs.

Will waited with his coat, eyebrow lifted, a wry smile on his lips. "I do believe you've been enchanted, Richard."

"Yes, enchanted."

"Be careful, Richard. Come back to us."

"I will, I promise."

He walked out into the night, heedless of the cold.

FOUR

It is thus certain that pity is a natural sentiment, which, by tempering in every individual the act of self-love, contributes to the preservation of the entire species. It is this pity which hurries us without reflection to the aid of those we see in distress; it is this pity which, in the state of nature, takes the place of laws, manners, virtue, with this advantage, that no one is led to disobey her gentle voice: it is this pity which will always hinder a strong savage from robbing a female child, or infirm old man, of the living they have acquired with pain and difficulty if he has but the slightest prospect of providing for himself.

—Jean-Jacques Rousseau, *Discourse on the Origin and Foundation of Inequality Among Mankind*

As darkness fell, Heals Like A Willow remained huddled beside the rocked-up burial crevice. Snow continued to fall, spun into patterns by the wind rushing over the caprock and down into the valley. Cold had leached into her back from the sandstone. She shivered. Empty. Her insides felt like a rotted log. How numb and cold could a person get before all feeling faded away into nothingness?

The crunch of moccasins on the crusted drifts might have been a dream.

"Willow?" the scratchy voice barely penetrated her foggy hearing.

She didn't look up, content to drift among images from the past. Her son's bright eyes danced with joy as his father played a finger game with those chubby infant hands. Squealing giggles mixed with strong male laughter to echo hollowly in her memory.

"You can't stay up here." The thin voice was heavy with the *Ku'chendikani* accent. "Smell the wind. The clouds are going to break and the night will be clear, deep cold ... bitter enough to make the trees pop."

The words lost themselves in thoughts as muzzy as cattail down.

"Willow?" This time a hand prodded her shoulder, intruding bluntly.

She blinked and twisted her head to stare up past the snow-crusted hood of her buffalo robe. Two Half Moons, her husband's aunt, appeared as a dark blot in the indigo twilight.

The old woman reached down to poke her again, harder this time. "Come on, girl. Dying up here won't do anyone any good."

"Freezing," Willow whispered absently. "It's an easy death. So cold at first ... and then the warmth steals over you until the shivering stops. Warmth ... out of painful cold. Strange, isn't it? That freezing to death is that way?"

Two Half Moons looked up at the murky sky. "Hot and cold. Man and woman. Night and day. Front and back. Two sides to everything, girl. That's how *Tam Apo* made the world. All we see is one side at a time, but look through the night and you will see dawn."

"And death?"

"Look through death and you will see life, *peti*." The old woman made a frustrated gesture. "But why am I telling you this? You're the one with more questions than is good for you. You're not going to change, are you? Stop questioning old Slim Pole? Stop annoying the *puhagan* and elders with your ideas?"

Willow resisted feebly as the old woman pulled on her. In the end she needed simply to remain limp to defeat Two Half Moons' efforts.

"All right," the old woman sighed, settling against the sandstone next to her. "I've seen five tens and five winters, girl. Perhaps that's enough, eh? I'll just sit here and freeze with you. We can talk about the two sides of things as our flesh grows colder and our souls grow warmer."

Willow remained silent.

Two Half Moons grunted, then said, "Of course, people

who freeze to death don't think too straight after a while. I've seen men forget which way they were headed . . . walk off trails they'd used for years. So, a couple of hours from now, as the cold sets in, we might be mumbling and cackling like sage grouse hit on the head—and making just as much sense."

Through her robe, Willow felt the old woman shiver, and could hear the elder's jaws making a slapping sound that would have been clicking had any teeth remained in her mouth. "*Napia,* why don't you go back to camp?"

"If you're fool enough to die up here for no reason, why can't I? You're still young. But me, I'm old. Can't do much any more."

Willow endured another attack of shivers. Two Half Moons would make this a matter of wills. Out of stubborn contrariness, she'd force herself to die here, too.

"I just want to be left alone." Willow hugged herself. The chill had eaten through the layers of her moccasins and her feet ached.

"Alone, hmm? How many have I buried in my years? I couldn't bury my mother and father. I can remember that day very clearly. We were up north, on the Musselshell River. The bottoms are good there. Plenty of room to run horses. The *Pa'kiani* came out of the trees . . . killed my father outright as he started out of the lodge. A *Pa'ki* shot him in the face with a gun. I was inside and he fell back on top of me, his blood and brains all over my dress. They took my mother captive, made her a slave. I heard later that the warrior who took her beat her to death. It was in the winter. She was pregnant with that Blackfoot's child. A boy who escaped the next spring said that the camp dogs ate her, chewed on her frozen body where it lay in the snow."

Willow closed her eyes.

"No, I didn't get to bury them, but I did bury three of my children . . . all very young. My sister and two brothers. Cousins, so many cousins," Two Half Moons continued. "Twice the White man's spotted sickness has come and taken people, one after another, from my family until I thought no one was going to be left. Once there were so many we just left them lying in their lodges where they died, and fled to the high mountains, preferring to take our chances with *Pandzoavits,* the rock ogres.''

Willow shook her head. *We live in an age of unhappy ghosts.* ''Better to die and let our souls find their way to the Land of the Dead. No smallpox. No sickness at all. Plenty to eat. Animals always willing to be killed. No pain, or cold, or misery of any sort. That's what Slim Pole says.''

Two Half Moons snorted. ''I thought you didn't believe the *puhagan.*''

Willow stared into the gloom. The snow fell in small crystals, like a powdery dust. ''Later, when this is all over, I won't. Up here . . . with my husband and son so close, I have to. It's for them, you see. I believe with all of my soul. I followed the rituals as the *Ku'chendikani* teach them.''

''And your *Dukurika* don't?''

''Grandmother used to tell me that the *Ku'chendikani* had learned so much about horses that they forgot most everything else that was important.''

''Such as?''

''Such as the way the people used to be. She says the *Ku'chendikani* used to stay in one place, moving through a smaller territory. They weren't concerned with wealth, with horses and White man goods. She thought I was a fool for running off with my husband. That I'd be treated like a pack dog instead of a person.''

''You've always been different.'' Two Half Moons grunted as she resettled herself. ''But your grandmother may not be wrong. I remember my grandmother saying the same thing. She was young when the horses came. She always thought we were crazy to have chased the *Pa'kiani* out of their lands, pushed them far to the north. But then, we had horses and they didn't.''

''And what did it get you in the end, Aunt? They traded for the White man's guns—and got horses of their own. Now look what's happened. They've pushed us clear back into the mountains. I've heard they want to kill us all. When you push on a sapling, you must expect it to spring back.''

Two Half Moons chuckled. ''You've always had that way about you. Had your husband not been such a great warrior, someone like Iron Wrist would have beaten it out of you.''

"Only once, Aunt. I'd have vanished into the mountains and that would have been the last anyone would have seen of me."

Two Half Moons considered for a moment. "I can remember my grandmother talking just like that. Perhaps you are right. We have changed. Horses are things for men, not women. When the elders died out, so did women's voices in the councils. I remember . . . yes. In the old days, the women spoke. They knew the places where the plants grew, where to find water and which camping spots were good. As the years passed, such decisions began to be made by warriors. The old camps weren't any good because they didn't have enough grass for the horses, or the trails were too rough for horses to travel down the sides of the rimrock."

Willow watched the snow fall and looked for patterns in the swirling flakes. "And women started doing all the work, processing the hides, sewing the lodges, carrying the firewood. They became as captives, more like slaves. Among the *Ku'chendikani* I have seen men who love their horses more than their women."

Two Half Moons frowned in displeasure. "I've thought about it from time to time. Who doesn't think back as they grow older? Your grandmother knows what some of the rest of us are too blind to have seen because it was right in front of us." She shook her head in the gloom. "When I was young, I told my children about life in the old days. About men, women, and children working together to trap the animals on the fall hunt. I told them about roots, and storage pots. And then I told them how much better life was when men started to ride out on fast horses, and we traveled constantly in pursuit of the buffalo. I told them that even when we were starving during the dry years—and starving worse during the bad winters. Funny . . . how we fool ourselves."

Heals Like A Willow knotted her hands inside her mittens. "Among the *Dukurika* we starve, too, but it's only when all the caches have been eaten. And even then we remember to strip the pines of bark, to lay snares for the elk along the trails to the feed grounds, and to stretch nets in the trees to catch waxwings. At least we have a *little* food in our bellies. Not like the *Ku'chendikani,* who have to boil their moccasins for the broth and chew hard strips of leather.''

Two Half Moons endured a violent fit of shivers, bowing her head. ''What does it mean for the people, girl? What is going to happen next? Something with these White men, I'll bet. It won't be good.''

''I don't know, Aunt.'' Willow pushed herself to her feet, snow cracking from her robe. Her cramped muscles ached, and the cold tightened around her body. ''But for now, here, take my hand. As dark as it is, we'll have trouble enough getting you back down to the camp.''

Two Half Moons shivered hard, rattling like a cottonwood leaf in the wind. With movement, however, their bodies would warm.

Heals Like A Willow began picking her way along the rimrock, glancing back only once for a final look at the rocked-up crevice. Snow clung in the recesses among her carefully placed rocks—a pale spider's web that had snared the last of her dreams.

As dreams of Laura faded, Richard blinked his eyes open to pale morning light filtering through the cabin window. The rattling, shaking, and clanking of the *Virgil* brought him back to the river and the journey's incredible tedium.

His blankets were pulled up around his chin and when he exhaled, his breath rose frost white in the dim light. Loath to leave the warmth of his bed, he snuggled into a ball and let his eyes trace the white-painted wooden walls of his little prison. He could hear footsteps on the Texas deck above his head.

Curse you, Father, for doing this to me. Boston, ah Boston. If only he were home instead of racing downriver toward God alone knew what fate.

In his memory, Richard relived that fateful Saturday night in Will Templeton's home—Laura would wait for him.

Great God, here he was, traveling ever farther from her and the wondrous opportunity she represented.

It's not forever. All you need to do is go to Saint Louis, then return. All will be as it was before. On his very soul, he'd never leave the city again!

After that last bittersweet Boston weekend, Jeffry had roused Richard out of bed before the sun rose. He'd dressed by lamplight, pulling on his warmest things.

Breakfast had consisted of Sally's bread pudding, pork, and eggs. Richard had been seated across the table from his father. Phillip watched him eat, then said, "I've had Jeffry pack a pistol in your grip. Given the nature of your—"

"I won't need it, Father. You know how I feel about firearms."

Phillip's face twitched, eyes narrowing. "We protested the Stamp Act. We threw their tea into the harbor in defiance of their tea tax. We told them that if they wanted to tax us, we damned well wanted representation. What good citizens wouldn't? When they shot us down in the streets of Boston, we remained loyal. We wouldn't have—"

"I don't need to hear this again."

"We wouldn't have risen against them had General Gage not ordered the confiscation of our rifles." Phillip pointed a meaty finger, emphasizing his point. "We didn't resort to warfare until they marched on Concord to seize our powder."

"I know. I know."

"Then you also know that no Massachusetts man worth his spit—let alone a man from Boston—will *ever* travel without his weapons. And where you're going . . ."

"I *won't* need it!"

Phillip closed his eyes, shaking his head. "Here in Boston you might not, Richard. But you must face the fact that no matter how much you despise weapons, the day will come when you *will* need one. Either to protect your life and property, or as the counterbalance to tyranny."

"Father, I am an enlightened man. There is nothing I can't cope with by employing logic and an appeal to human rationality." Richard wiped his mouth and steepled his fingers. "That was the challenge, wasn't it? My belief in my philosophy against your ruthless and brutal 'real' world?''

Phillip wadded his napkin and threw it to one side. "As you wish. You may leave the pistol behind—and I will discard any notion of my thirty thousand dollars making it safely to Saint Louis."

A long silence settled over the table, Richard simply playing with his food. Phillip watched him with resignation.

Jeffry entered and announced, "The carriage has arrived and awaits your convenience, sir."

Richard pushed back from the table. "Excellent breakfast. Jeffry, please give Sally my compliments." To his father he added, "There's no point in my lingering. The sooner this is over, the better."

Tight-jawed, Phillip jerked a short nod and got to his feet. "Jeffry, if you would be so good as to bring the grip from my office."

Jeffry nodded and left.

Richard paced to the hallway where his things waited: a satchel of books, and a trunk. When Jeffry handed him the grip containing the banknotes, Richard quickly opened it and extracted the heavy pistol. He hated to touch it, as if his flesh might be corrupted by the inherent violence contained in that polished wood and cold iron. Like a snake's flesh, it felt cool and slick. Holding it between thumb and forefinger, he laid it carefully on the hall chair. With a calculated swirl, he wrapped his coat about his shoulders, pulled on his hat and gloves, and opened the large front door.

Misty orange light slanted across the city, shooting through the smoke pall over the snow-crusted rooftops. The biting winter chill brought a rush to his blood as his frosty breath rose on the still air. A bundled carriage driver waited by the step, slapping his arms and rocking from foot to foot. He reached up, touched his hat, and muttered, "G'day, suh."

Phillip limped through the doorway and made his halting way down the stairs. Grim-faced, he handed Richard the grip. Jeffry followed, delivering the satchel and trunk to the coachman, who placed them in the boot.

At the door of the coach, Phillip cocked his head. "Richard, you . . . I mean . . ."

"Offering advice, Father?"

The gray gaze hardened as Phillip stiffened. "I wouldn't presume. You seem to have all the answers already." He half turned, then stopped, looking back sadly. "I just wonder is all. I wonder how you and I could have grown so far apart."

"Keep wondering, Father. A Greek philosopher once stated that the unexamined life is not worth living."

As anger reddened his father's face, Richard placed his foot on the step and climbed in to seat himself on the cold leather. He leaned out the far window to stare at the familiar Commons, the snow now crisscrossed with tracks. The carriage rocked as the driver climbed up.

The leather crackled as Richard settled in and the rig jolted forward. He didn't look back, preferring to watch the Commons as it slid past and dream of the look in Laura's eyes as she listened to his every word.

God, how I'll miss this.

January 24, 1825
On the Ohio River, four days from Pittsburgh

Dear Laura:

I hope you received the letters I posted from Pittsburgh. What a horrid little town! It has few amenities for either the civilized man or woman, though the poor residents do make a show of gentlemanliness and aristocratic pretension. I doubt, however, that the place will ever amount to much.

I am on the river now, aboard a steamboat named the *Virgil*. The boat itself is quite a marvel in that it smokes, rattles, and shakes, but makes excellent speed. The shore seems to race past.

How do I tell you about the river? Imagine, if you

will, dark water winding through wooded, snow-mantled hills. I've spent hours staring into the depths, sensing the inevitable power of moving water. Were I not the rational fellow that I am, I'd swear I could feel it, like something alive. It has a purity, perhaps something baptismal.

Water and land, it is an ancient duality, but one that is pressed upon a person out here in the wilderness. Where the river is pure and clear, the land is foreboding, dark and brooding. As we pass along the shoreline I can see small fields cleared from the somber trees. The fields lie fallow, and snow-covered. Tiny cabins—little more than rude huts—are situated off to the side, and traces of blue smoke rise from the chimneys.

What sort of rude beings huddle next to those feeble flames? As terrible as the land is, the people who inhabit it are beneath contempt. Laura, I have entered the dark heart of the benighted wilderness. The only solace which is mine is that you will be waiting anxiously for my return.

I cannot tell you how much I dwell on that happy day when we shall be reunited. Each minute passes so slowly as to be an hour.

I hope you don't think that I'm being presumptuous. Perhaps the wilderness has given me courage to write such things as I would never have had the temerity to do were I not so far removed from your presence.

> Obediently Yours,
> Richard Hamilton

Father, you've exiled me to Hell.

The steamboat clanked loudly, intruding on the wistful memory. He opened his eyes to his tiny stateroom aboard the *Virgil.* He could hear voices in the hall: men discussing the chill in the air as they walked forward.

Richard stared dully at the whitewashed wall. He kept to his cabin except when cold drove him to the forward parlor and the stove. Succor came from thoughts of Laura and his precious books. He need only open to a page and drop into

the convoluted prose of Hegel, or the intricacies of Descartes, and this tawdry world slipped away. The other men aboard congregated to enjoy card games, drinking, and planning explorations along the shore during wood stops.

In Richard's productive imagination, he had metamorphosed into a sort of Moses in the wilderness, isolated within his own mind. Such thoughts dominated his letters to Laura and the journal he'd begun to keep the day after he left Boston. His scribblings had become so voluminous, he'd been forced to purchase a large ledger book in Pittsburgh.

By the Lord, anything to break the monotony of being trapped aboard this floating cage with its benighted passengers.

The *Virgil* made stops at each of the squalid little hamlets along the Ohio. Places like Economy, Cincinnati, Wheeling, Louisville, Portland, New Harmony, and Paducah. They consisted of a mixture of frame and log houses—the latter little more than hovels with sod roofs. People lived in dirt, even to the point of covering the decks of their fragile flatboats with it—perhaps so the inevitable bone rick of a milch cow could feel as much at home as the filth-encrusted humans. Such ungainly craft now floated downriver in ones and twos. Richard had overheard that those intrepid voyagers hoped to make homes before spring planting.

Dirt into more dirt.

He'd seen them from the steamboat as they passed cleared patches in the trees: generally the homestead of a gnarled man and a hard-boned woman laboring to raise kids, corn, and pigs.

And this is the great destiny my father believes in?

Any semblance of civilization had stopped at Pittsburgh. That rowdy town at the confluence of the Monongahela and Allegheny might have met the approval of a Saxon chief, but little more.

Despite his disappointment in the people, the eternal voices of earth and water had captured his imagination. The majestic river amazed him. At first it had been cluttered with floes of ice. The Ohio exuded a sense of power and propriety, bounded by its tree-furred bluffs and somber, wooded banks. Staring out over the water instilled in him a feeling of tranquillity he'd never experienced before. As the river gained a hold on his soul, he began to fill the pages of his journal with poetic musings, an amorous tone apparent in his flowery words.

Beyond the river lay the forest, perpetually somber, a place of labyrinthine shadows and secrets. Richard had grown acutely aware of its presence. Once, at a wood stop, he'd walked out into the leaf-matted silence and stared up at the patterns of mighty limbs that blocked the sky. He'd run his fingers down the rugged bark of oaks, hickories, and walnuts, sensing the age and power of the land.

What was it that touched him? The prickle of danger? The warning that his soul was somehow in jeopardy? At the first threads of fear, he'd turned and bolted for the boat, relieved by the sound of human voices, the clank of metal, and the soothing reassurance of men and their works.

Even now, safely huddled in his bed, he shivered at the memory. It was out there, just beyond the thin wall of his cabin: a terrible presence he could not understand. The rational mind told him he'd seen nothing but trees: wilderness. What had made him feel so small, so meaningless?

Ever since, he'd watched the forest as it passed, uneasy at what might lurk in those dim shadows.

Like a child hearing ghouls in the winter wind. You're a fool, Richard.

His growling stomach finally drove him to throw back the blankets and climb to his feet. Shivering, he dressed, tied a thick white scarf about his neck, and broke the crust of ice out of his wash bowl to wet his face and slick his hair. Fingers numb, he unlocked his door, plucked up the grip containing the money and his copy of Kant, then stepped into the cramped corridor. Narrow black doors, each designated with a white letter painted by a wobbly hand, lined the way. The boards creaked underfoot as he proceeded forward to the parlor. The boat shuddered, the deck swaying in a most unsettling manner.

The boat is going to shake itself apart and I'm going to drown.

After his arrival in Pittsburgh, the *Virgil* had been the first steamboat making passage to Saint Louis. She was a small sternwheeler, no more than one hundred and ten tons. Two black smokestacks rose from behind the capstan in the bow, and through the forward gallery. Richard could see them through the large windows as he entered the main cabin. His fellow passengers, some twenty in all, had already filled the room with a blue haze of tobacco smoke that mercifully covered the taint of unwashed humanity. They sat at the tables, some engaged in cards, others in companionable talk over steaming tin cups. Most glanced up, noted his arrival, and returned to their conversations and games.

"Good morning, sir." The Virginia planter spoke with his usual politeness. He wore a gray beaver-felt hat, charcoal frock coat, and a silk scarf that contrasted with his blue eyes, pale face, and black hair.

"Good morning to you, too, sir." Richard gave a slight bow and turned toward the pantry where what remained of breakfast—crumbled corn bread, a well-hacked joint of venison, and shreds of smoked side pork—rested in tins on the warming shelf over the stove.

Richard seated himself by the window across from the Virginia planter and made the best of the fare. What would it be like to be married to Laura Templeton? She'd always be there, ready to listen to him, supportive of his studies of philosophy. He could imagine her bustling about the room, ensuring that the house was immaculate.

And later, they'd ascend to the bedroom. He swallowed hard, a flutter in his chest. Unlike the rest of his fellows, he'd keep himself sacred unto her, and her alone. In his imagination, he could feel himself snuggling under the covers, her warm body next to his.

What was it like, to have intercourse with a woman? Obviously better than those shameful occasions when he ejaculated in his dreams. Did the idea of intercourse worry her as much as it worried him? Or were women different when it came to such things?

The steward had no more than removed the plate when the Virginia planter rose and stepped to Richard's table.

"Cigar, sir?" The Virginian extended a prize specimen. "Charles Lamont Eckhart, at your service, sir."

"Richard Hamilton." Damn! The image of Laura had slipped away. Richard opened his copy of Kant and looked up. "Thank you, sir, but I don't smoke cigars."

The Virginian raised a dark eyebrow. "Now is as good a time as any to start, sir. I offer my private stock, produce of my own fields."

"I'm sure they are wonderful, but I must regretfully decline your offer."

The cigar was withdrawn to a deep coat pocket. "Boston, aren't you, sir?"

Richard stifled a sigh as the Virginian seated himself across the table. "Yes, Boston."

"Your speech gives you away." Eckhart used a thumb and forefinger to flick breadcrumbs from the scarred tabletop. "What brings you to the frontier, Mr. Hamilton? I would assume from your books, writing, and demeanor that you are a scholar."

"You are correct, sir. Philosophy."

Eckhart rubbed his smooth chin, eyes thoughtful. "You are going to Saint Louis to teach?"

"Business."

"Santa Fe trade, I suppose." Eckhart pulled out his cigar, lit it, and exhaled a cloud of acrid blue smoke. "Yes, a smart young man should do very well . . . provided, of course, that you have the ambition and character necessary for the frontier life."

Richard chuckled. "I can already tell you, I don't. My duty, sir, is to go to Saint Louis, see to some arrangements, and return to Boston with the greatest dispatch. Thereafter, I shall retire to the university, and never again endure such bad food"—he gestured at the pantry—"ill company, or the human dregs such as you see floating along on flat-boats.''

"Dregs, sir? Our fair countrymen?''

"I shudder to think of the society such men will create out here in the wilds. Anarchic ignorance does not breed greatness.'' Richard pointed at a flatboat coasting slowly along the south bank, the craft nothing more than a tent pitched on a log raft. Two men, dressed in what amounted to rags, used long poles to fend the craft from the bank. "Imagine, the noble red man has been made to give way before such as them. At least when Rome sent out her shining legions, they were followed by the administrators, engineers, and merchants. Now, in our modern world, at a time when the works of men like Rousseau should occupy the finest of minds, we've unleashed a horde of unwashed animals as the vanguard of our advance across the continent. How will history judge us, sir?''

"You speak of Americans more like Mongols than countrymen. Many of us see these settlers as the first foot soldiers of civilization in a virgin continent. Just as my own—''

"Civilization?'' Richard raised an eyebrow. "I pray you, sir, were you to ask that farmer floating along out there to discuss Plato's parable of the cave, I fully expect that he would reply that a cave was good for the storage of whiskey, and little else.''

"And Aristotle would be an excellent name for a mule, I suppose.''

"Indeed, sir. Thus, the question is: What sort of state shall these rude bumpkins build out here?'' Richard tapped his copy of Kant. "One based on rational and moral principles, or on the basest human passions? These frontiersmen are a bestiary of vermin. I fear any society they should create would reflect their animalistic propensities. Therefore, sir, I shall discharge my duty in Saint Louis, and be most hasty about my return to Boston with its enlightenment and a more genteel society.''

"I admire a man who knows his path so well.'' Eckhart smiled thinly. "If I might offer a word of advice . . .''

"You may.''

Eckhart pushed back his chair and stood. "Not all of your

fellow travelers can be counted on to share your, er . . . 'enlightened' sentiments. I would be careful of the manner in which I expressed such opinions. Good day, sir.''

"And a good day to you." Richard scratched his ear as Eckhart retreated to a table offering a card game.

Richard snorted in mild irritation, then found his place in Kant and settled back for a pleasant day, dissecting the problem of autonomy of will and the supposition of freedom. Later, in the privacy of his cabin, he would dream of Laura again.

Winter's hold was breaking. The first stars were flickering to life in the darkening sky as Travis Hartman shouldered a keg of gunpowder from the freight wagon's tailgate and carried it toward the low doorway that gaped like a black maw in the warehouse wall. The place had been built of squared blocks of gray limestone, the ashlars poorly dressed. Hickory and white ash had been laid crosswise for beams, then planks and a foot of earth had been used to complete the roof. A thick oaken door provided security in addition to the heavy iron hasp.

Muck clung to Travis's moccasins as he slopped along the trail beaten in the melting snow. The first robins were already flitting from branch to branch in the surrounding trees, greedily eyeing the places where the snow had melted. Spring would come, even after a winter like this one.

Travis ducked through the low doorway into the darkness. A single candle illuminated the stacks of crates and kegs, for everything had to be protected against rats and mice. The room smelled dank and musty, the way a dirt-floored warehouse should.

Dave Green stood braced over a flour barrel, which he was using as a table for his ledger. "Last one?"

"Yep."

"That's thirty kegs of powder. Ought to be enough for two years."

Outside, one of the mules snorted and shook its harness.

Travis blinked in the darkness, counting off tens on his fingers. "I reckon."

Green rubbed his broad forehead as his gaze darted from keg to keg. "We've got everything we need, Travis. Two hundred trade rifles, stacks of four-point blankets, foofawraw by the barrel, flour, lead, flints, mirrors, knives, copper kettles, vermilion and ocher for grease paints, strike-a-lights, a half ton of tobacco, ten tins of whiskey, and all the rest."

"But not enough men," Travis said dryly.

Green made a face. "You been around again?"

Travis kicked at the dirt. "T'ain't easy, Dave. Can't jist come out and say, 'Hyar, boys. Who's fer the Shining Mountains and two years on the Big Horn?' Do that and you'll have army folks swarming about like skeeters on the Platte."

Green braced his arms over his ledger. "Damn it! It's not enough that a man's got to trust himself to two thousand miles of snags, sawyers, and savages, all set to sink him or scalp him, but the damn gov'ment's against him, too!"

"I reckon it's Ashley, Chouteau, and Astor, hoss. Just like you said." Travis found a twist of tobacco in his possibles, slipped his knife from its sheath, and cut a chew from his twist. Green was silent while Travis got the quid juicing and spat. Travis then added, "I got fifteen men willing, no questions asked. That be all, Davey. I reckon if'n we was ter leave tomorrow, I could shanty up another twenty or so."

"We can't leave tomorrow. And damn it, we can't have it out that we're heading upriver to trade. I *need* that Godcursed license!"

"Wal, ye ain't gonna get it." Travis scratched his ear.

"Hoss, ye'll just have ter wait yer turn and hope the good Lord'll provide."

"My turn has to be now, Travis. Colonel Atkinson is upriver subduing the tribes with his army. Joshua Pilcher's Missouri Fur Company is weakened—half their forts are abandoned. William Ashley gave up on the river after the Arikara shot his brigade up in '23. He's way out west someplace, Meanwhile, Pratte and Chouteau have something in the wind. I think it's with Jacob Astor. It's like a crawling in my gut, Travis. American Fur is going to partner up with Pratte and Chouteau. If I don't get upriver and establish a trading post with the Crow, I'll be muscled right out of the trade."

"Do or die, eh?"

"Reckon so. When we head upriver, Travis, you've got to be my eyes, ears, and guard dog. I want you out roaming, scouting. We're taking more than enough risks as it is. I must be the first boat up the river."

"Like you said, the army is up there somewhere. How ye gonna handle that?"

Green half-closed his eyes, as if seeing upriver, into the future. "We'll know when they're close. Word travels downriver faster than keelboats. When we hear, we'll put up behind an island, maybe hole up in some creek. They'll drift right on past—and be no wiser for it."

"And Fort Atkinson?"

"I've got forged papers that say I'm carrying goods for Pratte. They won't stand close scrutiny, but by the time they find out different, we'll be long gone. Meanwhile, to avoid the whiskey embargo, you, my friend, will offload the whiskey two days downriver and bypass the fort to the west. We'll meet up two days' travel upriver."

"Risky bizness, Dave."

Green nodded. "That's why I sent for you, Travis. I don't know anyone else I could trust to get me through. You know the Indians, the land, the river. If I can't have a brigade, I want the next best thing. That's you, Travis."

Travis chuckled. "You do take all, Davey. Reckon it jist might end up fetch or spit, though. Yep, she's gonna swing according ter whether we get enough men ter make a go of her.''

Green nodded soberly as his gaze rested on the stacked goods. He'd bet the results of his years in Santa Fe, all that blood and sweat and danger. The scars on Travis's face pulled tight as he grinned. Dave Green was his kind of man. All he had to do was sneak his boat up a dangerous river, past powerful rivals, a hostile government, and build a fort in the wilderness where no one had been able to maintain a fort before. All that—provided Green could hire enough men to fill out the expedition without the authorities catching on.

February 1, 1825
Paducah, Kentucky

Dear Laura:

This is the first opportunity I've had to post you a letter from any place where it might conceivably be delivered. I am sending this letter, and the accompanying notes, to you care of the steamboat *Victory*. I am well, but somewhat thinner. Since leaving Pittsburgh, barbaric as it was, meals have been wretched—mostly salt pork and beans in the beginning. But as we have traveled farther downriver, the menu has tended more and more toward venison and corn, which farmers sell or trade to the boat during the frequent stops for wood to refuel the boilers.

Perhaps Sally might create something edible out of this crude fare, but for my part, cuisine within a monastery might actually come as an improvement.

Let me tell you something about how we travel. Steamboat speed, I have learned, comes at the price of quiet and solitude. In the beginning, the clanking, rattling, squeaking, and rhythmic shish-shishing of the paddle drove me half to distraction. Only after days has it faded into a dull monotony of the subconscious. When the boat shakes, the walls wobble and creak as if they will collapse around my ears. While I have become somewhat accustomed to it, I shall never be fully relaxed in this loose stack of kindling.

Laura, this you might find amusing. I've become quite familiar with the grim aspects of farming and husbandry, not by choice, mind you. Rather, I am forced—by virtue of the thin plank walls—to listen to the mindless babble of ignorant farmers seeking new land, merchants discussing prices and goods, and boatmen talking endlessly of water and vessels and ice in the river.

When we parted, you asked me to report all of my adventures. I must admit that, to date, I have nothing adventurous to report. The frontier, quite to the contrary of the stories, is dull, squalid, and about as stimulating as a lump of warm tar.

> Your Obedient Servant,
> Richard Hamilton

"Fort Massac!" came the cry from the pilothouse.

Richard marked his place in Kant and stepped out on the gallery with the rest of the men. The sky had gone blustery again, leaden clouds so low they seemed to skim the skeletal gray mat of trees. Chop smacked the gravelly banks, and the dark, clear waters of the Ohio had turned slate-colored.

A smell of rain carried on the cold air. Richard turned up his collar, the chill bracing to the skin. He was eager for exercise. The deck shuddered as the *Virgil* backed water. Foam rolled up from under the rocking hull to swirl away in sucking whirlpools. The crew shouted and gestured up at the pilothouse as the bow nosed in toward the landing on the north shore. Bells rang somewhere in the boat's guts.

Richard shook his head at the sight of Fort Massac. The settlement lay in a clearing cut from virgin forest. At the whistle's shrill blow, men had appeared from the log structures higher up on the bank. Fort Massac differed little from the other tiny settlements Richard had seen, its only distinction being that it rested on the last suitable landing above the mouth of the Ohio. Below this spot, the land was susceptible to flooding.

Deckhands threw lines out to the waiting men on the bank and dropped the plank. Dugout canoes, a couple of pirogues, and a canted keelboat had been pulled up on the mud.

Richard tapped his hat securely onto his head, picked up his grip, and descended the stairs to the deck before following the excited swarm of people ashore. Everyone was talking at once, calling for the news, asking about conditions upriver.

Richard found the inhabitants as distasteful as their pitiful trading post. The only women were Indians, their round, brown faces expressionless as they watched from the rear. The most common sort of men were bearded American hunters, each dressed in fringed buckskins glazed in dirt and grease that made the leather shine blackly. French boatmen composed the second common group. These wore equally dirty cloth garments that bagged about the limbs, colorful sashes, and flopping wool hats—generally red in color. The third, smallest, contingent consisted of the type of ruffian Richard took to be half-breeds.

The sticky mud had been churned with God alone knew what sort of filth. He winced as the goo oozed around his polished black boots, but trudged up the landing. He glanced uneasily at the forest. Did it lie in wait for him? Was that where the sense of menace came from?

Men were packing wood from a rickety stack down to the boat, fuel for the ravenous boilers. Someone cursed, yelling that the wood was still too green to burn well.

"Take it or leave it!" came the rejoinder.

Stumps stuck out of the ground throughout the so-called settlement, as if Fort Massac had been built straight out of the wilderness. The air smelled of hickory smoke, decay, urine, and the mixed pungency of manure. Bits of broken crockery, shards of glass, excrement, and splintered bone littered the charcoal-blackened earth.

The low-roofed log huts, rough-notched, had been chinked with mud and roofed over with earth. The insides were dark as caves behind green-hide doors that hung on leather hinges.

"Dirt into dirt," Richard whispered. A filthy little girl of about five ran past—an image of sooty smudges, tangled dark brown hair, and a snot-wet nose.

Dogs were fighting somewhere, accompanied by loud whoops of encouragement. Richard pinched his nose as he looked out back of one of the rude cabins. Animal hides had been pegged to the wall and added their stink to the piles of human excrement. Two pigs were rooting through the mess, snorting and squealing at each other as they nipped and butted a ball of some sort before them. Brown, muddy, and tattered, the thing rolled awkwardly as first one pig, then the other, savaged it with its tusks, occasionally ripping a strip of pulp from the . . . Richard started, his hand tightening on the grip. *Dear God, it's a human head!*

"I would not worry, m'sieur. It is only an Indian, a Shawnee who was caught stealing, I think. The grave, you see, she was very, how you say . . . shallow." The words, spoken with an atrocious French accent, brought Richard around with a start.

A swarthy boatman leaned against the log wall, feet braced, head cocked. The man might have been a caricature. No human should have had shoulders that broad. The V of his chest tapered to an insanely thin waist. The wide black belt held a pistol, knife, bullet pouch, and hide sack. Corded muscle packed the man's arms until they matched the thickness of his bandy legs. Moccasins clad his feet and splotched leggings rose to his thighs. A heavy wool shirt, grimy gray, barely concealed a chest fit for a Greek god. His face was long, the nose thin and hooked. A light brown beard hung well past his chin, and greasy black hair fell over his filthy collar.

But the eyes—a predatory blue—had an icy quality that pierced Richard like frozen needles. Richard backed away as if stung. He'd reacted this way only once in his life, when he'd opened a box given to him as a practical joke—and discovered a serpent within.

Yes, a serpent. Cold . . . deadly.

The boatman casually returned his gaze to the pigs' prize.

"How a man is buried says a great deal about him, no? In his case, she could be said zat Indians who drink too much of another man's whiskey and are slow to draw zee knife get buried shallow, eh, *mon ami?*"

Words cramped in Richard's throat. Those blood-chilling eyes had fixed on the grip, seeming to stare through the heavy cloth to the banknotes within. Richard tucked the grip protectively to his breast. His knees had begun to wobble as he backed away.

"Ah, maybe you do not like Indians?" The man shrugged. "Very well. This *Virgil,* she is a good boat? Fast?"

Richard jerked a nod.

The boatman chuckled at Richard's unease. "I am called François, m'sieur. A . . . I suppose you would say native of these parts, eh?"

"*B—Bonjour.*" Richard spun on his heel, fighting the urge to run full-tilt back to the boat.

"*Un moment!*"

"*Qu'est que c'est?*"

"You go to Saint Louis, *ami?*" François was striding beside him, a faint smile on those deadly thin lips.

"Yes! Yes! Now, excuse me, please. I must go!"

A hand clapped on his shoulder, the grip tightening like a vise. Richard shivered in spite of himself. He shot a frightened glance into those frozen blue eyes.

"You travel well on this boat? She is good, *oui?*"

"I suppose . . . yes. I . . . er, it hasn't sunk yet." Richard tried to smile. His guts had gone runny. "If you'll excuse me."

He wanted to gasp with relief when the callused hand withdrew. By dint of will he kept his legs from quaking, but hurried for the plank and the safety of the *Virgil.*

When he'd climbed from the lower deck to the gallery, he glanced back. The boatman had followed to stop at the end of the plank. François's eyes narrowed as if in thought.

What was it? Richard ran a cool hand over his hot face. *Why did he make me afraid? It's irrational.* The swine-gnawed head, that was it. It would have unsettled Achilles.

Richard paused at the railing, the grip clutched to his

chest. Sanity began to replace his blind panic, his heart slowing, breathing returning to normal. The trickly feeling in his guts began to recede.

"Eh! *Mon ami!*" François called up from the landing. "I think we will become good friends, *non?*"

Shamed by his irrational fear, buoyed by the high safety of the gallery, protected now by the sanctuary of the cabin deck with its whitewashed wood, windows, and its stewards, Richard called down: "I think not, monsieur. I prefer the company of gentlemen to that of animals. Perhaps you had better go back and root with your hogs!"

François stiffened, eyes narrowing to slits. "François will not forget your words, rich man. Life, she is full of little surprises, *non?*"

With a deep breath, Richard pivoted on his heel and entered the main cabin. He returned to his reading chair beside the stove and settled himself. His heart was racing again, nerves tingling. Despite the cool air, he felt overheated. His hands shook.

What did you just do? Take hold of yourself, Richard.

Picking up Kant, he listened to the hissing sounds of the boilers, the banging and knocking as cargo was moved.

The man was so . . . bestial.

Dismiss it.

But the way those eyes had pinned his soul. . . .

Richard stood, easing up to the window overlooking the landing. Packs of furs were being loaded; the captain, standing by the plank, was making notations in a ledger book. François had vanished from the crowd milling on the shore.

You're being silly, Richard. He willed himself to return to his chair. On impulse, he picked up the grip and unfastened the clasps. Inside, the crisp banknotes remained perfectly packed. Nothing more than paper. Nevertheless, they seemed to have taken on a terrible weight.

FIVE

Errors do not occur just because we do not know some certain things, but because we undertake to judge even though we do not know everything requisite. A large number of false-hoods—indeed almost all of them—owe their origin to such impetuosity. Do you know some predicates of a thing with certainty? Very well then, make these things the basis of your inferences, and you will not err. But suppose you wish to make a definition with them, although you are not certain that you know everything requisite for such a definition? If, in spite of this, you risk a definition, you will fall into error. It is possible therefore to avoid errors if we seek certain and distinct cognitions without presuming so readily to give definitions.

—Immanuel Kant, *An Enquiry into the Distinctness of the Fundamental Principles of Natural Theology and Morals*

Coals burned bright in the firepit at the center of the lodge. The hearthstones—rounded river cobbles thrown into the fire—glowed eerily.

Fire has a puha *all its own.* Heals Like A Willow twisted a strand of her black hair around and around her finger. How did it happen that heating in fire would make dark, impenetrable stone glow reddish-white? She gave up twisting her hair and held her hands out to the radiant warmth.

"Better than freezing on the cliff, don't you think?" Two Half Moons asked. Somewhere in the darkness beyond the lodge, a horse snorted and stomped at the frozen snow.

The warm lodge, with its cheery fire, mocked the terrible cold just beyond the finely tanned buffalo-hide walls. The polished lodgepoles gleamed redly and reminded Willow of bone freshly stripped of meat and still slightly bloody.

Square parfleches, humped mounds of robes, backrests crafted from willow stems, and a stack of firewood furnished Two Half Moons' lodge.

"What will you do now?" the old woman asked.

"Wait out the weather," Willow replied. "Go back to my people."

Two Half Moons rubbed her leathery old face as she peered into the fire. The crimson light accented the tones of the old woman's weathered face. Age hadn't treated her nose kindly; it had a shape that reminded people of a mushroom. Her undershot, toothless jaw snugged up to make a flat line of the wrinkled mouth. Spirit still burned in those obsidian eyes, despite the silver-streaked braids that hung to either side of her round head with its broad cheekbones.

"You are young, girl. I know that your husband's brother will speak to you soon."

"White Hail is just a boy."

"He's a man now. Killed his first enemy. Sought out his vision. Married. And I know he's always admired you. Wanted his wife to be like you."

"Didn't succeed, did he?" Willow reached for the stack of sagebrush and dropped another gnarly branch on the fire. Flames leapt from the leaves and twigs in a bright display of white light, only to subside into coals as the layers of wood charred and peeled back from the stem.

Willow raised her hands in defeat. "Yes, yes, I know he's a man now. I just can't help but think of him as the daring boy with a joke on his lips, and the gleam of fun in his eyes. Remember all the pranks he played?"

"Time has a habit of scuffing such memories away. Live with him for a while and you'll think of him as a husband— no matter that he's younger than you are."

Willow shook her head. "I like White Hail. You know that. But I can't marry him."

"Don't want to be a second wife?" Two Half Moons stabbed at the fire with a cottonwood stick. "Is that it? Afraid he'd make you do all the work? Think Red Calf would make you miserable?"

"She's always looked at me with suspicion."

"Don't be too proud to be a second wife, Willow."

"It's not that. It's that . . ." *I loved my husband. Without him, I don't want to stay here.* Memories of High Wolf, her father, filled her. He'd look at her with that glint in his eyes, and tell her stories of the great *puhagans* again.

"Yes?"

"When the weather clears, *napia,* I'm going back to my people."

Two Half Moons sighed. "It's the middle of winter. Oh, sure, this cold will break. Probably be followed by a warm spell, but you know that spring storms will roll down out of the north before you can get home. Stick your hand out there in the snow and see just how cold cold can be."

"I know how to survive in snow. Besides, I'll be climbing. A person can always find shelter in the mountains, make it from brush, logs, and snow, if nothing else."

"You'll be wading in snow up to your breasts."

"Unlike the *Ku'chendikani,* I remember how to make snowshoes."

"How will you find your *Dukurika*? They could be anywhere up there in the Powder River Mountains."

"They'll be in the southern foothills. Probably camped in the south-facing rock shelters where the sun warms them during the day. They'll be hunting the slopes where the snow blows off, then melts. The deer winter there. That's also the first place the shooting star and biscuit root grow in spring."

Two Half Moons snorted in irritation. "You know everything, don't you?"

Willow gave her a humorless smile. "What can I say? I'm *Dukurika.*"

"It doesn't have to be White Hail. Fast Black Horse would be proud to make you his wife."

"Then I'd be a third wife."

"That's a third of the work you'd have to do if you were the *only* wife."

"Fast Black Horse has the largest horse herd in the band. He kills more buffalo than anyone else. That's why he needs wives. The more he has, the more hides he can process for trade with the Mandan and the Whites."

"And the more fine things you can adorn your clothes with.

You'd be looked up to, admired by everyone in the—''

Willow reached out and placed a hand on the old woman's arm. "I love you, Aunt. But I don't want those things. I don't want the things *Ku'chendikani* want." Silence stretched until Willow began to worry that she might have offended the old woman. She added, "And besides, Slim Pole and Iron Wrist will be happy to be rid of me."

Two Half Moons waved it away. "Perhaps, just a little bit. They're not used to a woman like you, asking questions, prodding and prying at what people believe. They don't trust a woman who uses *puha*. It smacks of something *omaihen*, forbidden. But despite their growling, I think they respect you, girl. Those dreams of yours leave them a little nervous. A woman shouldn't be having visions, shouldn't be fooling around healing people."

Willow shied from thoughts of her husband and son, and said, "Why not? *Puha* is *puha*. It comes and goes where it will."

"A woman can heal . . . but not until her bearing years pass."

Willow threw her hands up. "Monthly bleeding has nothing to do with visions, *puha*, or healing. Precautions have to be taken, that's all. I wouldn't try to heal someone while I was bleeding." She ground her teeth, staring down into the blinking red eyes of the embers. *But that's when the dreams seize me with the greatest power. That's when the visions are the clearest.*

"You do strange enough things when you're bleeding. Wandering off like that. Makes people suspicious that you'd leave the menstrual lodge and go up in the hills to do *Tam Apo* knows what. Some think you're flirting with rock ogres."

"*Pandzoavits* wouldn't want me. I just get bored sitting in the menstrual lodge. What is there to do? Lie around and gossip, make moccasins, do beadwork? *Napia*, let's be honest. I couldn't care less who is sneaking off into the bushes with whom. Most women want to talk about other women. I'd rather talk about why *Tam Apo* made the world the way He did."

Two Half Moons sucked her lips past her gums and nodded.

"I know. That's why I always appreciated you. I think that's why my nephew loved you so much. You were different. Beautiful, exotic, and worthy of his status and souls."

"And that's why I can't take another man here, Aunt. Who could follow in his place?"

Two Half Moons rubbed her face with a bony hand. "No matter what you might think now, with your husband freshly dead, someone always comes along. And you'd better prepare yourself. You'll have a handful of suitors seeking to claim you."

"I can understand White Hail, and maybe Fast Black Horse, but why would the rest want me? Most of them think I'm nothing but trouble, and I'd be the last woman most of their wives would want to see brought into the lodge to share their fire."

The old woman shrugged, extending her hands to the fire. "Some want you because you are young and beautiful. Some want you because by claiming you, they gain some of your husband's status. And then, there are those who see you as a challenge. Like a prize buffalo horse, you have spirit and strength. They are the ones who want to tame you to the halter, make you docile, and control your strange ways."

"They might as well try to trap the lightning."

"Men and women go together. *Tam Apo* made the world that way. I think, deep down in your souls, you know that, don't you?"

Willow bowed her head. "The world might be made that way, but I don't have to like it, do I?"

February 9, 1825
Mississippi River, just below the Chains

Dear Laura:

At last, we've entered the Mississippi. What a broad and manly body of water it is, but so different from the

Ohio, which I consider to be a Greek river, for it has the clarity, beauty, and grace that would inspire a Hellenic poet. This Mississippi, however, is Roman in its nature, brawny, without nonsense or faint virtue. Caesar would have approved. The water of the Mississippi has a very different taste than that of the Ohio. I've noticed the distinct bouquet of must lingering on my tongue after taking a drink. The morning coffee has begun to leave a film of grit on the teeth that was missing before. Not that I should be surprised: Flotsam and brown foam dot the surface.

As we travel northward, more farms have been cut into the forest. Unlike the high bluffs on the Ohio, the hills on the Illinois side of the Mississippi are low, generally farther inland. Ragged outcrops of gray rock, angular and cracked, stand on the eastern shore, while the western side of the river disappears into a maze of trees.

My dear Laura, the world is filled with trees, endless trees. The wary sense of a hunted animal has grown within me when I look out into those sylvan shadows. What a wretched country this is. I am not without my shield, however, against the wild tangle. I clutch my volume of Kant to my chest as a legionnaire would his *scutia*. Behind it, I remain invincible.

Dear Laura, how do I tell you this? Despite my education and rational mind, it defies acceptance that this could be part of *my* world. Does Harvard really exist? Does Professor Ames still lecture about Hegel and Rousseau somewhere on this earth? And, most of all, I ask, are you sitting, even now, your wondrous blue eyes shining? Boston, wondrous Boston, how distant it all seems. It is real, isn't it?

Or have I been carried by some terrible nightmare to a place as dark and ominous as Hades? High above, in the tortured morning sky, patches of shredded cloud are whipped and curled. The moist breeze carries a bitter chill.

As I write this, I am sitting on the gallery, nodding

to the now familiar faces of the other passengers as they pass. My comrades have all come to some sort of amiable relation, addressing each other by first names. But I have remained steadfast, and am still referred to as Mr. Hamilton, or simply "the scholar"—which suits me fine. Thus far, I have been able to maintain my bargain with myself. I remain a gentleman, no matter what.

Please do not feel that I presume upon our short acquaintance, but your face fills my dreams every night as I fall asleep. I may be bold, but you have become a source of strength for me, Laura. No moment passes but that I think of you, and count the days until I may pay my respects to you in person again.

> Your Obedient Servant,
> Richard Hamilton

PS: Give my best to Will, and tell him that I remain a fortress!

Chuffing and clanking, the *Virgil* steamed north into the Mississippi's current. The notion hadn't quite sunk into Richard's skull that speed was relative to current. Whereas the *Virgil* had raced down the Ohio, she now plowed along at a quarter her old speed while the stacks belched black smoke. At night, sparks streaked out of the scalloped tops.

As he walked along the gallery railing, he looked down on the heads of the huddled people who couldn't afford a stateroom. They camped on the lower deck amidst barrels, crates, and bales, wrapped in blankets or worn coats, and sheltered by bits of canvas strung to whatever was available. A shift in the breeze carried the odor of unwashed humanity to Richard's nose. A child squalled, and Richard located the young mother: little more than a bone rack surrounded by four other clamoring children. Without concern, the gingham-dressed woman bared a dirt-smudged breast and gave the shrieking infant her nipple. At the same time she harangued the older children in a twangy nasal voice.

"Dobe! Y'ain't t' knit at yer bruther! Stoppit! I'll lallup ya one if'n ye don't!"

The murdered English grated on Richard with the same irritation as sand on window glass.

And this, Father, is the frontier. They shall build a nation of brutes where once pristine nature flowered. Describing this wretched state to Laura would take the most delicate of language. How did one communicate such unpleasant truths to a lady?

"Good day, sir." Charles Eckhart walked up and leaned his elbows on the gallery railing. He wore a dark frock coat, tailored trousers, and white shirt. A pale pink scarf covered his throat, and his beaver hat topped his head.

"And a good day to you, too, sir."

"It appears we've made good time. When last I made this journey, the engine stopped. Evidently the piston needed repacking, whatever that means, and we lay tied off on a small island just below the Chains until parts could be brought."

Richard gestured below. "And the hoi polloi camped on the deck the whole time?"

"Some did. Others were ferried over to the western shore to walk the rest of the way into Saint Louis. They had the better of the deal, and reached the city before the rest of us."

Richard shook his head, watching the woman with her dirty children. She'd seized the oldest boy by the ear and was dragging him screaming into the shelter of her canvas, the infant still suckling her flattened breast.

Richard lowered his voice. "Look at them. How can human beings—*rational* beings—live like that? You've seen their farms, the flatboats. The difference between these wretched beings and mere beasts is but a distinction of language, not nature."

Eckhart reached into his pocket for the inevitable cigar, but having no light, simply rolled it around in his mouth like a brown stick. "My father always taught me that if every man was a king, we'd all die of cold and hunger because no one would build the castles, grow the food, or cut the firewood. Now, me, I've never been to Boston, sir.

I, however, find it difficult to believe that all men there are kings."

"Assuredly not, but they don't live in mud and excrement, either." The domestic squabble below ended with a meaty slap.

"People do what they must," Eckhart said. "I dare say, sir, that while you and I, both gentlemen with advantages of station, honor, and education, might abhor the conditions and actions of others, the Holy Book teaches us charity in thought and action. Opportunity comes of breeding, sir. However, a gentleman should also seek to understand the plight of those beneath his station."

"A philosopher, sir, does not concern himself with charity, but with truth and understanding. I have dedicated myself to the study of our nature, and what it means to be a man. I confess, as I watch these people, I find nothing outside of shape in common with them."

"And should your station change, Mr. Hamilton? As an educated man, I assume you have read Shakespeare. Kings, like all mortals, rise and fall."

Richard made an airy gesture. "Fall I might, but I can promise you this, sir. I will be dead before I ever consent to live as they do."

Eckhart carefully removed his cigar, bowing slightly. "A man of honor and integrity, sir, should never have to. Thank you for a pleasant discussion. Should you be interested, we will be starting a game within the hour. Just in case, sir, you'd be challenged by something so unscientific as luck."

"Thank you, but I believe I shall find leisure with my studies. As always, the conversation was my pleasure."

Eckhart studied him with thoughtful eyes, started to turn away, and then spoke in a low voice: "Mr. Hamilton, most of my companions on this journey consider you to be a most irritating young man. For myself, however, I think you're just frightened, hiding behind your books and arrogance so that you don't have to face the world. For a philosopher to hide seems counterproductive to the search for truth."

"I don't see that that is any of your concern, sir."

"Perhaps not, Mr. Hamilton. But . . . well, I suppose you could call it friendly advice. Something you may or may not have had acquaintance with in the past. Good day.''

Eckhart touched his hat and strolled along the gallery toward the forward cabin.

Of all the . . . Richard started to turn, then froze. François, the boatman from Fort Massac, leaned against a davit, arms crossed, beard and sash toyed with by the wind. Richard met those deadly blue eyes. His soul shivered for an instant before he forced himself to turn away.

Just coincidence, that's all. Many people travel to Saint Louis.

He'd made but a step when François's voice called up, "*Mon ami,* I have something for you. A gift!"

Richard kept his back straight and walked away. *He's an animal, nothing more. Ignore him.*

Heals Like A Willow slept, curled on her side. She'd drawn her knees to her chest, arms tucked tight, like a lost child. Layers of heavy buffalo robes covered her. Her long hair had twisted until it covered her face in a black web. Her hands twitched in time to the mewing sounds locked in her throat. Outside, the icy winter wind worried the thin lodge walls that protected her from the brunt of winter; they whispered around the narrowed smoke hole. In the firepit, faint eddies stirred patterns in the glowing coals. Patterns— like the shape of Power.

Willow dreamed . . .

I can sense it coming . . . something terrible. I look around, seeing the mountains in the distance, so clear that I could reach out and touch their rocky heights. Snow blows through the sagebrush around my feet and whispers through the tough stems. It seems to be laughing, mocking me. The feeling is worse; something is very wrong. I look around, searching desperately for the danger. I see nothing, only smooth bluffs and the glass-bead blue sky overhead.

And then, from out of the very air, I hear cackling laughter. I know that sound; it is very old, from the beginning of the world. Coyote the Trickster's laughter sends chills up my back.

I run.

As I do, the horror comes from behind, hurling itself forward with the speed of a racing pronghorn. I run harder, willing my feet to move like the wind. Breath tears in my lungs as I sprint eastward, driven by this unseen horror.

The dark threat is so close. I feel it tracing cold fingers across my back; tendrils try to close around me, to pull me back into its dark interior.

If I falter, allow myself to be drawn into the black depth, I am lost. My souls are screaming at the faintest touch of the blackness.

Fear rushes through me, and I leap arroyos, race up grassy hills, and fly down slopes faster than falcon on the wind.

Run! Panic curls around my guts, squeezing tightly to wring the last bit of energy from my burning muscles. The dark horror is bearing down, twining in the wind, searching to snare my soul and drag me down.

Run! my husband shouts from above. I dare not look up. A misstep and I will fall, the landing worse than any tumble from a racing horse. My bones would splinter, and my flesh tear when I bounced across the ground like a buffalo-hide ball. I'd lie stunned, and oddly painless in that moment before agony seeped through the bleeding wounds to crush me. I'd gasp desperately for breath, my shattered chest incapable of filling.

And then the black horror would settle over me like smoke from a burning forest. As it tightened itself around me, it would suffocate my souls and suck them down into the terrible eternity.

Run! I tell myself.

I race down a long slope, legs pumping, feet hammering the grass. Before me I see a line of trees. My hair is flying out behind me, the tips teasing the black horror. I am moving so fast the trees seem to rush up at me in an impenetrable barrier, the trunks gray, branches waving in the wind.

An arrow might see the world flying toward it in this way, the whistling passage, the end growing ever larger until . . .

I burst through the trees, and have vague memories of snapping branches, of lashing leaves. Then I hang, the sensation that of floating, feet churning empty air, as I am stopped short by a great river. A huge expanse of water flows before me, menacing, with secrets hidden beneath those swirling depths.

With water blocking my escape, I pant, a hand to my aching chest. Blackness filters away the world. The horror looms in the sky to the west, blotting out the trees. It has a shape: a huge creature with soulless eyes.

I back into the river. Better to drown, and free the *mugwa*, than to be swallowed by this horrible power.

And suddenly the mist dog appears. It comes from the side, a foggy white shape, and takes a position facing the menace before me. *Tam Apo*, it is too late. I have nowhere else to go. Water is up to my knees, and I am afraid to leap into those cold black depths.

The blackness arches over the sky. I have nothing left, no escape route. Only the misty white dog separates us. He is too small. How can mist defeat such terrible, evil power?

I crouch and scream as the black terror beast springs like a coyote onto a mouse. In that instant, I see the white mist dog leap. . . .

Heals Like A Willow cried out and jerked awake. She blinked her eyes open to see the familiar lodge. Her fingers were entwined in the thick neck wool of her heavy buffalo robe. Frost tinged the curly brown fur before her mouth, and hoary patches of breath had frozen where her long black hair lay close to her face.

The images remained as vivid as if she'd just lived them in the light of day. *A dream. Only a dream.* But so powerful.

She gasped in relief, happy to fill her lungs with the biting air. Beyond the tawny translucence of the lodge, two dogs were barking, and a man shouted at them to go away. The barking persisted until a hollow thump was followed by a piercing yelp, and silence.

Then a pack of coyotes sent their songs like thorns into the quiet night.

Coyote had laughed at her, as if daring her to run, knowing that nothing could save her from the terrifying darkness.

But what had been the meaning of the misty white dog?

Willow rolled onto her back. Since her husband's death, most of her dreams had been this way. Pursuit, panic, fear, and flight.

What is it? Is the Spirit World trying to tell me something? Give me some warning?

Her breasts ached, as if the exertion from the dream flight had settled within them. She reached up beneath the heavy robe and massaged them, a familiar tenderness in the nipples. As if her son were still there, once again drawing life from her. A shiver passed through her chest and down her spine to warm her pelvis.

The ache in her breasts hardened with the memory of his movements within the cradle of her hips. How miraculous that her husband's seed could take nourishment inside her, become that life that had been so much a part of her.

I gave him life from my own. A man couldn't do that. He but planted his seed and was done with it. *I* made *my boy. From my pain and blood, he was born. From my breasts, he drew his life.*

"From me," she whispered, and lifted her damp fingers to inhale the fragrant musk of her milk.

Then she turned her head and wept, the sobs choked so that no one outside the lodge might know the bitter depths of her grief.

She was called the *Maria.* Travis ran his hand along the cargo box as he walked down the *passe avant,* the cleated walkway that ran the length of the deck on either side of the boat. It was nothing more than a narrow path between the cargo box and the gunwales. *Maria* measured forty feet in length, with a twelve-foot beam. When loaded with thirty tons of freight, she drew less than three feet of water. Rude wooden benches in the bow provided a place for eight oarsmen.

Travis walked toward the stern and climbed atop the cargo box. Here the patroon, or steersman, stood and handled the long steering oar that extended out over the stern of the boat. A twenty-foot mast had been stepped into the middle of the box, and carried a square sail for those rare days when the wind was right.

"How's she look?" Dave Green asked, the weak winter sun gleaming in his blond hair as he clambered up the ladder to stand beside Travis.

"Reckon she'll do. From what I can see of the hull, she's somewhat scarred up, but the planks seem sound."

"I looked her over from painter to steering oar. I know something about boats, and I couldn't find much wrong with her," Green stated.

"Yep, wal, I've pulled lesser boats upriver." Travis stared out over the swirling muddy water. The Mississippi had a raw look, heavy with snow melt and churning mud. The Illinois bank to the east lay muzzled in patchy gray trees. Even from here, Travis could see the distant Trappist monastery on the big Indian mound above Cahokia.

"Come on." Green turned. "Let's look inside."

Travis followed Green down into the cargo box. Some of the trade goods had already been stored: barrels of flour and salt rested neatly between the ribs on either side of the deck planking. The six-foot clearance made him crouch. Ropes, to stabilize the cargo, had been tied off from the mast to rings bolted onto the ribs.

Loading a keelboat for the upper Missouri required special skill. The cargo had to be balanced to maintain the boat's trim in the water. Trading would occur throughout the journey, so different kinds of goods needed to be easily accessible at all times. Guns, shot, and other durables were placed low in case the hull was breached by a sawyer or some other underwater obstruction. Powder, cloth, and goods easily water-damaged rode higher in hopes they could be salvaged before the river exacted its toll.

"Wal, Davey, weather's turning. Ice'll be a-breaking upriver any day now. Time's about here."

Green fingered the edge of a barrel packed with hanks of colorful Italian glass beads. "And we're still short enough men for a crew."

Travis pulled at his grizzled beard. "The good Lord provides, or so I was told once upon a time."

Green knotted a fist. "Time? That's the one thing we don't have." He pursed his lips. "Huh! Seems like all of my life, I've been gambling. Well, all right. I say we bust a gut and sail within the week." He leveled his gaze at Travis. "Find me the men, Travis. We've got to go. The sooner the better. Too many people know what we're about. If word gets to Clark, he'll stop us cold."

Travis rapped one of the barrels with his knuckles. "I'll find us enough crew ter get out of Saint Louis—provided ye ain't picky about what sort I gets. We can recruit as we go, too. Reckon we ought ter be able to fill out a boatload. Won't be a brigade like Lisa could muster, but by Hob, we otta be able ter piece together a boatload."

"That . . . or there'll be hell to pay."

Travis made a clicking sound with his tongue. "Waugh! Yer headed for the mouth of the Big Horn, smack inta Injun country, an yer worried about Hell? Reckon we'll git enough of that ter fill a lard eater's gut and then some." *An' we'll be pilgrim lucky if'n there's a one of us with his topknot left by next spring.*

The sun shone brightly in the cloudless blue sky. With characteristic suddenness, the terrible cold snap had broken, driven away by west winds that had howled out of the night.

White Hail squinted up toward the bright sun, shielding his eyes with a callused hand. Their camp lay in the Warm Valley bottoms of the Big River. To the west, the Warm Wind Mountains rose in tall peaks capped with a bright, aching white against the deep blue of the sky. To the north, the tall, snow-clad heights of Coyote Penis Mountain rose as a symbol of the Trickster's culpability. In the beginning times, Coyote had paid dearly for unmitigated lust, his member being turned into rock as a reminder to all who saw it that moderation was often prudent.

White Hail studied the distant mountain for a moment,

thinking about his beloved brother, about death, and about desire, if not lust.

No. I never lusted after Heals Like A Willow. But I have desired her all these years. Desired, yes. Loved, definitely, but not lusted. White Hail glanced around, aware that a man had to be careful about such things. He wasn't sure, but it seemed that the Spirit World listened in on a man's thoughts sometimes. That, or perhaps it was the *Nunumbi,* the little people who hid in the brush, behind logs, and in holes. They had strange abilities and did no little mischief.

"Where are you off to?" Red Calf asked, walking up behind him. Her belly was swollen with their first child, and she'd been nothing but bother throughout her pregnancy. She acted more like a bitter hawk than ever before.

Red Calf would capture any man's fancy. Her oval face, large dark eyes, and shining long hair had only accented the saucy sway of her hips when she walked. People had warned White Hail about marrying her, but somehow he'd misled himself into believing that Red Calf's tart answers, her resolute defiance, and unquenchable spirit paralleled the qualities of Heals Like A Willow.

Fact was, White Hail had married the human equivalent of a snappy bitch who'd nip the fingers off the first person who tried to be kind to her.

"You're going to see her, aren't you?" Red Calf narrowed her lustrous eyes to slits.

"She's my brother's wife. You know what is expected of me."

Red Calf's smile hardened. "Indeed, husband. It all worked out, didn't it? You've always done everything you could to follow in your brother's tracks. Now you can slip your lance into her sheath, see if you fit her as tightly as your brother did."

He balled a fist. The sudden anger, mixed with the pain, would have made it easy to flatten her. No one would have sucked their lips, or looked away in censure. The muscles in his arms knotted, but as always, the promise of retaliation in her dark eyes quenched any thought of striking back.

She'll take the child away from me. That, or she'll find

some way of disgracing me, publicly humiliating me. So he said, "I ought to divorce you."

"Go ahead."

White Hail turned on his heel, striding for Two Half Moons' lodge.

"She's trouble!" Red Calf called behind him. "Goes out into the hills during her bleeding. Why? So that the rock ogres can feel her with their pitch-sticky hands? She dreams about things a woman shouldn't! Is that it? You want to bring a witch into our lodge?"

White Hail willed himself to deafness. *Brother, I'm sorry it came to this. I cry out that your spirit may know. I have always loved Willow. That was no secret between us. But, brother, I would give her up forever to have you back alive.*

High above, an eagle screamed. White Hail looked up. Eagle, the messenger from the Spirit World. His brother understood.

White Hail slowed as he approached the doorway to Two Half Moons' lodge. He pulled his buckskin shirt straight, checking to see that the eagle-bone breastplate lay flat and the horsehair tassels swung free. The glossy scalp locks—coup he'd cut from a dead *A'ni* warrior's head—hung down from the tops of his sleeves.

He cleared his throat, scratching on the leather of the lodge. "It is White Hail, come to see Heals Like A Willow. Is she within?"

"Come, *teci*," she said. "I've been expecting you."

His heart leapt. White Hail pulled the doorway back and stepped inside, crossing to the man's side and seating himself. It took a moment for his eyes to adjust to the dim interior.

She sat on the buffalo robes across from him, Two Half Moons' backrest between them. Dying coals in the firepit radiated enough heat to keep the temperature comfortable.

As his vision improved, he noted the puffiness around her eyes, the drawn look around her mouth, and the disheveled hair. Was this the same wondrous woman whose laughter sparked like flint on steel, whose eyes laughed and danced like dew on grass?

Despite the haggard look, her beauty remained. Her heart-shaped face, delicate, straight nose, and full lips were meant to be admired. Even uncombed, the thick wealth of her raven hair contrasted to the firm lines of her forehead and accented the thin arches of her eyebrows. He wished he could reach out, run a fingertip along the smooth hollows of her cheeks.

He'd seen his brother do that. Seen her melt at the gentle touch. And his heart cried out at the pain stirred by the memory.

"My soul cries for him, too," White Hail began.

"I didn't know it would be so hard," she whispered, looking down. Her slim hands occupied themselves with the fringes of her dress. If only he could hold those slender fingers, quiet them.

"I want to thank you for attending to him the way you did. I would have been there, helped you to sing for him, pray for him, and for the infant, too."

"I know. But you were hunting, my brother. Attending to your duty to your family. I only attended to mine."

"I thought . . . thought that if I could bring him fresh meat, hot liver, that it would help. Make him strong. I didn't expect him to go so fast." White Hail gestured with his hands. How perfectly futile.

"No one did." The corners of her lips trembled.

White Hail took a deep breath. "I came here to ask you to share him with me. Together . . . over the years. I cannot replace him. I would not want to. My brother's lodge is gone. You have no lodge to go to. I would have you come to mine, as my second wife."

SIX

As long as men remained content with their rustic huts;
as long as they were happy with clothes crafted from the
skins of animals, sewn with thorns and fish bones; as long
as they continued to consider feathers and shells sufficient for ornaments, and to paint their bodies in different
colors, to improve or ornament their bows and arrows,
to fashion little fishing boats with sharp-edged
stones, or clumsy instruments of music; in a
word, as long as they undertook such works as
a single person could accomplish, and stuck to
such arts as did not require the joint efforts
of several hands, they lived free, healthy,
honest, and happy, as much as their nature
would admit.

—Jean-Jacques Rousseau, *Discourse on the Origin
and Foundation of Inequality Among Mankind*

No change of expression crossed Heals Like a Willow's face after White Hail made his proposal. She
sat in silence while he endured the hollow beating
of his heart.

"No," she said at last.

He squirmed, as if movement would vanquish the sudden
discomfort in his breast. "I would give you everything you
ever wanted." He swallowed hard. "If you wish, I . . . I'll
divorce Red Calf first. Make you *kwihi*, my first wife." *And
give up my son.* Other sons could be made.

She raised her tired eyes, shaking her head. "I cannot be
your *kwihi*, White Hail. Not your second wife, or your
first."

"But. . . . Have I done something to displease you?"

She smiled sadly. "No, my brother. Quite the contrary. I
like you a great deal. I will always think of you fondly. Of

the jokes and the laughter. When he looked at you, love filled his eyes. It will fill mine from now on as it did his. But not with a wife's love, *teci*.''

''I don't understand.'' White Hail frowned. ''Is it wealth? I'll bring you all you can stand. Horses from the *A'ni*. Scalps from the *Pa'kiani*. Mirrors, beads, colored cloth, and metal kettles from the White men. I'll leave tomorrow, and not return until I can shower you with—''

''Enough, my brother.'' She raised a hand and resettled herself on the robe-covered backrest. ''I have no need of those things—let alone the White man's wealth. It isn't a matter of wealth, and shouldn't ever be.''

''Wealth is proof. Proof of a man's ability to provide for his women.''

''That's a *Ku'chendikani* belief. Not mine.''

''I would see you decorated in colors, each step you take accented by the chime of bells. I would have all people look up as you pass and say: 'There goes Heals Like A Willow, wife of White Hail.' ''

She arched one of those shapely eyebrows. ''To hear that, you would ruin yourself?''

''Ruin?''

''Isn't that what Red Calf wants? Wealth and status, to be drowned in the White man's magical colors, metal, and looking glasses? Isn't that why you've been gone more than you've been at home?''

He sighed and studied the worn parfleches stacked along the lodge liner. They added to the old lodge cover's musty smell of leather. ''A man must travel a long way, across very dangerous country, to reach the Mandan territory and the *Ha'nidika*. When he gets there, he finds that he needs a great many beaver hides, buffalo robes, and horses for the poorest of the White man's wonderful things.''

''Yet you've been across the Plains twice.''

''I have.'' He grinned proudly. ''And I'll go as often as I like in the future, too. I'm careful, cunning, and fast as the wind.''

''And if, let's say, the *Pa'kiani* catch you with your horses, pelts, and robes?''

''They'll kill me. That's why I don't intend on getting caught!'' He clapped his hands to accent the point.

''My husband didn't intend to die from soul wasting, either.'' Her challenging eyes met his across the fire. ''If I had a husband I loved, I would rather walk in hole-riddled rags than think he was dead over something as silly as White man's goods.''

''A man gains honors by taking such risks. So does his wife. Would you have people think I am a coward?'' He glanced up to where the lodgepoles were blackened with soot from the smoke hole.

''I would have you be as brave and courageous as I know you are. I would also have you be wise and intelligent. Let me ask you, is it better for a man to lose his life way off someplace trading for White man's goods, or fighting bravely to buy time for his wife and children to escape the village when the *Pa'kiani* attack?''

White Hail stifled a growl and shifted again. ''You twist words around, did you know that?''

''Do I?''

''All right, the *Pa'kiani* have guns that they trade for with the British. I must have a gun to fight them. How do I get a gun if I don't travel across the Plains to where the traders are?''

''Ah! A gun!'' She clasped her hands in excitement. ''And then you must trade for powder and bullets. After a season, you must trade for more powder and bullets. And then the little iron spring breaks inside the gun—and you have nothing more than wood and metal. It's awkward to swing it, so you can't even use it to club mountain sheep to death in a trap.''

White Hail glared at her. "You try a man's peace."

"And you would marry me?" She cocked her head slightly. "Besides, I thought I heard Red Calf shout just before you came here. I think she called me a witch?"

"She needs time to think this through."

Willow gave him a level stare. "I see. White Hail, I meant what I said. My eyes will always shine with love for you, but only as your friend, and sister by marriage. I ask you, stop risking yourself to provide Red Calf with White man trinkets."

He paused thoughtfully. His *puha* had been with him on each of the dangerous trips to the Mandan country. As long as he listened to Power, remained pious, it would protect him. "Death is part of life. All things die. And the things the White man brings upriver . . . well, they're magical."

"Such magic, like their guns, comes at a cost, *teci*."

He fingered his chin thoughtfully. "I was only a boy when the Astor men came into our camp. I'd lived barely five summers then. I see it as if it were yesterday. They were headed west, across the mountains. I remember the story they told. A canoe, so big it carried more men than could be counted, with white wings that the wind blew. They were to meet this magical canoe. I followed the White men everywhere they went about our camp. I jumped at the thunder sound of their guns, and touched their colored cloth. I decided then that I wanted to be like them."

"You will remember," she countered, "that the Astor men got to the mouth of the Western River, found that their magical canoe had sunk, and most of them starved their way back through our country a year later."

"They are still magical."

"We would be wise to stick to our own magic. I've heard of their medicine water, how it makes warriors lose their souls and go crazy like mad buffalo."

White Hail spread his hands wide. "I've tasted their medicine water. I never thought anything could taste more vile than phlox tea, but after it hits your stomach, it makes up for the horrible burning taste. It sets your soul free."

She seemed unimpressed. "Seek the high places to free your soul, my brother."

"For someone who's never met a White man, you don't seem to like them very much."

"I don't think they're good for us. I've heard that horses were brought to our world by White men. I don't think that was good for us either."

"You've got funny notions, my sister. I think I love you all the more for them. I only wish you would reconsider and move into my lodge."

"You would live to regret the day I entered your lodge. It wouldn't be good for any of us. Not for you, or Red Calf, or me."

He looked awkwardly down at his hands. "I have always loved you. Therefore, it would be good for me to have you as a wife. You will make me think of many things, as you made my brother think. As to Red Calf, she will adapt, or I will move her things outside the lodge. As for you, you will have my love and protection. I will cherish you, provide for you, and give you my souls. Wouldn't that be good for you?"

Her dark eyes never wavered as she said, "I could never lie with you, my brother."

White Hail managed to keep from squirming under her gaze. He'd dreamed of her full breasts pressed against his chest. Of the warmth of her skin against his as her legs locked around him. "After a period of time to—"

"I'd always be with him, White Hail. No matter how much you think you love me, it would slowly drive you crazy to know that when we lay together under the robes, I would be coupling with your brother—no matter how many years dead."

February 30, 1825
Mississippi River north of Kaskaskia, Illinois

Dear Laura:

Tomorrow I will finally land in Saint Louis and discharge my final duty to my father. Immediately thereafter, I shall set forth upon my return voyage to Boston. It is possible that I shall arrive at your door before this post. After my task is completed, I shall have no more to do with my father, or his business. And what good riddance it is.

The weather has been terribly dreary, and I reluctantly admit, my spirits have been flagging. I have had enough of gray clouds and endless rain. The ceiling leaks here and there, and you should hear the jokes that pass back and forth about our leaky ark. Please excuse the spots where the ink ran. A new leak has sprung overhead, and I have had to relocate to a drier table.

I have been thinking a great deal about you, and about the possibility of our future together. Since it was Will who first broached the subject—and since he favors such a union—I hope these words are not too forward. I want to let you know that you have changed my life. For the first time, I have envisioned the future with clear eyes. As a professor of philosophy, I won't be a rich man, but I will be able to provide you with a warm hearth, cherished love, and a respectable future. If I win your hand, you will have made me the happiest man in all of America.

I will seal this now, and post it upon arrival at the Le Barras Hotel. Know that I send you my fondest regards and brightest hopes. Give your wonderful brother my regards—and, of course, your parents as well.

> Your Obedient Servant,
> Richard Hamilton

Richard sat at the table nearest the wet window in the main cabin, a blanket wrapped tightly around him. He thoughtfully turned the pages of his copy of Kant, squinting in the leaden light. Beyond the plank walls, the patter of cold rain shifted with each gust of wind. Wood creaked in complaint as the *Virgil* rattled and churned her way upriver against the roiling current.

The monotonous drone of conversation within the cabin had faded into the background, no more annoying than the coffee-shop babble or tavern talk where Richard had done most of his studying. Every now and then, cries of "Full house!" were followed by groans, hands slapping the table, and the clatter of pasteboards at the card game.

Ah, Laura, what can I tell you about these barbarians? How I wish I could see you again. Your smile would soothe the depths of my soul.

If nothing else, this terrible journey had brought home an understanding of how lucky he was to have Boston to return to. Boston . . . and Laura.

He closed his eyes, imagining her as she sat beside a warm fire, needlework in her hand. He'd do nothing but study her by the hour, and count himself the luckiest man alive. She'd look up, meet his eyes, and they'd share that singular intimacy of a man and his wife.

He'd rise, take her hand, and together they'd walk through the Commons, planning their future together. When he tried hard enough, he could imagine her hand in his.

With irritation, then, Richard looked up as the Virginian, Eckhart, stopped beside his table. He wore a charcoal gray coat over a frilled white shirt.

"Still reading, I see. May I?" Eckhart pointed to the chair. "It appears, sir, to be the only seat left."

Richard hesitated, remembering Eckhart's parting words. "Of course."

Richard resumed his study as Eckhart sat and pulled one of the inevitable cigars from his frock coat. Kant's pedantic language was difficult enough without blue plumes of pungent smoke drifting in front of his face.

In defeat, Richard closed his book and lifted an eyebrow at the planter.

"What is that?" Eckhart indicated the book with his cigar. "Must be engrossing, sir. You're the only man I know who could cross half the continent and see nothing but words."

"Immanuel Kant. A German philosopher. This book is his *Groundwork of the Metaphysic of Morals.*"

Eckhart waved his cigar. *"Groundwork for the Meta . . .* I see. Indeed. And, what, pray tell, does your Mr. Can't say?"

"Kant, sir. K-A-N-T." *Think of it as a challenge of rationality.* "Kant wrote his *Groundwork of the Metaphysic of Morals* to elaborate on the ideas introduced in his *Critique of Pure Reason.* I refer, of course, to the second edition, the 1788 revision."

Eckhart blinked and cocked his head.

Richard steepled his fingers. "Kant makes the following assumptions: He observes that man has two conflicting states. The first is the sensual, or, if you will, the emotional aspect. In opposition is the rational element of our being. Our sensuous nature provides the basis for most of our actions. For instance, the thought of revolution may indeed be a rational course of action—but only when passion is stirred do we find the will to act. Rational action is generally, therefore, the slave of our emotional nature. However, when we rise beyond our natures, moral decisions can be ipso facto the reason for undertaking actions. From reading Kant, it is my personal opinion that, as men, it is our duty to act from moral principle rather than emotion. Only when we reach that state will we improve the human condition."

Eckhart drew on his cigar and muttered, "I see," in the thick cloud of exhaled smoke.

"The problem becomes more distinct when placed in context with Newton's discoveries in physics." Richard flexed his fingers. "Kant is the first man to realize the importance of Newton's work *vis-à-vis* philosophy. Newton believes the universe to be predetermined, functioning just as reliably as a clock. And if this is the case, what role will autonomous play? As men, we must define the nature of moral decision on its own merit, and not just in relation to the attainment of a certain goal. Otherwise, we become as mechanical as the clock."

Eckhart nodded politely, his eyes oddly unfocused.

"Science, passion, and morality must all be brought into focus in our modern world. Thus, if you remember my reference to revolution, we must ask ourselves: Are we engaging in this action to attain something, for our own gain''— *as my father would do*—''or for a grander moral purpose?''

Eckhart sniffed. ''Revolution, sir, is for freedom from tyranny.''

''Indeed, sir? And do the slaves working in your fields feel free from tyranny?''

Eckhart stiffened. ''I have heard, sir, that such notions were gaining popularity in Boston. Am I to understand that you, Mr. Hamilton, are an abolitionist?''

''One need but read Epictetus to question the very nature of slavery, sir. And Rousseau indirectly brings the entire debate into focus in his *Discourse on Inequality,* but lest you should become offended, I might add that my father, a Bostonian of no little influence, keeps slaves in his house.'' *And if you knew how offensive that was to me, you would no doubt demand satisfaction on the field of honor, or something equally . . . Virginian.*

At Eckhart's relaxation, Richard experienced an unexplained relief. *But why did I back down?*

The cigar stabbed in Richard's direction. ''Then, sir, I take it that you have no objections to the institution of slavery?''

''I do—but within the groundwork I have just outlined. In Kantian terms, I believe it is morally improper. One human being should not dominate another.''

''You are assuming, sir, that the Negro is as much a human being as we are. I find your words curious, however.'' Eckhart pointed at the rain-slick window. ''I have noted, Mr. Hamilton, that you have similar reservations about many of your fellow passengers, white though they might be. I refer to the ones huddled under their tarps on the main deck. From your own lips, I have heard you call them animals. To the contrary, I do not believe my slaves to be animals, though I think we can agree to accept that their race is not equal to ours in intelligence, ability, or nature.''

''Well done, sir,'' Richard said softly. At the hard look in Eckhart's eyes, his nerves had begun to prickle. Somewhat uncertainly, he continued: ''I must argue, however, that the human condition which I abhor is an artificial one. The ignorant and unwashed masses have been created by the very nature of our civilization. I think we can agree that the institution of slavery is also an artifact of social, religious, and commercial aspirations. The question remains: What is the state of man in nature? To find truly free men, we must go beyond the frontier, beyond the reach of the slavers, and find the pure man in his unspoiled state. If Rousseau is right—and I believe he is—only there will you find man living in a truly free and egalitarian condition.''

For a long moment, Eckhart stared thoughtfully at the ash on his cigar. ''I think, Mr. Hamilton, that you've been too long in your books. If I follow the current of your conversation, you think that all the things that make us great, our institutions, our industry and independence, are, at their core, evil.''

Richard tapped the heavy pages of his book. ''It is only after you begin to examine the nature of civilization that you begin to understand; but to do so, you must uproot the entire thing. Look beneath the very foundations. Civilization, by nature of its very existence, must exploit the many for the advantage of the few. It finds itself, therefore, in constant opposition to the moral progress of humanity.''

Eckhart watched Richard through thoughtfully lidded eyes. ''You have the most interesting ideas, Mr. Hamilton. However, were I you, I would consider this: It's this same civilization that you so decry, along with its institutions, that allows you to ride up here in warmth and comfort while your rabble down there on the deck are wet, miserable, and shivering. Civilization, sir, keeps the savages from dragging you out of your door at night and using your books for firewood. You may talk philosophy all you want, but without civilization, you'd be out in the forest as we speak, and I dare say, fairly unwashed yourself.''

Richard chuckled. ''Indeed I might, Mr. Eckhart. Assuming, that is, that my mind was less keen than it is. However, it is an incontrovertible fact that I have the knowledge that I have. *Fait accompli.* No matter what the circumstances, I will always remain a moral man dedicated to the study of philosophy.''

''Sir, I don't believe you heard a single word I said to you on the deck the other day.'' Eckhart paused. ''For your sake, I hope you can always hide your true self behind your books and speeches. My father once told me that a man's values had to be lived, and not talked. If you will excuse me, I see a chair has opened up at the card table." Eckhart stood, tapping the brim of his hat. "A most refreshing conversation, sir. Good day."

Richard wet his lips as he resettled his book. *I do live them, you oafish Virginian baboon! Did I not, I'd most assuredly be anywhere but here, consorting with the likes of you.*

The *Virgil* huffed and rattled, and no one seemed to pay any heed to the rain that dripped through the plank ceiling. Tomorrow they would arrive at Saint Louis.

And then, Father, I shall deliver your money, spend a night in Saint Louis, and rebook passage on Virgil's *return voyage to Pittsburgh.*

He gave the grip a reassuring nudge with the tip of his toe as he stared out at the stormy dusk. Slanting rain marred the river with patterns of rings. The forest dripped with cold water, shadowed and ominous. How perfectly dismal. He shook himself, throwing off the dark sense of despair. By June he would be back at Harvard and his father would have been defeated. The old man hadn't understood just how easy it was to travel to Saint Louis these days.

And I've been able to continue my studies the entire time. Richard forced his attention to the page, only to have Eckhart's words creep into his thoughts.

Richard rubbed mist from the glass and gazed uneasily at the thick forest. In the twilight, his imagination conjured faces out of the interwoven trees. They mocked him like the masks from a Greek tragedy.

He retired late that night, jumpy and irritable, not even bothering to light his lamp. He discounted the smell of rot as something coming from below decks. Thus it was that he didn't discover the package until the following morning.

Only after he splashed icy water onto his face and blinked in the gray morning light did he perceive that his trunk wasn't quite closed. He made a quick check, ascertaining that while someone had been through his clothing, nothing

was missing. His satchel of books had been searched. And then he saw the bundle of cloth.

When he lifted it to the small washstand, the noxious odor filled his nostrils. The cloth was filthy with dirt, dried mud, and grease stains. The whole had been tied up with twine.

Throw it out?

Some perversity made Richard untie the string. The cloth stuck to the heavy bundle, and had to be tugged away. For a moment, Richard stared, seeking to identify . . .

He gasped, backing away until he came up against his cabin door. A panicked scream stuck soundlessly in his throat. He'd seen it once before, being savaged by hogs.

There, on his washstand, rested the grisly, rotting remains of a human head.

Heals Like A Willow exhaled slowly to watch her breath rise, delicate, in the lavender morning air. Then she followed the trail worn through the crusted snow. The way led down among the winter-nude cottonwoods to the ice-cloaked banks of the river. Frosted grass crunched under Willow's moccasins, and the dank odor of brown leaves and last year's vegetation filled her nose with pungency. She carried an extra blanket and a section of dried buffalo gut.

To the east, pink tipped the high clouds that huddled just above the silhouetted horizon. Morning would break soon, and with it the chore of moving camp. In the stillness, she could hear people already calling to each other in the village behind her. The horses had eaten all of the grass within a half-day's ride. Despite the time of year—raiders seldom traveled in winter—it was too dangerous to pasture the herds beyond the camp's protective warriors.

Horses, always horses. Willow shook her head as she reached the edge of the river. People had already broken the thin film of ice that had formed during the night. This place had been chosen because the water ran fast beside the bank, so the ice didn't thicken.

Willow dropped her blanket and gut container before she shed her robe, then quickly doffed her dress. Her warm skin prickled in the chill as she untied her moccasins. Cold burned into the bottoms of her feet. Sucking a deep breath, Willow waded out, gritted her teeth, and lowered herself into the cold rush, using handfuls of sand and gravel from the riverbed to scrub herself.

Her flesh prickled from the shock of the icy water. Breath seemed to stick in her lungs as her heart raced against the cold.

But at least I can feel something. Only my soul is dead . . . not my body.

Ducking her head, she used a wet fingertip to clean her ears, and then wrung out her long black hair. Shivering and puffing, she scrambled back up onto the bank and found the blanket. She used it to dry herself as thoroughly as possible. Her hair had already frozen into a stiff black mass.

"How's the water?" Red Calf's voice intruded.

Willow looked up as White Hail's wife walked out of the dawn-shadowed trees. In the gray twilight, Red Calf's blanketed form blended with the rough bark of the cottonwoods.

"Cold, just what you'd expect in the middle of the winter. Be careful. Don't slip on the ice."

Red Calf walked forward and shrugged out of her blanket before she pulled her dress over her head. She shucked off her moccasins and straightened, rubbing her hands over her distended belly. Petite, thin-boned, with small hands and feet, she carried her child high under her pointed breasts. Secrets hid behind her large dark eyes, and her full lips looked poised for laughter, but more often produced bile. Men had always found her physically attractive, but White

Hail had had no competition when he asked for her as a wife.

Now she watched Willow suspiciously. "I'd rather you left. I don't trust you here, Willow. You might do something, send some evil up my vagina and into my baby."

Willow laughed as she dressed. Before pulling on her moccasins, she stepped down to fill her section of buffalo gut with water. She quickly tied off the open end and wrapped her robe around her shoulders. She endured a bout of shivers as her body warmed within her clothing. "Go ahead and bathe in peace, Red Calf. I'm no threat to you."

Willow slung the buffalo-gut water bag over her shoulder, and stopped to look back. Red Calf waded into the water and gasped at the piercing cold. She looked impish in the reddening light of dawn reflected off the ice.

"Red Calf, why do you think I'm evil? Exactly what is it about me that makes you think I'm a witch, or that I'd hurt anyone?"

Red Calf watched her warily, hands still held protectively over her belly. "You're different, Willow. Strange. You're not a proper woman. You don't know your place, and these other things, ideas about plants and animals. You make people worry. I wish . . . I wish you were gone."

"I will be. Just as soon as the trails clear."

"I think *you* killed them."

Willow stiffened, heart skipping. "I killed . . . You mean my husband and child? My own family?"

"You meddle in things a woman shouldn't," Red Calf said smugly. "Slim Pole says so. Women aren't supposed to be healers. Not until after their bleeding stops. I think your husband found out you were a witch—so you killed him and your baby. A witch would do something like that." Red Calf waded out into the deeper water, lowering herself and splashing water over her arms, belly, and breasts. In the gaudy light, her skin looked as slick as the surrounding ice; then gooseflesh rose, spoiling the image.

"A witch might, I suppose." A dead weight had settled in Willow's souls. "But I guess I'll never make a very good witch, will I? A witch would have killed cleanly, without remorse. Watching my husband and my boy die wounded my souls forever. I'd have done anything to save them. And if . . . if I *were* a witch, I'd have known how."

"I don't believe you." Red Calf watched her warily.

"Don't you? I would have gladly traded their souls for yours, Red Calf." She lifted an eyebrow. "But then . . . you're still alive. So, maybe I'm not a witch after all."

At that, Willow turned and followed the trail toward the camp. *Fool! You let her goad you into saying things you shouldn't!* Anger began to drive off the last of the river water's chill. *It doesn't matter. Soon you'll be gone from here.*

Morning was reaching out with gentle fingers. In the soft light, lodges were coming down, women and older children knocking loose the pegs that held the lodge skirts, then unpinning the flaps on the front before peeling the buffalo hide away from the poles.

Willow hesitated at the edge of the clearing. She could see old Two Half Moons, bent over and worrying the stakes loose from the frozen ground. A small herd of children charged past, giggling and screaming, camp dogs barking and yipping in their wake.

Instead of hurrying to help Two Half Moons, Willow cut across the village, dodging as blanket-wrapped youths herded ponies around the lodges for packing. An infant squalled with displeasure. Mingled with the calls of people, buffalo hide rustled and flapped as lodge covers were folded. Tipi poles rattled as they were taken down and stacked. Horses snorted and stamped, some in anticipation, others in irritation. Woodsmoke hung low and blue, vying with the odors of lodge leather, horses, and earth.

Willow marched up to the old man who carried brightly painted parfleches from inside the pole skeleton of a lodge. The *Puhagan* wore his gray hair in twin braids to either side of his head. Flank steak, left in the sun for days to dry, had the same look as his weather-burned face: dark, wrinkled, and parched. For some reason the old man's fleshy nose had grown with a bend in it. He looked up with obsidian-dark eyes, and watched her approach. He clung to one of the brightly painted parfleches with swollen fingers that looked like pemmican.

Willow stopped before him, aware that Slim Pole's two wives had ceased their chatter as they folded the lodge cover into a big square. They watched her with wary inquisitiveness.

"Good morning, Willow." Slim Pole's voice sounded scratchy, belying the fact that he sang with deep rich tones during the ceremonies. "I had dreamed many things, but not that you would come seeking me this morning."

Willow crossed her arms. "Could you walk with me for a moment?"

Slim Pole grunted, turned, and carried his parfleche to the waiting stack. The squares of hard rawhide contained the medicine elder's healing herbs and paraphernalia for the Sun Dance and vision quests. He patted the stack as if making sure his sacred possessions were out of the way of trampling horses' feet. Then the old man turned and ambled out toward the west, away from the camp.

Willow walked beside him, watching his short, shuffling steps, reading the pain in the old man's hip joints and the wobbly balance caused by his fading vision.

"You wish to speak?" He glanced at her, his eyebrow raised. "My eyes are bad, but I see from the ice in your hair that you've come straight from your morning bath."

"Red Calf is going to accuse me of being a witch."

"I see." A pause. "Are you?" He slowed, staring out at the gray-brown buttes to the west. Snow-filled gullies streaked their sides like white veins. Beyond them, burning orange in the morning, the fir-covered slopes of the Warm

Wind Mountains rose to white-capped majesty against the paling sky.

"I am no witch—as you know, elder." Willow kicked at the hoof-flattened snow. Piles of frozen horse manure lay like black warts here and there in the scrubby sagebrush. "You have not approved of me, of my *Dukurika* ways. As a good elder should, you have sought to give me advice, to guide me to behave more like a proper *Ku'chendikani*. I have always listened with respect."

"And continued doing things just as you did before."

"That is true, elder. Each soul has its way. As *Tam Apo* made us. Perhaps there is a little of Coyote in all of us. An urge to follow our desires because we must."

"But there is also Wolf in us," Slim Pole replied. "To accept and do our duty. To act in a way which is responsible to the People."

"I agree, *Puhagan*. That is why I came to you this morning, inconvenient though it may be. I wanted to tell you that Red Calf is going to make trouble. I have the responsibility to tell you about it in order that you may give the matter thought before trouble breaks out."

He nodded slowly, eyes fixed on the distant mountains. Slim Pole could still see into distances with some clarity, but people said that even that sight was growing hazy. Only the bright colors of his parfleches allowed him to locate his things.

"And what responsibility do you have to the People, Heals Like A Willow?" He cocked his head.

"I also came to tell you that I will be leaving the *Ku'chendikani* within the next moon. I would go now, but the snow is too deep and I might not be able to carry enough food to reach the *Dukurika* winter camps."

"In another moon, the snow will have melted off the ridges. The ice will still be thick enough to allow you to cross the streams. But food will be a problem for another two moons at least."

"I can find food in another moon. The first sprouts of wild parsley and shooting star will be up."

"Ah, I forget, you are the one who thinks in terms of plants, and not of buffalo." He paused. "Perhaps this is for the best." He glanced at her. "I would have Heals Like A Willow know that Slim Pole, while he may have found her troublesome, enjoyed his talks with her."

"And I with him."

"I am sorry about your husband and son. Two Half Moons told me that you followed the rituals necessary for their souls to find their way across the sky. For that, I thank you. But, yes, I think perhaps it is better if you return to the mountains. White Hail wanted to marry you. Fast Black Horse may yet ask you to marry. And if he does?"

"I will say no." Willow let her eyes search the mountains, tracing the jagged lines of peaks. "I gave all the love in my souls to my husband and my son. I have none left to give to anyone else."

"Like a clay bowl? Poured out until there is nothing left?"

"Yes, like that."

He chuckled dryly. "Mostly you are a very clever woman, Heals Like A Willow. You surprise me by the questions you ask, and the things you know about life, about *Tam Apo* and the way He created the world. But then you say something like that, and I realize that for everything that you know, parts of you are still secret to yourself."

She stood silently, refusing to respond.

"I think you are no witch," he said at last. "I have watched you work with the sick. A woman should not do such things until after her bleeding stops. Until that time, she is unclean. Woman's blood is offensive to Power."

"Do we want to argue about this again, *Puhagan?*"

"No. You and I have argued so many times we each know the other's words better than our own. I was just saying that I have never seen evil in you, and while the Spirits have come to me to complain about you, it was just to tell me that you were polluting them with your woman's blood, not doing evil."

"We will disagree about that forever."

"Yes, we will." He glanced at her. "*Tam Apo* made women to bear children. If I would offer advice to Heals Like A Willow, I would say that she should stop worrying about Power, bear her children as *Tam Apo* meant her to, and worry about *puha* and healing when her bleeding finally stops.''

Willow smiled wearily. "I will consider Slim Pole's words. In the meantime, I thank him for his understanding and consideration. Within a moon, Heals Like A Willow will be no more trouble to him, or to the *Ku'chendikani*.''

"I wish you well," the elder said. "And . . . I think it is best for you as well as for my people that you leave. In the meantime, Slim Pole will see that Red Calf makes no big trouble for anyone." He smiled then, the wrinkles on his face deepening. "However, Red Calf will continue to make a lot of little troubles. It is her nature to make people miserable; she is like cactus to a barefooted man.''

"I will miss you, Slim Pole. I will especially miss arguing late into the night about good and evil, and the nature of *Tam Apo,* and about responsibility and life and death as we have done so often.''

His expression turned wistful. "Yes, well, who will challenge me from now on? Eh? Your souls see very clearly about many things, Willow. Your questions cut like obsidian. I have learned many things from you . . . and your irritating questions. For that, I thank you. And, I fear, for all the complaining I've done about you, I will find myself missing you, wishing for another of your annoying arguments.''

"May *Tam Apo* guide your way, Slim Pole.''

"Yours, too, Heals Like A Willow.''

Richard shivered as *Virgil* nosed in toward the Saint Louis waterfront. He stood at the rail with the rest of the passengers, witnessing the end of the long journey. Below him, the bedraggled masses craned to see. Richard watched them in turn, nervously searching for François. Even the thought of him brought tickles of fear to Richard's stomach.

A practical joke, the captain had said. A quick search that morning had produced no sign of the vicious Frenchman.

After all, who else could it have been? And where had he disappeared to?

Richard shuddered and tightened his hold on the grip containing the banknotes. At last he would be able to relieve himself of that albatross. Two days in Saint Louis, and then he'd be headed home. Home to Laura.

French calls and jokes mixed with English and carried on the air as the men caught lines and waited. The *Virgil* strained one last time, her paddle churning as she drove into the muddy bank.

Saint Louis didn't disappoint him. In the late afternoon light it looked as squalid as he'd anticipated. High on the bank stood an open-sided market building. The streets were mostly mud despite some attempts at brick paving. Along the shore, the men looked barely better than those he'd seen at Fort Massac.

"Mr. Hamilton?" the steward asked, working his way down the line of passengers crowding the gallery. "Would you like your baggage delivered, sir? And if so, to what address?"

"Yes, thank you. The Hotel Le Barras, please."

The plank was dropped and the deck fares crowded forward in a mass, pushing and shoving, their few belongings held high. Refugees fleeing Napoleon might have appeared thus, ragged and mindless.

"Mr. Hamilton?" Charles Eckhart thrust out a hand, cigar puffing in the corner of his mouth. "It's been a pleasure, sir. I wish you all of the best."

"And you, sir."

Eckhart stared out over the throng, then up the slope toward the low brick buildings on the bluff. "I know Saint Louis will seem strange and savage to you, Mr. Hamilton, but opportunity often arises from the most unpromising of circumstances. More than one young man has come here to test his mettle. I hope you find yours."

Eckhart touched a finger to the brim of his hat, smiled, and strode off. Richard glared at his departing back. How arrogantly Virginian, to think worth came from physically challenging the world. It was the keenness of a man's mind that made the real difference. All else was illusion.

Richard returned his attention to the settlement and sniffed; the odor of rot—mixed liberally with woodsmoke and coke from the brick factory—carried to him. Then he followed the others down the stairway from the gallery and across the wagging plank. The muddy shore had been churned into a morass.

"Carriage, sir?" a driver called to him.

"I'll walk, thank you," Richard returned. Dear Lord God, after all those weeks aboard the cramped boat, a walk was definitely in order. Besides, walking would give him a sense of the place, if only so that he might recall its crudity over the years.

He set out, grip in hand, climbing up from the waterfront and reveling in the solid ground beneath his feet, even though most streets in Saint Louis consisted of ruts worn through the rich black soil and into the pale gray limestone. Horse and cow manure left a bluish-and-brown film on the puddles.

Glancing back, he noticed Eckhart following along behind him. Wishing to avoid an unnecessary encounter, Richard slipped into the market, quickly crossed to the other side, and ducked behind a wagon trundling up the hill.

French, English, and Spanish were spoken, the three languages often intermingled in a hodgepodge. There, right there, stood a real Indian dressed in cloth and skins, with feathers woven into his hair. Richard stopped to gawk. The Indian stared back, black eyes hard and wary.

Following the Indian came two white men dressed entirely in skin clothing decorated with bright beadwork; the long fringes swayed with each step. They carried slim rifles and each had a belt pistol and large knife. Richard blushed as he came under their wolfish scrutiny. For the first time, he felt real excitement at the proximity of the untamed frontier. He climbed to Third Street, looking west along Olive.

He tried to soak it all in, to remember it in detail to tell Laura. What would she make of his stories? That enchanting smile would curl her perfect lips, and her eyes would sparkle with wonder.

He took a deep breath, swelling his chest, and looked westward. Out there, beyond the trees and rolling hills, not more than one hundred miles away, lay the last real toehold of civilization. Then, onward, across the plains and mountains, lay the vast emptiness—peopled only by the Indians and a few fearless traders. For the briefest of instants, the heady rush built. What would it be like out there? Pure and innocent, as Rousseau maintained? Or the brutality described by Hobbes?

Richard forced himself to be sensible and let his steps carry him where they would. He marveled at the old French houses with their second-story verandas and whitewashed walls. The city evoked a feeling of rambunctious youth grappling with an older society—and the older was losing.

The large Indian mounds, in perfect north-south and east-west alignment, piqued his interest. He climbed the tallest, well over seventy-five feet high and two hundred feet long, and tried to fathom its secrets. From the summit, he peered out at the river to the east, the forest to the west, and the city below. What ancient society had caused the construction of such piles of dirt, and what could their purpose have been?

Rousseau, you would marvel.

The gathering dusk finally overcame his thirst for exploration. He turned down Olive Street, holding the precious grip to his breast as he entered the shadows.

A woman's laughter issued from one of the open windows. Giggling children ran past in a wild game of chase. The odor of baking bread twisted something in Richard's innards. He'd passed most of the houses now, and found himself surrounded by dark warehouses.

His ebullience ebbed, leaving him nervous as he hurried down a muddy street, confused by the darkness. All he need do was find the hotel, contact Blackman, and be on his way back East.

I'm here, Father. Saint Louis! And I am as resolute about my future as ever. But which way was the hotel? Surely, he'd missed a turn.

"*Pardon, monsieur!*" a voice called. "A moment, if you please. Could you help me?"

Richard could see a man in the shadowed darkness between two buildings. Something about that crouched figure . . .

Richard backed warily away. A rasping laugh came from the shadowed man, who started forward, calling, "Eh? Monsieur? You 'ave time for talk, *oui*?"

"I don't know you," Richard cried, and started to retreat the way he'd come. Two men cut him off. Richard dodged to the side; a cry strangled in his throat. He fled down a narrow passage, making better speed as he ran downhill toward the river.

"Run, *bourgeois*!" a hauntingly familiar voice cried. "We are coming for you, *mon ami*!"

Richard ran for all he was worth, footsteps of pursuit thudding in the twilight. He darted down toward the river, aware that only open fields lay between him and the water.

"Leave me alone! Go away!" Richard stepped in a hole, wrenching his leg as he half-fell. *Dear Lord God!* "Help me! Someone . . . help!" He ran on.

"No help, Yankee! We catch you!" The pursuer was barely straining to keep up.

A quick glance over Richard's shoulder sent a horrible start through him: He looked into François's leering face.

"*Mon ami,* we will party and sing songs," François crooned, and a muscular arm snagged Richard from behind, cutting off his wind. "Repayment for a gift, no?"

Richard clawed at the choking arm. His scream became a gurgling sound. Another dark figure wrenched the grip from his arms as if plucking a petal from a flower. Richard flopped and twisted, powered by panic. The chokehold only tightened.

"We 'ave him, François!"

His vision had gone gray . . . floating. A roaring filled Richard's ears, growing ever more faint. Even the pain at his throat was fading . . . fading. . . .

SEVEN

What seems at this point to be the individual's power and force, bringing the substance beneath it, and thereby doing away with that substance is the same thing as the actualization of the substance. For the power of the individual exists in conforming itself to that substance, that is, in emptying itself of its unique self, and thus objectively establishing itself as the existing substance. Its culture and its own reality are, therefore, the continual process of making the substance itself actual and concrete.

—Georg Friedrich Wilhelm Hegel,
Phenomenology of Mind

Through groggy dreams, Richard shied from the pain. Lurking shapes huddled in the darkness. Voices, echoing hollowly like ghosts, mocked him with indistinct words. Spectral creatures reached out from the depths with tendril fingers to ensnare him. . . .

In a blind panic, Richard ran down dark cobblestone streets. Like a coiled serpent, the pain hissed and slithered as it waited for consciousness. Richard whimpered and ran on, his breath tearing at his windpipe. He'd do anything to escape, to drift smokelike and unseen through the streets of Boston.

Professor Ames's soft voice filled the empty lecture hall. Laughter rang out in Fenno's Tavern on the Charles River. Gleaming spars on the ships in the harbor were webbed with black rope. Boston. Peace. . . .

But the precious images faded away into soggy obscurity. Spears of white agony replaced them, and slowly dragged Richard to consciousness with each beat of his heart.

My skull is cracked and broken. The jagged pieces are grinding against each other. He tried to bring his wounded mind into focus. The wretched stabbing in his head failed to mask the smaller pains at his wrists and ankles.

Oh, God, where am I? What's happened?

No whiskey-head had ever tortured him thus. His numb flesh bordered on shivers. Cold—everything cold. He lay on his side, cheek pressed against something gritty. Dirt, from the smell of it. He tried to bring his hands forward, met resistance, and gave up.

What's happened to me? A wadded rag filled his mouth and tasted foul. Swallowing hurt. His throat felt as if a splintered broomhandle had been pushed down it. For a horrible instant he wanted to throw up. *No! Gagged like this, you will strangle in your own vomit.* His eyes ached as though sand-filled, and rheum stuck the lashes together. He blinked to clear them.

In the faint light he could see the dim outline of a rude table—little more than rough-cut boards—a rickety chair, and mud-chinked log walls.

As he flopped on the dirt floor something scurried along the wall. To Richard's horror, a rat ducked through a gap where timbers rested on the rock foundation.

Again, he tried to bring his hands around, then realized they were tightly bound. When he sought to straighten his legs, a cord behind his back pulled down on his wrists. He could only flop like a fish on a dock.

Memory returned: the ambush on Olive Street. The chase and capture. François. Robbed! His father's money. Thirty *thousand* dollars. Gone. . . .

He slumped back on the floor.

Time passed. Something rustled in the darkness.

God help me. Now that they have the money, why don't

they just let me go? Questions led to answers he didn't care to embrace. Shivers started as the cold deepened and his full bladder demanded relief.

How long do I have to lie here? He chewed on the rag in his mouth. It had gone soggy, and grit rasped against his teeth. Damn it all, someone had to come or his bladder would burst!

In the end, he lost that fight. The several drops that leaked out onto his legs became a warm rush. Shamed, he lay there while urine cooled and filled his nose with its tangy odor.

This isn't happening. I'm a rational human being. They have the money; now, why can't they just let me go?

Tears leaked from his eyes, while fear charged his imagination with images of torture and death. He couldn't shake the memory of a hog chewing at a human head as it rolled in the mud.

Stop it! Think back ... remember ... Yes, the last night on the way to Will Templeton's. That's right. Boston. Two days before you left. The night you fell in love with Laura. Think about it. Bring it all back. Walking the snowy streets ... remember ... Remember the lights? The passing people? Pastries in windows ... Boston, my Boston ... The shops, the books, musicians, enlightened conversation, and prosperity. Ships from the ends of the earth brought cargoes, ideas, and learned men to Boston's safe harbor. Within the walls of her colleges, the intellectual torch of the Americas burned with resplendent brilliance. There, Richard Hamilton had enfolded himself within the womb of philosophy and had drawn its nurturing protection around him. How could his father *dare* send him away from this, the only life he'd ever known, or ever wanted?

Laura? Please, God, let me see her again.

Had it been real, that night of revelry? Or simply illusion? Prone in the darkness, still and numb on the shack's dirt floor, Richard could no longer be sure. He started, gurgling against the gag as something scampered behind him. Rat ... yes, it had to be. They ate people, didn't they? Bit them until the blood ran?

He thrashed until he could hear the foul rodent scamper away, and, exhausted, closed his eyes in the cold darkness.

How had he managed to get from Laura's parlor, so warm and happy, to this place?

Laura, I'm going to die here. I'll never hold you in my arms. Never share your love. Tears trickled down his face.

The pack weighed more than she had expected. Heals Like A Willow took a firm grip on the leather straps and grunted as she swung it onto her shoulders with the easy grace of one long accustomed to heavy loads.

"That sits just about right." Two Half Moons ran her pink tongue over her thin brown lips as she shoved the pack up on Willow's back to check the straps. "If you start getting a headache, tighten the shoulder straps and pull this higher over your hips."

"You shouldn't have given me so much to carry." Willow stared out over the village, newly settled among the winter-gray trees. As always, the *Ku'chendikani* placed their winter camps in the cottonwood flats beside the river. Only in such places did enough grass grow for the large horse herds, and on those occasions when terrible winters snowed the people in, they could augment the grass by stripping cottonwood bark for the horses. To Willow's eyes, the disadvantage was the cold that lay in the bottoms with its fog and bone-numbing chill.

Now the tawny lodges with their soot-darkened tops sent streamers of thin blue smoke into the clear morning sky. The happy sounds of children squealing at play carried over the muted voices of adults talking. Somewhere behind the willows, a man whooped as he broke through the ice for his morning bath.

"You just be careful." Two Half Moons squinted toward the west and the snow-crowned peaks, pink now in the morning light. "If the weather warms, you keep an eye out. You know how this country is at this time of year. A real nice day, and you better get ready to hole up like a beaver in a bank, because you know it's gonna turn real cold and snow hip-deep to a tall horse."

"Yes, *Napia*, I know."

The old woman waved it off. "I'm not your aunt anymore. Your husband and child are dead. That bond is broken."

Willow hunched her shoulders to reposition her pack. "To me, you'll always be my *napia,* relative or not."

"Ah, girl. I'll miss you."

"The *Dukurika* keep track. Some fall, when you're wintering close by my mountains, I'll come visit."

Two Half Moons sighed, turning her squint to Willow. "Are you sure you don't want a horse?"

"You only have two, Aunt. And you'll need both of them to move your lodge." Willow smiled wryly. "Besides, you *Ku'chendikani* only have one form of wealth, your horses. I couldn't impoverish you."

"That nephew of mine, White Hail, he thinks he's going to be a big man. He'll steal me another horse. You wait and see. He's so busy stealing horses, the *A'ni* and *Pa'kiani* won't have any left."

Willow turned, heading toward the edge of the trees. "Red Calf doesn't know what she has. She'll waste him, Aunt. She has no sense, and he doesn't know when to say enough. She'll want more and more, beyond what is good for her and her family. What good is wealth if you're a widow?" *Like me.*

"A young man must try. That is the nature of young men. Sometimes they grow wiser as a result."

"Lessons from the winter stories, Aunt? Like the ones told about the Bald One, *Pachee Goyo*? Is that what you mean? Just because the Bald One grew wise through his adventures doesn't mean White Hail will."

"Not many old men are fools, girl. And the stories of the Bald One teach good lessons."

"Yes, they do. Red Calf should take heed. One of the lessons the Bald One teaches is that greed leads to disaster."

"So does ignoring the advice of your elders. Look at you! Wandering out there to be eaten by the rock ogres! You shouldn't be traveling alone."

"I'll be fine. It's still too early for trouble. War parties aren't out at this time of year. Our enemies are in camp, snug by warm fires, waiting out the weather and winter grass. By the time the *Pa'kiani* come south, I'll be safe in the mountains with my people.''

''I will pray to *Tam Apo* that you make it safely.'' The old woman leaned forward, touching her cheek to Willow's.

Without another word, Willow took a deep breath and started eastward, feet crunching on the crusted snow as she passed the line of trees and started up the bluffs. Climbing the last terrace, she could see the distant Powder River Mountains rising like mounded buffalo backs against the morning sky.

Taking a final look back across the frosty bottoms, she saw the horse herd clustered just south of the village, animals pawing at the snow. The camp lay under a blue haze of woodsmoke. The warm brown tones of the lodges contrasted with the tawny grass, the grizzled trees, and snow patches.

Farewell, Ku'chendikani. *Good-bye, my husband and son.*

And with that, Willow turned her back on a vanished life.

Travis scraped his moccasins free of manure-filled mud on the sides of the tavern doorframe. The sign hanging over the door would have been worthless to Travis but for the faded, if rather optimistic, rendition of a fully leafed tree.

Travis was no stranger to the Green Tree Tavern. Old John Simonds, the proprietor, gave him a nervous squint when he walked past the scarred oaken door, remembering, no doubt, the night a somewhat younger Travis Hartman had gouged the eye out of a squealing and thrashing boatman.

And I'd a done a heap more, too, if'n Davey Green hadn't a-busted a cider keg over my noggin.

No two tables were the same, since they'd been scrounged throughout the city, and had proved rugged enough to resist pounding, hammering, dancing boatmen, and occasional flying bodies. Long ago, Simonds had turned from chairs to benches, the latter being heavier and less likely to be thrown.

The walls were blackened from years of candle soot and tobacco smoke. Across the room, a young man in a smudged white shirt polished tin cups with a rag. He started at the sight of Travis's mauled face, and hastily looked away.

Walking to the plank counter, Travis nodded to the young man behind the bar. "Ale, lad."

Four men, three already deep in their cups, sat on one of the benches. Even from the back, Travis recognized François.

Ale in hand, Travis dropped a coin on the scarred wood before sauntering over to François's table and seating himself. His arrival brought an instant quiet—and the sense that he'd walked into something at just the wrong time. One by one, Travis nodded at each of them, taking the measure of their suspicious eyes.

"Sorry to interrupt, lads. Come ter talk bizness. Nothing more."

"Travis Hartman," François said softly, a faint smile on his thin lips. "What's this? No Ree has lifted your louse-infested scalp?"

"Yourn neither, it appears." Travis lifted his mug and drank, white foam sticking to his mustache. He wiped it off with a sleeve. "How ye been, François? Long time since I seen yer carcass. Three . . . four years?"

"Four at least, Hartman. You 'ave not grown any prettier since the last time. The scabs, they were just falling off as I remember. Now, even the red ees gone. You look like . . . yes, a man who has let chickens walk across his face."

Hartman ignored the snickers from the other men. One, a big fellow with black hair and a bristly beard, had been around. Travis knew him by sight. The other two were strangers, but from their sashes, boatman's caps, and baggy white shirts, Hartman might just as well have known them. He'd traveled with enough *engagés* over the years.

The *engagés,* mostly French, were the hired boatmen who worked for a regular wage. Each signed a contract to fulfill certain obligations to a *bourgeois,* or "booshway," as the Americans called the expedition's leader. The contract might be to reach a certain destination, to complete a journey, or for a period of time.

"I'm looking for men." Hartman sucked at his ale. "Pay's good and fair. Two-year contract. Hauling a boat upriver."

"Two years?" The black-haired man watched Hartman through flat eyes. "A long contract, *oui*? It makes me wonder, why have I not heard of this? No one has been talking. I ask myself, where would this boat go for two years? It could not be the upper Missouri, for I would have heard that."

Hartman watched him through narrowed eyes. "Boats go a lot of places, coon. Maybe we just want your skinny arse for two seasons instead of one. Think of it like this: Long-term pay, eh?"

François chuckled, glancing at the black-haired man. "Relax, August. What interest is it of yours? You no longer work for Bourgeois Chouteau."

Travis gave August an even harder look. If word leaked to Chouteau, it would blow the whole thing higher than a spark in a powder keg.

"I need men," Travis said softly. "No questions asked. And jist from the looks of it, yer not the kind interested in questions. That, or I'm a pilgrim when it comes ter reading sign on men's souls."

August tensed, fists clenching. François reached out to restrain him, saying, "You want no part of Hartman, *mon ami*." François chuckled then, fingering his bearded chin as August relaxed. "I think, Travis Hartman, that we all have our secrets. Fortunately, we know more of yours than you know of ours, eh?"

"Reckon so. Now, if'n ye'd have an interest in the river—"

"*Non! Pardon. S'il vous plais.*" August had nevertheless reached down to the handle of his belt knife. "Now, if you will kindly take your—"

"*Un moment,*" François said thoughtfully. In French he added, "Perhaps this can work to solve our little problem." In English he said to Travis. "Two years? Upriver? No questions asked?"

"Yep. Hard work up, and lard eating for the winter. I'll not lie to ye. Thar'll be a sight of danger. Cowards need not apply. But, boys, I give ye my word, stick her out, and ye'll come back rich men. Reckon thar'll be a share of the profits divvied out to the hands."

"*O, mon Dieu!* Madness," August hissed, hand still on his knife. "I am not stupid! This thing you plan, the upper Missouri! *Pied Noir,* Blackfeet! That is who you seek. Or perhaps the Crows, *hein*? You think you can trade with them? *Non, impossible.* They kill you in *trois mois.* Four at most. It is suicide!"

François smiled. "Two years? No questions asked? How desperate are you, Hartman?"

"We leave day after t'morrer, short-handed or no."

"*Sacré infant du grâce!* You 'ave gone crazy?" August stared incredulously at François. "To go upriver, now? Why? You 'ave *everything*!"

François gestured for silence. To Travis he said, "What if I told you that I have a man for you? He's not much of a boatman, understand? I would not sell you false goods, Hartman. He's skinny, weak, and worthless. A liar of the worst kind, he will tell you the most fanciful of tales. Of being robbed. Of being a bourgeois gentleman. You must watch him every moment, for he will try to escape from your boat. Are you that desperate, eh? Do you want to buy his contract?"

Travis rocked his mug thoughtfully. "If'n I'm desperate enough ter think of hiring the likes of you, I'm desperate, all right."

August had begun to grin, shooting a crafty look at François, and then Hartman.

Travis sipped his ale, trying to fathom the trap.

"You need men to cordelle and pole the boat, *non*?" August shrugged, expression blank. "He's a man. And . . . who knows? If he does not do the work, you must have to shoot him, *non*?"

François shook greasy black hair off his shoulders. "I own his contract, Hartman. How you say, an indenture?"

Travis cocked an eyebrow as he stared into his ale. "I ain't enough of a pilgrim ter pay money fer no shirker.

Sorry, boys. I need men, strong, hale, an' hearty."

"You 'ave not asked how much." François slapped the table, clearly enjoying himself.

"Ter buy a man's indenture? How long's he got on his contract?"

"How long you want?"

"Two years."

"*Très bien*, I sell you this man for two years. Take him up to the *Pied Noir*. Make him haul your boat. I will take leisure in my great house in New Orleans, or perhaps Paris. I will caress my Lizette, and I will think of my indentured servant, hauling the boat upriver." François laughed happily and the others now joined in.

Hartman pulled at his chin hairs. "Yer a damned devil François. Reckon ye've always been, too. Ye've nothing but trouble in that damn black heart of yern. Still, even a pig falls into a sweet spring of an occasion. 'Cept in yer case, if'n yer flush, it's through murder or robbery."

François's gaze hardened. "No questions asked. You are interested, or no?"

"How much fer this pilgrim you took?"

"One *sou*."

The boatmen howled in delight.

"Fer a legal contract?"

"*Avec certitude*. All legal. Signature and all. You may even 'ave your lawyer . . . even Monsieur Ferrar, if you like, inspect the document. No money until you are 'appy with the agreement. I make but one condition. You give me your word, Travis Hartman, that he fill his contract."

"And give ye time to skip out from whatever's owed ye, eh?"

August added, "He will see the river one way or another. For the price of a *sou*, Hartman, you can become a Good Samaritan in the process!"

Travis toyed with his mug as he thought it out. François was a cutthroat. Plain and simple. Whatever his game, his victim would end up dead anyway—another body floating downstream. And Green was plumb desperate. Better half a man than no man at all.

"Hell! He's cheap for the price—provided the contract's

legal. If'n 't'aint, I swear, I'm coming after you, François. Reckon ye know me. Know I don't give my word less'n I mean it.''

"The contract, she shall be good." François slapped a callused hand on the table. "You promise me, Travis Hartman, that you do not let him go. That you keep him for the duration of his contract."

"I'll do 'er." And at that Travis stuck out his hand. "A *sou,* ye say? If'n I cain't find one, will a penny do?"

"Naturellement!" August cried. "Of course. And on that, we will drink."

"Reckon so," Hartman agreed, lifting his mug. After he swigged the cool ale, he asked, "Who's Lizette?"

August smiled wickedly. "You 'ave not heard? Lizette, the Creole woman, eh? The dark beauty of the Bourgeois!"

"Her?" Travis squinted suspiciously at François. "She's rich man's meat, coon. What's she doing squiring about with the likes of ye?"

François grinned, exposing yellowed teeth behind his dark brown beard. "Perhaps she finally has come to know a man, eh?"

"Oh, yer flush, all right." Travis nodded. "She don't smile at a man without he's dripping gold from his pockets. So, tell me, she tied a ribbon on yer pizzle?"

"That story about her . . ." François leered. "It is true!"

"Uh-huh, wal, fer what it's worth, this child wouldn't trust her ahint me with anything sharp."

"I don't want her, how do we say, 'behind' me, eh? But I 'ave been behind her, and her bottom is as good as they say, *non?*"

"Yer funeral, coon. Now, where can I find real men?"

EIGHT

The question is whether, assuming we recognize in the whole series of events nothing but natural necessity, we may yet regard the same event which in the one instance is an effect of nature only, or in the other instance is an effect of freedom; or whether there is a direct contradiction between these two kinds of causality.

—Immanuel Kant, *Critique of Pure Reason*

A door slammed, jerking Richard from his dreams of Boston. He had been walking through the Commons, talking to his long-dead mother. An odd dream for him, but it kept his mind from dwelling on his growing thirst.

"*Leve!* Wake up!" a harsh voice ordered. A boot jabbed at his ribs.

Light filtered through the cracks beneath the roof. Morning had come. Richard twisted his head and looked up. A big man with a black beard gazed down at him. He wore the boatman's loose white shirt, red sash, wool cap, and high, laced moccasins. Like the others of his kind, his arms and shoulders bulged with muscles.

"You rest up, *mon ami*? Sleep good, eh, bourgeois? I should tell you, so did we. In the Le Barras Hotel, eh? Imagine, poor *engagés* like us, living like kings with so many fresh banknotes to spend!"

Richard wriggled around and tried to sit up. The big man flattened him with a vicious kick to the ribs. The pain made him gasp.

"You be still, pig." The boatman pulled a long knife

from his belt. The honed blade gleamed in the slitted light. Richard moaned into his gag.

"François and I have talked, *mon ami*. You have made our fortunes. More wealth than we would have seen had we counted every *sou* to pass through our lives since the day of birth. But, if you lived, told the wrong person . . . like Chouteau, perhaps, or Judge Lucas, it could be very bad for us. You understand, do you not? We are not, how do you say, wicked men. Just practical."

Richard closed his eyes and tensed, waiting for the stab of cold steel and the pain that would follow. Instead, he could feel his arms being wiggled and one hand flopped onto the ground in front of him. He opened his eyes. His hand looked horrible, blue in color and mottled. Then it began to hurt worse than even that blinding headache.

"Get up!" The order was followed by another kick.

A rough hand jerked the gag out. Richard's mouth and tongue felt made of canvas.

"Who . . . are you?" Richard croaked.

"Get up!" The big bearded man repeated. He bent down, lowering the long steel blade until Richard stared cross-eyed down the shining length. The sharp point dimpled the tip of Richard's nose. "I do not have to leave you beautiful, *mon ami*. Perhaps you 'ave seen men with their nostrils slit? Among the Maha, it is said that a man can run faster that way. Get more air to the lungs."

Richard jerked back—only to flop about on the floor as his numb hands and legs refused to support his weight.

"I *can't*!" Richard wailed. For that he got kicked in the ribs again.

He sat up, hoping the man would be satisfied.

A big hand reached down and lifted him effortlessly into the rickety chair. Richard wobbled on his perch and peered owlishly around the room. "Where am I? Please. Let me go. I haven't done anything—"

"Shut up!" The fellow slapped a tin bowl down in front of Richard. "Eat." A spoon rattled across the table.

Richard lifted his purple-mottled hand and tried to grasp the spoon. His fingers might have been made of wood for all the control he had.

"Lick it up." The man leaned across the table with a baleful black stare. "Eat, damn you . . . or I'll feed you!"

Richard dipped his head into the bowl and began sucking up the contents. The stuff tasted like watery oats, bland and tasteless. Each gulp passed his bruised throat like a length of hemp. Richard did his best, thankful for the moisture, hopeful that the hunger pangs would lessen in his belly.

Food? Does this mean they won't kill me?

"Where am I?" Richard raised his head, aware that liquid was dripping from his chin and bits of gruel had stuck to his face.

"You are in Saint Louis . . . animal."

"You weren't on the boat. Why do you call me that?"

"Let us just say I owed a man a favor. You made several men very rich, you know. It leaves us with a problem of what to do with you. Some think you would be best served with your throat slit, adrift in the river."

Richard's bowels loosened. They'd do it. His throat went tight. He started to tremble again, but forced himself to concentrate in an effort to forget fear. But his voice squeaked as he said, "That is not rational."

"What? What do you say?" The big man pulled tobacco from his pocket.

For God's sake, Richard. This is your only chance! You're arguing for your life! "Be . . . Because, men are rational. I can . . . can understand why they took the money, but to kill me for having had it? That makes no sense. Why not let me walk out of here? I have . . . have already failed at what I was supposed to do. How much more do you want? Only . . . only to humiliate me? What have I *done* to you?"

The big man leaned forward, toying with his knife. "You do not understand. François, he told me you were different, eh? A little stupid about things. Listen, *mon ami.* Think, eh? If you can get that bourgeois mind to do that. You could tell the authorities who took your money, *non*?"

"I suppose." *God, they're going to kill me after all.*

"You called François an animal. What would it mean to you, rich man, to see us hang, eh? If François is an animal, then so am I, *non*? A boatman . . . a Creole. But what is that to you, bourgeois? You have not worked like a dog on the boats for all these years. You have not sweated your guts out in the sun, frozen in the snow, ached and cursed and slapped the mosquitoes. You have not seen your home go from France to Spain to France to America. You know not what it means to lose everything." The fierce eyes bored into Richard's. "You, rich boy, 'ave lived like a pampered prince!"

Richard stared at the tabletop, a numbness in his soul. He barely saw the rat droppings and honey brown urine that stained the dusty wood.

"So, bourgeois? Does it not make more sense to cut your throat? If you are feeding fish, you will not be telling the governor that François and August 'ave robbed you."

Richard licked his lips. "Listen to me. We are both rational. We can find a way. It comes from the proper perception of life. I could give you my word that I'd tell no one who took the money. I am a *moral* man, an intelligent man. Don't you see?"

August laughed again. "Your word? What means a word? Eh? What is your word? Nothing but air! Moral, you say? 'I'm a *moral* man!' *Sacré merde!* Tomorrow you will walk into the governor's office and say, 'I am a moral man. François and August have stolen my money.'"

"If I give you my word, it would be a bond. Between the two of us. Surely you can see the rational—"

"You 'ave much to learn about morality, boy."

"I'm talking about ultimate morality. One's duty to himself and—" *Acting out of principle. So, where does the principle lie, Richard? Keeping your word? Or allowing robbery to go unpunished?* He swallowed hard. *And by giving my word, I become a participant in the robbery—in the immoral action.*

"Duty?" August used the tip of his knife to peel dirt from under his thumbnail. "But, of course, François and I have done nothing more than our duty to ourselves. And, for the rest of our lives, we will see to it that we live like bourgeois."

"There is more to life than money. There is honor and responsibility to oneself and—and one's conscience."

"*Mon Dieu!* Honor! What is honor? Honor does not fill the belly of a man. You would expect me to believe that? How can you tell this to me, eh? I have lived long, monsieur. Not always have I lived well. Honor, *mon ami,* is a worthless term. Did Napoleon act with honor when he sold Louisiana to the Americans, eh?" The big man spat a stream of tobacco juice on the ground. "You are a fool, boy. But, then, a wise man would still 'ave his money, and would not be tied up like a pig waiting for slaughter, *non*?"

Richard shook his head. "Listen. There's a dignity to human existence. You should know that if you are a man. It's deep-seated. It's what separates us from animals. It—"

"Animals, *mon ami*?" the big man interrupted. "You have just lost your own argument. For it was you who called my friend an animal." August cocked his head. "Ah! And he even gave you a gift! Sent you the head that fascinated you so!"

Richard stared into those hard black eyes, seeking any hint of compassion. "But . . . but there's got to be something inside, in the soul, don't you see? That spark of . . . of . . ."

August spat on the floor again. "You tell me, eh?"

"That essence that makes us human! That necessitates introspection. The concept must be nurtured by investigating a man's life. From study—" Sweat trickled down Richard's brow.

The big man stood. "Your words are like garbage in the streets. They blow about and do nothing but add stink to the air."

"But there's *truth*!"

"Truth? You tell me what is truth? Truth is cold and fever and pain and death! It is life, monsieur. You tell me of your rich American truths. They mean nothing to me. Let me ask you—you ever killed a man, *copain*? You ever see the truth in his eyes? You ever find your friends cut apart by the Indians? Eh? Have you?" August leaned over the table and glared into Richard's eyes. "Look into the face of death, *mon cher,* there you will see the only real truth."

"No. No, there's got to be—"

"When you have lived with these things, then you come back and tell me of truth." August struck like a snake, the callused hand slapping Richard hard across the face.

Blood tasted salty on Richard's lips as it leaked from his nose. He cowered lower on the chair, trying to crawl into himself and away from this hideous man. Tears of fright began streaking down his face.

August paced to the side, chewing gristle on his thumb. "I tell you what. You want truth? I give you truth."

Richard looked up as August pulled a piece of paper from his pocket. "Sign that!" August produced a quill and small bottle of ink. "I will give you life, *mon ami,* and enough truth to fill your belly for the rest of your days . . . such as they may be."

Flexing his fingers, Richard picked up the paper and started to scan the scrawled words.

"Don't read!" The voice thundered. "Just sign!"

"But I never sign any . . ." One glance into those terrifying eyes and Richard picked up the quill and dipped it into the ink. His numb fingers shook as he scratched his name at the place August indicated.

"Ah, now you will live, *mon ami.* Just that simple, *non?* You 'ave signed for your life. A life of truth. Live long, and thank August for the gift he has given you."

Richard wobbled to his feet and tried for the door, but a big hand grabbed him and threw him sprawling. No sooner had he hit the ground than a knee landed in the pit of his stomach, driving out his wind. A second later, Richard threw up.

"Cowardice is also truth, *chien,*" August crooned as he quickly bound Richard's wrists and feet. "You might want to lick up what you have thrown up. You will need your strength."

August snorted his disgust as he stood. "Good day, *mon ami.* Perhaps, before we deliver you to your new life, we will dunk you in the river, eh? You stink of piss and bile. No man should voyage off in search of truth when he smells like the privy behind a whorehouse!"

August stepped out and closed the door. Richard could hear the latch being fastened on the outside.

The wetness on his chest was growing cold. What in God's name had he signed? He flopped over on his side, only to rest his cheek in August's tobacco-stained spittle.

Is this the reality you wanted me to find, Father? Is this what you wanted me to come to? Damn you to Hell, Phillip Hamilton!

Years of rain and wind had created a hollow in the age-rounded rocks. The young warrior crouched in its shelter, squatted over a small fire so that his heavy buffalo robe trapped the rising heat around his hunched body. The rock outcrop blocked the bitter wind that howled out of the west bearing flakes of granular snow. Dark clouds scudded low across the sky.

His horses, a scruffy gray gelding and a rangy brown mare, stood with their rumps to the storm, heads down. He'd picketed them between two gnarled juniper trees, now clotted with snow. The crusted white that lodged in the grass at the animals' feet hid the heavy twisted leather hobbles.

Among his people, the Skidi Pawnee, he was known as Packrat: "the one who collects things." The name, like many among the Pawnee, had been given as a joke. In Pawnee eyes, Packrat was less than a commoner. He was *pira-paru,* a hidden child, one born without family.

The Pawnee traced descent through the women, and it was they who owned the property and controlled the food. A man married into a woman's household, moving in to live in her half of the large, round earthen house, taking a place among the members of her family. Living in their communal houses, the Pawnee shared many things, including sexual favors; provided, that is, that all parties concerned were amenable to the idea. Strict rules existed, however. A woman kept track of which man she coupled with, always being careful to observe the incest taboos and avoid her blood kin. Beyond that, Pawnee law prescribed that the man who sired a child, and the woman who bore it, were forever responsible for the child's health and welfare. Responsible women knew who fathered their children—and Packrat's troubles stemmed from that.

His mother's true name was Braided Woman, from a family of status and standing. Unlike many Plains peoples, the Pawnee recognized three distinct social ranks based on familial heritage. Braided Woman not only was born of chief-rank parents, but at the moment of her birth, the Star Priest had studied the constellations, finding them auspicious of greatness.

With property and chiefly heritage—she was the daughter of Knife Chief—not to mention the blessing of the heavens, Braided Woman seemed to have everything a young Pawnee woman could desire. After her first menstruation, she had married old Makes His Enemies Tremble as a third wife. But during the spring planting, the year after Braided Woman's marriage, Half Man had arrived.

In Pawnee eyes, Half Man was exactly that: half Omaha and half Pawnee. His Pawnee mother had been captured by the Omaha, taken as a slave, and later escaped back to the Pawnee. Since she was a respected woman, from a respected family, her sisters had taken her in. Against the wishes of her family, she had allowed her half-breed son to live.

The boy, Half Man, had borne the stigma of his Omaha blood with little grace. He'd grown into a surly young man who finally ran off to claim his Omaha heritage. Over the years he had drifted between the two peoples, always mistrusted, always suspect, yet able to claim sanctuary with either people. Since the Pawnee traced kinship through the females, Half Man was a full member of his mother's lineage. The Omaha traced descent through the males, making him a full-blood Omaha in their eyes.

On the day that Half Man arrived at the Skidi village, he brought with him a tin of the *La-chi-kuts'* spirit water: White man's whiskey.

That night, after council, Half Man had given Makes His Enemies Tremble whiskey until the old man went to sleep. Then he let young Braided Woman drink some. And then some more.

"*All I can recall is waking up,*" Packrat's mother had told him. "*My head hurt. I thought for a moment that I had been attacked, hit in the head with a war club. I was lying in the grass outside of the village. Thirsty, horribly thirsty.*

I sat up and vomited into the grass. That's when I discovered I was naked. Looking down, I could see that I had been with a man. I had bruises on my breasts and my neck had been bitten. Semen had dried on my thighs.

"I found my blanket and covered myself before I walked back to the village, shamed, trying to hide myself. A couple of days later, when I felt better, I went to Half Man, who was staying in his sister's house, and asked him if we'd coupled. He laughed, and said no. He said it before his family."

Packrat lifted his head to stare out at the stormy skies. Wisps of white snow blew around the hollow, finally to pile in the lee of the granite boulders.

Everyone knew that Half Man had lied. The old and familiar anger throbbed in Packrat's chest. From the time of her menstruation until Half Man took her, Braided Woman had not coupled with her husband. No other man could have fathered a child in her. Yet Half Man, with the honor and respectability of a weasel, had shamed her in public. The reason was understandable: He wanted to keep his relationship with Knife Chief and Makes His Enemies Tremble. A man did not lie with another man's wife without permission.

Therefore, Packrat was *pira-paru*, a hidden child, one unrecognized by others. A pariah who lived at the margins of Pawnee society, but one step up from a slave.

"I'll tell you what to do," Pitalesharo had said. *"You must always remember that you are* Panimaha . . . Pawnee. *Because of an accident, your life will never be easy,* tiwat. *But we are a forgiving people, a fair people. It runs in our blood—the gift of Evening Star when she bore the First Woman. Everyone knows who your father is, and what he did to your mother."*

Packrat threw another twisted sagebrush onto the fire. As flames licked up around the dry branches, the pungent honey-eyed odor of sage lifted around him and lit the smile on his thin lips. "I told him I should kill Half Man."

"But no!" Pitalesharo had cried as he lifted his hands. *"That is not the way of the cunning* Panimaha. *True, people would agree that it would be a justified murder, but you'd still be suspect, always considered dangerous, not really*

*right for the people. Tiwat, you must be more cunning.
Think back to the stories we tell, the lessons we teach. You
must prove yourself a better man than all others in finding
your revenge. You must do it in a manner that will honor
yourself, Morning Star, Evening Star, and the White Wolf.
You must be cunning, tiwat . . . ever cunning!"*

Packrat tilted his head, allowing the cold snowflakes to
settle on his hot face. Pitalesharo, Knife Chief's son, called
him *tiwat*, nephew, the most affectionate of Pawnee terms
used between men. Of them all, no man was as brave, kind,
and strong as Pitalesharo.

Packrat had considered the lessons taught in the stories,
and from them, a plan had been born.

"I have found my way, *tiwatciriks*," Packrat answered
his distant uncle. "The stories have shown me the way."

Indeed they had. Packrat had taken two horses and ridden
out from the Skidi winter camp, traveling up the river to
this place where the Platte vanished into worn rocky gorges
and bent south into jagged mountains. He would travel farther west, into the lands of the Shoshoni, and there, he
would find a woman. Once he'd captured her, he would
return to the Skidi villages, and there he would have his
revenge on his father—and in a way that would elevate him
in the eyes of his people, and restore the standing of his
long-suffering mother.

The wind howled harder, white wraiths of snow streaming
past. Packrat, "he who collects things," glanced up into the
darkness. Evening Star's guardians shook their rattles and
danced furiously to produce a storm like this one.

Thinking of Evening Star, and the war at the dawn of
time, made him smile. Retribution could come in many
ways. The people would talk forever about Packrat and the
way he had repaid Half Man for his perfidy.

Packrat stood for a moment, looking westward into the
wind and storm. Somewhere, out there in the blackness, he
would find a woman. Then, all he needed to do was carry
her safely to the big Skidi village. After that, he could take
his place among the people, and no one would doubt him.

A sleet-mushy rain fell from the black spring sky as Travis Hartman followed the trail that led down toward the muddy bank where the *Maria* was tied off. In the distance, beyond the murky Illinois shore, lightning flashed against the night: the first of the year.

And just maybe an omen, Travis told himself.

The treacherous trail snaked down between trunks of green ash and pin oak; their roots stuck up to ensnarl the unwary foot. Travis slipped and slid, but kept his balance. As he stepped out of the trees he crunched across riverbank gravel to reach the *Maria.* Travis hoisted himself onto the wet deck and rounded the corner of the cargo box before ducking inside through the low doorway.

An oil lamp cast a glow over the interior. Green lay in his blankets, a ledger propped up on his knees. Green had thrown his blankets over stacked bolts of cloth to make a soft, if lumpy, bed. He glanced up, recognized Hartman, and lifted an eyebrow as he set the ledger aside. "Bit early for you to be in, isn't it?"

"Trouble." Hartman took off his soaked hat and shrugged out of his dripping coat before reaching down into a gap between flour kegs to retrieve a salt-glazed jug. Twisting out the wooden stopper, he lifted the jug and took a deep swig before grimacing and wiping his lips with a sleeve.

"T'ain't just water staining your coat, is it?" Green gestured at the wet jacket. Dark red smears had run in the rain.

"Reckon not. Chouteau's starting ter take an interest in Dave Green, Travis Hartman, and the *Maria.* A couple of Chouteau's *engagés* wanted a little talk with me." Travis grinned. "I guess one of them boys must'a busted his nose when he hit the side of Smith's Tavern. Them logs is all hickory and ash and walnut. And thick, too. A feller shouldn't otta run his face into 'em like that." Hartman rubbed at one of the red stains. "I guess his head did a little leaking whilst I was a-dragging him away."

"And the other one?"

"Oh, wal, I reckon he jist plumb passed out when I whacked him 'longside the head with that ax handle ol' Smith was whittling down fer hafting." Travis smacked his lips, shaking his head. "I figger it like this. Them boys surely ketched the worst of it, and I got ter feeling a mite upset that they's all bunged up. So what, I asks meself, would do them shady lard eaters good? Why, a boat ride, I tells meself back. That's what they wanted ter ask this ol' coon about in the first place.

"Wal, sure 'nuff, I drug their heavy carcasses down ter the water, tied 'em up right pert, and dropped 'em in a pirogue. Then I sort of cast the whole shitaree off into the current and figgered that they'd get a sight of traveling in afore they fetched up on an embarrass, or else reached Natchez. One or t'other."

Green gave him a hard stare. "I don't reckon you could have just lied to them and sent them on their way?"

Travis fingered his chin, frowning, and shook his head. "Wal, Dave, I might'a . . . but I ain't sure they'd a taken ter such palaver. One of 'em was old Jacques Valmont. Didn't know the other feller. Reckon I knew his kind, though. Big, mean, had half his ear bitten off, and a nose what looked like somebody tried to make hominy outa it."

"Jacques Valmont." Green grunted. "Correct me if I'm wrong, but you killed his brother a couple of years back up on the Heart River, didn't you?"

"Something like that, I reckon." Travis took another swig from the jug. "Hell, Dave, they jist come outa the dark and Jacques starts in asking about ye and the boat and where we was a-headed. Wal, thar's bad blood atwixt us anyhow, and I plumb didn't like the tone in his voice. That other feller with him had his hand on his pistol, and Jacques had his knife out. I reckon I jist laid into 'em."

"Jacques had his knife out?" Green mused, looking someplace far away. "None of the Valmonts ever bluffed for a damn. I reckon they meant business." Green looked up. "You're sure you didn't kill 'em?"

"Wal, I didn't lift their topknots."

Green rubbed his square jaw, eyes slitted. "We've got thirty-one men. Barely enough to move the boat."

"They'll do. Dave, we're outa time. We been lucky as it is. I don't think we got more'n a day afore someone important perks up and takes serious notice. Not with Jacques and his pal up and missing."

Green brooded in the lamplight. "You know, Travis, I've bet the world on this."

"Reckon ye could sell 'er out. Cut a deal with Chouteau, a boat full of goods . . . delivered."

"Can't. I already thought some about that. I mean, well, what am I? I'm a trader—always have been. What would I do? Just build me a nice house, sit in Saint Louis, and sip wine? No, old friend. I'd rather take my chances on losing it all. Here I could waste away in comfort, but out there, I have the chance to build an empire."

Green stared down at his hands, working his fingers back and forth. Weather had browned the skin like leather. Those calluses had come of hard work, and the man behind them had a soul built of the same sinew, bone, and muscle.

Hartman grunted and sucked at the jug again. "Reckon I foller where yer stick floats, Dave. Tain't neither one of us a gonna die in bed. Now, that's fer sure." After a pause he added, "Don't know much about this crew I done scavenged. Some'll make her with the rye on, some we might have ter shoot afore we make it upriver. Hell, I even bought one fer a penny from old François."

Green glanced up. "François? He still around? I'd have thought he'd have been hung by now."

"Nope. Last I heard, he done floated over inta Illinois someplace ter trade liquor. Something happened and François kilt a couple of men. Heard he slipped off south ter Fort Massac, and now he's back here. Seems as if some poor Yankee Doodle from back East got crosswise with him, that's sure, and François got him in the end."

"Huh. So what's the matter with François? He get religion or something? Why didn't he cut the pilgrim's throat and dump him in the river? It's not like him to fart around."

Travis hitched himself onto a barrel, his head bent low

under the plank ceiling. In the light, Dave Green's blocky face looked as if he saw all damnation looming before him. Everything Dave had hung by a thread, and the saws of fate were fraying that single hope.

"Wal, you know François. He's always been a bit notional. Reckon it's jist my guess, but he's playing some sort of joke."

"Is that so? François's jokes are usually funny only to François. Remember that time up at Fort Manuel? François had those spectacles he was clowning around in? That Oto boy stole them one night, and François caught the kid, poked his eyes out, and gave him them spectacles afterward. Said it would help him see better."

"Yep, I remember. François's got a mean streak that'd make a Blackfoot plumb proud."

Green lay back on his blankets. "Only a fool'd cross someone like François. Knowing that, why'd you pick this man up?"

"Figgered he was one more body. Whatever François's reasons, the pilgrim's better off pulling our boat than floating face down in the river. François swears himself blue that he's got a legal paper on this feller. Said we could have the Yankee Doodle's contract of indenture for a penny. All I had ter do was promise ter make the pilgrim fill out his time—or shoot him if'n he cut and run."

Water lapped on the hull, and out in the trees the wind sighed in the dripping black branches.

Green continued rubbing his hands together, the hollow sound loud in the silence. Then he said, "If François is involved, something's rotten. Keep that in mind."

"I did. Told him if'n he pulled a fast one, I'd kill him. 'Course, I ain't expecting much outa the Doodle. But like I say, I reckon he's better off a-pulling on the cordelle than he'd be as fish food." Travis paused. "Ye've heard of this Lizette? The Creole whore?"

"She ain't exactly a whore." Green gave him a wry look. "A woman like that, well, they call her a courtesan. I've met her. Couldn't afford her."

"Wal, it appears François can. Says she's done tied a ribbon on his wang."

"His funeral, then. She's more'n he can handle." Green nodded to himself. "All right. Time's up. Dawn—day after tomorrow, Travis. Get the men together." Green closed his eyes, and lay completely still in the lamplight. Only the rising and falling of his chest distinguished him from a corpse.

Travis took another swig from his bottle, and cocked his head as a rat scampered somewhere behind the packed cargo.

NINE

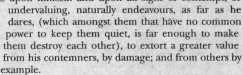

Again, men have no pleasure, but on the contrary a great deal of grief, in keeping company, where there is no power able to over-awe them all. For every man looketh that his companion should value him, at the same rate he sets upon himself: and upon all signs of contempt, or undervaluing, naturally endeavours, as far as he dares, (which amongst them that have no common power to keep them quiet, is far enough to make them destroy each other), to extort a greater value from his contemners, by damage; and from others by example.

—Thomas Hobbes, *Leviathan*

Richard lay shivering in the dark. Lonely and forgotten. *But then, I've been lonely all of my life, haven't I?* If only his mother hadn't died. How different would his life have been? He might have been able to grow up like the others, like Will Templeton. Will never had to live with the knowledge that his father often slipped away in the night to lie with a mysterious woman.

I'll never forgive you for that, Father. Mother lies in her grave, and you sate yourself in another woman's arms.

Once, Richard had thought to discover his father's mistress's identity, but Phillip had been as canny as an old fox about keeping his secret.

No matter what, Laura, I will be yours alone. If I live through this, I swear I will never betray this sacred trust between us. He nodded to himself, savoring the solemnity of his vow.

Then he heard the door open. Fear crawled down his nerves as he stared into the blackness. Two men, burly shadows, entered, then came a third man bearing a lantern. The man opened the lantern's shutter and a feeble light played across the room.

"There he is. Goddamn, he stinks worse'n a privy."

Richard squinted into the light, unable to make out the figures. Rough hands grabbed him by the shoulders and feet.

Dear God, what now? "Who . . . who are you?"

"Shut up!"

"Where are you taking me? Help! *Help!*"

A big fist lashed out of the darkness and sparks blasted through Richard's vision.

"Keep yer mouth shet or you'll git another one o' those," a voice rasped in his ear.

"*O mon Dieu!* He has pissed himself," another of the men cursed.

I'm going to die. How would it be? His throat cut? A blow to the head? He twisted, driven by panic, but a hard cuff to the side of the head stunned him. He swung slackly in their arms as they carried him out into the night.

Dear God, don't let me die! Those mocking words, spoken so long ago in Boston, slipped loose in some desperate corner of his mind. Three weeks and he'd run the country? The material world could be molded by perceptions? Think of me as an animal tamer? Why don't you start a government? A warrior, conquering with the sword of philosophy!

Gripped by terror, he was barely conscious of his shivering body swaying between the men as they hustled him along night trails. The dark boles of trees rose into a black filigree of branches. The smell of the river—mud, water, and rotting vegetation—filled his nostrils. Then he heard voices, soft in the night, growing louder.

"Hartman?" one of the abductors called out.

"Hyar, coon!"

Richard's captors turned toward the voice, cursing as they stumbled and slid down a steep embankment and out of the protection of the trees. A plank bounced under the men's feet and Richard was dropped on a wooden deck. He stared desperately at the stars, waiting for the discharge of a pistol or the bitter sting of a knife. Water slapped a hollow rhythm against the hull.

"Here's your delivery." One of the captors smacked his hands, as if to clean them. "I been told I get a penny."

"And I get papers," a tall shadowy form replied. "François said this was all legal."

Paper crackled. "Here. François told me the pig signed it."

"Yer sure?"

"Sure? What is writing, eh? Chicken tracks on paper? Who knows? I was just told to bring him here. François has given his word, *non*?"

The tall shadow pointed with a hard finger. "I reckon, and I give him mine. If'n he's crossed me, I'll drive a knife inta his greasy French belly, down low, and saw it right up through his brisket ter his jawbone."

"I do not think, *mon ami*, that François would trick you."

A low chuckle erupted. "No, I don't reckon he would. I figger he knows this child too good. Hyar's yer penny. Give my regards to François . . . and old August, too, eh?"

"*Bon voyage*, Hartman. Just don't let him break his contract, eh? That was François's only condition."

Richard closed his eyes as footsteps retreated across the deck and down the bouncing plank. When he looked up, dark shapes had gathered like blots against the stars.

"Christ," a voice muttered. "He stinks like pig shit. Dip him in the river for a while."

"You know, there's people downstream might want'ta drink that water."

"Reckon so . . . but then, what they don't know ain't a gonna hurt 'em none."

"Oh, God," Richard mumbled as hard hands picked him up. "Leave me be, please?"

"Shut up!" A voice hissed from the dark. "It's bad

enough we gotta smell ye, let alone listen to ye whimpering like a sheep.''

As his buttocks hit the cold black water Richard let loose with a squalling sound, then he was under, still grasped by strong hands, trying to hold what breath he had left.

His head broke the surface and he gasped before he was pushed under again. The cold ate into his limbs while his heart pounded. He came up, and was ducked yet again.

They held him down longer this time. The current gurgled and tugged at him. Darkness and cold, like leaching death, caressed his chilled skin with a lover's touch. His lungs began to labor, sucking at the bottom of his throat. In panic, he thrashed against their hold. Their iron grip held and they pulled him—wriggling—from the water like a gaffed fish.

They laughed as they dumped him on the deck. Richard coughed, spent and trembling, as water ran from his soaked clothing. He broke into sobs then, wishing for death, barely aware of the men as they walked away. He began to shiver as the night wind blew across his sodden body.

He heard himself start to mutter incoherently. *Is that me?* a distant part of his brain wondered. Dark forms moved in the night around him.

''Oh God. Why is this happening to me?''

The cold crept through his numb joints—a cold unlike anything he had ever experienced, teeth chattering, bones shaking. It intruded into his soul as water did the pages of a book.

What kind of nightmare was this? One from which he could not awaken, a terror to be lived, not dreamed.

Someone relieved himself over the side of the boat.

''Please,'' Richard called softly. ''Help me.''

''Waugh!'' a gruff voice called. ''Who be thar? That you, Doodle?''

''I'm c—cold.'' Richard gritted his teeth to stop them from chattering.

''Huh!'' the gruff voice continued. Richard had heard him called Hartman. The man disappeared for a moment, then approached on silent moccasined feet. He dropped a blanket over Richard, peering down curiously in the darkness. ''You're that Yankee Doodle I done contracted fer?''

"Help me . . . *please*! I've been kidnapped."

"Now, I reckon that be a matter of opinion. Yer a-headed upriver, lad. We bought yer contract from ol' François. Has your sign on it, they say. You just stay plumb put, pilgrim."

"You don't understand. . . . Dear God, I'm going to die, I just know I am. Can't you *do* anything?"

"Well, it don't seem right—"

"God, no! I've been kidnapped!"

"—just ter leave ye a-layin' on the open deck this a-way."

The man reached under Richard's shoulders and lifted him against the cargo box. "Hyar now, pilgrim. Ye just take a mite o' this hyar jug o' mine. Reckon it otta light a little fire in yer Yankee belly."

The cool jug was tilted to Richard's mouth. He could smell the stuff, almost pure alcohol. He drank, and sputtered on the harsh liquor.

"Thar ye be."

"Thank you. No one's been nice to me in days. I'm Richard Hamilton." He gasped at the warmth building in his stomach.

"I be Travis Hartman. My pleasure ter meet ye, Dick."

"What did you mean, a contract?"

"Reckon it's a paper what ye signed, a-sayin' ye'll go with us up ter trade with the Injuns upriver. I been havin' a time gittin' hands fer this hyar trip. Ain't got no permit from ol' redhair Clark. So ye see, lad, this's all from under the boards."

"Under the boards . . . what's that mean?"

"Means we got ter sneak. Like rats under the floor. Means we ain't got no license fer trading. We're gonna have ter get past Fort Atkinson slicker'n fat on a Ree woman's rump. But I reckon we'll do 'er."

"What do you mean—upriver?"

"Why, up the Missouri, Dick." Hartman sounded annoyed. "We're gonna go trading with the Crow for plews, boy. Got this here boat packed clean full of foofaraw."

"And you *bought* me?"

"Wal, way I hear'd it, it was that or François and his crew of pirates was a gonna slit yer gullet and feed ye to the fishes.'' Travis laughed. ''Reckon, come down to it, yer hair's worth passage.''

''My hair?''

''Whar ye be from, boy, that they don't talk no English?''

''Boston. I came here on business. François—and his friends—they robbed me and beat me up. They tortured me and . . . and you simply *must* set me free! Let me go to the authorities. Travis, cut me loose. *Please,* I need somebody to help me. I must get away from here.''

''Nope,'' Travis stood up. ''Can't go a-doin' that. Reckon I done told ye 'nuff as 'tis. Ol' Dave Green needs all the help he can get ter make her upriver. Yer in. Come low water or high. Best cling to it, boy. Like I done told ye, sure beats what François had in store fer ye.'' Hartman fastened his callused fingers into Richard's shirt and pulled him into a sitting position. ''Reckon ye otta be sleeping, Dick. Shore 'nuff, ye'll get a bellyful of boatwork come sunup.''

''Don't leave me, Travis.''

''Best shut yer mouth now, boy. Git yerself some sleep.'' Hartman stood, a black silhouette against the night sky. He tilted the jug against his lips, and strolled down the *passe avant* on cat-silent feet.

Curled in the blanket, warmth fought the chill to a draw. The only sounds were the whisper of the breeze in the trees, the muted slap of waves against the hull, and the haunting cries of the night birds. Richard never felt the difference when he slipped from consciousness to sleep.

Heals Like A Willow walked steadfastly across the open plain, her moccasins crunching in the wet snow. The bright sun on the virgin snowfields forced her to squint to protect her eyes. The day before, she'd found shelter in the lee of a sandstone outcrop as a vicious spring storm blew through. While the wind howled, and the snow drifted, she'd slept, eaten, and recouped her strength.

She could see her destination to the north: the snow-bright slopes of the Powder River Mountains. The *Dukurika,* her people, were waiting there, camped somewhere up in the foothills. They had always done it so, hunting the south-facing hillsides where sun and wind kept snow from the winter range so beloved by deer, elk, and mountain sheep.

"It won't be long," she promised the distant mountains. "Mother, Father, I'm coming home."

There, in the warm rock overhangs, and among the tawny lodges of her kin, she'd find solace. The smiles of her brother and cousins would blunt the keening ache of death. The jokes her people enjoyed would help patch the gaping emptiness within her.

She could see it, the crackling fire casting yellow light on weather-brown faces. Her father, High Wolf, his eyes crinkled, spreading his arms wide as he told the Winter Tales of Wolf and Coyote, and *Pachee Goyo,* the Bald One. Alder, her mother, would be smiling, her worn teeth like stubby pegs behind her brown lips. Willow could almost smell the succulent mountain sheep haunch roasting slowly over the coals of the cookfire, its aroma mingling with the scents of juniper and limber pine on the crisp night air.

"Soon," she told herself as she wound through the snow-crusted sagebrush, each with a tapered drift that stippled the land.

The dazzling morning was already warming in the wake of the storm. Spring was like that, bitterly cold one day, warm and sunny the next. Within a day, the broad basin she crossed would become a quagmire of sticky mud, pooling water, and rushing drainages.

Up in the mountains, rock and gravel on the slopes would make travel less treacherous. It might take days to find a camp of the *Dukurika,* but find them she would. By the time the biscuit root, shooting star, and desert parsley sent forth new shoots, she'd have begun the long process of healing herself.

Unbidden, her dead son's voice gurgled in the back of her memory, and an image of his round face tried to form. Tight-jawed, Willow forced it away, focusing herself on the distant mountains and memories of youth spent among the cool forests and sun-glazed meadows. Yes, it would be like that again.

Because of the sun's glare, Heals Like A Willow kept her eyes in a narrow squint. As a result, she didn't see the rider until too late. Perhaps it wouldn't have made any difference, out in the open as she was. He crested the ridge, nothing more than a black dot skylined against the ceramic blue sky.

She slowed and watched. The man and two horses picked their way down the snow-humpy sage slope. Their tracks dimpled the pristine white. A heavy buffalo robe disguised his tribal identity, and the horses wore Spanish tack from far to the south.

All right, what do I do now? Willow wet her lips and lowered her pack from her shoulders, dropping it into the snow. Behind her, her tracks, winding through the snowy sage, were the only visible break across the basin. Ahead of her, still far away, the foothills of the Powder River Mountains mocked her, white and gleaming in the morning sun. No drainage, no prominence, nothing lay close enough to offer protection. Even if she could outrun him, the snow would allow him to track her.

You must face him, Willow. With your digging stick as your only weapon, you'd better just hope he's Dukurika *or* Ku'chendikani.

As the rider reached the flat, he trotted his horses forward. She could see him now, a young man, wearing moccasins. And yes, she knew that style of decoration. For the most part, Pawnee hunted around the forks of the Platte, preferring to raid south, into the Spanish lands and into the territory now held by the *Yamparika*, who many now called Comanche—distant cousins of the *Ku'chendikani*.

A dryness settled in Willow's throat as she braced her feet and gripped the heavy chokecherry-wood digging stick. Each end was fire-hardened and sharpened.

He pulled up on his horse and studied her, head slightly cocked. As if he had all the time in the world, he glanced back along her trail, then toward the mountains ahead.

Willow swallowed hard and slowly tramped the snow flat, feeling with her feet to learn the footing. She tightened her grip on her digging stick, checking the balance. Everything would depend on the young Pawnee. If he rode close enough, tried to brain her with the war club hanging on his saddle, she had a chance. If he strung the bow hanging on his back and shot at her from long range, she could dodge and try to deflect the arrows. If he tried to ride her down, she could set her digging stick, leap out of the way at the last moment, and hope the horse hit it at the right angle to impale itself and throw the rider.

Long chances, Willow. He's going to kill you. And at that thought, she chuckled, then laughed out loud.

To her ears it sounded like he said, "*Cheshay mowhat atshak ahat.*" But then, Willow didn't know the first thing about Pawnee talk.

"I'm laughing because it is a good time to die, you two-legged piece of filth. Do you hear? I'm not afraid. Come kill me! My husband and son will thank you. Come on, you pus-infected penis, come kill me!" *But not without a fight, worm!*

He grinned at the challenge in her voice and threw back his robe to expose his head. Like many Pawnee, he'd chosen to shave the sides of his head and leave a long roach that fell into a braid down his back. With careless ease, he pulled the bow over his shoulder and artfully strung it on the saddle.

He's too close! No dodging, no matter how violent, would save her.

She started forward, desperate to distinguish herself as a woman of the *Dukurika* with pride, attacking her enemy.

The Pawnee laughed, heeling his horse back. He continued to jabber at her in Pawnee, but with one hand he motioned for her to put her digging stick down.

Willow slowed, seeing that no matter how she charged, he'd circle and skip out of the way. When she glared into those bright eyes, death didn't lurk there. Instead, she saw wry amusement. Willow hesitated, then used her hands to sign the message: "What do you want?"

He signed back, "You, woman. You are my captive. Come with me."

She gave him the "It is finished" sign, and gripped her digging stick. What would death be like? Would there be a horrible pain as his arrows sliced into her? The initial fear had receded with the realization that death brought relief from guilt, an end to the lonely grief. She'd be with her husband and her son soon, a warrior returned to her family.

The Pawnee shook his head, unhooked his war club, and slipped nimbly off the side of his horse. He continued talking to her in irritated tones the way he would to a fractious horse.

"So you think, corn eater." For good measure, Willow took a swipe with her digging stick, listening to it tear the air. "That's going to be your head, fool!"

He stopped no more than four paces in front of her, gesturing again for her to put her stick down.

"You think I'm as silly as a sage grouse?"

He didn't look more than a boy—barely old enough to be a man by anyone's figuring. But the eyes broke the illusion; they were wise in the ways of the world. In another time and place she would have considered him a handsome boy, tall, muscular, with fine features and a mouth made for laughter. His nose was broad and straight, his cheeks slanting to a strong jaw.

He gestured once again for her to put her digging stick down.

Willow shook her head, and saw him slowly nod. He muttered something under his breath and began to close, his war club held out before him.

The weapon had been crafted of some hardwood, bent slightly, with a knob on the end. Willow circled, holding her digging stick defensively. If he lunged, she could block the blow, and perhaps poke him in the face before she skipped out of the way.

Instead, he walked right up to her and swung the club in an arc. Willow easily blocked the blow, but the power of it threw her back and the resilient chokecherry wood stung her hands. Off balance, she jabbed at him. The Pawnee sidestepped, and whacked her on the elbow.

The impact didn't break her arm, but pain caused her to gasp as the nerves tingled and flashed. From the corner of her eye she barely saw the war club coming around—before lightning blasted through her vision and the ground swam slowly up to enfold her.

Men began to move about the boat before dawn. Someone stepped on Richard, then kicked him. *"Leve! Mangeur du lard!* Get up!"*

Richard pulled himself back out of the way, huddling in his blanket as he stared at the burly boatmen who had swarmed aboard in the gray light. Where was Travis Hartman? Wouldn't someone here help him?

"C'mon! Goddamn ye! Dawn's a-coming! Let's go, you lazy whelps!" a harsh voice snarled out in English. "We got wind to fill the sails! Let's not waste it, eh?"

Richard watched as men joked under their breath, poking fun at others who were obviously drunk. Two were brought aboard unconscious, feet dragging as they bobbed between the shoulders of companions who sang softly in French.

"Eh? Jules? They 'ave to pry you out of Rosette's arms, eh?"

"Pry him out of her arms? *non!* They pry something else out of Rosette!"

"You better have enjoyed it! There be no more soft woman for you until we reach the Rees!"

"And they might sell you a woman just to split your head in two as you go down to poke your pizzle into some greasy squaw!"

"Knowing you, Trudeau, not even threat of death will keep you from a woman. And as for the Rees, eh, they do things to a man not even a Saint Louis whore would consider!"

Richard winced. What kind of barbarians were these?

"Eh! Booshway! We are ready!" a man called.

"Any time, lads. Sooner we're gone, the better she'll be," an American shouted from the top of the cargo box.

"Cast off! Cast off, you curs!"

"Eh! Patroon! You are all mouth and gut! Do we 'ave to listen to you the whole way?"

"Sacré enfant du grâce!"

Men made clunking noises on the shore side, and Richard felt the *Maria* move off and away from the dark bank amid low curses and grunts. From where he lay, Richard could crane his neck and see the crewmen as they shoved long poles into the water. Like a lumbering monster, the keelboat swung out into the current.

"We've still got our breeze," the American called from above. "Reckon it's a sign! Henri, drop the sheet! Let's use her while we got her!"

Amidst more cursing and commands, the sail flapped down, lines being run out to the gunwales to stay the sheet. Someone struck up a nonsense song in French about fishing in springs, girls in wells, and hearts in guerdon, all punctuated by a "Ding-ding-a-dong" chorus.

Richard resettled his cramped body and sought to ease the chafing ropes that bound his wrists. *This is going to be horrible. Escape—I've got to escape.*

That was it, slip off the boat, make his way back downstream to Saint Louis, inform the authorities and . . . Well, no matter. Someone would advance him the necessary funds to buy passage back to Boston.

He pulled hard against the ropes, and gasped as the bonds burned his raw skin. Too tight. Even if he slipped over to the side, he'd plummet into the water like a dropped stone. And sink like one.

As the sun came up, Richard took stock of the keelboat. She was built of weathered oak planks bleached white by the sun and storm. Keelboats were not creations of great beauty. The big square cargo box filled the hull with limited fore and aft deck space. The *passe avant* was a narrow, cleated walkway that allowed passage from the bow to the stern along each side of the cargo box. A single mast rose from the keelboat's center. The patroon, or helmsman, stood atop the rear of the box and grasped a long tiller that controlled the rudder.

A big man with blond hair and a blunt face walked over to Richard and cut the bonds around his wrists. The pain of restored circulation made Richard gasp as he stared at his mottled and puffy hands.

"Mornin'." The big man grinned at him. "I'm Dave Green. I bought your contract from François."

"Mr. Green," Richard sighed. "Thank God I've found you! I've been through a terrible ordeal. This François robbed me and tied me up. I have been victimized by the most horrible of crimes. I must get off this boat, make my way back to Saint Louis, and inform the authorities."

"Authorities, huh?" Green squinted out over the water. "Now, that's a matter of disagreement between us, boy. A contract is just that, a deal. You are Richard John Charles Hamilton, aren't you?"

"Yes, sir. I am, but I—"

"And you did sign that paper, didn't you?"

"But I had no choice! You don't understand what he was—"

"Then it's a deal. Fair and square."

"Deal! He had a knife to my throat! You can't—"

"Look here, boy. I don't know what François did, and further, I don't really give a good God damn. François is a black-hearted son of a bitch, I'll grant. But your trouble with him is your own. My trouble is that I've got to get this boat upriver and I don't have the men to do it. What I do have is a contract with your signature on it."

"But this is abduction! The laws . . ."

"Lad, don't go spouting law at me. You're on the river. Law is far back East." Green laced his fingers together and cracked his knuckles. Richard stared at those powerful hands and swallowed dryly. "From the moment you signed that paper, you became an *engagé*. You know what that means?"

"Contracted labor. But I wasn't—"

"Damn right. Contracted labor. You're going to work this boat upriver, boy. I'm the booshway on this trip. That means the chief, understand? Travis Hartman's the little booshway, my second in command. Henri is the patroon, head of the boat. When it comes to camp, you're in Trudeau's mess. You're bottom of the heap, boy. You do what others tell you, and you'll get along fine."

"But I've got rights! Rights guaranteed under the Constitution of the—"

"You don't have shit, boy. Not here, not on the river. You'll work . . . or you'll wish you had. Understand?"

The *engagés* were watching, drawn to the commotion. Someone snickered, and another big muscular man grinned and elbowed the man next to him. Wolves would watch a sheep with eyes like those.

Green chuckled grimly. "Let me lay it out for you, boy. Let's say you jump ship and make it back to Saint Louis. What the hell do you think's going to happen to you? François's gonna get wind of it, and he's gonna kill you. Dead. Got that? The miracle is that you're alive at all, but then luck slips into just about anybody's life once in a while."

"Luck? You call *this* luck?"

"Yep. You're floating on the water instead of in it. Now, look at it from my side. I'm short-handed, and I damned sure can't have you going back telling people that the *Maria* is headed upriver. Provided you lived long enough to tell anyone, and provided they believed you, Clark would send an express off to—"

"Express?"

"A rider . . . with a message to Fort Atkinson that I was headed that way. Understand? They'd stop me just as sure as François would stop you. They'd just throw me in jail, boy. But you, well, you're a heap better off on this boat than rotting in the mud along the bank someplace."

"But I've been robbed!" Richard cried. "They hit me. I never signed any contract. Not of my free will!"

Green fumbled in the little leather sack tied to his belt. He unfolded a wrinkled sheet of paper. "That your signature?"

"Yes, it is. But you don't understand. They *made* me!"

"Uh-huh. Tell you what. You help get this boat up the river and you can go free as a bird. Till then, your meat's mine."

"But I—but you . . . you . . . ."

Green looked up. "Travis! Come here."

Hartman appeared from behind the cargo box. Long fringed leathers, grease-stained and shiny, covered his muscular body. He moved with a powerful grace, padding like a lion on moccasined feet. Silver-streaked hair streamed down over the beaded shoulders of his buckskin jacket. Seeing him in daylight, Richard gasped. Something had once tried to rip Hartman's face from his skull. A mass of scar tissue arced across from his left cheek, through the mangled nose, then thinned into parallel lines on the right side that ran back toward his ear. A full beard did little to hide the damage.

Hartman lowered himself to a crouch, thick thigh muscles giving his squat a springy resilience like that of a hunting animal poised to leap. Richard looked into blue eyes that froze his soul. Up close, more scars were visible tracing through Hartman's hair in marbling patterns.

Green indicated Richard. "If he tries to jump the boat, Travis, hunt him down and shoot him. I'll have no man breaking his contract."

Travis narrowed one eye. "He do that an' he'll be wolf-meat, Davey. Reckon as how I'll do 'er."

"My God, you *wouldn't*!" Richard stared from one to the other.

"Ye'd better check yer topknot, Doodle. I give me word ter old François. Reckon ye'll fill out yer contract." Hartman's frigid blue stare froze Richard to his guts.

"Get yourself some breakfast." Green pointed forward. "Then get to work. We don't get upriver any faster if you set on your skinny 'butt, boy."

Then Green stood and clumped his way aft to shout up at the patroon.

"I reckon ye heard the man," Hartman said as Richard gaped in disbelief. "Fetch yerself some vittles and pick out one of them poles stacked on the cargo box. They's some old, but we'll cut new ones up past the settlements."

Richard backed carefully away from Hartman, wobbled to his prickly feet, and made his way forward. A pot containing the remains of diced meat and vegetables—now stone cold—was propped against the plank wall of the cargo box. Richard's soul crawled at the sight of the congealed grease in the bottom. In God's name, how long had it been since he'd eaten? His gnawing stomach overcame squea-

mishness. With nothing but fingers to eat with, Richard scooped the last dregs out of the pot and fought down the desire to vomit.

Maria coasted gracefully along the shore. The west bank was high here, gaps in the trees marking occasional fields. The Mississippi ran dark and deep, water roiling and choppy from the south wind. The boatmen were singing yet another of their songs, this one some nonsense about walking footpaths, being made to laugh, and being afraid of wolves. They glanced curiously at him, several with the bloodshot eyes as a result of their revelries the night before.

Richard huddled beside the empty stew pot and stared dully out over the gunwales at the river and the malignant trees beyond. Miserable as he was, he could sense that presence, as if the land watched him from deep within those shadowed ways.

"God, I'm going to die out here. What kind of a place is this? What kind of men are these? A land of demons . . . peopled by a race of devils."

"*. . . No arts; no letters; no society; and which is worst of all, continual fear and danger of violent death; and the life of man, solitary, poor, nasty, brutish, and short.*" The acid words of Thomas Hobbes filtered through Richard's brain.

"Wind's dying!" came the cry from the cargo box. "Break out the poles, boys!"

Richard dropped his head into his hands. *Father, why did you do this to me? This isn't true. It just isn't true!*

"Dick?" Hartman's voice intruded. "Ye'd best be getting yer pole down like I told ye."

Richard glanced up into that cold stare.

"Best get on, now," Hartman said.

Richard rose unsteadily. He'd seen this kind of activity on the river. A man set the end of his pole in the mud at the bow of the boat and walked to the rear, pushing off on cleats pegged to the *passe avant,* no more than fifteen inches wide. Upon reaching the stern, he pulled the pole out of the mud and walked back forward while the boat coasted on momentum before he set and pushed again. The pole had a large knob set in the end to cushion a man's shoulder.

The *engagés* watched him pull one of the long poles from the pile. Snickers gave way to guffaws as he grunted, teetering to balance the weight. With all the bravado of a terrified mouse, he picked a place between two burly *engagés* who stared suspiciously at him.

He handled the pole awkwardly, lowering the end into the water, hunching over the knob, and pushing as the boat moved slowly under his feet. At the end, he pulled, twisting to break the mud's hold, and started back toward the front of the boat.

He made three trips before he began to gasp for breath.

TEN

❖

With passions so tame, and so salutory a curb, men, instead of being wild and wicked, and no more attentive to ward against harm than to cause any to other animals, were not exposed to any dangerous dissentions; as they kept up no manner of intercourse with each other, and were, of course, strangers to vanity, to respect, to esteem, to contempt; as they had no notion of what we call yours and mine, nor any true idea of justice; as they considered any violence they were liable to as an evil that could be easily corrected, and not as an injury that deserved punishment; and they never so much as dreamed of revenge. . . .

—Jean-Jacques Rousseau, *Discourse on the Origin and Foundation of Inequality Among Mankind*

The short-coupled, rough-gaited mare that Willow clung to cantered relentlessly across the sage. Whenever the mare slowed, the stubborn young Pawnee warrior who kept his own mount close behind used a willow crop to quirt the mare's rump. An equally stubborn Willow clung to the horse's mane with cramped fingers. The Pawnee had tied her feet beneath the mare's belly, and if she lost her hold and slid around the mare's barrel, she'd be kicked half to death—or, worse, the animal might fall and crush her into the sagebrush and rocks.

The wiry mare stumbled now, driven to her limits. With each jerking misstep, Willow's heart skipped. For four days, they'd alternately ridden, walked, and ridden some more, straining the endurance of the horses and themselves.

Fool, Willow mentally told the Pawnee, *no one even knows that I'm missing. And worse, if they did, no one would follow.*

The mare caught a hoof and lurched forward, jolting Willow's hold. If the mare fell and killed her, at least the agony of cramped and screaming muscles would be over. The numbness had started in her thighs. Then a terrible ache had eaten into her knees and calves. It had spread to her hips, climbed her back and shoulders, and ended in her pain-knit fingers.

The day had been warm, and the snow had melted to create a slick, pale gray mud treacherous to anything two- or four-legged. The Pawnee had chosen to ride up, away from the river, where the uplands provided better footing for the horses, and better points of vantage for him to study the backtrail.

Now, as the winter sun dipped behind the transected plains to the west, the Pawnee slowed the killing pace, once again glancing back at the purple mountains that rose in points against an orange and lavender evening sky.

The Pawnee kicked his horse up alongside of Willow's. He signed, "We camp," and led the way down into a drainage.

He had an eye for campsites, picking a concealed location with a southern exposure. The weathered sandstone would remain warm through the night, while the hollow protected them from both the west wind and the seeking eyes of pursuers—of whom there would be none. Juniper and tall sagebrush filled the hollow, while one lone cottonwood had taken root where the drainage trickled over the rocks.

The Pawnee slipped over his horse's side, deftly hobbled Willow's pony and his own. Only then did he untie the thongs from around Willow's ankles. When she slid down, her rubbery legs betrayed her. For a long time she lay staring at her hands where they propped her on the grass.

The Pawnee eyed her warily as he began twisting sagebrush out of the ground for firewood. She met his stare with one equally as wary. She knew his name now: Packrat—the knowledge rendered by sign language. Of the Pawnee people, she knew only a little: that they lived far to the east; mostly raided to the south; and were very warlike. Among other things, Pawnee were known to sacrifice young women to Morning Star. The gift of a woman to repay the female powers who had created the world.

Is that why he wants me? She cudgeled her memory. The Pawnee captured a young woman, treated her well, and finally took her out and tied her to a scaffold. Then, precisely at dawn, when the stars were right, they shot her full of arrows.

Willow calculated the exact spot on his skull where she'd land a blow the first time she got her hands on anything suitably lethal.

Packrat used his lips to point the way he wanted her to go. Willow pushed up, stood carefully, and walked on brittle legs toward the base of the sandstone outcrop. At his gesture, she settled herself on the pale sand. Their eyes held for a moment. What was he thinking behind that serious expression? Curiously, he looked slightly concerned.

"What do you want, boy?" she asked.

He said something in his own tongue.

"Well, don't worry about me. I'm not going anywhere.

Not tonight. Every bone and joint in my body aches. Even if I wanted to run away, I just couldn't.'' *Besides, you're still wary, ready for me to make a break. But down the trail, when you begin to relax, that will be different.*

Packrat muttered something in Pawnee. Then he bent down, pulled charred tinder from his leather bag, and used a strike-a-light to start a fire. With care, he nursed his glowing spark to flame, then added bits of sagebrush twigs until he had a suitable blaze. From Willow's pack he pulled what was left of her jerked meat, handing a hard piece to her.

As she chewed, she signed, ''What are you going to do with me?''

''You are a gift,'' he returned, watching her.

''To your gods?''

He chuckled at that before signing, ''Not as you think, but I hope Morning Star will be pleased.''

From the stories told, captive girls were kept for almost a year, pampered and jealously guarded before the spring morning when they were taken out, tortured, and killed. The hunt, capture, and return of the prisoner were highly ceremonial. Packrat's dress and actions hadn't reflected anything of the stories Willow had heard.

''A gift for whom?'' she signed.

''My father.''

''To be a slave to him?''

''Yes.''

Willow chewed thoughtfully on the tough jerky. As the night darkened overhead, the temperature dropped. Packrat, she noted, kept a careful fire, never letting it flame up, making sure it burned at a red glow, enough for heat and some light but not enough to disclose their position to watchers.

The horses simply stood where they'd stopped, heads down, as raggedly weary as she herself was. She forced herself to eat the last piece of jerky Packrat handed her. Strength was important. One day soon, she'd need all she could muster.

''You will try to escape,'' Packrat signed.

''Not tonight. Too tired.''

He considered, chuckled dryly to himself, and motioned her to roll over.

"Why?" she signed in defiance.

"Tie your hands and feet."

"No. Too tired to escape. I hurt everywhere."

He cocked his head, a slight smile giving his handsome face a mischievous look. Dimples formed at the sides of his mouth. "Better that I tie you. I, too, am tired. Too tired to want to chase you down or have to defend myself when you sneak over and grab my war club to brain me."

Was she that obvious?

He was so young. Undoubtedly inexperienced. And somewhere therein lay her final victory. She signed, "Heals Like A Willow wouldn't hurt you."

He laughed aloud, exposing straight white teeth. His flashing hands responded, "You think I'm stupid?"

"Not at all. You caught me, didn't you?"

"It wasn't very hard. Why were you out there, all alone like that?"

She considered, weighing her responses. He expected pursuit, and thus far had dealt with the flight from *Ku'chendikani* country like a seasoned warrior. Since he expected pursuit, lull him another way? "I was going back to my mother and father. My husband and young son are dead. Nothing remained for me among my married-into people."

He nodded with sudden understanding. "That is why you had no horse. I have heard how you wild people live. Had you had the luck to have been born Pawnee, you would still have your house, horses, fields, and family. A woman owns everything. If a husband dies, she does not end up poor, like you."

"I am rich enough," Willow insisted. "Not all wealth is in the form of horses or guns."

Packrat leaned back, evidently having forgotten he was going to tie her. "How rich can a woman be who rides tied to a Pawnee horse?"

Willow gave him a confident smile. "I am rich in dreams and visions. Several nights before you captured me, I dreamed of running as fast as an arrow, right for some trees. Then I tore through the trees and was flying." *Yes, that's right. This might be the way to beat him.* "Power brought you to me. It is all happening the way it is supposed to."

Packrat reached up to scratch his ear, jumping as a wolf howled in the gloomy distance.

And then she remembered a story she'd been told once. Wolf—in the Pawnee legends—was killed just after the Creation. Because of Wolf's death, men, too, must eventually die. Yes, and the willow was Wolf's tree, the one that symbolized death in the Pawnee ceremonials.

"You are a wild woman," Packrat signed with irritation. "Don't tell me your Snake people stories. I do not believe them."

"Do you know that star?" Willow pointed to the southwestern sky. "That is the star in my dreams." As well as the star that the Pawnee associated with death.

Packrat followed the way her finger pointed. He glanced at her and narrowed his eyes. His hands flew as he told her, "You are a foolish woman. Now, roll over. I'm going to bind your hands."

The lines at the corners of his eyes had gone tight. Like a small thorn in the flesh, it would fester, work on his confidence. She gave a harsh laugh as she rolled over, submitting her wrists to his thong.

After he had finished, he dropped her buffalo robe atop her and settled himself by the fire, his own robe draping his shoulders. He yawned, head nodding.

The howl of the wolf carried again on the quiet night.

Teetering on the verge of sleep, Willow opened her eyes to a slit. For long moments the tired boy stared up at the Wolf star—the Death star of Pawnee legend. Then he growled something to himself, shook his head, and lay back on the sandy soil.

Think about it, boy. Dream about it.

Images of captivity played through Willow's mind. What would it be like? She'd be beaten by the boy's father to teach her submission and to break her spirit. One wasn't a slave without being beaten on occasion. She'd have to spread her legs to any man who wanted her. And at that thought, she glanced again at the young man who slept just across from her. This night he was too tired to think of it. Soon, however, he would take her.

And when he does, Willow? Fighting him would prove useless. He'd simply beat her until she couldn't resist. Better to save her strength, perhaps lull his suspicions. As young and inexperienced as he seemed, he might make a mistake, leave himself open. Men often lost their wits when it came to driving their *we'an* into a woman. And, after all, it wouldn't be the first time a man had pumped his seed into her. *It will be unpleasant, girl—but nothing you can't endure.*

And for that, she would have to prepare herself.

The wolf howled again, and Willow heard Packrat stir uneasily.

Despite the night's chill and rain, the morning proved warm and bright as *Maria* coasted slowly along the west bank of the river. Travis sat with his back to the mast, alternately dozing, honing his skinning knife, and checking his possibles: personal effects like tobacco, needle-and-thread, gun flints and spare springs, whetstone, and so on. He'd made many of these journeys upriver, usually as one of the sweating *engagés,* never lying around like a lazy turtle on the cargo box, sunning himself. Behind him, Dave Green plied the long-poled rudder, and talked to Henri, the patroon who stood cross-armed, watching the current.

The patroon served as boat boss. Henri had been steering boats for over twenty years, and had a chest like a barrel. A thick mane of black hair hung down past his shoulders and matched his full beard. His fists looked capable of driving hardwood pegs through an oak post, and bristly black hair covered his forearms.

On the *passe avant,* someone cursed the poor Doodle. From where he sat, Travis could see Richard Hamilton's expression. Christ must have looked like that as he hauled the Cross up to Golgotha. The young man's mouth was set, cheeks sweaty and flushed, his eyes glazed. Hamilton staggered against the pole more than he pushed it. Stringy muscles shook as he struggled to keep up, a task made urgent since Trudeau, the burly *engagé* behind, cuffed him for being slow and clumsy.

Green, having turned the boat over to Henri, walked up and settled himself on the planks beside Travis. He squinted up at the sun, pulled a twist of tobacco from his pocket, and cut off a chew. His cheeks worked as he softened the quid and got it to juicing.

"Good day fer taking leave," Travis noted.

"Yep. Nice weather for a change. I've heard two different sets of beliefs on that. One is that it's an omen for good, the other says that the better the weather, the shittier it's going to get on the trip."

"Reckon I'll settle fer the first one."

"Me, too." Green paused thoughtfully. "Well, no matter. We're off, and the Devil take the hindmost. I'll tell you, Travis, I never thought I'd see this day. Look at her . . . my own boat, my own goods. For years I dreamed about this."

"I 'member." Travis closed his eyes and leaned his head back against the mast so the sun could warm his eyelids. "Always reckoned ye were a mite teched, Dave. As I recollect, first time I heard ye spouting off about being a booshway was that time on the Knife River."

Green chuckled. "Yeah, I remember. You and me, lost, shivering under that blanket while the wind howled and blew the snow so hard you couldn't see your hand in front of your face. We didn't dare fall asleep—scared to death the snow would drift up, cover us, and we'd smother to death before we could freeze."

Travis smiled, the scars around his mouth going tight. "Yep. Ye talked all that long black night about being a booshway. Bigger than Manuel Lisa, as I recall."

"Funny how things can change a man's life. The dream was born that night out there in the snow." Green crossed his arms over his knees, watching the heads of the *engagés* as they bobbed past the cargo box in the endless chore of poling the boat upstream. "But bigger than Lisa? Nope. He was the canny old lobo of the high Missouri, Lisa was. Travis, I'd just be happy with my share of the trade. Lisa wanted it all—and he'd have had it, but for dying too soon."

"Reckon we all worry about dying too soon. And in this country, 'tis high to probable that's how she'll happen. Too bad ye warn't fixed to head upriver the year after Lisa gone under."

Green shook his head. "Time wasn't right. I'd have lost everything a couple of years back when the Rees closed down the river. As it was, Ashley took that loss instead of me."

The bank sloped down to the river here. Periodically they passed an opening that had been cut in the trees where a couple of cows grazed a small field.

"I'll tell you, coon, it won't take too many more fights like that'un ter ruin this whole damned country fer white men fer good. Leavenworth taking troops up ter fight the Arikara jist made fools out of all of us. Not only did the Rees escape, but the Sioux reckon we're worse than old women when it comes ter a scrape."

"Leavenworth was a fool. He should have pressed his first attack on the big town. Everybody knows that, including Atkinson and O'Fallon. They're no fools." Green clenched a fist. "That's why the time is now. The army's up the Missouri. They've got four hundred and fifty soldiers on eight keelboats. That's the biggest expedition ever sent upriver. They'll take the fight out of the tribes. O'Fallon's got enough temper for five men, and Atkinson's all cat scratch and honor. And we're slipping right up in their wake."

"So long as they don't just run right over us."

"We'll know."

"Best hope so, coon."

Green lowered his voice. "Chances have to be taken, Travis. If I make this work, we'll all be set. Think of it! We'll build us an empire on the Yellowstone. Joshua Pilcher can have the headwaters of the Missouri clear up past the Three Forks. Let him take the rough off of the Blackfeet. They'll pretty near suck him dry, and Pilcher will keep their attention for a while. Meanwhile, we fort up and sink roots. First we build a post at the mouth of the Big Horn . . . maybe right there on top of Lisa's old post. The first season we establish trade with the Crows. Second season, we expand the post, build it permanent. Maybe out of stone. Third season, we start scouting up the Big Horn. I've always hankered to put a post up at the hot springs where the Big Horn runs out of the mountains.''

"That's Snake country."

Green pulled at his beard. "That it is, Travis. First the Crow, then the Shoshoni. If I can corner the trade for both tribes, I'll die a wealthy man . . . and so will you."

"Me?"

Green reached over and slapped Travis on the leg. "You're my right arm, Travis. The only man I can trust. You know the mountains and the Indians. The men respect you. You've been over most of that country. Who knows it better?"

"Lots of coons. Colter, Glass, lots of 'em."

"*Bête âne!*" came an angry cry.

"Stop it! Leave me alone!"

Travis stood, stepping over to where the *engagés* had piled up in a little knot to frown down at Richard Hamilton. The man from Boston hunched, quivering, while Boulette snorted and stomped.

"Hyar, now!" Travis snapped, glaring down.

Boulette looked up, hands gesturing Gallic disgust. "Why you have this man? He's worthless! Weak!"

"Dick! Git to work, now. We ain't got all year to git upriver."

"I can't . . . can't," the Yankee panted, trembling.

The other *engagés* looked on, braced on their poles so the boat didn't slip against the current. Expressions ranged from humor to disgust.

"Reckon ye'd better, Dick."

Green stomped across the deck, a large horse pistol filling his fist. "What's the matter here?"

"Reckon young Hamilton hyar's about done in." Travis sucked thoughtfully at his lip as he studied the situation. The sunlight was glittering off the water; the trees on the near bank looked bronzed with the new buds ready to burst.

Green's jaw had set; the pistol was pointed at Hamilton's

blanching face. "How much we pay for him? A penny, didn't you say, Travis?"

"Yep."

"Think I ought to just shoot him? Hell, it don't look like he's going to be worth the bother, not with us being held up because he can't work."

Richard's eyes widened and he grew oddly still as he stared into the black muzzle of the pistol.

Travis hawked and spat out beyond the gunwale. "Wal, Dave, if'n ye shoot him, thar'll be no doubt among the *engagés* that we mean what we say." And indeed, it might forestall any further trouble upriver.

Green thumbed back the cock on the pistol, the click loud in the suddenly quiet air. Boulette and the others backed carefully away.

"Oh, my God," Hamilton whispered dryly, hands clutching the thick pole as he rose, the action as slow as the opening of a flower. "Damn you . . . *damn* you!"

In that instant Travis saw something in those desperate brown eyes. Yes, there it was—angry defiance driven by an animal lust for survival. He'd seen it before, and it didn't match what he'd expected of this rabbit of a man.

"Hold on, Dave." Travis dropped to a knee, meeting Richard's smoldering glare. "Yer life's on the line, pilgrim. Reckon ye can pole till midday? Ye got the sand fer that?"

"I'll pole." Richard's muscles had begun to tremble again, and this time Travis could see that the tremor came from fatigue, for the defiance remained in those hard brown eyes.

"Stow yer pole, Dick. Flop down up forward and catch a rest." Travis turned a hard eye on the rest of the *engagés*.

"Reckon the rest of ye can cover fer young Dick hyar. He ain't been on the river afore. I'm giving him five days to toughen up. After that, he's fair game—if'n Dave don't shoot him first."

"How about me?" Trudeau called up from where he slouched on his pole. "Do I get five days?"

Travis grinned, knowing how it contorted his scarred face. "Reckon so, if'n it suits you, Trudeau. But afore ye do, yer a gonna do five minutes with me. That's the word, boys. Any of ye want to try me? See if'n yer man enough?"

Heads shook slowly.

"Let's git back to work, lads. We're making the mouth of the Missouri by nightfall."

At that Travis nodded to Green, who uncocked his pistol and stuffed it into his belt. They walked slowly back to the mast as the *Maria* began moving forward. Surly grumbles passed among the *engagés*.

"You sure I shouldn't have just up and shot him?" Green asked.

"Hell, I don't know."

"Why did you stop me, then, Travis?"

"Something in his eyes, Dave. Wal, reckon I give him five days. Maybe I'm a sight tetched for thinking it, but either he's got grit in him, or he don't. Sometimes a man just needs a chance ter find out. Reckon little Richard, thar, why, he ain't never had that chance."

"He does now."

"Yep. Five days' worth."

Richard lay sprawled on the hard oak deck. Somewhere, during the hellish day's long hours, his brain had simply ceased to function beyond the routine of the pole and keeping his feet as he staggered along the *passe avant*. When his feet became too clumsy, he'd drag his pole from the water and stumble to one side. He'd even grown oblivious of the boatmen's contemptuous glares as they passed him.

Inevitably, the image of that black gaping pistol barrel

would grow in the back of his mind, and he'd stare into that dark eternity until it filled his entire world. Then, Dave Green's implacable stare burned through the darkness like a death's head. Travis Hartman's twangy voice would say, *"Yer life's on the line, pilgrim... Ye got the sand fer that?"* and Richard would force his wobbling legs back to the line. Once again he would fit the pole to his throbbing shoulder and endure the pain and the *engagés'* cruel jests.

Just at dusk they'd followed the curve of the bank into the mouth of the Missouri River, where it vomited mud-choked water, floating branches, debris, and brown, soapy-looking foam.

His ribs moved on the smooth wood with each desperate breath. Though the urge to sob tickled within him, exhaustion had robbed him of the energy even for that relief.

Boston. ... Oh, to be home again. Images flickered through his cartwheeling fantasies: narrow streets, North Church, Faneuil Hall, and the Charles River Bridge spanning the sparkling waters. Laughter mixed with the lapping waves against the *Maria*'s hull. This world, or that? Silver clinked against fine china as diners lifted forkfuls of steaming beef. Men conversed in genteel tones, while women in snowy dresses smiled and greeted each other. The salty odors of the damp air carried the aroma of baking bread, spices, and coffee. Faint whiffs of rich tobacco tantalized his nostrils.

Laura's face hovered before him. She reached out, her slim white fingers seeking to trace the lines of his face. Her blue eyes were so serious, as if doubting she'd ever see him again. Then she faded like mist.

"Laura?" his voice croaked.

Dear God, to be home again. Boston ... beautiful Boston, where even the cobblestones gleamed in the spring rains ...

"Dick?" Hartman's rough voice burst the image with the surety of a plow mule amid piled glasswares.

"My name is Richard," he insisted numbly. Hartman was kneeling down next to him. The faint traces of tobacco strengthened, and now new smells, of roast pork, potatoes, corn, and onions, made him open his eyes.

"Brung ye vittles, Dick."

"You speak like a heathen."

"Ye got no call ter take that voice with me, Dick. Reckon ye'd best eat up. Long day starts come sunup."

"Maybe I'll just let Green shoot me."

Travis seated himself beside Richard, putting the wooden bowl down before his nose. The tobacco smoke came from Hartman's pipe.

Richard groaned, every muscle knotted and painful. He couldn't stifle a gasp as he sat up.

"Reckon yer some sore."

"I feel like I've been pulled through a keyhole."

"Figgered that. Reckon once ye've eaten I got a cure for that."

Richard shot him a wary look, the rich smell of the food triggering an angry growl in his stomach. Richard lifted the spoon that had been stuck in the stew. The handle was bent, but it served its purpose as he blew to cool the first mouthful. In another life, he would have scowled at the bland flavor; in this one, he wolfed the contents of the bowl as if it were one of Sally's masterpieces.

Hartman watched him with thoughtful eyes, and Richard surreptitiously studied the ugly scars. Thin strips had been ripped from Hartman's left ear, across the cheek, the tears thickening until the nose had been nearly torn away. An ugly patch of wrinkled tissue hinted that much of the right side of Hartman's face had been shredded. What could ruin a man's face like that?

When Richard cleaned out the bottom of the bowl, Hartman stood and extended a callused hand, saying, "C'mon, coon. I got an Injun cure fer ye."

Richard gritted his teeth as he was hauled to his feet. Every joint had gone stiff. "What cure? Beating me with clubs?"

"Wal, she's some better than that. But ye'll howl a mite afore the medicine works its way."

Twilight had fallen. The river looked glassy and silver before giving way to the dark forest on the north bank. Hartman led the way onto the plank that crossed to the muddy shore. The camp was set back from the water in an open field. Several yellow fires flickered, and knots of men hunched around them, smoking, talking in low voices. Beyond them, the forest brooded, the treetops etching dark patterns against the still-luminous sky. The chill was settling, damp, and promising of the cold to come.

Richard stared uneasily at the forest. Why was it so eerie? Surely hidden menace prowled out there among the shadowed trees.

Hartman reached back, steadying Richard as he negotiated the bouncing plank. ''Yer balance will come, lad. Reckon all them fancy Boston streets never taught ye no grace.''

''Apparently you and I have vastly different concepts of grace.''

At that, Hartman laughed, but they'd stepped onto the soggy ground. Evidently this camp was used often, for the grasses lay beaten flat. A wall tent had been pitched, and Green and Henri sat cross-legged on a blanket before it. The booshway was jabbing at the fire with a long stick while Henri talked softly, blocky hands fluttering in emphasis.

The *engagés* watched curiously as Richard passed, some stopping in the act of unrolling blankets. The smell of coffee carried from steaming pots that hung over the smoky fires.

''They're all wondering about ye, Dick. Trying to figger if'n ye'll make her or not. Most is laying bets ye won't. Odds is that Green or me will shoot yer lights out in another four days.''

Richard darted nervous glances at the sober-eyed men as he made his way through the camp. A sheep would feel this unsettling shiver as he walked through a pack of wolves.

''Bets?''

''Got to do something on the river, lad.''

''Betting on whether a man gets shot?''

''Wal, they'll fall ter monte, euchre, and stud afore long.''

''I see.''

They'd passed the fires and followed a faint track past a brushy stand of hazel that, from the odor, served as the latrine. Richard's muscles had warmed, and some of the stiffness had left his legs.

''Hyar we be.''

Richard squinted in the gloom, seeing a firepit of red

coals dotted with rocks. A low dome covered with blankets stood behind the fire; a triangular opening gaped blackly where one of the blankets was folded back.

"Shuck out of yer clothes, Dick."

"But I—"

"Tarnal Hell, child, jist do 'er." Travis was peeling out of his hunting shirt and then started to unlace his greasy pants.

Richard's heart began to pound. "You're not . . . I mean . . ."

"Yer not a woman under them britches, is ye? Wal, if not, I ain't interested. Now, take what's left of them fancies off and skedaddle inside."

"What *is* this?"

"Injun cure. Sweat lodge, coon. Now skin that shirt and britches, or I'll whittle 'em off."

Richard's fingers shook as he fumbled the buttons and undressed. The night blew cool on his skin as he dropped and scuttled into the black interior of the low tent. Sore muscles protested. Inside, he huddled against the far wall, scratchy blankets against his back.

I'm going to be tortured, maybe raped. The man's an animal. Animal? Wasn't it the use of that word that had brought him to this horror?

Hartman's bulk filled the doorway, a silhouette of muscle and long grizzled hair. The hunter carried a hot rock pinched by two smoking sticks. It glowed an evil red as it was laid in the center of the floor. Hartman scuttled back out, then returned with another, and yet another.

An Injun cure? The glowing stones seemed to stare at Richard with demonic eyes. Hartman returned yet again, and the flap settled in place to leave them in complete darkness.

"Now, Dick, I'm splashing a bit of water. Yer not used to such doings, I'm thinking. Breathe deep, lad. Let the heat soak into yer hide. They's medicine in it. Yer muscles will loosen like old wangs in a rain."

"What's a wang?"

"Leather strap—usually. Don't they larn ye nothing back East no more?"

The instant the water hit the hot rocks, it popped and

crackled into steam. At the same time, Hartman began chanting in a strange language.

Easy, Richard. It's just some silly superstition. Some barbaric custom this berserk Mongol has concocted.

Warm steam curled around him, thickening, moistening his nostrils. Water trickled and more steam swirled in the darkness.

Richard nerved himself. "Where did you learn this?"

"Injuns. Most of the tribes I've had truck with sweat. Makes the body pure. Reckon I believes it. Most figger they don't get clean lessen they sweat. Funny thing, ye lives around Injuns, an' sure's snow in the winter, ye starts ter suck up their way of thinking. Reckon that otta do ye fer now."

Perspiration had begun to bead on Richard's face. He gasped for breath. Heat was biting into his flesh, and the muscles were loosening. About that, at least, Hartman had been correct.

"Feel better?" Hartman asked.

"I think so." Talk. Do anything but concentrate on the stifling heat. His hair was dripping. "I still can't believe this is happening to me. Today, Green was really ready to kill me, wasn't he?"

"Yep."

"Why? It's irrational! Nothing makes sense! How can a man's life be worth so little?"

"Reckon ye've got her backwards, Dick. Best ask yerself, what makes yer life worth so much? Folks never turn questions inside out. Can't larn a damn thing till ye turns life inside out, like pulling a hide off a beaver."

"So, why did you stop him? Why are you doing this for me? I don't understand."

Hartman grunted. "I get notional sometimes. Reckon I got a dose of curiosity is all. Turning things inside out again, wondering what's really in ye, lad. Wondering if'n ye've any idea yerself."

"I know what's inside of me." *And I sure don't want to be here.*

"Huh! That's so, is it? Look old Ephraim in the eye, lad. Where ye been? Boston? All yer Yankee life?"

"That's right."

"Shit."

"What do you mean?"

"Jist what I said. Shit. Lad, ye jist don't know shit. Not about the world, and not about yerself. Folks in cities, they get these ideas they know all about living, and right and wrong."

"If it's a discussion of ethics that you're looking for, you've come to the right place. The philosophical basis for—"

"What was that ye said? Ethics? What's that?"

"The rules of civilized conduct. Right and wrong, Mr. Hartman. And, I might add, you're in the latter category. You are an accomplice to robbery and abduction. Just as guilty as François and August. Your actions are in violation of every tenet of ethical behavior."

"Better that I'd jist let François slit yer gullet open and dump ye in the river?"

"Absolutely not. Better that you had gone with me to the authorities in order that François's unethical and immoral behavior be brought to an end, and justice served."

"Yer some, Dick. Still looking at the outside of the beaver and thinking ye knows the whole critter. How much did old François skin ye fer?"

Richard's skin felt as if it were peeling away. He kept sinking lower and lower, seeking cooler air. He hesitated, then said, "Thirty thousand dollars in banknotes."

"*Tarnal Hell!* How'n Hob's name did a sprout yer age get so rich?"

"It was my father's money. Money to invest in the Santa Fe trade. I was just supposed to deliver it."

"And yer father give it ter ye? A wet-eared boy?"

"I'm no boy!"

"Wal, I reckon that's ter be seen. And I'll wager ye come off all high, mighty, and rich, and that's what set François off. That French varmint can smell money a day's ride away. Ye done something ter him, didn't ye?"

"I did nothing to him."

"Painter crap, lad. If'n François was jist a gonna rob ye, he'd a slit yer throat and dumped ye. I couldn't figger why he was so set on sending ye upriver like a lard eater, and now I got ter know. What was it ye did?'' Hartman dribbled more water on the rocks.

"We had words."

"And ye called him something?"

"I stated the obvious."

"Uh-huh."

"I told him he was an animal."

Hartman sat silently.

"You should have seen him. Bragging about killing an Indian. The hogs were worrying the poor man's head like . . . some obscene melon.''

"Reckon yer father don't know shit neither, sending ye out alone into country like this. Proves my point about city folks back East. 'Specially Yankees."

The heat had melted Richard's natural caution. "He thought it would be good for me. He wanted to teach me responsibility. As if Aristotle, Rousseau, and Locke hadn't.''

"And where did them fellers work? Fer yer father?"

Richard rolled his eyes, feeling ill in the stifling darkness. "No, no. They're philosophers. Teachers who wrote books. I was studying them. I want to be a professor of philosophy. My father and I had a disagreement about that. That's why I'm here. He sent me on this trip to learn something about the world.''

Travis scratched his ear. "Reckon ye did that, all right."

"Travis, I've got to get out. I'm going to be sick." The heat made him sway.

"Lift the bottom of the blanket there."

Richard reached out with an arm that worked like soggy flour. Air rushed in along his boiling skin and he sucked cool relief into his lungs, drafting it inside like a bellows. For long moments he lay limply on the grass.

"How's yer hurts?" Travis asked.

"I don't know. I'm not sure I can feel anything anymore.''

"Reckon ye'll be feeling plenty tomorrow, coon. When ye picks up that pole, think back on how bad it would a been without the medicine lodge hyar.''

From under the edge of the blanket Richard watched the

stars twinkling over the inky treetops. Was that way east? Were they twinkling like that over Boston? "I want to go home, Travis. Can't you and Green just let me go? Would my skinny little butt, as you put it, really make that much difference to you?"

He could hear Hartman scratching his scalp before he answered. "Yep, I reckon so. François'll be looking fer ye, fer one. Fer two, the rest of the *engagés* might get the cute idea that they could skip out same's you. Fer three, I'd never figger out if'n I's right or wrong about ye, Dick. Yer stuck with us, lad."

"And if I get the chance, run off?"

"I'll hunt ye down. I can track painter cats across slickrock, so I don't suppose no pilgrim Yankee kid from Boston's a gonna hide his sign from Travis Hartman."

"What's a painter cat?"

"Lion, coon. Cougar, puma, whatever ye wants ter call 'em. Kilt a mite or two of 'em, I have. Plumb shot their lights out."

"And you'd shoot me? Just like that? Just as Green would have today?" Richard wiped the sweat from his face. Damp strands of hair lay plastered to his scalp.

Hartman's voice turned low and serious. "Dick, they's times a feller's just got ter do what he's got ter do. Listen close, boy, hyar's facts. I can't let you get crosswise atwixt me and the crew. Ye got that? Whar we're headed, there ain't none of them ethics yer so full of. Dave's word has got ter be law. If it ain't, the whole party can be wiped out. The whole shitaree. Ye savvying that?"

"You're telling me it's life or death?"

"It ain't Boston out hyar, Dick. Them's the only two rules that count. So, yep. To keep discipline, I'll shoot ye dead if I have ter. I might sit around of a night afterwards and feel a mite blue, but that passes through a man's soul same as green corn through a fella's belly."

"I guess I've never quite thought of life like that."

Beyond the hazel, over by the river, the *engagés* were singing a nonsense song about woodpeckers.

"Best start, coon."

ELEVEN

Thus it is that every man has an empirical character of his arbitrary will, which is nothing more than a certain causality of his reason. It demonstrates in its actions and effects in appearance, a rule according to which one may infer the motives of reason and its actions, both in degree and kind, and therefore judge of the subjective principles of his will. Since that empirical character itself must be inferred from appearance as an effect, and from their rule which is supplied by experience, all the acts of a man in the appearance are determined from his empirical character and from the other concomitant causes according to the order of nature, and if we could investigate all the manifestations of his will to the very bottom, there would be not a single human action which we could not predict with certainty. . . .

—Immanuel Kant, *Critique of Pure Reason*

Her people were known for their endurance, and Heals Like A Willow had worked hard all of her life, hauling wood and water, scraping hides, digging roots, and carrying packs. The relentless flight eastward, however, was taking its toll. Her legs ached from clamping onto the horse. Stitches of pain prickled in her shoulders and back. The only justice—such as it might be—was that Packrat looked just as haggard.

They had passed the last of the rugged sandstone bluffs that rose, pale yellow, south of the river. Now they rode across endless gentle uplands, the country grassy and open, flatter than anything Willow had ever seen. Here, however, the spring grasses were greening. Buffalo stood out like black dots on the horizon, their worn trails winding down from the ridges to the river and its life-giving water.

Their only companion had been the wind. At night, just after dark, it would let up, until by dawn the air was still and a person could hear birdsong across the miles. Then, as the sun rose higher into the crystalline sky, the breeze would pick up in the west, increasing in strength as it gusted through the afternoon.

It still blew as Packrat led the way down into a cotton-wood-filled hollow along a brush-choked creek. Twilight darkened the east. Willow swiped at long black strands of hair that had escaped the severe braid she'd adopted to keep it from turning into a snarl worse than a horse's tail in fall.

Packrat hobbled the horses and collected fallen cotton-wood branches for fuel. He built a fire from his strike-a-light, and leaned back on his blanket. In silence, they ate the last of the jerked meat from her pack.

Packrat signed: "Five days and we will reach my people."

Willow shot a glance at the weary horses. Their heads were hanging and she could see their ribs through their patchy hair. Within her, a faint hope stirred.

Despite bound hands, she signed: "Travel faster. Arrive in four days."

He pursed his lips, curious. "Why? You should want to go slow. You'd have a better chance of rescue."

"I'm tired. Let's get this finished."

He dropped another branch on the small fire, thought for a bit, then signed: "You make no sense. A buffalo doesn't walk willingly to the hunter."

"It does if the Power is right."

He cocked his head, noticing her quick glance at the horses. A slow smile spread across his face. "You are crafty, like a coyote. The horses are worn out. One might falter, go lame. Then we would be forced to go much slower."

Her sudden hope flickered out.

Packrat chuckled to himself. His fingers said, "You are a worthy catch. My father will reap his reward. I could not have done better if I had given him a panther to warm his bed."

"You hate your father that much?"

A glint sharpened in Packrat's eyes. "More than you could know. He dishonored my mother."

"Why not kill him?"

"It is better this way." Packrat picked up his war club, stood, and walked over to her. "Roll onto your stomach. I'm going to scout. If your feet are bound, and your hands are tied behind your back, you will not be able to run."

She glanced at the club, sighed, and then rolled over, allowing him to truss her ankles with a long thong. Perhaps while he was gone . . .

But he didn't leave. Instead, he tied yet another thong snugly around her neck. He signed: "I am going to lie with you now. If you fight me, I can twist the thong around your neck with one hand. A woman with no air cannot fight."

Willow licked her suddenly dry lips.

Packrat loosened his fringed pants and stepped out of them. He signed: "My father dishonored my mother. Lay with her without permission. I will lie with you before I give you to him. My triumph will be that much greater."

Willow nodded wearily. Taking a deep breath, she lay back and locked her gaze with his as he tugged her dress up past her hips. The evening breeze cooled her thighs and belly as his hands slid over her skin, under her dress, and cupped her breasts.

His incomprehensible words were spoken gently, as if calming a horse.

I could make it difficult. The thought ran around her head. With her ankles bound, she could stiffen her legs, resist until he got a hand around the thong and choked her into submission.

And to what purpose? He'd been wary this time. But the next time? Or the next?

She slid her ankles up and spread her knees as he moved to cover her. She was dry, his entry difficult but not painful. Staring into his eyes, so close to hers, she thought, *My time will come. No one is forever vigilant. If I get the chance, I will cut that penis from your body.*

He'd barely started to move before he gasped and stiffened. She felt the warm fluid release within her. *I'll take this little victory from you. I don't know how, but I will.*

The knob of the pole was eating a hole in Richard's bruised shoulder when his stomach cramped. Thinking it was just another strained muscle, he kept pushing. Then his gut cramped again, and his bowels demanded relief.

He called to Trudeau behind him and indicated his need for relief. Walking to the offside, he squatted out over the gunwale of the boat and voided.

The ever watchful Green approached and cocked an eye. Almost solicitously, he put a hand on Richard's head. "Got the scours. Take it easy, Hamilton. Work too hard like this and it'll kill a man."

Richard nodded weakly and voided again. His stomach knotted and his bowels wrenched. For long moments he held the position, legs trembling. Unable to straighten up, he waddled over and sat in the shade, shaking and sweating. He could hear the booshway's voice telling the other men. Jeers and laughter erupted.

Then the sweats and chills began. The deck he lay on grew hazy, then shimmery. Time lagged. He slept and drank and ate and slept again while strange dreams played through his mind. Occasionally Dave Green would bend over him and place his cool hand on Richard's burning head. Once, when that happened, he blinked and looked up—but into Phillip Hamilton's piercing eyes.

"Satisfied, Father?" he croaked. "This what you wanted me to see? Reality? This isn't reality . . . it's Hell."

Phillip laughed harshly and Richard cowered from those mocking gray eyes. The face shimmered and lost focus.

The deck, yes, the deck lay below him, wet with his own sweat. *Maria,* the river. A different Hell.

The silvered visions wavered. Once he walked through Boston's narrow curving streets, past coopers, blacksmiths, silversmiths, ceramic shops, bootmakers, bookshops, printers, tailors. As he continued, he nodded and exchanged greetings with warm, friendly people.

Then he rounded a corner, and to his horror, Thomas Hanson stood there. Laura was enfolded in his arms as she kissed him passionately. She melted against him, sighing as she pulled his head down and pressed her lips against his.

"No!" Richard screamed, his heart breaking. They turned then, and Laura's eyes flashed, mocking him for a fool. Hanson lifted a cool eyebrow, then laughed as he slipped an arm around her slim waist. They turned and walked away while Richard stood rooted to the spot. Her hips were swaying in time to Hanson's steps.

A sweltering gray haze surrounded him, and somewhere water dripped on dirty stones.

Suddenly old Professor Ames took his hand, pulling him away. Together they strolled through Market Square toward Merchant's Row.

"You didn't really think she'd be yours, did you, Richard? Nothing is permanent—least of all the loyalty of a woman. She's better off with Thomas," Ames told him with an engaging smile and twinkling eyes. "But, tell me, how was your trip? What observations did you make? Is a rational mind enough to overcome social contract?"

Richard struggled to think. Laura and Tom? No, he couldn't accept that. Wrong, somehow. Not real. But when had Professor Ames ever lied to him? "No, Professor."

"Then you have not tried hard enough, Richard," Ames told him. "You have given up without attempting to elevate yourself above the baser desires."

The vision drifted away. Then, out of the warped silver waves, his father's cynical scowl formed. "I had not intended to raise a weakling, Richard. No wonder Laura married Thomas Hanson."

"I am no weakling!" Richard cried at the apparition. "I am superior! I have truth! The real is the rational! Damn you, Father, don't you understand?" Hot rage boiled. "You are evil, Father!"

"Of course, you would think that," Phillip told him.

. A terrible rage burned in Richard's breast. He gathered himself to strike—only to recoil as François leered back at him through icy blue eyes. "What is rational, eh? I will give you truth. Truth is life, weakling. Life is suffering in the wind and the sun. Life is the river and the land. Take your life and think of the truth I have given you, *rich* man!"

Richard cringed.

"Well, Richard?" Professor Ames asked from a great distance. "All that you claim to believe is challenged. To prove yourself, you must survive. Can you?"

"I . . . don't know. I just don't . . ."

"Fool!" The words echoed from the darkness of Green's pistol barrel. An image formed in that crucible of death: himself, smartly dressed and arrogant.

"Stop it! Damn you! *Stop it!*" Richard screamed. "There *is* rationality in the world. I have not yet failed. I *will* be stronger. Damn you both! You watch me! I am an animal now, but I will win. I will escape and return to Boston. You'll see! You and your kind. You'll . . . see . . ."

He frowned uneasily. His tormentors had vanished into the bleary light. Dear Lord God . . . thirsty . . . so very, very thirsty. Richard gasped, blinking into the night.

Darkness, stars, water lapping against the keelboat's hull. The plaintive hoot of an owl carried from the trees.

"Boston," he whispered hoarsely into the night. "I won't die. God be my witness. I'll live. Prove them wrong."

"How are ye, pilgrim?" a gentle voice asked. Phantom, or real?

"Travis?"

"Reckon they's some devils ye been a-wrassling with."

"Water? Please?"

A tin cup was placed against Richard's lips, the rim cool. He drank greedily.

"Heard ye had a case of the collywobbles. Figgered ye'd be needin' a mite of curing, coon. I fetched medicine fer ye. Snuck up and kilt a farmer's cow, but I got what ye needs. T'aint buffler, but it'll do."

"What?" Richard leaned back against the plank walls of the cargo box. The night sounds of the forest carried to his ears.

"Hyar, lad."

Richard squinted in the darkness as Hartman held out a teardrop-shaped bag no bigger than a green walnut.

"Gallbladder, coon. Best cure they be fer collywobbles. Reckon ye'd best eat it. Like I said, cut her right out'a the cow. Fresh as could be. Though, I reckon that farmer's a gonna be peeved come sunup."

"No, I—"

"Eat'er, lad. That, or I'll sit on ye, clamp yer nose off, and douse ye good when yer breath runs out."

Richard took the little sack with trembling fingers, glanced at Hartman to see that he really meant it, and plopped the resilient gallbladder into his mouth. He started upright as the vile liquid filled his mouth.

Hartman anticipated his reaction, clamped an iron hand over his mouth, and pinned Richard to the deck.

"Swaller it, Dick! It ain't a gonna kill ye. Reckon the better the medicine, the worst the taste. I done cured meself a time or two with gall."

Richard wriggled under the iron grip and gulped the wretched stuff down. Nothing on earth could taste that bad.

Hartman nodded to himself and released his hold, handing Richard another tin of water. "Wash her down, coon. I'm thinking ye'll be a-healing, now."

"Lord God, that was horrible," Richard gasped, the taste still violating his mouth.

"Strong stuff. Cure ye, or kill ye."

Richard slumped limply onto the deck. "Let me die."

"An' lose me bet? I got ten plews bet again ol' Henri that ye'd live."

"Plews?"

"Beaver skins. Yer ignerant, Dick. Even fer a Doodle."

"My name is Richard."

"Uh-huh."

They sat in silence, Richard watching the stars.

"Fever's gonna break." Hartman said after a while. "I seen it afore. Must have been some visions ye was having. Raging and muttering. I reckon I figgered out who yer father was, but who's Ames?"

"My professor. At the university."

"Philos'phy?"

"Yes."

"Injuns, they put a heap of store by dreams, visions, and such. Heard you say ter stop it. That ye was an animal. Ain't that what we got ye in all this mess?"

Richard grimaced at the lingering taste of gall. "I saw myself in the dream. Arguing with Ames. They thought I was beaten. I'll get away, Travis. Go back to Boston. I swear it."

Hartman bowed his head for a moment. In the darkness, Richard couldn't see his face. "Don't try it, Dick. See her through. Then ye can go back."

"You'd still kill me?"

"I figgered we'd been across that trail already, Dick. Like I said, yer ignerant. Upriver, Dave's word has got to be like God's. I been in outfits that fell apart. Men work together, or people die. A booshway's gotta make decisions, and have 'em stick. I don't know how ye'd philos'phy it, but killing you now might save my life, and Henri's, and Davey Green's a couple of months from now when the Rees get a fight on. Or when the boat's in danger in the rapids. Folks got ter depend on each other. Follow whar my stick floats?"

"As in an army?"

"Reckon yer on the scent now, pilgrim."

"So you give up freedom in exchange for a chance at survival."

"To yer way of thinking, maybe." Hartman turned his head to gaze upriver, his voice softening. "Freedom's up yonder, boy. Freedom like ye've never knowed. Reckon I cain't tell ye, not in words. But, Dick, if'n ye reaches down inside yourself, pulls up them guts ye've never used, and buckle down, ye'll have a chance to see. I reckon once ye've seen sunrise on the Shining Mountains, outskunked the wily Crows, eat hump steak off'n a fat buffler cow, and foxed the Blackfoots, ye'll know what few other men ever will.

Not in yer noodle, lad, but in yer guts. In yer soul.''

Would the vile taste of gall ever leave his tongue? Vision was going shimmery again. "You sound like a poet, Travis."

"Waugh! That's some, it is. Me, a poet?"

Sleep had begun to drift into Richard's thoughts. "Indeed. A poet"—*who's as ready to butcher me as that poor cow he killed.* "Tyranny comes in many forms, Travis."

Something was forming in Richard's soul, but he lost the answer as he fell into restless dreams of Laura and Thomas, walking hand in hand, laughing.

Willow lay limply as Packrat stiffened and moaned for the second time that morning. She watched his face, his eyes clamped shut, jaw muscles tensed. Then he slumped, dead weight pressing her down. Would he withdraw now, or lie on her again until his manhood recovered?

Packrat took a deep breath and opened his eyes, running his fingers along the sides of her head. She took the opportunity to stare into his eyes, spearing his soul with her hatred.

Today, Pawnee filth, I have given you more than just pleasure. Get up. Look at yourself. See what Heals Like a Willow has done to you.

He grunted, pushed himself off of her, and looked down. She chuckled dryly, enjoying the consternation on his face.

Three days had passed while they camped in the cotton-wood bottoms. Packrat had used the time to allow the horses to recover their strength while he sated himself inside her. On the first day, Packrat had tied Willow tighter than a load of firewood, and led his horse out to hunt. Hours later he'd returned with choice cuts of buffalo wrapped in a quarter hide. That night, she'd gorged herself, rebuilding her own strength for the moment Packrat's guard slipped.

Each time he had climbed onto her, parted her legs, and pumped himself empty, her menstruation had been that much closer. Now, as he stared wide-eyed at his bloody

penis, her satisfaction grew. Pawnee males feared the
monthly cycle as much as *Dukurika*, or any other men she'd
heard of.

Horror filled Packrat's face. He shivered, then grabbed up
his clothes and broke into a panicked run for the river.

Willow sat up and laughed until her sides shook. Now, if
only he hadn't trussed her up like a grass doll. Her hands
were secured behind her, with a thong running from wrists
to bound ankles. She wriggled around, searching for something to cut herself loose. He'd taken his knife and quiver
along with his clothing. Previously, she'd searched in vain
for anything sharp and found nothing but grass, twigs, and
soft dirt.

She scowled, muttering, "*Tam Apo*, this would have
made a very good place for a flint outcrop." The only stones
were crumbly sandstone cobbles that Packrat had placed in
the firepit.

She lifted her head. Tendrils of smoke rose from the
ashes. Suppose she found a stick and managed to light one
end. Could she prop it so that the ember would burn the
leather thongs in two?

Wriggling like an inchworm, she snagged up a stick and
hitched herself to within a length of the fire. She craned her
chin over her shoulder to see as she poked the stick in the
coals.

How long did she have until Packrat's return? The river
was just over there, beyond the trees. If she guessed right,
he'd scrub and scrub, desperate to cleanse himself.

There. Smoke had begun to curl up around the end of the
cottonwood she held so precariously.

All right, Willow, let's see if this works.

Her neck had begun to cramp. She rocked herself and
wished she had a neck like a heron, but managed to pull
her feet close to the smoking end of the stick. If only the
position weren't so awkward! The harder she strained, the
more the stick jiggled. The muscles in her neck, back, and
sides ached. Jaw cocked, tongue parting her lips, she managed to touch the smoking branch to the thongs.

After a few moments the heat began to sting the skin of
her ankles. To her frustration, the ember went out. Grousing,

she prodded it into the fire again, glancing toward the river. Blood and dung, she didn't have all day!

It took four tries, and painful burns, before she could snap the thong that held her ankles.

"Thank you, *Tam Apo,* and now, help me!" She lurched to her feet, hands still bound behind her. With time, she might use the bark on the cottonwoods to wear the thongs in two—as well as to scrape the hide off her wrists. Better to get away now, and worry about that later.

The horses foiled her attempts to loosen their rawhide hobbles. They'd let her approach forward, but shied the second she twisted around to fumble at the leather with her fingers. After the third time the mare dumped her on her butt, she glared up.

"I *hate* horses! You've brought nothing but trouble to my people! I hope a rock ogre eats you. Slowly."

Her time was running out. The hobbles were hopeless, and she couldn't ride with her hands behind her back, unable to control the horse with more than kicks to the ribs.

She studied the bluffs to the north, and broke into a trot— the fastest pace she could manage with her hands tied. On foot as she was, Packrat couldn't help but overtake her. She crossed the first of the low ridges, slowed, and stepped out onto sandstone. With infinite care, she backtracked to the crest of the ridge where the gramma grass lay in thick patches interspersed with wind-deflated gravel. There she sidestepped, each foot placed delicately so as not to disturb the coarse gravel.

Packrat would work it out, of course. She made several steps, hopped to a patch of gramma grass, and hurried off to the west. She ran desperately, throwing frightened looks over her shoulder, then tore across yet another of the low ridges, dropped over the side until hidden from the east, and sprinted northward again.

She'd bought time. If she could hide her trail well enough, cut the bonds on her wrists, and hide in this flat land, she might have a chance.

As the sun slid westward, she zigzagged to the northwest. Topping a low rise, she glanced back and saw him, on horseback, cutting for tracks.

Heals Like a Willow ducked low, scuttled over the crest, and ran like a frightened antelope. Breath tearing in her throat, she prayed to *Tam Apo* for a miracle.

Richard awoke to a gray rainy morning. He sat up, weak and wobbly in his water-soaked blanket. His gut tortured him, but he crawled to the big stew pot and ate. The cold stew might run right through him, but at least it didn't come back up. With careful fingers, Richard probed at his belly and started at the tender spots. His raw butt felt like whip-sawed meat.

Beyond the gunwale, the dense forest passed, many of the branches no more than a foot beyond the laboring polers. They might have been fingers, reaching out for the *engagés*. Richard closed his eyes and shook his head.

"I'm seeing monsters."

"How's that, coon?" Hartman asked as he stepped around the cargo box.

"Monsters," Richard mumbled. "Out there, in the forest. They've been after me for . . . well, since I left Pittsburgh. You can feel them, sense them in the shadows."

"Huh!" Hartman rubbed at his beard, the scars looking paler on this gray day. "There be painters, black bears hyar and there. Ye'd find a rattlesnake in amongst the leaves. Reckon a feller might stumble onto a wolf on occasion. Them don't shine fer monsters, Dick. Not like Old Ephraim. He be some. Some, indeed."

Richard glanced up uncertainly.

Hartman pulled his pipe from his possibles, gesturing toward the trees with the stem. "Them woods be plumb dull, Dick. Right friendly when ye comes down ter it. Why, a feller can hide himself like a tick on a dog. He can feel safe, comfortable. Everything a man needs right there to hand. Deer, coons, and squirrels fer meat. Nuts fall like hail every fall. All a feller has to do is pick 'em up. Wind don't blow a man till his eyes sting, and the deep cold don't settle until a man's fingers freeze, blacken, and fall off. Sun don't burn

ye so dry yer pizzle shrinks up and fergits what it's fer. Wood and water everywhere. The forest's safe. It's the plains and mountains as will kill ye.''

"Why do I feel it, then? Like eyes, always watching."

Hartman tapped tobacco out of his little leather pouch, pressing it into the pipe's bowl with a hard finger, the cracked nail lined with dirt. "Taking yer measure, I'd guess."

"Taking my measure? What are you talking about?"

Hartman cocked his head. "Judging ye, Dick. What do ye think? That the land's dead? Hell, look at it, ye ignerant Yankee! Everything ye sees out thar be alive."

"Only men have souls, Travis."

Hartman hawked and spit into the river. "Do tell, Dick? Prove it."

Richard scowled. "The philosophical works of—"

"Painter crap! Ye been living all yer life in buildings and cities a-reading books. Get out there in the forest, Dick. Listen, boy! That's what yer ahearing . . . feeling. It's the soul of the land, the trees, and critters."

At Richard's blank look, Hartman shook his head in disgust. "Aw, ter hell with ye! Damn Yankee son of a bitch! Gets ter feeling the land, and 'cause he's never felt it afore, he figgers it's old Hob hisself spinning evil."

"I didn't mean to make you mad."

Hartman's lips pinched. "Ye cain't larn everything outa a book, Dick. Some things ye got ter larn with yer soul. Now, how're ye feeling?"

"Better. Weak, miserable, but better."

Hartman pointed at the *engagés* who'd been poling along

the *passe avant,* listening to the conversation. "Reckon ye can fetch a pole, then. A body mends quicker when it's a-working."

"I'm just better, not well! If I strain I have—well—accidents."

"Hell, I never said ye was plumb fit, did I? A man's got ter haul his pack. Go do what ye can, and run squat when ye got ter."

"Travis, I—"

"Reckon I'll go find me an ember fer me smoke. By the time she's lit, ye'd better be a-hustling yer butt, Dick."

"But you don't—"

"We just slid them four days back, Dick, on account of ye being down with the scours, and all. Green's still aching ter shoot ye, and old Trudeau there, he done put a month's wages that yer a gonna be dead afore then."

Hartman disappeared around the corner of the cargo box and Richard stared dully at the battered oak deck. He could barely stand up, so how was he supposed to pole?

Glancing up to the side, he could see Trudeau's smile, so wide the white teeth gleamed below the black mustache.

Richard gathered himself, pulled a pole from the top of the cargo box, and worked in between the boatmen.

"Don't shit where we walk, *mon ami,*" Louis hissed. "And stay back, yes? Don't spread your contagion around us."

"Sleep well?" Trudeau asked as they made the next trip. "About time zee booshway get some good out of you, *non?*"

"You're all nothing but a pack of—" Richard caught himself. "Leave me alone. I'll do what I can today."

Someone snickered.

To Richard's relief, Henri began the "Ding-ding-a-dong" song, and the voices turned to singing instead of tormenting him. Then his gut twisted, and he almost lost his pole as he ran for the far gunwale.

◆

Packrat's life was shattered like a dropped pot, his soul wounded and broken. She would *pay* for this!

He pulled his horse up and scanned the country. What appeared to be flat grassland was in reality a deceptively rolling terrain cut by shallow drainages working their way down toward the river. The scrubby gramma and buffalo grass was broken by low patches of sagebrush and gray-green splotches of prickly pear, none of it tall enough to hide a person. A small herd of antelope watched him from a distance while a hawk sailed above, uninterested in his plight.

Triumph had become a disaster. Heals Like a Willow had profaned him with her menstrual blood and broken the purity of his manhood. The Spirit World would turn its back on him, withdraw its protection. A warrior depended on Power to protect him, to give him luck. But now . . .

He glanced self-consciously up at the sky and remembered stories about young men who had been profaned, and how lightning had struck from clear blue skies, and how they died in freak accidents.

I must return to the Skidi and be cleansed. He winced at the implications. The Doctors could cleanse him, but the ceremonies would cost his family a fortune. The Singers and Doctors would have to be paid, feasts provided for dances and sweats.

Not only would his folly cost his family's wealth, but he would pay a terrible price in public humiliation. The jokes told at his expense were already ringing in his ears. "Packrat, the *pira-paru*, so desperate he dipped his lance into a bleeding captive!" "Hey, Packrat! If you were so desperate, why not stick yourself into a camp dog? The shame would have been the same, but you wouldn't have made your family destitute in the process!"

I'll find her even if I die in the process. A likely event, since the Spirit World would shun him now. *And then I'll kill her!*

Until he had been purified in the ceremonials, people would avoid him. In his current state of defilement, no one, not even his own family, would allow him into their houses. They'd refuse him entry into the village.

Adding to his humiliation, the woman had taken what had been a dashing coup, and thrown it in his face.

I curse you, you Shoshoni bitch!

All those great plans! His only chance to establish himself, repay his father for that long-ago perfidy! His guts went hollow at the thought of Pitalesharo's reaction. *I'll no longer be tiwat. He'll disown me.*

He kicked his horse forward. *It's all her fault. She'll pay . . . and very dearly.*

He found the thongs on a low hilltop. Willow had obviously located a sharp stone and managed to slice through the rawhide straps. Inspecting them, Packrat smiled at the flecks of blood. It wasn't easy to cut one's bindings when one's hands were tied behind one's back. Too bad she didn't bleed to death in the process.

Bit by bit, his keen eye worked out her trail. The grassy gullies drained from north to south, and Willow had to keep to their bottoms.

The drainage he now followed was broad, offering little concealment. He took a chance, kicking the horse to a canter, watchful of low humps and swales. He couldn't be that far behind her. She'd had no more than half a day's head-start, and despite the tricks she'd used to hide her trail, the country didn't offer many hiding places.

The shallow drainage came to a head at the base of a low knoll, but no sign of Willow could be seen.

"Fool!" Packrat balled a fist and smacked himself in the leg. "Better to have slowly worked out her tracks." He glared back down the drainage. The sun lay half-a-hand above the horizon, casting thin shadows in the rolling grass.

"All right, Packrat. She's crafty and cunning. No fool, this one. She didn't lose her head and run like a pronghorn, so where would she be?"

He heeled the horse around and headed back down the drainage. He almost rode past her a second time, barely giving the little sandstone ledge a second glance.

It had formed where the water undercut a thin layer of golden-brown rock. Just a gravel-filled hollow screened by a thin beard of grass. Not even room to hide a jackrabbit, really.

Some odd sense, that feeling of being watched, caused him to pull up. He looked twice, and, yes, there she was, prone, barely hidden by the ledge.

"Perhaps my Power hasn't been broken completely, Willow," he called to her. "But yours has, Snake woman!"

He jumped lightly from the horse, swinging his war club. Savoring the anticipation of the impact as it broke her skull. "I shall have your scalp . . . little as it is to repay me for what you've done!"

She stood warily, poised to flee. In the setting sun, she looked magnificent, her skin bronzed by the light. The breeze teased her gleaming black hair, and Packrat remembered those full breasts and how they'd filled his hands.

But then, that was what had caused all the trouble in the beginning, wasn't it? For the briefest of instants his resolve wavered. Such a shame to kill a woman this beautiful and smart.

She read his indecision and signed: "Do not hesitate. Kill me."

Packrat chewed at his lip, overcame the urge to leap forward and crush her skull, and signed: "You should be afraid, for you see your death standing before you."

A flicker of a smile touched her full lips. The gleam in her eyes challenged him. Her graceful hands made the sign for, "Strike. As soon as you do, I will have won."

Packrat cocked his head. "You'll be dead."

"And you'll have nothing. Finished." She lifted an eyebrow, mocking him.

Packrat kicked at the sandy gravel with his toe. He'd have

her bloody scalp. Wasn't that enough? He glanced at her from the corner of his eye. She knew something he didn't.

"You've done enough to me. It is finished!" He made the signs with a flourish.

Her white teeth flashed. "Tell your father how close you came."

Packrat lifted his war club, tensed, and slowly lowered it to his side. Was there a way out of this? No matter what she'd done to him, some redemption would come of handing her over to his father.

Packrat stamped his foot. In Pawnee, he said, "Giving you to Half Man would be too good for you—and he's no better than a flea-bit camp dog!"

Willow signed: "Kill me."

Packrat shook his head, disparate ideas forming. He told her, "No. You'll live. With Half Man, you'll pay for making me unclean. At least a little. And, who knows, maybe you'll do the same thing to him."

His Pawnee words were lost on her Shoshoni ears. Packrat signed: "You don't win. I'm taking you to my father."

He couldn't be sure as he studied her blank face, but somehow he perceived that she'd beaten him. With his war club, he pointed southward toward the river. "Walk, woman. Darkness is coming. And if you try to run, I won't hesitate to drive an arrow through you."

Willow turned, and doggedly started down the drainage. Packrat watched her straight back, the way her hips swayed, and the proud set of her head. Her movements conjured memories of coupling with her. He shook his head, viciously kicked a scrubby rabbitbrush, and turned back to his horse.

TWELVE

The Missouri differed from the Mississippi as night
differed from day. The Mississippi might be dangerous, but the Missouri was downright treacherous. As
the current twisted like an angry brown serpent, it under-
mined the banks, toppling huge trees. Once in the river's
grip they floated down the muddy channel like giant rollers,
jagged branches slashing the water. Pity the keelboat that
ran afoul of one. Sooner rather than later, the trees would
ground, snagged by the roots. Thus anchored, the trunks
bobbed up and down in the water: They called these nightmares sawyers, for they'd cut the bottom right out of a boat.

The trees often piled up, creating huge logjams that lined
the sandbars like some perverted beaver dam. Such an obstacle was called an embarras. The river's channel would
weave around the devilish tangle of trunks, roots, and
branches, to undercut yet more of the bank and topple yet
more forest giants into a watery grave.

The spring flood was the most perilous time on the river,
for as the water rose, entire rafts of embarras would break

free, spinning down the river en masse, branches and roots interlocked.

Travis watched an embarras float past, splintered branches dripping like bloody spears as the current toyed with the jagged snarl of wood. Brown water slapped at the slick black trunks, and scummy white foam bobbed.

"Glad that one missed us." Green rubbed his face. "Mess of junk like that comes down on you, there's not much you can do."

"Cast loose," Henri said, powerful hands on the steering oar. "Outrun it downstream."

Travis nodded. "Times come, old coon, when ye've got ter cut and run."

Green reached up under his cap to scratch his head. "Yes, I know. Downstream. Every inch you lose is another you've got to make up. It's a long way to the mouth of the Big Horn, Travis."

"Better alive than dead, hoss. This child'd rather get there a mite late than not at all. Compared ter going under, a winter spent at the mouth of the Yellerstone appears right pert."

Green propped his hands on his hips, squinting upstream, searching for planters and sawyers. "You know what will happen if we do. Assiniboin will come in. Trade us out of everything we've got. We'd have to pull our stick come spring and head back downriver. No, I want two years, Travis. That means the mouth of the Big Horn. Time to get established."

"Wal, ye might do 'er." Travis watched the sweating men pole the boat against the current. Unlike the ocean, where wind did the moving, every ounce of boat, line, and cargo had to be tugged upriver with human muscle and sweat. Hell of a poor way to run a boat. But then, no one had found a better one. Steamboats rarely dared the Missouri's bars and snags. Break a boat up here, and you might just as well leave it behind.

"*Faible chien!*" Trudeau cursed. "You are worthless as a pig without legs!"

"Leave me alone!" Hamilton's voice called back.

"Then work, *bébé*!"

Green glanced at Hartman as the polers walked the boat against the current, their heads bobbing just beyond the edge cargo box. "Think that pilgrim Doodle will make it?"

"Cain't say."

"I swear to God, Travis, I'm not sure his skinny carcass is worth the trouble of feeding him."

"He ain't caved in yet."

"Lord knows, he gets babied enough. He still hasn't worked a full day. A boy would have been more help."

Travis caught Henri's eye and shrugged. "Wal, think of 'er this way. The *engagés* got all their attention on him. Not a one's thought ter start gritching about the boat, the wages, or the work—'cept what Hamilton ain't doing. I ain't yet had to bust a single head. Reckon by the time Hamilton breaks in or gets hisself kilt, we'll be up past the Platte."

Henri was grinning.

"Can't believe you," Green said. "Nursing that skinny bone pile like he was a sick calf. You of all people."

Travis jabbed Green playfully in the ribs. "I recall yer not so bad a nurse yerself. Pulled me through, ye did."

"That was different. You were a man."

Travis studied Hamilton's head as it bobbed along, slightly out of rhythm with the rest of the polers. The kid hadn't quite got the way of it yet. "He might be. One day."

"Hell might freeze over, too."

"Folks what don't take a long shot now and again never gets nowhere, Davey. Or do I need ter remind ye what a savvy man would say about this hyar expedition of yern?"

Green continued his scan of the river, watchful for eddies in the current, or the humping of water that might mark a submerged planter. "So, what is it about him?"

Travis hawked and spit over the side. "Don't rightly know. He's a queer sort. Book-larned better than any feller I ever met. He spouts off about them Roman and Greek fellers like he was telling winter stories in a Sioux lodge."

"And that's why you took up for him? I could have brought an old squaw along if stories was all you were interested in."

"Reckon it's more than that, Davey." Travis pulled at

his beard. "Looks like a sawyer up there. Near the bank where that water's a mite muddled."

"Steer wide," Green ordered Henri.

"*Oui*, booshway. I see her." Henri bent to the steering oar.

"Reckon the pilgrim's got sand, Dave. I jist don't think he knows it. The way I figger, he ain't never been pushed. Them Boston folks hid him away in books all his life. He ain't never had him no chance to see what he's made of. Can't tell how stout a hickory stick is till ye bends it."

"And what if he breaks?" Green asked.

"Reckon life never gives none of us no promises."

Green sighed. "Well, I'll be honest. We've passed the Osage. I never thought he'd make it this far. Must have hurt to take in all them bets."

"Yep," Travis mused. "I'm one rich child fer sure. Man can't have that much owed and feel right. Fact is, I done bet the whole caboodle. Wagered he'd make the mouth of the Platte afore we had ter shoot him."

Trudeau bellowed, "You are worthless! A woman would work harder!"

Richard almost tripped over his feet as he stumbled along. Sweat dampened his flushed skin, and he made desperate gasping sounds.

"You have more faith in him than I do," Green muttered.

The only sound in the camp was Packrat's soft snoring, and choked whimpers that couldn't quite break free of Heals Like A Willow's lips.

Two field mice dared the presence of the humans, slipping stealthily between sleeping forms, whiskers quivering as they followed familiar scent trails. Their watchful eyes like black beads, they picked through the grass for the bits dropped by the humans. They froze each time the woman made one of her piteous sounds.

Bound tighter than a stack of green willow sticks, Heals Like A Willow slept with her back propped on a half-rotten cottonwood log. Her head bowed on her chest, and her hair hung like a black veil to obscure the pained expression on her face and the eyes flicking back and forth beneath closed lids.

As the power of Willow's dream grew, the mice scurried for cover, content to seek their food in other, less troubled territory. . . .

I stand on a grassy point high over the plains. Sunlight fills the land with a soft golden glow that blurs the harsh edges of the bluffs and the tree-choked stream bottoms. I look down and see a steep drop-off, and far below at the bottom, a river is shining silver in the sun.

But such a river? A strong man couldn't shoot an arrow halfway across the shimmering waters. As I watch, the river changes, the silver surface turning murky and dark. Looking closely I can see that it has been fouled, clotted with floating bodies of dead men.

The water is black now, the color of old blood. The corpses continue to float past, men, women, and children. Some are dotted by sores from the White man's pox. Others have coughed until their lungs have shredded and protrude from their mouths. Here and there I can see wasted bodies. They look like winterkill with the skin shrunken into a rawhide tightness around the bones.

So much death. But why? Where has it come from? I want to step back, away from the sight. But when I look back toward the west, I see my people, *Dukurika* and *Ku'chendikani,* watching with worried eyes.

I will do anything to avoid their questioning gazes, so I look back into the blood-black river—and the corpses are staring up at me while waves of stinking water slap into their eyes.

My chest feels tight, as if a great weight is pressing on me. I can't seem to fill my lungs. Fear steals along my backbone. The suffocation increases.

That's when I hear the laughter coming from far away. I know that laughter, but for the moment can't place it.

I see them as dots first. They charge forward like fleas in a blanket, jumping and bounding, racing up the river of the dead. They look like grasshoppers, coming in wave upon wave, more than a man could count in a lifetime.

The laughter rings out of the sky again. This time my souls chill at the sound. Yes, I know that laugh, have heard it before when Coyote sends me one of these Power dreams.

The golden sunlight has faded to a dirty gray, so I must squint to see that coyotes, not fleas, are running up the river. Why? To what purpose? And what has killed all these people?

A low moan rises from the floating dead as they bob and twist in the current. In return, the coyotes alternately cry and yip with excitement as they race onward.

From a great distance I hear thunder, rolling and muffled as if from an exhausted storm.

I close my eyes. A soul-deep sickness makes my guts squirm. I can smell only death and rotting flesh.

What is happening? What do you want from me, Coyote?

When I can finally open my eyes, I look down on the river once again. Now the water is calm, as if the river's soul is sleeping. The air is silent, unstirring. The entire world might be holding its breath, waiting.

The only thing that moves is a dog, a white dog. I look closely. It appears to be nothing more than mist. It chases around and around the way it would if it were trying to catch its tail in its mouth. Around and around it goes, while the world waits in deathly silence.

The dream of escape grew in Richard's breast. He was stronger now. He could pole most of the day and not collapse into instant sleep after stuffing himself with dinner. Memories of Boston filled his hours. He dreamed of the shops, the fine food, the company of educated men like Will Templeton and George Peterson.

Laura waited for him, soft and warm. He could feel her reaching for him, wrapping her arms around him. There, in that ephemeral safety, the world was far away, unable to harm him.

When I come to you, dearest Laura, nothing will ever part

*us again. I swear it. I'll make you a queen, shower gifts
upon you. You and I will be together forever.*

Boston became a magical city: the antithesis of what he
suffered during the day. While Green cursed him, and the
engagés glowered at him, Richard retreated into himself,
despising their miserable animal lives. Trudeau was the
worst of the lot, a burly, arrogant tormentor. Trudeau
seemed to take pleasure in torturing Richard in little ways,
like the night he tripped him face-first in the mud.

Another of his messmates was Toussaint, a giant of a man
with muscles knotted like intertwined oak roots. Toussaint
watched Richard with oddly flat, emotionless eyes. He
worked like a human draft horse, always silent and intro-
spective. Forever brooding. The rest of the *engagés* cautiously avoided him.

Louis de Clerk and Jacques Eppecarte were the other two
men in his mess. They had both come from Saint Louis, old
hands at the river and its ways. Like the rest, they, too,
despised Richard, but rarely went out of their way to add to
his misery. Rather, they did their best to ignore him.

Each night, Richard would stagger ashore and flop down
to look at the leaping flames of the fire. He'd wolf down
his supper, and stare out at the dark trees. The *engagés*
watched him like wary hawks lest he try to escape. The
irony was that nightfall found Richard so exhausted that he
could do little more than collapse into his blankets and sleep
like the dead until the morning call.

"Hamilton!" Green ordered one morning. "Today, you
work the cordelle."

They hadn't trusted him on the cordelle before. On the
bank he'd have had an opportunity to slip away into the
brush. But where would he go? The days and miles had
passed. Names and places, the litany of the river, had disappeared behind them like the roiling brown current: The
coal mine at La Carbonier, the squalid village of La Char-
ette, the cave called Montbourne's Tavern; the mouth of the
Osage; Booneville, Franklin, Chariton; and finally the mouth
of the Grand River.

So. Maybe today he would get away. As he stepped onto
the muddy bank, Travis followed him, rifle in hand.

Green was talking to Trudeau. "Keep an eye on him. If he slips off, holler. Hartman will hunt him down. If he tries to run, beat the hell out of him."

Trudeau nodded wolfishly and threw Richard a hard glance.

Yes, you'd like that, wouldn't you, Trudeau? With resignation, Richard took his place in the middle of the line, Trudeau behind him.

The cordelle was a long rope, thick and bristly. Pulling it used different muscles than poling did. Richard rubbed the tender spot on his shoulder bruised by the pole, then took up the rope.

"Hurry up, pull, damn you!" Trudeau cursed behind him.

The long day began. Cursed and cuffed, Richard pulled, building his hatred of Trudeau as he struggled with the heavy rope, tugging the boat against the rippling current.

Like oxen. The thought settled into his brain. *I am no more than a two-legged ox.*

What miserable work. They slipped and trudged their way along the bank, stepping over fallen trees, slogging into muddy little creeks, and forcing their way through thickets of sumac, hazel, and tough grapevines. The brush was the worst. Hell must be full of these thick twisted brambles, for only the Devil could torment a man so.

The air grew hot, muggy, and stale. Sweat beaded and trickled as they wound their way along the river's edge. Flies buzzed around their heads as men mumbled, swatted mosquitoes, and pinched ticks off their flesh.

Richard tripped and fell. He was kicked to his feet again and forced on. Muscles quaking, he clawed through the brush, planting his clumsy feet in the steps of those before him.

Around him, the *engagés* sang. What sort of men *were* these? They had none of the virtues which he had thought common to all. This life had nothing to do with the teachings of the philosophers. Reason dominated the philosophical quest, yet here on the river, among these savages, it seemed as ephemeral as the breath of God.

"Why do you beat me?" Richard asked over his shoulder.

Trudeau scoffed, "To make you work. You are lazy and soft, like the maggot, *non*?"

"But why do you beat me? Why do you not just encourage me to achieve the same purpose?"

"Eh? You would leave us at the first opportunity, *oui*? The *bourgeois*, he say so."

"You have no proof that I would leave."

"*Sacré!* It is what I would do were I walking on your feet! What you get out of this trip? Nothing! So you leave, you get away, and you be free sooner."

"Perhaps. But why should you care? What is my leaving to you?"

"Ah, *mon ami*, if you run, the boat has one less body to help pull it upriver. My burden grows heavier while yours is less. Besides, we 'ave hauled you this far. Perhaps I want you to haul me now."

"Yes, but what about the morality of the situation? I have been sold like a slave. I am a man, Trudeau. I'm not a draft animal. What was done to me was wrong. Doesn't that mean anything to you?"

"*Cochon!* What do I care of your problems? What do you care of mine? My problem now is that you do not pull hard enough. You pull harder, or I shall kick your skinny ass so high you fart through your ears. Pull! I've had enough talk."

Richard threw his full weight against the rope. After straining for several minutes, he called over his shoulder again:

"Trudeau? I'll tell you what. I'll pull my hardest, I give you my word on that. If I make the effort, will you not make the effort to treat me better?"

"*Oui!* You pull like the mule, and I no kick you to keep you moving."

Soon Richard was grunting and gasping for breath. Still he struggled. *All right, Richard, if your mind is truly superior, you should be master of your body, protesting though it might be. This is nothing more than a problem of perception. I am fit for this job. I can do it.*

A couple of hours later he wasn't so sure. He stumbled more than he pulled. Trudeau began to curse again.

"I'm giving it my best," Richard grumbled to his tormentor. "How many years have you been hauling boats up the river?"

"All my life, rich man," Trudeau growled. "It does not take skill to pull the cordelle. Pull."

Richard strained against the weight. "I have pulled a boat for one day, now. It will take me at least a week to become as strong as you who have done this all your life."

"Ha! We shall see. I think you never make good on the cordelle. I think you'll die soon, weak man."

"A week," he gritted back and strained at the cordelle. "Tell you what. I'll bet you ten fine plews."

"And where will you get these? Everyone thinks you will be dead."

"Bet me."

"It is done." Trudeau raised his voice. "You hear that? This *Yankee* says he can pull with the best of us in a week! Ten plews, that's what the *vide poche* bets!"

Laughter rang out.

At long last, the sun settled blood-red into the distant trees. After the bow line, the one they called a painter, had been run out from the *Maria* and was securely tied, Richard reeled to the gangplank. He staggered onto the deck and propped himself against the cargo box. The cool evening breeze blew across his face. He swatted a mosquito that landed on his neck and scratched at the older bites on the back of his neck and along his arms.

Another itch pestered his leg, and he lifted his fraying pants to see a tick embedded in his calf. He pinched the bug off and threw it into the river. Damn this country! He looked across the opaque brown water at the trees on the far bank.

God be my witness, I'm tired.

What would Will Templeton think of him now? He stank of sweat and filth. Scratches crisscrossed his arms and face. He hadn't had a true bath in weeks. His tattered clothes were almost black with filth and grease, coated with mud.

"I was a gentleman," he mumbled wistfully. "Now, I look like a wretched criminal."

Very well, Father, you son of a bitch. You wanted me to see reality, and if this is it, I don't find it uplifting at all.

"Be talking ter yerseff?"' Travis asked, dropping next to him with a plate of food.

"That I am, jailer."

"Hah! Jailer, be I?" Travis grinned, and it didn't help his ruined face at all. "That be some, after where I been a time or two, Dick."

"The name is Richard. If I must be condemned to this damned voyage of yours, I might at least get a little respect as a man."

"Watch yer tongue, pilgrim. If'n yer wanting respect now, ye've yet to earn it."

"Or what? You'll beat it out of me?"

"Might," Travis said through a mouthful of food. He wiped his jacket sleeve across his lips and swallowed. Then he glanced at Richard. "So ye comes from Boston town, do ye?"

"Yes, that's my home. God, how I wish I was there now."

"Been there onc't upon a time. Got skunked on good likker and woke up next day on a brig headed fer J'maica. Spent two years on that bark. Then we made port at New Orleans and this coon skipped, I'll tell ye. Made me way upriver to Saint Loowee and took ter the Plains. Seen me a sight of places since then. Seen the Shining Mountains and trapped me a plew or two."

"Want to go back to Boston?" Richard shot a shy glance at the man.

"Hell, no! This child never lost nothing in them waters." He forked another mouthful and chewed thoughtfully.

"I could make it worth your while. My father has a lot of money. You could be richer than you ever thought to be."

Travis chuckled. "Do tell? Don't reckon I'd take kindly to them doin's, though. Reckon as how this child couldn't put up with them Yankee sops."

"Never know until you try."

"I know's 'nuff 'bout them diggin's." Travis gestured with the bent fork he held. "Saint Loowee is enough civilization fer this coon, an' that's some, it is. Naw, I reckon

I'm fer the mountains. Man can float his stick where he will.''

They were silent then, and Richard went and dished him up a plate from the big pot. The stew had been built around fresh venison that Travis had shot that day. He returned and sat next to the old hunter.

''I want to thank you for giving me that whiskey the first night.''

The hunter nodded.

''What's it like upriver?''

A strange light grew in Hartman's blue eyes. ''It be some, Dick. Thar's open land as far as ye can see. Makes a man sit right pert, it do. Thar be open prairie an' high mountains that shine in the sun. Ain't no people but the Injuns, and they be few and scattered. Thar's buffler, and prairie goats, and elks, too. Open land, Dick. Free land, where a man's what he's meant to be.''

''True freedom? Why do you say that? Freedom only exists in the mind.''

''Waugh! Them words'll rot in yer gullet after ye been in the wilds fer a season or two.''

''Freedom comes from philosophy, Travis. It comes from investigating your actions and motives by logical frameworks and manipulating your environment by perception. It's from reason—not a physical thing. There is an inward path, a quest for totality of experience, the primacy of will and nature as spirit. The world around us works according to rational plans and can be understood when we develop our perceptions.''

''Whar'd ye figger that from?'' Travis arched an eyebrow.

''You need to read Hume, Hegel, and Kant.'' Richard set his plate down to gesture with his hands as he talked. ''Hegel, for instance, in the *Phenomenology of Mind,* documents how men can grow. Right now, you're in a master-slave relationship with the world. Dave Green is the same as my father, a master. Others work, like you and me, or my father's employees, so that the master can consume the fruits of their labor. But that's only one step on the way to truth.''

''Do tell?''

''Indeed, I do. The master-slave relationship leads to what

Hegel calls 'the unhappy consciousness.' That is the condition in which we all seek more than material satisfaction. It's the search for a higher truth. Let's see if I can remember. Hegel says, 'It is in thinking that I am free because I am not in another but remain completely with myself.' That's where your freedom lies, Travis. In overcoming the myth of civil institutions such as the master-slave relationship, breaking the bonds our civil conditions have placed us in, and being free to pursue higher truth through reason.''

Travis sat silently and pulled his pipe and tobacco from what he called his possible sack. He tamped the tobacco into the bowl, rose, and walked across the deck toward the gangplank, his moccasined feet silent on the wood. The somber trees seemed to watch Richard, an unforgiving presence. An owl hooted in the forest, and he could hear the distant lowing of cattle from a farm hidden somewhere back from the river.

Richard picked up his plate, satisfied with his translation of Hegel's complex ideas into something the hunter could understand.

Hartman returned, having found an ember to light his pipe. He puffed contentedly and settled cross-legged on the deck.

''Well?'' Richard asked as he chewed.

Hartman finally looked at him pensively. ''Maybe so, Dick. Reckon though ye better sit back and wonder about this hyar. Seems ter me that's there's a hitch in all that. This coon sees two kinds of freedom. Thar be the ability ter use yer noodle fer thinking, and thar be the ability ter pull yer traps and head whar ye will. Reckon a man can't be free lessen he can do both. Them thar Boston folks can't just up and skeedaddle fer the timber if'n they get the urge. Reckon they can think all they wants, though. See whar me stick floats?''

''It's your mind that is important, Travis. Your mind is your ultimate freedom.''

''So's a good smoke, warm blankets, and a hunk of buffalo haunch roasting in the coals while all the stars are twinkling overhead.''

''But that's only catering to the animal instincts. You

must rise above a base state of nature. That's what civilization has attempted so poorly to do. You must free your mind, and the only way is through reason."

Hartman exhaled a blue cloud and removed the pipe stem from his mouth. "Yer still seeing one side of the beaver hide, Dick. It ain't the whole beaver. Yer claiming that to be whole, you can only be a half. Ain't nobody, not even yer mister Haggle—"

"That's Hegel. Georg Wilhelm Friedrich Hegel."

"All right, all them fellers, too. They can't jist think their way through life. It's like walking on one leg. A feller can only hobble."

"You're missing the point."

"Do say?"

"Or you're purposely being thick-headed."

"Tell me, Dick. Did ye ever see a bear what'd been raised in a cage?"

"I did, once. A bit barbaric."

"Do ye reckon that thar bear be free to think anything he'd want ter, huh?"

"Bears don't think."

"Painter crap! Bears think as good as the next critter. So ye don't know shit about bears. Wal, that don't matter, let's just agree he can think, all right?"

"All right."

"So, yer bear's been raised in that cage. He can roll back on his arse and think from Hell to breakfast. Still, he'd not know the first thing about what it be ter be a bear, now would he?"

"Men and bears are different, Travis." Richard sighed. "It isn't the same thing. Men have different needs than bears. We have the ability to transcend earthly needs. We have spirits and souls. We are not base."

Travis gave him a level stare. "Reckon ye been in a cage too long yerseff, Dick. Be best if'n ye took that noodle yer so proud of and did ye some more thinking." Travis stood up, nodded politely, and walked off.

"Damned old fool," Richard muttered. "He has no idea what I was trying to teach him."

Packrat had never felt so utterly miserable. The woman's blood had stained his very soul. At night, his dreams were tormented; horrible images of Heals Like A Willow capered through them. The eye of his soul saw her consorting with mole, weasel, and owl—all evil spirit helpers. Packrat had taken to sleeping with his blanket covering his face lest Willow shoot a witch pellet into his mouth.

By day, he couldn't shake the jittery sense of impending doom. Any confidence he'd had in himself had evaporated like cool spring rain from sun-warmed ground. Even now, he checked himself for pains, for sores, for any indication that his health was failing.

They'd passed the sand hills, always following the north shore of the river. These were familiar hunting grounds. He had ridden here as a boy, full of dreams. Now, returning on what should have been his first great triumph as a man, Packrat felt as empty as the grassy plains that spread around them.

He shot a nervous glance at his captive. She rode her mare with a particular grace, head high, back straight. How could she look so calm and proud when disaster lurked everywhere? His gaze darted at the sky and then around at the hillsides, expecting Sioux raiders to top each hill. His horse shied at nothing. Packrat mumbled his prayers, hoping that some spirit beast wasn't lurking nearby to steal his soul.

I ought to kill her, find myself some peace.

But if he did, he'd be haunted by her ghostly face, grinning at him in triumph. After all, she knew about the Death star, and Wolf, and the other powers sacred to the Pawnee. Wouldn't she come back in death to haunt him?

At no time did he allow her out of his sight. Once, encamped, he'd stripped her, searching through her clothing.

"What are you doing?" she finally signed.

In Pawnee, he'd told her, "Searching for an owl claw, mole skin, weasel hide, or sole skin from a corpse's foot. That, or anything else you could witch me with."

She'd studied him with those penetrating dark eyes and signed, "Why don't you let me go?"

"You would win," he had told her.

Packrat looked out over the rolling plain. The river ran just to their south, its course marked by the thick band of cottonwoods that had begun to bud out in a green haze. Piled white clouds built against the blue vault of the sky to the north. The grass had greened; some, like the junegrass and bluegrass, was already heading out. Wildflowers dotted the earth in white, yellow, and blue.

Spring, the time of renewal. The stars known as the Swimming Ducks had appeared in the night sky to rouse the animals and inform the Pawnee that ceremonies were due. Thunder had awakened in the sky. Careful hands would have prepared the Evening Star Bundle by now. The ground-breaking, the Pawnee planting ceremony, would have just passed, the fields tilled and corn planted.

And here I am, far away, riding with a Snake woman who may be a witch.

If nothing else, the long days and hard travel should have worn her down. Where did she get the stamina to maintain that poise? His gaze strayed to her muscular brown legs, and followed the rounded curves of her calves, up along those sleek thighs until they disappeared under the leather of her dress. How slim-waisted she was, lithe and supple. The fringes on her dress swayed with the horse's gait, accenting the full swell of her hips. At the same time, her hair, washed glossy the night before with yucca root, gleamed with blue tints in the sunlight.

How he longed to run his hands over her smooth skin, cradle her soft breasts in his hands and . . .

Fool! That's how she polluted you in the first place! "I can't believe myself. Here I am, dreaming about a witch!"

She turned at his voice, raising one of those perfect eyebrows into a questioning arch.

"Nothing," he growled. "I'm just wishing I'd never captured you." With his hands he signaled, "Turn around. Ride."

"You do not seem happy."

"Why should I be?" he signed. "You have ruined me."

Her quick hands replied, "Do not take women captive. And if you do, don't lie with them."

He listened to the trill of a meadowlark and signed: "What do Shoshoni men do with women they take?"

"They lie with them. That doesn't mean a woman likes it."

"You're a captive. Not even a real person."

"Only Pawnee are real persons?"

Packrat snorted derisively. "Everyone knows that."

"And the Sioux?"

"Worse than animals! Homeless raiders, too lazy to work for what they can steal. One day, the Pawnee will kill them all for the vermin they are."

She laughed. Her fingers signed: "People are the same everywhere. If you were raised Sioux, you would say the same thing about Pawnee."

Raised a Sioux! By the light of Evening Star, what a ludicrous idea! "Sioux can't even speak in a human tongue!"

"And you can?"

In Pawnee, he told her, "Yes, I can. Only Pawnee speak like real people."

Her smile was flirtatious. "Good. Me human," she told him in passable Pawnee.

Packrat's mouth had fallen open and he closed it foolishly. "Where did you learn Pawnee?"

"I listen. Have some words. You teach." She tilted her head innocently. "Keep talk to me. Signs help me learn. You say Pawnee-talk make real person. In you rules, me real person."

"You'll be Snake—and not a real person—until the day you die, witch."

"No understand all your talk."

"Good. I'm going to keep it that way!" He shook his head. Of course she would learn to speak. Captives usually did, if they lived long enough. "And I'd better stick to making signs."

To his irritation, she'd heard that.

Preoccupied with this new problem, he was slow to notice the riders, no more than two black dots in the distance. Heat waves shimmered off the spring grass, but even that far away, Packrat could tell the difference between men on horseback and buffalo.

He glanced suspiciously at Willow. She seemed unaware, riding with the stately grace of Evening Star herself.

Packrat called, pointed toward the trees, and angled away from the riders.

With her hands, Willow signed: "You wish to avoid them? Afraid they will kill you with your Power broken?"

He hadn't seen her look in the direction of the riders. "What are you talking about?"

She lifted her bounds hands, pointing toward the strangers.

"How long have you known they were there?"

"Don't know words," she answered.

He repeated his query in signs.

"Saw horses before we talk," she told him simply.

"And you didn't say . . . ? Oh, forget it. I should have taken my father a bear instead of you. It would have been a lot easier." *There, figure that out, witch.*

The trouble was, the riders had seen them, and were even now racing toward them.

"Wolf, help me. I may have to fight, and this accursed woman has robbed me of Power."

"What say?" Willow asked.

"Nothing." He wet his lips, kicking his horse into a run. "How can I win with my Spirit Power broken, woman? When they kill me, you'd better hope they are as kind to captives as I've been!"

And they would kill him. No warrior could win a battle when his spirit helpers had turned their heads away. Not even when fighting against animals like the Sioux.

THIRTEEN

◆

Every man carries about him a touchstone, if he will make use of it, to distinguish substantial gold from superficial glitterings, truth from appearances. And indeed the use and benefit of this touchstone, which is natural reason, is spoiled and lost only by assuming prejudices, overweening presumption, and narrowing our minds. The want of exercising it, in the full extent of things intelligible, is that which weakens and extinguishes this noble faculty in us.

—John Locke, *Why Men Reason So Poorly*

Phillip Hamilton carefully lowered his stiff leg to the carriage step until it could take his weight, then following with his good leg, and repeated the process to reach the ground. He did that now, helped by Jeffry's stabilizing hand.

His black carriage was parked beside a rutted road that transected a rolling grassy field. To the south, the Charles River and Boston Harbor sparkled in the morning sunlight. The harbor islands made black lozenges in the silver.

The horses stamped in their traces as Phillip grasped the head of his cane and slid it out of the carriage. Bracing himself, he turned, looking at the low grassy knolls that gave way to trees several musket shots to the north.

Everything seemed to burst with life. The breeze off the bay carried the musky scents of saltwater and tidal marsh. The gulls cried raucously, their voices mingling with the melodious trills of the inland songbirds. Wildflowers bobbed and waved in the verdant spring grass.

Once, nearly fifty years ago, before the harbor defenses had been built, this undulating terrain had been vital to the defense of the city.

"Sir?" Jeffry asked. "Are you all right?"

Phillip pointed with his cane. "Look. Cows grazing out there as if nothing had ever happened. Where once our feet trampled, now only winding cow trails remain. It's better that way, I suppose."

"You say that every year."

"Perhaps I do. It's only once a year I see it like this. The rest of the time, I see it in my mind. Hear it. Dirty white puffs of gunsmoke, the popping clatter of the muskets, men yelling, screaming. Battle is incredibly loud, Jeffry. The funny thing is, you barely hear it when you're in the middle of it. A bullet makes a sound when it hits flesh. Did you know that? A mixture of a pop and a splat. Men were shot down all around me. Through that roar of cannon, yelling, and clattering of ramrods, I heard those balls hitting home. But, you know, I never heard the one that hit me. One minute I was charging forward, and the next I was down. No pain. Just down, and I didn't remember how I got there."

He relived that moment, lying facedown, men bellowing and the screaming hiss of balls cutting the air. How puzzled he'd been, that he could have taken a fall when his blood was up. How silly to trip at so important a moment. Had he stepped in a hole?

"I didn't understand until I tried to stand." Phillip rubbed his nose, remembering. "My leg, it just wouldn't work. Wouldn't hold me. I rolled over, looked down, and saw the blood, the ripped breeches. It still didn't hurt. I just lay there with the battle raging all around me. It might have been an eternity . . . refusing to believe."

Phillip used his cane to point part way up Breed's Hill. "Right up there. When I finally collected myself, I used my musket to pull myself up. And then I hobbled back, right through the middle of the battle and . . . Oh, I'm boring you to death. You've heard it so many times."

"You may tell me again, sir." Jeffry smiled.

"You're a good man to humor me so." Phillip stumped out into the grass, Jeffry at his side. "It was more important than usual to come this year."

"Because of Master Richard?"

"I'm worried sick about him. I let my anger goad me into something I never should have considered. I could have sent him West, yes. But not with the money, Jeffry. How incredibly foolish of me. Had I the sense God gave a rock, I'd have sent the money with you, and Richard could have been your cover. You could have protected them both."

Jeffry frowned thoughtfully at the grass. "He must have a chance to find his way to manhood, sir. You, of all men, know the risks that entails."

"Do you think I made a mistake?" Phillip turned to meet Jeffry's eyes.

"Yes, sir."

"Why didn't you tell me?"

Jeffry's smile flickered at the corner of his mouth. "The only subject I cannot advise you on is Richard, sir. Your relationship with him provokes you beyond your normal prudence."

An emptiness yawned within Phillip. "My grandfather was a prisoner in England, a debtor. He took out loans. Unfortunately, he went into competition with the squires. They broke him. Made him lose everything because he was running his business better than they, taking a share of their market.

"I remembered that lesson and fought here to make a better world. I was such an idealistic young man. I had determined at that early age that I would be a soldier. Take my chances on death."

"To fight for equality in trade?"

"Hah! You know better than that. There is never equality in trade. He who is smarter, more industrious, and more ambitious will always dominate trade. Equal? Never. No, I was a soldier so that I could have the chance he never did, and my father barely had. The chance to make something of myself, no matter who I was descended from."

"You were a soldier so that you could build your fortune, marry a beautiful lady, and allow your son to become a philosopher."

"That's right." Phillip pressed the tip of his cane into the soft soil. "And I achieved all of those things. But at such a cost, Jeffry. When Caroline died, she took the light out of my soul. Now, I wonder what I have done to Richard. Why didn't I just leave him alone? Better by far than to have sent him to his death.''

He looked down at the holes he'd poked in the rich earth. Holes, like men, were ephemeral. The grass would reclaim them, and the birds would sing as if nothing had happened.

''He's not dead.''

''Are you so sure? Feeling something in your African soul?''

''Perhaps.''

''Did you ever long for a son?''

''Once, sir. A long time ago. I thought you among the luckiest of men in the world. When Mrs. Hamilton died giving birth to Richard, it was a shock. Seeing what it did to you made me uneasy. Then, watching as you tried to raise Richard, my desire evaporated.''

''You could have married, you know.''

Jeffry chuckled dryly. ''We've had this conversation before, sir. Nothing has changed over the years.''

''My Caroline, your Betsy. What miserable old men we are. Each defeated in love, I by death, and you by an institution. Pathetic, aren't we?''

''No, sir. We live, and have our health. Only our dreams are dead.''

''And now I've cast my son to the wind.''

''At least you had him to cast, sir.''

''That is true.'' Phillip propped himself on his cane. ''If he survives, he'll inherit the estate. Idealist that he is, he'll make you miserable. Give you lecture after lecture on freedom, self-responsibility, and free will. He'll do his damnedest to cast you out on your own.''

''Yes, sir. I'll handle him, sir. Just the same as I do you.''

''I'm sure you will.'' Phillip placed a hand on Jeffry's shoulder. ''And thank you for helping me to believe that he'll come home one day. An old man needs his fantasies—no matter how foolish he's been with his life.''

FOURTEEN

When I see freeborn animals, through a natural abhorrence of captivity, dash their brains out against the bars of their prison; when I see multitudes of naked savages despise European pleasures and brave hunger, fire, and sword, and death itself to preserve their independence, I feel that it is not for slaves to argue about liberty.

—Jean-Jacques Rousseau, *Discourse on the Origin and Foundation of Inequality Among Mankind*

Shivers ran down Packrat's back as he watched the horses charging in his direction. He and Willow had pulled up just inside the grove of cottonwoods that covered the floodplain of the Platte.

"Make a fort?" Willow signed. "Pile up logs?"

Packrat gave her a dull stare. "Why fight? Dirtied by your woman's blood, I can't win. My Power is *gone!*"

She said something in her language, and watched him with expressionless eyes.

Weasel eat her guts for the trouble she was, he had other problems.

You are going to die now, Packrat. These warriors will kill you. How will you face the Spirit World? What will happen to you when your soul arrives in a profane state?

He ground his teeth. Loneliness and fear, old companions that they were, had never filled him with such hopelessness. The warm place deep inside, between his heart and backbone, had turned cold and empty.

My soul is dying.

Packrat glanced unsurely at Willow, met her mocking eyes, and slumped. His arm might have been stone as he reached out, took up her halter, and kicked his horse forward, back toward the nearing riders.

"Come, woman. Together, you and I will die. You have destroyed me. I shall die in shame. My soul will be hounded forever. And you? I hope these are Sioux riding down on top of us. I hope they kill you slowly, maybe pour hot coals into that cunning vagina of yours. Make you suffer until you howl as I will . . . for all of eternity."

No change of expression crossed her maddening eyes. Packrat tightened his grip on his war club, his thumb rubbing the familiar grain of the wood. He should kill her now, achieve that small satisfaction before death swallowed him.

As jumpy as a woodrat in a snake's lair, he tensed to strike, and glanced again at the closing horsemen.

As determined as he was to encounter bad luck, it took a moment for Packrat to recognize that style of dress. These were not Sioux, not bloodthirsty, howling enemies, but Skidi hunters!

Packrat's soul slipped from resigned defeat into weary acceptance. Willow had noticed the change in his demeanor, read it correctly, and now turned her hard gaze to the riders who thundered over the last of the grassy rises. Their horses' hooves chopped through a patch of prickly pear, dust and bits of cactus flying up behind.

"Screams At His Enemies and Blue Bull Robe," Packrat identified the hunters. But what were they doing out here?

"Packrat!" Screams At His Enemies waved, whooping and shrieking.

The two yipped and slapped their sweating horses, cutting circles around Packrat and Willow in a mad display of horsemanship. Through it all, Packrat sat quietly and considered his options.

Screams At His Enemies was the first to notice his reticence. "Hey, Packrat!" He pulled up on his horse, trotting closer. "You look as if you haven't slept for days! This woman you have captured, she's that much of a wild one, eh?"

"By the stars," Blue Bull Robe muttered, "she's beautiful. I'll trade a couple of horses for the likes of her!"

Screams At His Enemies nodded. "Good catch, Packrat.

When you steal a woman, you take the most comely, don't you? No wonder you look tired! If I had her in my robes at night, I wouldn't sleep either!''

''What's the matter, Packrat?'' Blue Bull Robe shouted. ''Have you pumped her so full of your seed that there's nothing left inside you?''

Packrat chose his course of action. He would preserve as much of his honor as possible. He raised his hands, imploring, ''Come no closer!''

Blue Bull Robe cocked his head, but reined in his horse. Screams At His Enemies slowed his animal and trotted it over beside Blue Bull Robe's.

''This woman!'' Packrat cried. ''She is bad luck—she breaks a man's Power. Since I captured her, my friends, I have dreamed, seen her consorting with Weasel, Mole, and Owl. Keep your distance!''

Screams At His Enemies slumped forward, arms crossed on his horse's neck, a quizzical look on his face. ''So, if she's so bad, what are you doing with her? Why not whack her in the head, take your coup, and be done with her?''

''I have started this thing. If I kill her, she will win. I think it's a matter of Power, something that I don't really understand yet. No, I must finish this the way I started.''

''But if she's evil,'' Blue Bull Robe noted, ''why stay close to her?''

''A man must trust the voices within him. Mine tell me that the only way I can survive this is by finishing what I have started. You know the stories, about the way the Spirit World tests a man. I must succeed or fail. Power will judge me.''

''Ah!'' Blue Bull Robe nodded. ''You have caught the bobcat by the ears. Now, you must find a way to let loose without getting scratched and bitten. But I don't understand. If she's dangerous, where are you taking her? A smart young man like you wouldn't bring a sorcerer into our village.''

Packrat chewed his lip. When a polluted young man brought a Snake woman who might be a sorcerer into the Skidi village, no matter what happened, all the bad luck, illness, and death would be blamed on him. Of course he'd be guilty. People would know he was paying the Doctors for healing and soul cleansing.

Packrat rubbed his face as he thought. That bobcat analogy fit better than a new pair of stitched buffalo-calf britches. "She is a gift, my friends. For Half Man. A tribute from his son, if you will."

Screams At His Enemies tilted his head. "Give a woman to Half Man? After what he did to your mother? Of all the worthless . . ." A sudden glimmer of understanding lit in his eyes. "By Morning Star! You wouldn't!"

"Yes, he would!" Blue Bull Robe cried, catching on. "What a way to pay the old weasel back! Oh, Packrat, you will shame him. People will nod knowingly, and laugh at Half Man behind their blankets. How clever and cunning you are! Worthy of Evening Star's grace!"

Packrat watched woodenly. "But first, I must be cleansed, my friends. She has polluted me with her woman's blood. Do you understand?"

Blue Bull Robe backed his horse away.

Screams At His Enemies inspected Willow with interest. "She is a Snake woman, what do you expect? Don't look so wounded, Packrat. The same thing happened to my cousin, Takes Things. You know him, don't you? Lives over with the Loups. You just have to go to the Doctors. It will cost you everything you own, but they will cleanse you."

"It could be worse," Blue Bull Robe called from his greater distance. "At least you can be cleansed . . . and then you can call your Power back."

"What are you doing out here?" Packrat asked, more than ready to change the subject.

"What does anyone do out here? The keeper of the Skull Bundle sent us. He saw a strange formation in the stars and thought someone should go and scout before the Chiefs don their costumes to become Heaven in the opening ceremonies for the hunt. We're looking for buffalo, checking the grass to see how it is growing and where it will take the summer herds."

"The grass isn't as good as it could be." Packrat pointed back to the west. "Not as much rain this spring. We've seen buffalo all the way from the Snake lands, mostly scattered in small herds.''

To Packrat's annoyance, Screams At His Enemies kept staring at Willow with open admiration. "Hunting will be easier. The buffalo will be close to water."

"The rains could always come," Blue Bull Robe noted. "Maybe that's what the keeper of the Skull Bundle saw in the stars."

The summer hunt was one of Packrat's favorite times of year. Unless he could be ritually cleansed, he'd miss it this year. During the hunt a young man could prove his prowess to his peers, and, of course, the young women would be watching. But in his current state, the Hunt Chiefs would never let him close to the animals, for his pollution would offend the buffalo, and enrage the spirit helpers.

"It is good to see you, friends," Packrat told them. "I, however, must hurry on. The sooner I get to the Skidi and give this woman to Half Man, the sooner I can be cleansed and take my place with real people again."

Screams At His Enemies grinned sardonically. "Your luck is truly gone, Packrat. After the Breaking-Ground ceremonies, Half Man left for the *La-chi-kuts'* fort on the great river. He's going to trade for their medicine water, maybe stop and grovel with his 'other' people." Screams At His Enemies wouldn't even deign to speak the name of the Omaha.

Packrat knotted a fist and shook it in empty rage. Through slitted eyes he glanced at Willow. *You did this, didn't you? Made sure that he wouldn't be there.*

"I wouldn't take *her* to the village," Blue Bull Robe added. "Not if you think she might be a sorcerer. No one would welcome that. Not even her beauty would do her— or you—much good."

"Half Man will return before the summer hunt?" Packrat could hang around the vicinity of the main Skidi village, waiting until the proper moment to bestow his gift.

Screams At His Enemies laughed as he fingered his horse's mane. "You know Half Man. He'll time his return to the moment the hunt is over. Just like he'll leave again just before the harvest. He won't dare take the chance that he might have 'to work!''

"Why is this happening to me?'' Packrat wondered.

"Were I you,'' Blue Bull Robe called, "I would take her to him at the *La-chi-kuts*' fort. Who knows, maybe it will be better that way. It will give you time to be cleaned before he brings her to the village. Then, if anything bad does happen, it will fall on Half Man's shoulders instead of yours.''

Screams At His Enemies nodded, smiling. "And think on this, friend. You might be able to steal something from the Sioux, or maybe even the *La-chi-kuts,* to help pay for your cleansing. These Doctors, they charge a great deal for their help.''

Packrat mulled the idea. The White man's fort drew a great number of horses, wagons, and goods. He could rid himself of the woman, and who knew what kind of wealth he might stumble across?

That, or I'll be killed by the first war party to pass my way. But then, he'd grown used to the idea of being dead. Why did he care that both Pawnee hunters were staring so raptly at Willow? A man about to die had more serious things to worry about.

"I shall go straight to the *La-chi-kuts*' fort. There, I shall give this weasel woman to Half Man. After that, I will search for something to pay for my cleansing. Tell my mother . . . tell her that her son will do this thing. If she sees him again in this life, he will have succeeded. If not, he has failed, and neither she, her family, nor any other Pawnee must weep for Packrat.''

"I will tell them,'' Screams At His Enemies promised. "In the meantime, Packrat, I'd keep my penis out of the woman.'' The words didn't match the hungry look in the hunter's eyes.

You have no idea, Packrat thought as he turned his horse away, driving Willow's beast before him.

Throughout the conversation, she'd sat rock-still, a knowing look on her beautiful face.

"Ride with care, Packrat!'' Blue Bull Robe called.

The last Packrat heard was Screams At His Enemies saying, "By the Evening Star, when did you ever see such a magnificent woman!"

Packrat never looked back.

The storm broke in the middle of the night, cold air blowing out of the west. Gaudy blue-white lightning bolts illuminated tormented clouds. The wind howled through the spring-budded trees then brutalized the camp, ripping at blankets and flapping Green's tent. Tin cups, pots, and kettles rolled clanking across the ground, chased by groggy, cursing *engagés* who tripped on their blankets.

The rain followed, pelting them from the black sky. One furious assault after another hammered them until morning, when cold breakfast was served, and the cordelle was lined out.

The misery Richard had endured to date paled in comparison to this. Rain beat on his unprotected head, trickled down his numb skin, and disappeared into his already soaked clothing. With each sodden step, Richard's breath misted in the chill. As Toussaint passed, wet branches slapped him. His boots slipped from under him and he fell into the churned mud.

"Why?" he asked. "Trudeau, why work on a day like this?"

"We are going to the mouth of the Big Horn. We will be lucky, *enfant,* to make it there before first snow. Each day, she is ten miles, no?"

"This is madness."

"Work, pig. Your muscles will warm you."

Work he did, through that interminable gray day. Step after step, in the churned slop left by those ahead of him. His worn boots squished and sucked, water gurgling around his swollen toes.

Only the cordelle and the backbreaking exertion remained constant. Sometimes he looked up, as if in supplication, to the leaden sky and the interwoven branches of newly budded ash and elm.

To his right, just spitting distance away, the river coiled and flexed, water brown and scummy with bits of foam and flotsam. Rain stippled the muddy surface, tracing patterns on the rippling muscles of current. How broad it was, more than a rifle shot across. All that water, fighting them, fighting him.

Lightning flashed, followed by the crash-boom of angry thunder.

Richard tightened his grip on the thick rope, leaning into it. His legs trembled: half from exertion, half from the shivers. *Work! Turn off your mind. Don't listen to the land.*

Earth and river, each as much a presence as the indefinable essence of God. How silly of Green to think that he could pull a boat through a country like this. How silly of all of them.

"We're doomed," Richard mumbled as water dripped from his brow and nose. "No one can do what we are attempting."

"What do you say?" Trudeau asked.

"I say we're going to die up here. The land, the river, maybe together they will kill us. Like swatting a fly, Trudeau. And in the end, for all of your bullying, you'll be just as dead as I am."

"*Oui,* if God wills."

"God?" Richard's wet clothing chafed as he clung to the cordelle. "What does God care?"

"God is God, m'sieur."

"Care to engage in theological epistemology?"

"Eh?"

"Nothing. I was just about to tell you . . ." A crack opened several feet to Richard's left, the ground moving outward, slanting toward the rushing water. Toussaint, in position ahead of him, reeled, arms windmilling. The crack gaped blackly.

"Jump!" the cry came in French. "Swim outwards! Away from . . ."

Richard lost the rest. He fell, pummeling the air as the loosened earth pitched into the rain-torn river, and smacked face-first into the crashing spray. The tons of falling dirt propelled a huge wave into the current that rolled over the struggling *engagés*.

Richard slashed and kicked in the muck, surrounded by screaming men. The cordelle slithered past him like some tortured reptile. Most of the *engagés* had recovered from their shock and were striking out, swimming downstream, cursing and bellowing.

Powered by panic, Richard battled his way toward the shore, feet kicking off clods of mud that melted underfoot. The current surged, sucking him along the clifflike bank. Mindless with terror, screaming, he clawed futilely at the sheer wall.

A strong arm clamped around him from behind, jerking him back, away from the bank.

"Fool!" a voice roared in his ear. "Stop fighting me! You'll only kill us both!"

Richard panted his terror, a catch in his throat making a sobbing sound.

"*Merde!* Easy. Like a baby in Mama's arms, *non*? You be safe, you see."

"Help . . . help me!"

"I was taught to swim like the otter! What you do, eh? Only a fool swims against the bank that way. The current, she drags you down . . . that, or more bank falls on you."

Limp in defeat, Richard watched the shore growing farther and farther away, bobbing in the strong grip of his savior. Toussaint. That's whose voice it was.

Toussaint, who worked like a stubborn ox, said little, and smiled rarely. Whose hard black eyes watched Richard as if he were some sort of insect.

"You no swim?" Toussaint asked.

"N-Never learned."

"You learn now, eh? Kick with your feet. Legs straight. It will help me."

"Kick?"

"Like mermaid, eh? Legs straight. That's it. Good, *mon ami*. Oui, you do good. *non!* Do not bend knees. That was me you just kicked."

"Where . . . where are we going?"

"To the *Maria*. I see her. Just there. A little way, no

further. Stay calm, Reeshaw, we are almost there."

Richard kicked, clinging to the brawny arm that circled his neck. Raindrops continued to pelt his face and waves slapped him. The taste of mud filled his mouth.

Then he was alongside the *Maria,* and hands reached down to pluck him from the water.

"Of all things," Trudeau asked as he bent down to give Toussaint a hand, "why did you save *him*?"

Toussaint came over the side, jerked from the muddy water like an ungainly fish to flop wetly on the deck. "Practice, Trudeau. Just in case I 'ave to save you next time, eh?"

Richard coughed and sat up, gasping for breath. Beyond the gunwale, the river had taken on a silver sheen, roughened by the slanting sheets of rain. He glanced at Toussaint. "*Merci beaucoup.* I can't thank you enough."

Toussaint waved it away. The hard glint returned to his eyes. "Such things, they are done on the river. Speak of it no more." The *engagé* stood and made his way forward to help the others pull in the wet cordelle.

"Come on." Trudeau reached down and pulled Richard to his feet. "Back to work, *mon ami.* Now we 'ave to make up what the boat lost when the bank collapsed."

Richard managed to lock his wobbling legs, and wipe the muck from his wet face. "I . . . we almost died back there!"

"Then come, *enfant.* The sooner you are back to work, the sooner you will 'ave the chance to die again, no? But next time when the bank collapse, swim out, eh? No sense to rush to death. It find you quick enough."

Richard swallowed hard and followed the *engagé* down the *passe avant.* Until he died, he'd relive that moment of the ground tilting, falling out from under him. What kind of insanity was this?

Order has gone from the world. I live only in chaos, and await the approach of death.

Men braced themselves on poles, holding the keelboat against the current as the plank was dropped to the bank. One by one, the *engagés* trotted across, passing the dripping cordelle from hand to hand. It unspooled from the coil on the deck with uncanny grace, a thing alive.

Trudeau beckoned and Richard nerved himself to step

onto the plank. By some lucky streak, he didn't tumble into the ugly brown current again, but found his place. Rain stippled the water pooled in their pocked tracks. His fingers wrapped around the cordelle. He placed each foot in the marks left by Toussaint's big feet, taking the weight of the rope and boat.

The endless agony resumed. He only recognized where the bank had collapsed by the reduced number of footprints in that place. Half the morning lost. Five miles that day instead of ten.

FIFTEEN

◇

Pure insight, therefore, is the simple ultimate being undifferentiated within itself, and at the same time the universal achievement and result, and a universal possession of all. In this simple spiritual substance self-consciousness gives itself and maintains for itself in every object the sense of this, its own individual being, or of action, just as conversely the individuality of the self-consciousness is there identical with itself and the universal.

This pure insight is, then, the spirit that calls to every consciousness: be *for* yourselves what you are all essentially *in* yourselves—rational.

—Georg Friedrich Wilhelm Hegel, *Phenomenology of Mind*

Travis Hartman wound through the cottonwoods and green ash, a heavy whitetail buck slung over his shoulders. The first taint of woodsmoke came to his nostrils. Camp was right where he'd expected it to be—in the flats, just north of the mouth of the Kansas River.

Hartman had run his rifle through the buck's tied legs and used it as an aid to carry the deer. Now he adjusted his hold, his hand protectively over the pan to keep it dry. Rain continued to fall in wind-whipped fits and starts.

"Reckon a frog would drown in this," he muttered to the heedless deer.

Looking back, he could see where his heavy steps had broken the wet grass. Water trickled from the fringes on his pants and soaked moccasins. Fortunately, the prickly pear didn't grow in the taller floodplain grasses. Out in the prairie, however, the thorns would find their way through his water-logged moccasins and make travel hell.

As he passed through the last of the trees, he could see the *Maria* looking somber in the gray twilight, her deck and cargo box water-slick. On shore the *engagés* huddled about smoky fires, blankets propped overhead to keep them merely miserable instead of rain-sopped. Green's tent had a hunched look, the dark canvas sagging.

"Hello the camp!" Hartman bellowed. At his words, heads popped out to stare. "Whar in Hob's Hell are the sentries?"

Trudeau called back, "In this rain?"

"Hell, pilgrim! Yer in Kansas country. Never know what them weasels is up ter. Git two men out, and not lessen a hunert paces from camp. Them Kansa braves would have yer topknot before ye'd even have time ter whistle!"

Trudeau turned, barking orders.

Green poked his head out of the tent flap. "Trudeau! Devil take you, I told you to put out guards."

"*Oui*, booshway. I make the order. No one listen."

Hartman dropped his deer beside a fire, slid his rifle out, and strode up to the gathering *engagés*. He stopped before Trudeau, staring at the man through slitted eyes. "Reckon yer not up ter the job?"

Trudeau's eyes lowered. "It will not happen again."

Travis remained motionless, water dripping. "I reckon not, coon. If'n it do, I'll have yer ears."

Trudeau nodded and backed away.

"What's the news?" Green called, refusing to step out into the rain.

Hartman stuck a thumb toward the deer. "Thar's dinner.

Cut 'er up.'' Then he walked to Green's tent. "How do, Davey?"

The booshway grinned. "Crossed the Kansas. According to the calendar, tomorrow's May first. We're just about on schedule. Sometime this year, the government wants to build an agency right here at the Kawsmouth. I'm thankfully glad we beat them."

Hartman ducked into the tent, owl-eyed in the darkness. Henri, hunched on a whiskey keg, nodded. A small fold-up table stood in the back, on it a ledger book, quill, and ink.

"See anything?" Green asked anxiously. "Any chance of a Kansa raiding party? Osages?"

Hartman wrung out his beard and long hair, water trickling onto the trampled grass. "Nary a sign older than a month. I reckon so long's the storm holds, we're going ter sail right on past without a lick of trouble."

Green rubbed a hand over his blocky face and indicated a second keg. Travis settled himself gratefully, noting the drawn look in Dave's eyes. The endless worry was eating at him, tightening the corners of his lips, lining his forehead.

"I've heard the Kansa are keeping themselves up country. Letting the traders take the risk of traveling. Iowa, Oto, Sauk, and Fox are too powerful. The Sioux and Pawnee have taken to raiding them pretty hard."

Hartman grunted, straightening his legs. "Osages are pounding them, too. Heard tell that most of the tribes are heading inland as soon as they get the corn planted. The buffalo are gonna be running good—lessen, of course, this rain moves them out west."

"The demand for hides is increasing." Green smiled happily, pointing at his ledger. "When we get to the Big Horn, we can obtain winter hides. They're worth a sight more."

Hartman slipped his pipe from his possibles, emptied a bit of tobacco into it, and stared at it thoughtfully.

"I will light it for you," Henri said, rising. "You 'ave come far enough today, yes?"

"Hit her plumb center. Many thanks, Henri."

The patroon took the pipe and stepped out.

Hartman glanced up as Green sat on the other keg. "Anything happen?"

Green spread his hands. "Bank caved in yesterday. Damn near drowned the Doodle. Toussaint pulled him out. We lost a couple of hours. This morning a big drift of embarras came corkscrewing down the channel. Had a couple of raw moments, but Henri steered us right through it, slicker than eggs through a hen."

"He's a good man."

The patroon reentered, Hartman's pipe smoking.

Travis took it and puffed contentedly. "So Hamilton come close to being fish bait?"

Green arched an eyebrow as Henri crouched on his heels. "That kid might make it after all," Green admitted. "Each day he gets better at the job. He's still got that look of surefire disaster, but he hasn't collapsed yet."

"It'd help if'n he had an outfit." Travis inspected the glowing bowl of his pipe. "How'n hell do ye expect him to get fit if'n he's out freezing his arse off?"

"I suppose." Green rubbed his hands together. "I've got an old leather coat in the cargo box. It's lying on the flour kegs."

"I'll give it to him." Travis took another puff. "What about Fort Atkinson? Ye given any thought to that little problem?"

Green nodded. "Think you could go in? Maybe barter for a string of horses? Let's say we drop you two days downriver from the fort; you could cut wide around the fort, rendezvous with us two days upriver?"

"I could skin that cat." Travis paused. "Hamilton might cause trouble. Might see that fort as the answer to all his prayers. Reckon it wouldn't do fer him ter jump ship. Whatever officer's in charge might listen to his story."

Green took a deep breath. "He could put a stop to us right quick. It's a wonder he hasn't made a break yet."

"Yep, wal, he's a bit a-feared of the country. Yankee's sure some bear's gonna eat his lights. 'Course, it might do the pilgrim good ter see a sight of country. Maybe so I'll take him with me. If'n he's packing whiskey, he sure ain't a gonna be telling no tales to soldiers."

Green frowned, then met Travis's gaze. "If you get in a

scrape, he'd be more hinder than help. Another thing you'd have to keep your eye on.''

Travis shrugged.

''Oh, hell,'' Green relented. ''Take him. Good riddance. I won't have to worry about Trudeau breaking his neck.''

''Trudeau riding him?''

''No more than you'd expect. The *engagés* don't like him much. Think he's a weakling puke. Not worth the wad in a shotgun.''

''But old Toussaint pulled him out'n the river?''

''Toussaint's a curious sort.''

''That he be. If'n he warn't so moody, I'd set him in charge of the *engagés*. Catch him in the wrong mood, and he might try me. Trudeau, now, he knows he ain't up ter my kind of trouble.''

''Not many men are, Travis.'' Green sighed. ''Lord knows, just having you aboard has saved us a heap of trouble as it is.''

Travis puffed his pipe cold, knocking the dottle onto the wet floor, and stood. ''All right, I'll go find Dick a coat. How's them boots of his?''

''About to fall apart.''

''Reckon I'll fetch him a pair of moccasins at Fort Atkinson. Won't hurt him to get used ter good footwear. 'Sides, an *engagé*'s like a hoss. Can't pull fer shit when they's lame.''

''You're too kind to that skinny kid. You just wait, Travis, he'll pay you back with an empty bedroll some morning.''

Travis nodded, dropped his pipe in his possibles, and stepped out into the rain. He squished through the wet grass to the plank and stepped aboard the *Maria*. Overhead, thunder rolled across the prairie.

The cargo box was darker than Satan's pit, but feeling around, Travis found the coat where Green had said it would be. He stepped out into the night and trotted down the plank in search of the Doodle. Hamilton huddled under the shelter of a sagging blanket that he'd rigged between two cottonwood saplings.

"Hyar, pilgrim! What in Hob's name have ye got this done up like a sunshade fer?"

"Travis?" Richard blinked awake, shivering. Water had collected in the sagging blanket to drip with a maddening plop, plop on his back.

"Yankees don't know shit. I ever tell ye that? Who'n Hob's name ever told ye ter build a shelter like this?"

"Why . . . er, no one."

" 'Tis a wonder yer not dead of the consumption. Hyar, now. Put this on."

Richard took the coat, running cold fingers over the leather. "For me?"

"No, fer yer brother Jack. Reckon yer not worth spit to us dead, boy. Now, put that coat on, and run out an' fetch a stick. Aboot as tall as yer leg. Then I'll show ye how ter tie up a shelter so's the water slicks off'n the back. By then, them lard eaters otta have that buck cut up."

Richard shrugged into the coat, gave Travis a rabbity look, and scrambled for the trees.

Travis crawled into the shelter, lifting the blanket to hear the water gushing down the backside. What drained off ran right into the hollow where Hamilton had laid his bedding.

Travis stared at the water-soaked blankets. "Ah, hell, I'd rather try teaching a preacher ter sin."

The fire didn't burn well. Most of its heat went into drying the wood before it had a chance to cook the skewered jackrabbit. The meat would be smoked rather than roasted.

Heals Like A Willow poked at the rabbit, then looked over at Packrat, huddled in his blanket. Rain leaked down through the limbs they'd laid tipi-fashion against the trunk of the big cottonwood tree that bore the storm's brunt.

She'd tied a blanket as a skirt around the leaning branches and it provided some protection from the rain, as well as helped to hold what heat there was. Water traced patterns on the gray-white bark that still clung to the wood. Drips fell on them, but not nearly so many as would have done without the primitive shelter. Some protection was better than none at all.

She picked up another wet stick, broke it, and pulled the fibrous bark away before setting it on the struggling flames.

"Tell me." She looked at Packrat, using signs to fill the gaps in her Pawnee words. "Giving me to this father you dislike. How does it help you?"

He watched her for a moment, eyes dark and resentful. Finally he told her: "Half Man shamed my mother. Got her drunk on the *La-chi-kut's* whiskey. He coupled with her without her permission, or the permission of her husband. Then, when she was with child, he would not claim me. I would be justified to kill him. No one would say that it was wrong, but no one would say it was right, either. Such a murder would bring suspicion and people would look at me, and wonder."

Packrat reached out, tested the rabbit, and sighed before leaning back. "There was a better way, a way to shame Half Man in a clever manner. A way with honor for myself in the eyes of the Pawnee. I would capture a woman, and give her to Half Man. A woman given for a woman taken. Then I would renounce him in council. To the people, such an action would show that I am a great man, worthy of respect. Not just a killer."

"But your father would get me. A slave."

"He is not my father. He is only the man who sired me. But that is the point. Such an action would shame Half Man. To repay perfidy with a gift is a greater insult than murder. When Half Man showed up, people would laugh at him, mock him. No one would invite Half Man to share his fire. He would be unwelcome."

He leaned forward, gesturing. "Pawnee are not like other people. We don't like trouble among us. People look up to a man who can solve his problems without creating trouble. A wrong must be righted, but in a way that brings honor and respect, not suspicion. Suspicion breeds trouble. No one would say, 'Packrat killed the man who made him.' "

Packrat leaned back. "I would gain a great deal of respect. A man who repays injustice in such a clever way would be listened to in councils. My mother's disgrace would be wiped out. All the shame she has borne would be heaped upon Half Man.''

Willow crossed her arms, staring at the smoldering coals. "So you will give away my life for yours?"

"You are not a real person. Just some Snake woman from beyond the mountains.''

"I see myself as a very real person. So did my—"

"What you see doesn't matter. You are not Pawnee. I am going to find Half Man, give you to him, and ride off. You've caused me more than enough trouble as it is. What should have been talked about for generations will only be mentioned in passing.''

She arched an eyebrow. "From what you tell me, I have repaid you in a very Pawnee way.''

"Tell me," he hissed, "do you lie with Snake men when you are bleeding? Is that why your people are so weak? Do you pollute your own men with woman's blood?''

Memories of the menstrual lodge in her head, she said, "Of course not.''

"Just me, is that it?" He reached to his side, running his fingers over the handle of his war club.

"Do you take just any woman without her permission? Or, are you your father's son?''

He stiffened, face going hot. "You are *not* Pawnee! You are a slave! A slave is nothing more than a dog!''

Easy! The wrong word would incite him enough to kill her. "If a dog bit you, you'd kill it, wouldn't you?"

"Yes!"

"Then kill me now. That's what I'm trying to get you to do.''

"And leave me polluted, without the means to repay Half Man for what he did?" Packrat sank back, fingers still on the war club. "You are indeed crafty, woman. You think you can goad me, make me do what I don't want to. No, the best way to settle this thing between us is for me to give you to Half Man. I will have to steal some horses, steal some things from the Osage, or the Kansa, to pay for a cleansing. For the rest of my life, however, I shall dream of *you* . . . and *him,* together, under the robes. And when I do, when I think of your cries, I shall smile. You can't work more of your weasel ways on me.''

''So, we go to the *La-chi-kut* fort on the river. And then what?''

''I will give you to Half Man. That is all. Then I shall ride away and hope I can do what I must, despite having the Spirit World turn away from me.''

She smiled inside. *Yes, brood on the loss of your spirit helpers. The more dejected you become, the weaker you will be when my time comes.*

Willow plucked the rabbit from the fire and twisted off a back leg. The stringy meat steamed in the damp air and filled her nostrils with its aroma. Packrat seemed oblivious, drowning in his bad luck.

She finished the back leg, and used a thumb to peel the heavy back muscles from the spine. She chewed thoughtfully, then asked, ''How many days to the *La-chi-kut* fort?''

''Four, maybe five,'' he told her sullenly, then realized that she was eating. He leaned across the fire, ripped the rabbit out of her hand, and attacked the carcass like a starved dog.

Four days, maybe five. And in that time, I must find a way to escape. She placed another smoldering stick on the fire. Until the right moment came, she would continue to slowly grind away his self-confidence. *You are not as smart as you think you are, Packrat.*

A drop of water splattered into the hot coals with a hiss.

The military post now called Fort Atkinson had had plenty of names, and been located in two places. Travis had seen both. The first name had been Camp Missouri, located about a mile north of the present location on the Council Bluffs. The army changed the name to Cantonment Missouri and expanded the post, then, with their usual wilderness prescience, had watched their fledgling fort wash away in the spring flood. After the engineers had relocated to the top of the bluff, the place was known as Cantonment Council

Bluffs, and then, finally, Fort Atkinson, named after the commanding officer who was even now upriver pacifying the tribes for Dave Green's benefit.

Or so Travis sincerely hoped. Fort Atkinson, perched on its bluff, was little more than could be expected for the American military's most distant outpost beyond the frontier. The fort had been laid out in a square, the buildings constructed of log, rock, and clay plaster. From its location more than one hundred and fifty feet above the river, it dominated the Missouri, and theoretically could sink anything that tried to sneak contraband upstream without the proper licenses.

The latter theory had always remained a point of curious conversation at the trading posts and among the fur parties. No one had ever been shot at, least of all fur hunters paddling downriver in bateaux loaded with pelts. In fact, Travis had once watched the artillerymen shoot at the river, practicing with their sights, levels, and trajectory tables. Several seconds after the squat howitzer belched gray smoke and rolled back on its carriage, a satisfying white plume spouted in the river. How close it would have been to an offending boat had, of course, remained academic. No one gave the artillery much thought, or respect, particularly after their less than sterling performance shooting up the Ree village for Leavenworth. All the shot had been too high—and the Arikara had escaped.

Suffice it to say that military or not, the traders made a stop here. This was the last toehold of the United States in the wilderness. Letters could be sent from Atkinson, messages left, and news gathered. Here, too, final supplies could be had, for the most outrageous prices, from the military contractors who maintained their own trading establishments.

Travis slogged his way through the gravelly mud, his nose twitching at the septic smell of urine, garbage, night earth, manure, and rot. He carried his rifle over his shoulder, and a pack of deer hides on his back. Rounding the corner, he nodded at a vicious-looking Pawnee who squatted against the trading-post wall.

Travis kicked some of the mud off his feet, lifted the

latch, and stepped into the smoky interior of the old Missouri Fur post. Tobacco, candle soot, and stale air added new insults to his nostrils.

The good Lord knows why it bothers me, he thought. *I reckon this child's done spent more'n one winter a-smelling smells just like this. T'aint never bothered me afore.*

"Travis Hartman!"

Travis cocked his head as he looked across the barrels and bales. A muscular black man sat lounging at a table behind the factor's bench. Travis grinned and said, "Baptiste de Bourgmont! I reckoned ye'd be dead afore now. Most likely the Ree would'a lifted yer topknot."

"Figgered they'd a lifted yers," Baptiste replied, then he smiled. The Negro wore a long, fawn-colored leather jacket that dangled waves of carefully cut fringe. His canvas pants were tucked into tall moccasins dyed maroon and decorated with tin bells, beadwork, and silver conchos. The broad black belt snugged around his hips held knife, pistol, bullet pouch, and pipe bag.

Baptiste was tapping an empty tin cup on the table with the tip of a knife blade. The charcoal black of his skin contrasted with the bright white of his teeth. Like thick wool, his kinky black hair had been pulled back into a severe ponytail.

"What brings you to Atkinson, old coon?"

"Same's always." Travis stepped behind the counter and threaded past barrels and tins, leaned the Hawken rifle against the wall, and unslung the tightly rolled deer hides from his back. Baptiste stood, then wrapped his arms around Travis in a bear hug, pounding him on the back. "It shore is good to see you, coon!"

Travis pushed him back, slapped him on the back, and used a toe to snag out the bench opposite Baptiste's table. "Yer looking fit. Chopped off any heads of late?"

Baptiste shook his head as he sat down again. "Lord God, Travis. I forgit just how ugly you are. I reckon as I always had the idea that time would make yor face look more like a man's."

"I could take my knife, whittle a bit on yers. Ye'd be

surprised how them squaws take ter a man with a face like mine. Figger I'm chockful of medicine.''

Baptiste chuckled and studied his knife. ''You'd make my face look like my back, eh? The last man to scar me lies dead in a grave in Louisiana.'' He glanced up. ''But I think I'd have my hands full killing you.''

''Didn't do so well last time ye tried down ter Natchez— but I reckon we'd make a scrape of her, all right.'' Travis wiped his nose. ''What's news?''

''Not much. Everyone is waiting to hear what Atkinson and O'Fallon accomplish upriver. Otoes, Omaha, and Sioux been picking on each other. The usual. Prices fo' plews are going up. People wonder if Ashley has fallen off the face of the earth.''

''That would be some, it would. That Ashley, he's a canny old beaver if ever there was one. Maybe craftier than Manuel Lisa.''

Baptiste shrugged. ''Yor with Pilcher again this season?''

''Nope. Just roaming. Seeing whar my stick floats. Come up from Saint Loowee. Travel's a mess. These rains played hell.''

Baptiste's eyes narrowed. ''Uh-huh.''

''You hunting for the fort?''

''Among other things. Like so many, I wait to see if the army can open the river. It'll take a heap big show to undo the damage Leavenworth did to the trade.''

''Atkinson ain't Leavenworth.''

''The gov'ment sent a new agent upriver. Fella name of Peter Wilson. Gov'ment thinks it's going to try and make treaties with the Kansas, Pawnee, Oto, and Ioway.''

''Won't hold. Never does.''

''Nope. Reckon not.'' Baptiste cocked his head. ''You're up to yor neck in something. I can sense it . . . like a wolf around a weak buffalo.''

''This child don't know nothing. If'n I did, I reckon I'd be plumb fat and sassy, sitting in Saint Loowee in a big house, with a fat woman tending my needs.''

Baptiste leaned forward. ''You? Don't feed me no poor dogmeat and tell me she be fat buffler, Travis. Not after what you and me been through.''

"Ye never was much a one fer fancy palaver."

"They beat it out of me when I's a slave."

Travis glanced around. "Whar's the factor?"

"Probably asleep." Baptiste looked around the packed storehouse. His eyes rested on a keg of beads. "They's little trade now. Most of the tribes are planting, or out fo' spring buffalo."

Travis kicked the roll of deer hides. "Thar's eleven green deer hides. Spring stuff with their hair slipping. Reckon that'd fetch me an outfit?"

"Such as?"

"Good pair of moccasins, set of good britches, a heavy shirt. Maybe a knife."

"I reckon. Yor particular about the moccasins? Want any tribe?"

"Got Crow?"

Baptiste studied him with half-closed eyes. "Mountain moccasins."

"They got ter have heavy soles. Made outta bull buffalo. Reckon yer figgering whar my stick floats."

"I think they gots a pair. Your size?"

"Smaller."

"A woman's?"

"Not that small. Let's say, wal, about the size of yer foot thar, maybe a tad smaller, but not much."

"Mountain moccasins, not fo' a woman but fo' a medium-size man. They got a pair in the storeroom. Good Crow work. And you expect such fo' green spring deer hides?"

"Reckon so." Travis grinned. "Maybe fer the time I kept the Sioux from lifting that curly black hair of yern."

Baptiste gave Travis a crooked smile. "Or fo' the days on the river, or the time in Louisiana when I hid in the tree. Or the time you got me that job. Or the time—"

"Reckon I'd be right obliged if'n ye didn't go a-palavering all about the fort with yer ideas, coon. Reckon maybe ye seed me, done some swapping, and old Travis Hartman just up and left."

"I reckon that might happen."

"Waugh!" Travis took Baptiste's hand and shook. He glanced around, and then added, "Reckon a boat'll arrive a couple of days from now. Dave Green's hauling supplies for Pilcher. Carrying them upriver. Pilcher's business, understand?''

Baptiste's interest visibly sharpened.

"Now, I reckon this hyar's just atwixt the two of us. Don't need to be nothing said.''

Baptiste fingered his chin, thinking. "I work fo' the Company. Not many people would ask me what yor asking.''

Travis shrugged.

Baptiste grinned then. "But then, yor not just anybody.''

"Thanks, friend. Reckon I'll owe ye one.''

Baptiste shook his head. "No. You took a big chance fo' a runaway slave. They'd a hung this nigger. Fed my carcass to the dogs as a lesson to the others. If'n they caught us, they'd a hung you, too. Baptiste don't forget.''

"That's some, it is.'' Travis chuckled. "Saw something in ye, I did. Figgered ye was worth the risk.''

"Perhaps they gonna hang you this time if they catches you? And maybe Green?''

Travis studied the tip of his thumb as if he'd just found something fascinating there. "Wal, ye knows Davey and me. Just hauling a load upriver fer Pilcher. But ye wouldn't know whar a feller might hire a string of hosses, do ye? Say seven or eight? Maybe fer a week?''

Baptiste pursed his lips. "They'd be questions. But . . .'' His eyes narrowed. "No, wait. There's this Pawnee. Half Man. Last I seed, he was hanging around out front. He has hosses. No questions—but a passel of trouble.''

"Half Man? Reckon I heard of him. Runs whiskey, hosses, and plews back and forth atwixt the Pawnee and the Omaha? Likes to play heap big man with the chiefs?''

"That's him. Now, let's say a man wanted to sneak whiskey past the army inspection. He'd help. And he'd kill you fust time you turned yor back on him.''

Travis frowned, remembering the mean Pawnee leaning against the logs. "Thar's times a coon's got ter take a chance.''

Baptiste reached out, powerful hand grasping Travis's shoulder. "Watch yor back, coon. If'n ye don't, yor gone beaver.''

SIXTEEN

For in absolute freedom there was no reciprocal interaction either between an external world and consciousness, which is absorbed in the manifold existence, or sets itself determinate purposes and ideas, or between consciousness and an external objective world, be it a world of reality or thought. What that freedom encompassed was the world totally in the form of consciousness, as a universal will, and along with that, self-consciousness gathered out of all the dispersions and manifoldness of existence, or all the manifold ends and judgments of mind concentrated into the naked and simple self.

—Georg Friedrich Wilhelm Hegel,
Phenomenology of Mind

Fort Atkinson. The name had mingled itself with Richard's dreams to become the promised land, and the Platte his River Jordan. He splashed through the shallows, slipping in mud, back breaking. Despite the cool day, sweat trickled down his face to sting his eyes and drip from his nose. The endless weight of the cordelle lay like the great earth on Atlas's shoulders.

"*Sacré!* Careful!" the cry came. "Hold on! Don't let it slip!"

Behind them, coursing like a huge fish on a line, the *Maria* curved out from the shore, driven along the arc of the cordelle line by laboring polers as the boat passed wide of the sandbar she'd grounded on earlier that day.

What a Herculean labor that had been, to free her. Now she had to swing wide around the sandbar at the mouth of the Platte—that or drop back downriver, cross to the far bank, and recross once the boat had passed the Platte.

Dear Lord God, all they did was pole and cordelle. Didn't the wind ever blow from the south in this wretched land?

A signal came from the patroon.

"Go!" Trudeau cried. "Run! No slack in the cordelle, or she slip right back on the sand!"

They stumbled forward, sloshing through the shallows, scrambling for footing in the quicksand. Breath rasped in Richard's throat.

At the end of the cordelle, the mast bent under the stress. But *Maria* held her place. Brown water curled white at her bow, and the grunts of the polers could be heard as they braced their bare feet and leaned into their poles.

The mouth of the Platte was a terrible place, shoaled with sandbars, dotted with small islands of willow, for the Platte spilled into the Missouri in interwoven ribbons of water. But beyond the Platte, up there where the bluffs rose above the tree line, lay Fort Atkinson. There lay all of Richard's hopes for escape.

He'd never paid the slightest attention to men in uniform. The only interest he'd had was a philosopher's: lofty and abstract. The military, as Hegel had noted, was for the protection and furthering of the state's interest *vis-à-vis* other states. The pomp, pretty dress, and regulations had appeared rather ridiculous. Those officers he'd met had been possessed of an arrogance unbecoming their lack of either the education or ability to discuss complicated subjects. Philosophy, for instance.

Richard now chafed to see a soldier; the first uniform would mean deliverance from his living nightmare.

I'll throw myself at the first brightly dressed mannequin, clasp his knees, and plead that he take me to his commanding officer.

That would work, wouldn't it? Or could Green come up with a reasonable explanation for his *engagé*'s odd behavior? Claim he was crazy, driven mad by fever, or maybe drunk.

No. I'll hit him. Ball my fist, and whack him right in the face. They'll have to arrest me. No amount of Green's excuses will keep them from dragging me away. Then, at the inquiry, I'll tell my story.

That was it. Foolproof.

Green would try and keep him on the boat, of course; but Richard had heard the talk. The army searched all of the boats, turned them inside out looking for whiskey. It was against the law to trade whiskey to the Indians, and—in addition to the kegs allotted for crew ration—*Maria* was chockful of curious triangular tins of the stuff. Way more than the half-gill per man per day allowed by law.

This time you won't stop me, Mr. Green. Once I hit that soldier, I'm free!

And then? Well, no matter what he thought about the men in the army, the system was rational. A man didn't become an officer without some sense and training that set him above his comrades. When Richard told his tale to the commander, they'd drop charges. He'd be placed on the first boat back to Saint Louis. From there, he could find the means to buy passage back to Boston.

I'm coming, Laura. You'll see. It won't be long now and I'll be knocking on your door.

Boston! In defiance of his weary labor, he smiled dreamily. He could hear his boot heels striking the cobblestones as he and Laura walked down Washington Street. Her arm was tucked tightly in his. He touched his felt hat, tipping it to each passer-by, no matter how lowly. A silk cloak was swirling around his shoulders as he looked up at the familiar buildings. Just for good measure, he studied their reflection in the windows of a tobacconist, and straightened his cravat. Laura looked dashing in her long velveteen dress with a ribbon bow at the waist. The royal blue set off her long blond hair with its gathered ringlets.

Home. Boston. The cultured tones of intelligent people like music on his ears. *I will be a gentleman again.*

"*Merde!*" Trudeau shouted. "Pull, you women! She is backing water!"

Richard threw himself against the cordelle, just one more grunting animal in a line of beasts. Tendons burning in his hands, he tightened his grip on the unforgiving hemp. *Heave! Heave! Come on, damn it!*

Maria skated forward, rounding the head of the sandbar. To avoid an abatis of wicked snags that thrust up from the water like the splintered ribs of a water monster, Henri leaned on the steering oar, sending her in toward shore.

"Too much slack! Hurry! *Run!*" Trudeau cried, and they scampered forward like trained rats, churning muddy water with booted feet. They raced to take up the slack, diving into the willows on the Platte's north bank, clutching the slippery stems with one hand as they manhandled the heavy rope with the other.

Richard panted and gasped, humping forward under the swaying cordelle. Ragged breath sawed at his throat. Every muscle in his legs and back cramped and ached. Off balance, the cordelle pulled him sideways through the willows. With the last of his strength, he caught himself before falling. Springy stems tangled his feet so that he crashed forward instead of stepped. He fixed his attention on Toussaint's broad back. Whiplike branches slapped at him, smacking wetly.

Pull! Come on, Richard. Each step is closer to Fort Atkinson. Each step is closer to Boston. Boston . . . Boston. . . .

"We 'ave her!" Trudeau called from ahead. "We've crossed the Platte!"

Their screams and shouts sounded more like an Indian massacre than a celebration. Someone began singing *"A La Claire Fontaine,"* and Richard joined in between pants for breath. He didn't sing at first, not really, just hummed along.

They beat their way through the willows, cutting back toward the river through muck that sucked at their feet. Mosquitoes hummed up in clouds as they waded. Brain-numb, the *engagés* slogged their way out of the marsh like weary beads on the cordelle's string.

Richard, along with Toussaint and Robert, bellowed and roared as they dragged the thick wet cordelle through the marsh, crushing the long green leaves of cattails and flattening the round tubes of bulrush.

They could see the river here. *Maria* bobbed at the end of the cordelle, cutting water.

"Hand-over-hand!" Trudeau called, and like triumphant fishermen, they reeled in their prize.

Richard grinned happily. Let the *engagés* have their *"Fontaine,"* his reward would be Boston. A summer eve's stroll around the Commons, just to enjoy the yellow squares of candlelit windowpanes.

Distant thunder rolled down from the plains to the west, and far off over the eastern bank, lightning flickered in the clouds.

"We've crossed the Platte!" *Engagés* pounded each other on the back, capered and jeered, whooping and leaping, taking turns as they pulled the *Maria* in and coiled the cordelle into a big black ring.

Richard watched the keelboat ride in across the choppy brown water. Normally ungainly, she moved with a grace he'd never seen before. Almost beautiful.

"Whiskey!" Green cried, coming to stand on the deck. "A good day's work, lads!"

Men jumped, shrieked, and waved their red wool hats.

Richard looked down at his hands as the *Maria*'s hull whispered on the bank. The palms were caked with wet sand and grime, the skin reddened and callused.

His once white shirt hung in tatters about his shoulders. The duck brown pants—the envy of Boston gentlemen— were tied on with rope. Gaps hung in what had been the knees. The heel was missing from his right boot—and that was the good one. The upper had come loose from the sole of his left; the nails had rusted out, and the leather was rotten and torn.

He slapped at a mosquito and waded out into the river, washing the worst of the grime from his face and hands. He was the last to have a tin of whiskey handed down. He stared at it, fond memories in his mind of fine brandies, aromatic bourbons, sweet sherries. He could taste them, smooth, rich, and flavorful on the tongue. But that . . . that was Boston.

The clear liquid in the cup revealed sand floating in the bottom of the tin. A glob of fat, probably from last night's supper, clung to the rim. Nevertheless, he gulped the grain alcohol straight down, winced, and tried not to cough. The draught snaked fire all the way to his gut.

Stooping, he scooped up the muddy riverwater, and drank down all that his thirsting body could hold. The full flavor of the river no longer annoyed him; neither did the grit that stuck in his teeth.

"Line out, lads!" Green called. "We've an hour yet to reach a decent camp, but when we get there, double rations for all!"

Richard tossed his cup up on deck, combed his matted hair with his fingers, and waded back onto the beach. The cordelle had been coiled cunningly so the end could be unspooled from the inside out.

Richard took his place behind Toussaint, and shouldered the heavy rope. *Across the Platte. But this time, I'm going home. Each step is one closer to freedom.*

Without further incident, they brought the *Maria* into the camp Green had insisted that they reach. True to his word, the rations were doubled, and more whiskey was given out.

Richard strung up his shelter the way Travis had taught him, collapsed inside, and fell asleep to the humming of mosquitoes around his blanket-covered ears.

The dreams were so pristine and clear: Boston, gleaming in the morning sun as he and Laura ate their breakfast before an open window. She was laughing at one of his stories as she sipped tea from a delicate china cup.

"Oh, Richard," she said softly, her other hand reaching for his. "You've made me so happy. . . ."

"Hyar! Dick! C'mon, coon. Git yer kit together," Travis's rasping voice intruded. "*Leve!* Dick, we ain't got all day."

"Huh?" Richard shifted, pulled his blanket back, and peered out into pitch blackness. "Laura? I mean . . . Travis?"

"I ain't no Laura, coon. Best rustle, now. Got breakfast cooking. Tend ter yer needs and roll up yer outfit. I'll be over to the fire."

Richard rubbed his head, splinters of the dream clinging to him, fading . . . fading. . . . Well, so be it. By sunset, they should be within sight of Fort Atkinson.

He climbed to his feet and fumbled with the ties. He rolled his blanket carefully and wandered over to the fire. Hartman squatted over the low coals, his horrible face illuminated by the red glow. The scars made him look like something straight out of Hell.

"It's the middle of the night, Travis!"

"Be coming on light soon, Dick. Hyar, I done boilt up some coffee. Side pork's cooked and pone's crackling in the grease. Figgered I'd dip into stores fer the occasion. Dig in and eat up." Travis glanced curiously at Richard. "They didn't shave ye? Didn't pull no funning on ye?"

"Funning?"

"Pranks. Fer making passage past the Platte. Reckon it's like when sailors cross the equator. Means ye ain't a pilgrim no more."

"I'm not?"

"Hell, no. 'Course, given yer queer ways, ye'll be damn Yankee Doodle till ye dies. Some things cain't be overcome through travel, no matter how much a feller could wish."

"I didn't see any pranks, Travis. Unless you getting me up when I ought to be sleeping is one."

Hartman seemed to be thinking. "I reckon it's 'cause they's all been upriver. Every last man of 'em. Reckon, too, that yer not one of 'em. Yer no *engagé*. To their eyes, yer more like a tick. A . . . what do they call 'em? Partsite?"

"The word is parasite."

"If'n ye says so."

"Listen, Travis, I didn't want to be here in the first place. If you didn't wake me up as a prank, I'm going to go right back to sleep. It's a long pull into Fort Atkinson tomorrow."

"Who's Laura?"

"Nobody. Just a dream. That's all."

"Uh-huh. Drink yer coffee, Dick. Then eat yer fill. Soon's ye finish, I'll be needing ye ter give me a hand with the whiskey tins."

"Whiskey tins?"

"Wal, coon, it's like this. Cain't take whiskey upriver. It's agin' the law. 'Course the Injun trade works on whiskey. No whiskey, no trade. Now, Green don't want no more questions asked than need be when he reaches the fort. He'll have just enough over the limit on board to look normal, whilst the two of us packs the whiskey out around the fort.''

''That many cases? On our backs?''

Travis looked up with mild irritation. ''Tarnal Hell, Dick. I done fetched hosses, and a sneaking Pawnee ter go with 'em.''

''An Indian?''

Hartman handed him a cup of coffee. ''Ye fixing ter repeat every word I says?''

Richard dropped to his haunches and stared into the coals. He sipped the hot coffee, and glanced sideways at Hartman. This wasn't the watery brew the boatmen got on special occasions, but thick and black. Real coffee.

''Now, pay special attention, hoss,'' Travis said in a low voice. ''This Pawnee—Half Man. Don't trust him, hear? Don't never turn yer back on him. Yer a gonna have ter be cat-quick, and watchful as a hawk. If'n ye see him do anything odd, tell me, right fast.''

''If you don't trust him, why travel with him?''

'' 'Cause he's got hosses. I need hosses ter pack the whiskey. Now, I'd rather borrow 'em from Colonel Atkinson, but he's upriver. Reckon the only other choice is ter take my chances with Half Man, and hope I can keep the red devil buffler'd. Now, eat.''

Richard needed no second invitation, but stuffed himself with the hot venison and corn meal. These days he shoveled his meals into his belly, constantly looking for more.

''Yer full?'' Hartman asked, throwing out the grounds in the bottom of his cup. ''Wal, come on. Let's unpack them tins.''

Birds were singing by the time they carried the last of the heavy tins into the dawn-grayed trees beyond the camp. The musty smell of the river lay heavy on the damp air. Trees, like humped monsters, made a black silhouette against the glowing eastern horizon. A line of horses—scrubby-looking ponies for the most part—stood at their picket.

''That's the Pawnee,'' Travis said, pointing at a dark form rolled in a blanket. ''Reckon the coon's getting all the sleep he can. All right, Yankee, come watch me. This hyar be how ye packs a hoss. Ye ever packed afore?''

"No."

"Wal, watch then."

One by one they lashed the heavy tins onto the horses, and Richard suddenly understood why they were triangular—just right to be lashed to a horse with a complicated knot Hartman called a diamond hitch.

"And thar she be," Travis concluded as the last animal was loaded. "Whoa, there, hoss. Easy now. Dick, take up that slack on the rope. That's it. Now, bend down and look at that lash cinch. Setting pert, is it?"

"Looks so."

"Wal, then, I reckon I'll go kick that lazy Pawnee awake." Hartman half turned. "Huh, almost fergot." He pointed to a roll of tan hide. "Best put them on, Dick, whilst I roust out this hyar mangy half-breed. We got tracks ter make."

Richard bent over the roll, pulling out a pair of beautiful white leather moccasins, a heavy cloth shirt, and fringed leather pants. He cast an uncertain glance at Hartman, who was crouched several feet away from the Pawnee, talking in a strange tongue and gesturing with his hands.

How did they tan leather to be this soft? Richard stripped and slid into the pants, then pulled on the moccasins after stopping to feel the hard, thick soles. The shirt fit loosely, but how wonderful to wear something that didn't have a hole in it.

Travis walked up, rifle in hand. "Pawnee's up. Let's get a move on."

"Just a moment. I need to take my old clothes back to the boat."

"Reckon not. Wrap 'em up and tie 'em with a thong. A feller can always use rags."

"I . . . I'll pay you back, Travis. For the clothes, I mean."

"Fergit it, lad. It's on the jawbone."

"Travis?"

"What now?"

"You and I, we won't be going by the fort, will we?"

Travis stared around, as if to see if he'd forgotten anything. "Reckon not."

The deep sinking sensation hollowed Richard's gut. "Damn you. Damn you all."

Hartman's gaze went winter-hard. "Pay attention ter the Pawnee, Dick."

"Why? Maybe I'll help him steal your whiskey. That's what you're afraid of, isn't it?"

"Yep. 'Course, ye need ter be mindful, Dick. Ter lift our whiskey, he's gotta kill me first. Then, after he lifts my hair, he'll be fixing to lift yers, too."

"*Kill* us?"

"Reckon so. Keep your eyes open."

Heals Like A Willow sat stiffly on her horse, her blanket over her head for protection. A low bank of gray clouds sprinkled her and Packrat with a gentle spring rain. They trotted down a trail, winding through a copse of trees.

After two months of hard riding, she'd grown somewhat fond of the mare. After all, it wasn't the animal's fault that she'd been captured. The stolid pony had carried her resolutely across desert, plain, and prairie.

Willow winced and tried to shift her position. If only her hands weren't always tied; but then, after two moons of practice, she'd learned to do a great many things despite bound wrists.

Riding through the rain, they crossed hilly country covered with tall grasses and interminable patches of brush. The trees were of a kind Willow had never seen before, black-barked, with twisting branches. The wood was heavy, and burned into better coals than even sagebrush produced. And how hard it was! A digging stick made of such would last a woman all of her life.

"Here!" Packrat told her. "We are close now."

As they broke through the spring green trees, Willow gasped. There, before them, lay the *La-chi-kuts'* fort. She'd never seen the like of it. The White men had built their soldier village in a square—and such lodges, like giant baskets made of logs. And slanting roofs! A strong man couldn't shoot an arrow across the place in three shots!

She rode in silence, trying to comprehend what her eyes saw, remembering White Hail's claim that the White men were magical. Perhaps they were.

As they rode up to a big lodge, she saw her first White men. She could only stare as Packrat jumped off his horse. He bent down to hobble her animal, ordering, "Stay where you are. Do not leave your horse, or the *La-chi-kut* will catch you. They do terrible things to women."

She waited until Packrat had stepped inside the log lodge, swallowed hard to nerve herself, and carefully slipped off her horse. The White men were watching, their weird pale eyes gleaming, but no one shouted a warning, or even took a step in her direction. She hadn't made three steps when Packrat emerged from the black doorway and came flying after her.

He bellowed in rage, leaping to tackle her and slam her into the ground. "I told you!"

"What do you expect?" she hissed back.

"Get up! Get up, or I will beat you."

Laughter made her look up. More White men had gathered at the door of the log lodge. Packrat noticed, and colored. He cuffed her hard on the side of the head, to regain some of his shattered honor.

Willow stood with reluctance, and allowed Packrat to lead her back to her horse.

"Where is Half Man?" she asked.

"Not here," Packrat growled angrily. "Gone. Working for a *La-chi-kut*. Now we have to find him."

Willow leapt, caught the mane of her horse, and kicked onto its back. She stared down into Packrat's burning eyes. Hatred sparkled there, fueled by frustration. He blamed his bad luck on her, on her polluting woman's blood.

"Whoa!" came a cry.

Willow turned her head to see a *La-chi-kut* step out of the opening of the log lodge. Her breath caught. He had hair the color of the sun on winter grass. And such eyes! Blue, like a clear sky. By Wolf, the stories were true! His skin was as pale as hide bleached with white clay. And, yes, hair grew on his face! A dog face, like the stories said.

Packrat turned, watching the *La-chi-kut* warily.

"Your woman?" the *La-chi-kut* asked in crude Pawnee.

"My captive," Packrat replied cautiously.

The *La-chi-kut* studied Willow with calculating eyes. "Snake?" He repeated the word, "Snake?" Then he pointed at Willow, eyes inquiring. With his hands he made the sign of her people.

Willow jerked a curt nod. Her heart had begun to pound. A *La-chi-kut*! No telling what he might do to her. Even slavery among the Pawnee would be better.

"Make trade?" the *La-chi-kut* asked Packrat.

Packrat bit his lip, glanced nervously at Willow, and shook his head.

"A rifle," the *La-chi-kut* said.

Packrat shook his head.

"Two rifles."

Packrat's face betrayed a man in pain. In desperation, he signed, "The woman is not for trade. It is finished." Resolutely, he stalked to his horse and vaulted nimbly onto the animal's back. He reined the horse around, and gathered up the lead rope for Willow's beast.

Laughter broke out again as Willow's horse hopped, the hobbles forgotten in Packrat's hurry.

She'd never seen him so, the facial veins standing out as he slid down, soothed her mare, and worked the hobbles loose. The hoots and jeers might have been cactus thorns the way they stung him.

This time, they left at a run, Willow clinging to her mount, wind whipping at her, tearing her blanket from her shoulders. So desperate was the pace that she couldn't reach back for it, but had to let it vanish in the grass behind them.

They bolted across the flats, and up through the trees, before Packrat slowed, shoulders slumped, head drooping. From the heights, Willow could see the mighty Missouri River loop around to the south to meet the line of trees marking the confluence of the Flat River, and the route that would take her back west to her people. To the north, the big Missouri wound its way into the distance, water like a silver thread in the green land.

"Where is Half Man?" she asked, aware that any words might incite Packrat to violence.

"Somewhere. He said he would be back in four days, with whiskey to trade for guns, powder, and shot. He told them that then he would go back to the Pawnee. A rich man."

"I am sorry I ran. The *La-chi-kuts* frightened me."

Packrat glanced up, eyes smoldering. He sidestepped his horse close. Gripping the head of his war club, he cracked her on the side of the head with the handle.

She cried out in pain. Her mare shied at the sound and Willow's flinch.

"Next time, I use the head of the club, Weasel Woman. I won't kill you, but I will hurt you so badly that you will never be right again. Do you understand? I am *tired* of you! You are *evil.*" Tears glistened in his eyes. "You have ruined me!"

You have ruined yourself, fool! But she only bowed her head, squinting at the sting of his blow. *No, you only started it. I have driven you to this. Goaded you, driven poison barbs into your soul. Whatever kind of man you might have been, I have broken your Power, Packrat. You will never be able to trust yourself again. In the words of the Pawnee, you will always be pira-paru.*

"This way. They said he had horses, probably to carry something for the *La-chi-kut.* We will cut for sign. Do not blind me with your magic. If you do, I will take you back. Give you to the *La-chi-kut,* and be happy to be rid of you."

Behind his tormented eyes she could see crazy violence brewing. She swallowed hard, aware that the time for threats was over. Like a man climbing rimrock, he hung by his fingers. Were she to make his grip the least bit slippery, he'd fall into the darkness that had grown in his soul, and she would suffer for it.

Late that afternoon, Packrat cried out in anticipation, "It is here! I know his sign. Look! Half Man walked here. And here you see where one *La-chi-kut* walked. And here, another, wearing new moccasins!"

She glanced at the tracks, interspersed with those of heavily loaded horses.

"Come!" Packrat cried. "I will succeed after all! And, who knows, perhaps I can take this whiskey. Wealth enough to pay for a complete cleansing by the Doctors!"

She fingered the bruise on the side of her head, and remained passive. If an opportunity was to present itself, it had better be quick. If Half Man surmised just what his son was doing to him, he might well kill her outright.

She cocked her head. *What has changed? Two moons ago, I would just as soon have died.* Deep within her soul, the will to live had been rekindled—or, perhaps, it had been smoldering all along.

SEVENTEEN

If I strip this human being, thus constituted, of all the supernatural gifts which he may have received, and of all the artificial faculties, which he could not have acquired but by slow degrees; if I consider him, in a word, such as he must have originated from the hands of nature; I see an animal not so strong as some, and less agile than others, but, upon the whole, the most advantageously organized of any: I see him sating his hunger under an oak tree, and his thirst at the first brook; I see him laying himself down to sleep at the foot of the same tree that afforded him his meal; and there are all his wants, completely provided.

—Jean-Jacques Rousseau, *Discourse on the Origin and Foundation of Inequality Among Mankind*

Richard studied the Pawnee. He didn't look like much. Skinny, dark-skinned, with a protruding belly, he wore greasy black skins, a filthy blanket, and shabby moccasins with little metal bells on the tops.

The Pawnee's face might have been cast of weathered

bronze, and looked just as unforgiving as the metal. Those eyes were black, and hard as river pebbles, the nose hooked over thin lips. Half Man looked at Richard and Travis with a natural arrogance, as if he deigned to glance upon inferiors. But when they paused for a rest, Richard caught the crafty look as he appraised the whiskey.

Now they walked, single-file, each leading a string of horses, the animals tail-hitched. The Pawnee went first, then Richard, and finally Travis bringing up the rear. Richard had noticed that neither Travis nor the Pawnee went anywhere without his rifle in hand. Each might have been hunting a tiger, so alert were they to each other's movements.

They had passed beyond the trees and now crossed lush meadows of bluestem and wildflowers of every color. In the drainages, stands of mixed oak and ash were leafed out in a brilliant green that contrasted to the plum, hazel, and raspberry bushes.

A free wind tugged at the fringes on Richard's pants, playing with the wispy beard on his cheeks. After months of not shaving, he had come to resemble all the others. It wasn't a beard like the older *engagés'*, but it was good enough for the river.

Patchy white clouds scuttled across the sky, promising more showers. But how blue the sky was beyond them, how vast the distances. Down in the river bottom, a man didn't have this sense of eternity. Something deep inside him shivered at that. How easy it would be to get lost out there, naked to the eye of God.

"Ouch!" Richard hopped sideways, causing the horse he was leading to throw its head.

"Prickly pear," Travis noted from behind. "Told ye, Dick. Watch whar ye puts yer feet. Don't stop now. Walk on it fer a while. It'll sure larn ye where ter put yer feet."

Richard whirled around, glaring. "Damn you, Travis. You knew I'd be free by now. You and Green. You plotted this! Took away my chance! I ought to . . . to . . ."

The hunter stepped up to him, a hardening glint in his eyes. "Easy, hoss. Yer not up ter taking this coon. Not by a damn sight. Now, settle down—less'n I fetch ye up good."

Sudden fear, like a cool wind, blew through Richard's hot guts. He swallowed to still the runny feeling down inside.

"Glad ter see ye got sense, Dick." Travis nodded his head toward the Pawnee. "Reckon he'd be plumb happy ter see us take a go at each other. After I kilt ye, he'd only have me to worry about."

"Killed me?" Richard glanced uneasily at the Pawnee.

"Oh, reckon not. Yer not that dangerous. I'd just have to slap ye around a bit. A feller's good sense creeps right back inta his head when he's getting whacked around and the lights start a-popping behind his eyes."

Richard rubbed the back of his neck, turned, and started off again. The Pawnee was watching him. The Indian resumed his pace, rifle in his right hand, the lead rope for the horse in his left. Along with the rifle, the Pawnee carried a tomahawk and a knife.

"What about him?" Richard asked. "Why would he just kill us? I mean, he doesn't know us."

"What's to know? We got whiskey—he wants it."

"It's not rational, Travis. Look at him. A man raised in nature. How does he get tainted by the corruption of civilization? He's free! A free man doesn't kill others. It defies any philosophical dictum I've ever read."

"Philos'phy!" Travis snorted. "Ye thinks a man needs ter be civilized ter kill? Rot and hogwash!"

"That's not what Rousseau says. And I dare say, Travis, he's a great deal more thoroughly read than you are on the subject. In his *Discourse on the Origin of Inequality,* he makes a point that primitive man—and I assume our Pawnee is exactly that—keeps his dissensions to a minimum. Without the chains of property, or belongings, to bind him, he needs not resort to violence. What need does he have to strike another, when he can avoid the first blow? An insult can be easily repaired in a primitive society. A man need not seek revenge."

Travis stopped, his head cocked, mouth open. "Of all the foolish . . . Tarnal Hell! These Injuns war with each other just ter keep in practice! Don't ye know how they counts coup? By striking an enemy. The more the better! If'n ye wants ter start a war, just walk up and strike an Injun warrior. Afore ye can take yer next breath, he's a gonna lift yer hair, slit yer throat, and open yer belly so yer guts fall out fer the dogs to eat!''

"But that doesn't make sense. Rousseau—''

"Hang Roosoo with a rawhide rope!'' Travis gestured his frustration by shaking his rifle. Then he glared—all the more terrible for the hideous scars. "Dick . . . Dick, listen. Please, now. I'm a-begging ye. That Pawnee up thar, he's a warrior, half-breed or no. They's proud people. Honor and coup mean everything to 'em. Now, ye can't go around judging them by the likes of yer Mister Roosoo, or by the Bible, or nothing else. Understand? If'n ye do, I reckon you'll be dead right quick.''

Richard studied the Pawnee, trying to read the mind behind those obsidian eyes. "That isn't rational!''

"Hell! 'Course it's rational, so long's ye looks at it through their eyes! Strength, pride, honor. Hyar's how ye deals with Injuns, Dick. Foller these rules, and God willing, ye might see next fall roll around with yer topknot on yer head. Show 'em respect. Respect is just that. Don't never be weak. Not when they can see. They value strength and bravery. Last, keep yer word, coon. Injuns is getting used to whites breaking their word, but if'n ye keeps yers, they won't fergit. Now, that means yer not ter be making promises ye cain't keep. Think on that. Right now the Sioux'll spit on a white as soon as look at him, after what Leavenworth did up ter the Ree villages. Reckon ye don't promise nothing lessen ye can back her to the hilt.''

"But how is that rational?''

"Wal, how's it rational that a man can shoot another man fer fooling with his wife? That's ter say he didn't force her. Reckon if'n she says yes, and her lover says yes, they both want to be with each other. What right's the husband got to shoot 'em? Ain't no court'll convict a husband that shoots his wife, or her lover. Is that rational?''

"That fact is, it is indeed rational. The tranquillity of the hearth—''

"Horse crap! Rees, Kansa, Pawnee, lots of people let their wives sleep with lovers. So long as she's willing, and he's willing, thar ain't no upscuttle. They got rules, Dick.

Just like we do. By their rules, if'n ye acts with honor, shows respect, and ain't weak, yer a gonna do all right. But ye've got ter use yer noodle.'' Travis hawked and spit. ''Hell, I git along a heap better with Injuns than I ever did with white men. And Injuns comes in all kinds.''

''So, Rousseau is right? The savages are carefree in love, unlike civilized man, whose passions lead him to entanglements. Savages make love, then part. Satisfied to allow anyone to mate with whomever they choose?''

Travis screwed his ruined face into a disgusted look. ''Wal, among the Rees, maybe. But I'll tell ye, child. Don't ye never go fooling around with a Cheyenne woman, lessen ye wants ter marry her! They's worse than white men. Drive yer pizzle inta one of their young women, and her folks is gonna kill ye dead. But most peoples out hyar, they figger a man laying with a woman is plumb natural.''

A huge rabbit, bigger than any Richard had ever seen, broke cover and went bounding and sailing over the grass. ''What's that?''

''Jackrabbit,'' Travis said.

''How come they don't get cactus thorns in their feet?'' The burning spine still made Richard hobble, but after the altercation with Travis, he'd be damned if he'd stop to dig it out.

''They ain't got feet, exactly. Just gobs of hair between their toes. Turns the cactus, I guess.''

''So these women lie with anyone they and their husbands agree on. What about the bastard children?''

''Bastards? Hell, that's another way I don't cotton ter white ways. A child's a child. Given the number that dies young, who's to say? Injuns generally welcome a kid— lessen it comes from another tribe. Take that Pawnee, yonder—Half Man. Half Pawnee, half Omaha. He slips back and forth atwixt and atween. Home in both places—trusted by none. Talk among the Pawnee is that his mother'd have been better off to leave him out in the winter, let him die since he was planted by an Omaha when Half Man's mother was a slave.''

''Slave?''

Travis squinted at Half Man walking several paces ahead

of them. The Pawnee seemed oblivious to them, as if he were just out for a morning walk. "Reckon so. Most tribes out hyar, they takes slaves right regular. Used to be the Comanche stole Pawnee to sell to the Spaniards down south. Then the Comanche'd steal Lipan and Jicarilla kids and women, and sell 'em to the Pawnee."

"Morally reprehensible."

"Perhaps, lad. But watch yer tongue. Specially when we get up among the Crow. They steal anyone they can get their hands on. Kids especially. They love 'em, and raise 'em up to be good Crows."

"It doesn't sound like any slavery I've ever heard of."

"Reckon not, but then, ye ain't seen what the Osage do to an Iowa woman when they capture her, neither."

Richard skipped wide of a patch of prickly pear hidden down in the tall grass. "Rousseau can't be this wrong. Travis, we're missing something important. These people, they've been corrupted. That's got to be the answer. Like Half Man, here. He's been around whites for too long. Picked up too many of our vices: liquor, slavery, the drive to possess objects. I need to see someone who hasn't lived around whites, hasn't been affected by the traders with their guns and whiskey."

Hartman grinned amusedly. "Ye do take all, Dick. Ain't no such folks. Tarnal Hell, I seen 'em, from yer Boston to the Blackfeet. Folks has different customs, Dick. But they's all the same down deep. Some's good, some's bad, according to their lights. That's all."

"It's not rational!" Richard threw up his hands in protest, and to the horse's unease. "Whoa, boy." With restrained gestures, Richard said, "The closer to a state of nature, the closer man is to a state of innocence. Neither good nor bad, but like your Pawnee—"

"They ain't *my* Pawnee."

"—without binding morals. Morals are the result of ensuing stages of civilization placing ever more restrictive concepts of good and evil upon people. These Blackfeet, they don't have any sense of evil, do they?"

Travis made a sour face. "Yankee, yer gonna be dead within the month. I can feel it in my bones. Why on God's green earth did I ever stick my neck out fer an idiot? Listen up, Doodle, the Blackfoot will kill ye dead just because yer white. We call 'em Bug's Boys. They use that term in Boston?''

"The Devil's boys."

"And rightly so."

Richard tried to split his concentration between the argument and the patches of grassy prairie that gave way to groves of trees. But what was he supposed to see? With grass this tall, if Indians were crawling up on their bellies, they'd be invisible until the last minute.

Richard gave it up for a lost cause and said, "Then, well, name another people, even farther away."

"Wal, thar's the Snakes. Generally good folk, with the exception of old Left Hand, if'n he ain't gone under by now."

"Are they more innocent?"

"Naw, they damn near wiped out the Blackfoot a couple of generations back. Did such a damn good job of it, the Blackfoot ain't fergot. Them two tribes is in a fight ter the death. No treaties, no mercy. Just a fight till every last one's dead. And ye've got ter keep an eye on a Snake. He's a right smart trader, right up there with the Mandan. The story is that the Snakes used to trade with the Mandan before the Sioux, Cheyennes, and Arapaho cut the trade routes."

"Trade? I mean, Rousseau . . . Didn't any of these people ever just sit under an oak tree? Didn't any of them live off the bounty of the land? Aren't any of them innocent?"

Travis chuckled. "Yes, wal, as innocent as any other folks ye can think of. At least as innocent as that Yankee captain what stole me off on his ship from Boston." He looked at Richard. "Which might be one of the reasons I stuck my neck out fer ye. Hell, if'n I'd a stayed in the States, I'd been hung or jailed by now."

"You don't seem like a criminal."

"I ain't, not much, if'n ye judges me by the rules out hyar. Back in that civilization ye harps so on, I'd be a handful. Reckon I like the rules better hyar."

Richard glanced at the Pawnee. "Some rules. According to you, he'll kill us to possess this whiskey."

"Reckon so."

"It's irrational."

"Tell it to him."

"I intend to."

"Speak Pawnee?" Travis asked, raising an eyebrow and changing the lines of scars on his face.

"No, I guess not. You'll translate?"

Travis chuckled. "I'd better. Maybe I can keep ye alive after Half Man decides yer an idiot. I wouldn't try and philos'phy him. Half Man ain't noted fer his elocution."

"Oh, what's he noted for?"

"Stabbing people in the back."

"Travis?"

Hartman came awake in an instant, hands tightening on his rifle. "What's up, coon?"

"I can't stay awake any longer." Hamilton yawned as he spoke.

"Reckon ye done fine." Travis sat up, kicked out of his blankets, and studied the dark camp. Half Man lay rolled in his blanket, no doubt hearing every word. Hell, that Pawnee son of a bitch might be as good as his word. The dicker had been five gallons of whiskey for the use of the horses. Five gallons would allow Half Man to trade for a heap of hides. Maybe the red bastard wouldn't try and raise hair after all.

And all them book ideas the lad's been spouting have made mush outa my brain, too.

Travis walked out from the smoldering fire, sniffing the night air, damp and green-smelling after the rains. The land had needed that. Insect sounds carried to him as he checked the horses on their pickets.

All quiet.

Travis opened his senses, becoming one with the night. The sounds, the smells, the feel of the breeze on his skin. Overhead, stars made patterns against the black patches of clouds. The world had come alive again.

Travis made his careful way back to the fire, checking to

see that the Pawnee was still in his blanket. The attack would come without warning. When?

Morning, most likely.

How?

Knife or tomahawk. He'll try and whack me, silent like. Maybe cut my throat. Then he can deal with Dick any way he sees fit. The Pawnee would know Hamilton for a pilgrim.

So, how do I fox Half Man?

Don't give him a chance.

Travis tugged at his beard, and ran his fingers over the smooth ridges of scar tissue. That was the other thing about ever going back to the United States. He couldn't stand the way they'd look at him, like a monster. Out here, among the Indians, they understood what had happened and honored him for it. In the East, they'd stare, loathing on their faces, and they'd back away from him in horror.

Reckon I couldn't take it. Worst of all would be the women. The look in their eyes, like they done seed a serpent.

Better for him to stay here, where he knew the rules, was good at them, in fact. Like Baptiste, he could never go back. The planter had put the scars on Baptiste's back with a whip. The wilderness had scarred Travis's face, marking him as its own. *Each of us branded by his master.*

Travis settled by the low fire, warming his hands as he watched the darkness. Satisfied, he turned his attention on Richard.

Am I just stringing him along? Setting him up for some disaster he ain't prepared for? A wrong word, an insolent act, and some Sioux, Ree, or Crow would smack the boy's brains out. And why? Just because he'd read a book written by some damn fool who'd never been shot at—or seen what a Blackfoot did to a dying man.

Innocent—in this country? Travis shook his head. *Sorry, Dick. Reckon ye be the only innocent out hyar.*

He scratched his head. How in Tarnal Hell was he gonna give Hamilton an even break when every deck on earth was stacked against him?

For hours Travis thought on it, and finally made his decision. Wal, she'd be Katy bar the door, but he'd do 'er. Sunup was coming. Half Man might be waiting, figuring to make his play just at dawn when reactions were the slowest. Still, it never hurt to make the first move in a cat-and-mouse game.

"Dick? *Leve!* Daylight's a-coming. Half Man, come on, ye Pawnee devil. Let's get a move on."

"In God's name, Travis," Hamilton moaned. "Let me finish the dream. Pastries, and a fine claret . . ."

"Sun's nigh to breaking forth, coon. Let's get on with her. Sooner we reach the river, the sooner we're all on our way."

Half Man hadn't moved, but Travis could see the glint of his slitted eyes. *We're a pair, you and me.*

Richard was up. "Dick, rustle up them hosses. Let's get our likker tied on."

They ate jerked meat washed down with cold coffee. By the time the sky had turned pink, Travis had the pack string moving, never allowing the Pawnee the opportunity to act.

That's it. Keep him off balance. Don't let him have time to get the drop.

As the sun rose and shot glowing red rays across the cloud bottoms, Travis moved up beside Richard.

"These prickly pear, come fall they make a red fruit. A feller can eat 'em. Right sweet they are. The flowers, a feller can eat them, too. Takes a lot to fill a man's belly, but food's food, and can make the difference atwixt living and dying."

Richard stared quizzically at the cactus.

"Meat's meat. Ye got ter remember that. Don't make no matter what the critter. Mule or mouse. Fat cow buffler is about the best eating on the plains, but ye get into the mountains, and elk is some, it is. Better than these hyar plains elk."

"Any meat?" Richard asked. "Who'd eat a mouse?"

"Wal, if'n ye were starving, I reckon ye'd eat all ye could catch. Remember, lad. Meat's meat. Even lizards and buzzworms."

"What's a buzzworm?"

"Rattlesnake, coon. And they's good eating. Flaky white meat. Now the Shoshoni, way out west, they even eat ants. Collect 'em and grind 'em up on their slabs. Makes a kind of paste. I've heard coons tell it ain't bad eating, so long's ye don't dwell on it being ants. Grasshoppers, they's good, too."

"Travis, you're making me sick."

"Listen, coon. I ain't talking to hear my jaw flap." Travis pointed out at the grassy plains. "Thar's a whole big land out there. Reckon a feller that didn't know better, specially one full of book larning, wal, he might starve ter death surrounded by all the food in the world. He needs to use his noodle to think about the world a mite different."

"But ants? Grasshoppers?"

"Whar's an egg come from?"

Richard stared at him thoughtfully. "A chicken. They lay them."

"How?"

"Uh, well, I don't—"

"Right outa their assholes, coon. I hear they's rich folks what eat fish eggs. And didn't them Pharaohs eat birds' tongues?"

"I think that was Roman emperors."

Travis waved it away. "One's as good as t'other. Thing is, when it gets down to cat scratch, yer gonna do whatever it takes ter keep yerself alive. Remember that. Meat's meat. If it comes off a critter, ye can eat it. 'Course, meat ain't everything."

Travis pointed eastward. "Over thar, to Cantonment Missouri. Reckon they had three hunnert soldiers billeted through the winter about five years back. Most of 'em ketched the scurvy. Reckon they had plenty of meat. Fact is, they didn't eat the lights."

"Lights?" Richard frowned. "What are the lights?"

"The guts, coon. Heart, liver, kidneys, boudins. Remember that, if'n yer ever getting poor in spite of eating all the meat ye can hold. Injuns, they know. If'n the lights don't fix ye, ye need plants. I've even seed Injuns boiling grass to make tea. Balances a man's blood, I'm told."

"I've heard that lemons are carried on ships for scurvy. Do lemons grow out here?"

"Don't reckon so. Plants, now, they take a little larning. Reckon it's early, and we're a bit north fer finding *pommes de terre*, but they's other things. Sunflowers, fer one. Prairie turnips, a feller can make a meal of them. Sego lily, Yampa root, blue-flower camas. I've et 'em all. Like a cross between potato and carrot. Wild onions is everywhere. Look, reckon that's one.''

Travis led his horse over, and used his belt knife to lever a bulb out of the ground. He handed it to Richard, resuming his pace. ''Smell her. Onion, ain't it? Thar now. Knock the dirt off'n it and eat it. Ye'll know onion from death camas. She's always got that smell. And did ye see how quick it was to dig that out? A feller can eat on the run.''

''We didn't get killed by the Pawnee this morning.'' Richard ate the onion thoughtfully. ''Maybe you're worried about nothing.''

''Maybe.'' Travis slung his lead rope over his shoulder and lifted his rifle, checking the priming in the pan. ''This morning, notice how I loaded the packs? Always kept a hoss atwixt me and the Pawnee? He didn't have a clear target.''

''You always make him walk first,'' Richard noted. ''Is that so that you won't get shot in the back?''

''Yer larning, coon.''

''Travis, I don't know. He's strange. But how can you be so sure he's a bad man?''

''Maybe he ain't. But this hyar ain't a Christian land. Reckon old Half Man, he ain't heard of no Good Samaritan. Now, pay attention. If'n he makes a play, I want ye ter grab the hosses. Understand? I'll raise the Injun, you just make sure the hosses don't bolt.''

''Raise the Injun? I don't understand.''

''Kill him dead.''

''Oh. Is that a Christian reference, as in resurrect?''

''Reckon not.'' Travis reached in his possibles for a twist of tobacco and cut a chew. After he had it juicing, he asked, ''What's yer job if'n the Pawnee makes trouble?''

''I grab the horses . . . but what if he gets the best of you?''

Travis placed his twist back into his possibles. ''Then, I reckon ye'd best hope he's been a-reading that philos'phy of yern.''

EIGHTEEN

This appears to me as clear as daylight, and I cannot conceive from whence our philosophers can derive all the passions they endow to natural man. Except for the basic physical necessities, which nature herself requires, all our other needs are merely the result of habit, before which they were not needs or of our cravings; and we don't crave that which we are not in a circumstance to know. Therefore it follows that as savage man yearns for nothing but what he knows, and knows nothing but what he actually possesses or can easily acquire, nothing can be so tranquil as his soul, or so restricted as his understanding.

—Jean-Jacques Rousseau, *Discourse on the Origin and Foundation of Inequality Among Mankind*

After so many days of rain, the sun beat down hot and bright. Travis might have found that a welcome change, but for the muggy air that made a man's sweat just about useless. The trilling of a meadowlark, the chirping of the finches, and the colorful wildflowers helped to make up for the humid heat.

"Warm enough fer ye?" he asked Hamilton.

"I guess. After freezing for days, now I'd give anything for a couple of clouds."

"Later this afternoon. Reckon the thunderheads will come rolling in."

Travis never let his attention waver from where Half Man walked ahead of them. An Indian walked differently, planted his feet in a softer manner than a galomping, booted white man. Half Man didn't look like much, skinny, his eyes soulless. Made a coon figger he didn't have a thought in his head. But a man didn't skip atwixt and atween the Omaha and the Pawnee—mortal enemies—without having a heap of savvy locked in his noodle.

He's planning something. Knows we're smuggling, and if'n we don't show up, thar ain't gonna be no questions asked. At least, not by the gov'ment. If'n I's in his moccasins, I'd be thinking to raise Dick and me, skip off to the Pawnee, and make like a king. Pile up a heap of buffler and beaver, and trade it while prices are high. Probably down to Fort Osage.

"What are you thinking?" Hamilton asked.

" 'Bout the Pawnee. I got him figgered as far as the whiskey's concerned. What I ain't got figgered is when he's a gonna strike."

Richard made a face.

"Still don't believe this child, do ye?"

Richard's thin face looked pensive. "Travis, I can understand him wanting to steal our things. But unless we give him cause, he doesn't have any reason to kill us."

"Coup, Dick. I explained that to ye. Honor as a warrior."

"Such concepts of honor are irrational."

"Tell them soldiers they pin all them medals on."

Richard frowned as he walked, eyes on the grass.

"Best larn to watch around, Dick. Feller's got ter see everything. Front and back, up and down. Trouble can come on ye from any direction. Thar's times that seeing a danger first means ye can avoid it altogether."

"I was just thinking." Richard wiped sweat from his forehead. The distant trees were shimmering in the light, and delicate butterflies fluttered in the hot air. The sweet smell of grass seemed to grow stronger with the heat.

"Yep, locked in yer Doodle noodle. Last thing ye'll be wondering about is how that arrow come ter be sticking through yer guts."

"They just shoot people. Without any warning?"

Travis gave the young man a twinkling grin. "Reckon they's plumb rational about it."

They walked along in silence, and to Travis's relief, Hamilton had started to look around.

"See the deer over ter the trees? Two does, still as can be."

"Nope."

"Right yonder, down under the branches of that hazel. Just ahint that patch of daisy flowers."

"No, I don't. . . . Wait. Yes! I see them—or I think I do. How in God's name did you see them over there?"

"Got ter train yer eye, Dick. It's in the outlines, the way the light sits. Work at her, and ye'll larn."

Finally Richard asked, "What happened to your face? The scars, I mean. A fight? Indians?"

"Old Ephraim. He done it."

"You've talked about him before. Is he an Indian?"

"Waugh! He be the white bear, the grizzly!" Travis pointed at his face. "Time this happened, we's working our way west, outa Fort Benton. Made her clear ter the Great Falls of the Missouri. I was walking up ahead, scouting like, ye see. That's Blackfoot country, so a child's got ter be slick, see them red bastards afore they can sneak up on ye.

"Wal, thar I be, a-sneaking through these sarvisberry bushes, and lo, Old Ephraim just rared up outa a hole and whacked my rifle away. He grabbed aholt of me, and it was Katy bar the door! Pressed down like I was in them bushes, I couldn't hardly move. He bounced on me, but the bushes gave, ye see. Didn't crush my lights out. Then he took a swipe with his paw. That's what took my cheek and nose, and made these hyar scars that run round me ear. At the smell of blood, he started ter chew my head up. That's what made these hyar scars running up through my hair. Pilgrim, I reckon ye've never lived till ye hears bear teeth a-sliding along yer skull."

Richard blinked as if in disbelief. "How . . . how did you survive? I mean . . . Good Lord!"

"Davey Green heard my screams and come a-running. He saw the bear, but couldn't see me. Davey, he ups his shooter and drives a galena pill inter Old Ephraim's lights. Then Davey dives in with his knife.

"At the sound of the shot, Old Ephraim turns, and swats Davey half across the berry patch. Plumb knocked him cold, and woulda busted him up, but for the bushes breaking his fall. Then Keemle, Immel, and Jones runs up. Wal, Old Ephraim, he sees all this and roars. He's still a-standing

on me, mind. Keemle up and shoots." Travis chuckled.
"Funny thing. I was looking up at that bear's head. Big as
the world, it was. I saw that pill hit him. Took him square
in the nose. I felt that bear jerk and damn me if'n it ain't
true, but I knew what he's a-thinking."

"You did?"

"Yep. Don't know the why of it, but we might a been a-
sharing minds. He knew he's hit plumb center. That ball
had busted up his nose and cracked his skull. And way down
deep in that bear's soul, I felt the rage as he charged out to
take old Keemle down with him. 'Course, afore he got thar,
Jones shot him through the shoulder, and busted him down.
Then Immel busted his neck with another shot."

"What about you?"

"Ain't much ter tell after that. Reckon all the excitement
was over, and the real hurting started. They put me in a
pirogue and sent me back down ter the fort. Dave Green
went along, took care of me. Sewed up all the loose pieces
he could find. Reckon Old Ephraim woulda kilt me but for
Green running up ter give him something else ter think of."

"And Keemle, Immel, and Jones?"

"Ah, Keemle's printing the paper down ter Saint Loowee.
Immel and Jones . . . they gone under. Blackfoots caught
'em a couple of years back." Travis smiled sadly, voice
dropping. "And I'da been with 'em that day. They's under
a bluff on the Yellerstone. Blackfoots wiped out the whole
shitaree." The old wound in his soul opened again. "Makes
a coon wonder, Dick. I was the scout—the keen devil ter
slip on ahead. Now, if'n I'd a been thar—instead of a-laying
flat on me back in Fort Benton—would I a smelt out that
Blackfoot trap? Would I a saved them coons? Or would I
be a-laying up thar, topknot gone, and all turned to bones?"

Hamilton had a funny depth to his eyes as he said, "Perhaps God saved you for a reason. If Isaac Newton is right,
the universe is predetermined. Maybe God used the bear to
save you for the express purpose of torturing me." A faint
smile bent his boyish lips.

Travis chuckled. "Hell, Doodle, ye ain't worth the torturing. Now, skin yer eyes and keep a watch on that sneaky
Pawnee fer a while. Hyar, notice the way he walks, how his

feet mashes the grass. See? From the pattern, ye can figger which direction he's a-going.''

"What did Immle and Jones do to make the Blackfeet so mad, Travis?''

"Nothing. Blackfoots is just poison, coon. That's all thar is to it. They done declared war on whites, and by God, they'll fight her out.''

"Well, were Immel and Jones going up to fight them?''

"Tarnation, no! Child, ain't none of us interested in fighting. Wal, 'cept maybe fer some fools like the British. Ye cain't never trust a Britisher no more than a Blackfoot, or a Ree. No, it was like this. Manuel Lisa died of the fever down to Saint Loowee. Joshua Pilcher, he took over the Missouri Fur Company. He and Lisa had been palavering about setting up a post to trade with the Blackfoot. Figgered, just like yer a-doing, that with the right presents, and a peaceful delegation, they could open that country up. Hell, we didn't want no war with the Blackfoots! A feller cain't trade fer plews when he's being shot at. Rational, eh?''

"Maybe.''

"Wal, Immel and Jones, they met up with one band of Blackfoot, and sure enough, had 'em a peace talk. It was later that them Blackfoot all got together with the others and decided to wipe out the whites. And they done her.''

An eerie feeling of danger had drifted over Richard like a miasma. He gave the Pawnee's back an unsure look. Was he like the Blackfeet? "But why? Travis, I'm looking for the reason. War is not the natural human state. I can't believe that. They must have had a reason.''

"Who knows? They's just devils. Maybe their spirits told 'em to. Maybe it's because we're friendly with the Snakes, and Blackfoot hate Snakes as much as they hate anybody. Dick, listen close now. Out hyar, a feller don't need a reason. These Injuns don't think the same as ye. Larn their rules, or they'll kill ye. Get that philos'phy mush outa yer head.''

"It just doesn't make sense. Man is rational. Man *must* be rational. Otherwise, what's the difference between us and the animals?''

Travis scratched at the sweat running down his cheeks

and into his beard. "Wal, now. That's the first smart question ye've asked all day. So far as old Travis Hartman's concerned, thar ain't a whole lot."

If nothing else could be said for him, Richard Hamilton had a quick and agile mind. "Coneflower," he said, pointing.

"Good. Yer a-larning."

White fluffy clouds drifted across the endless blue vault of sky. Richard had never seen such blue. The warm breeze skipped across the grass, moving it like waves on Boston Harbor. Butterflies flitted past in dots of spectacular color. Insects were chirring in the grass.

"Seems like the whole land is alive." He wiped his sweaty face. "But I'd sure like a drink."

"Spring up ahead." Travis said. "Pawnee's been making fer it."

"You know this country pretty well."

"Reckon so. Worked out of the Council Bluffs fer Lisa, then fer the Company."

The Pawnee started down into a brush-and-oak–filled draw where water had cut through the caprock. Deer trails led through the trees to a little brook.

"Water them hosses downstream, Dick. Reckon we'll let them drink, then us."

When the horses had watered and began grazing along the trickle of creek, Richard dropped to his knees to drink his fill of cool water. Oak boughs dappled the ground with shade, relief from the heat of the day.

Half Man sat a short distance away, crouched on his haunches, rifle across his lap. He watched Richard with expressionless black eyes.

Richard asked, "Do you speak any English?"

Half Man continued to stare at him for a moment, then spoke, the language incomprehensible. At the same time, those brown hands formed different patterns.

"He says he wants to trade." Travis tied his lead horse

to a tree, and walked over to squat several paces from Half Man.

Richard shook his head. "I don't have anything to trade. I just want to ask questions."

Travis spoke slowly, haltingly, his hands tracing patterns in the air. When Half Man answered, Travis looked up and said, "He says he ain't got no reason to waste his time if'n ye ain't gonna trade. Says he's got better things to do with his day than jabber with a *La-chi-kut*."

Richard chewed at his lip for a moment, then slapped at a mosquito. "Tell him I'll trade ideas."

"Ideas? Hell." But Travis spoke, gesturing with his hands the whole time.

Half Man narrowed his eyes as he looked at Richard. When he spoke, the tone ridiculed. Travis translated: "Words are empty air. I want whiskey, tobacco, gunpowder, mirrors. You are poor, you are nothing."

"I'm not nothing," Richard said. "I'm a student of philosophy, of ideas. The things you speak of are meaningless. Truth, the nature of God, the way in which you perceive the world, those things are all that mean anything."

Travis glanced warily at Richard, then made the signs, adding the Pawnee words he knew.

The Pawnee spoke in mocking tones. Travis translated: "He wants to know if ye'll trade them fine moccasins. He says if ye gives him yer moccasins, he'll find a reason ter be bothered by yer questions. And, which God are ye interested in? Evening Star or Wakonda? First is Pawnee, second's Omaha."

"My moccasins?" Richard cried. "They're the only shoes I've got!"

Half Man made a hissing sound, barked a couple of words, and spit in emphasis.

"He says yer a fool, Dick. And I reckon we'd better call her quits, afore he gets riled."

"A fool? I've at least the decency to have an interest in his beliefs! What does he think? That men have only things—tobacco, whiskey—to tie them together? Damn him, he . . ."

Richard started as the Pawnee rose, expression turning to snarl. With the quickness of a striking cat, the Pawnee feinted at Richard, pivoted on his foot, and swung the butt of his rifle at Travis's head.

Travis ducked the whistling rifle, lost his balance, and fell against the Pawnee's knees. In that instant, Half Man dropped his rifle, whipped out his knife, and leapt on Travis, who blocked the slashing blade, growling like a wild animal. Half Man screamed like a panther.

Heart pounding, Richard backed away. The sudden fury of the attack stunned him. Terrified, his hands clutched spasmodically at nothingness.

On the leaf-matted ground, Travis and Half Man kicked and bit and gouged. Grunting now, straining against each other, their faces contorted. Travis got a knee into Half Man's belly and levered the Indian off.

Half Man landed on his side, but struck out with his blade. Travis rolled away, rising. Half Man knocked Travis off his feet. Before the hunter could recover, Half Man leapt. Travis shot his elbow forward, partially deflecting the vicious blade that sliced at his side. At the same time, he jabbed his other hand into Half Man's face, the fingers clawing the Indian's eyes.

Richard gasped for breath, slowly shaking his head. Travis howled with an unearthly fury that drowned Half Man's screams. The Pawnee jerked frantically at the hand clamped to his face, Travis's fingers digging ever deeper into his eyes.

At the same time, Travis jacked his knee into the Pawnee's crotch, again and again and again. Half Man's body jerked from the impact. In desperation, Half Man broke the hunter's grip, flinging himself backward. Cat-quick, Travis was on him, an insane moan breaking his scarred lips, gray-white hair flying. Travis tightened his hold on the knife hand, while his other caught the Pawnee's throat; they were face-to-face, panting, spitting in effort. Travis's strength slowly bent the knife arm until the blade hovered over Half Man. The Pawnee gave a last heave, letting the knife slip out of his fingers. At that moment, Travis butted the Pawnee with his head, battering the Indian's already bloody face.

Richard staggered forward as Travis grabbed a rock and hammered the Indian's head. The rock made a hollow thump like a stick on a melon.

"Travis, no! He's beaten!" Richard cried as he rushed forward. But again and again Travis slammed the rock home, using two hands.

When it was over, Travis rolled off the limp body and flopped on his back. He coughed, blinked at the sky, and closed his eyes.

Richard stood, numb. Blood welled in the ragged red holes where the Indian's eyes had been. The skull had been pounded to pulp from which streams of red leaked. What had been a man was now nothing more than meat. A big black fly landed on the dead man's ruined face.

"Travis?" Richard whispered.

"Dick? Come hyar. I reckon ye'd better take a look." Travis pulled up his shirt, the slice in the crimson-stained leather clearly visible. Blood ran in a bright red sheet from the cut in Travis's side.

"Come on, coon," Travis called. "Ye gots ter look at it. Tell me how bad. Stings like unholy Hell."

Richard stumbled forward, dropping to his knees. So much blood! He'd never seen anything like it before. "It's . . . Oh, my God, Travis!"

"Is there—is there guts hanging out, boy?"

"N . . . No. I . . . I don't . . . well, see any."

Travis gasped, lying back. With shaking fingers, he prodded at the long wound.

Richard watched those fingers as they worked carefully through the blood.

"Shit!" Travis growled. "Might not be guts out, Dick, but she's sliced clean through the side." He swallowed hard. "All right, coon. Ye gots ter sew her up. Savvy? If'n ye don't, old Travis is gone under."

"Sew?" Richard mewed. This wasn't happening! "God, Travis . . . I *can't*!"

"Reckon so, coon. Needle and thread's in my possibles." Travis felt around. "Must a busted the strap. Find 'em, Dick."

Richard crawled over to the leather bag where it lay in the trampled grass. He grabbed it up with shaking hands. "Got it."

"Come on, then. Let's get her done quick."

"Travis, I . . . I . . ."

Travis ground his teeth and swallowed hard. "Wal, now, Dick. If'n ye don't, who in hell do ye see around hyar to do her? The damn hosses?"

Richard closed his eyes, shaking. His soul went cold. "Can't we go to the fort?"

Travis propped himself on one elbow. "Dick . . . Richard. Look at me. That's it. Now, yer scairt plumb silly. But hyar's how it is, son. I got a slice in me side. It ain't a long one, or else my guts woulda spilled all over the ground whilst I's raising that red Pawnee son of a bitch. I checked the blood. Thar ain't no gut juice in it, so he didn't nick me boudins. If'n ye can sew me up, I'll be all right. It's on me right side, Richard. I cain't sew it myself, not without stretching. It's up ter you. So, fer God's sake, stop shaking like a puppy and dig around in my possibles. Ye'll find a needle all wrapped up with strong thread. I'll talk ye through it."

"Travis, I don't—"

"Thar *ain't* no choice, Richard. It's gotta be done. If'n ye cain't, step over thar, pick up my rifle, and shoot me through the head. I don't want ter die slow with my guts leaking out. It's up ter you, now. Yer gonna kill me, one way or the other, if'n ye don't dig out that needle."

Richard opened the bag, finding a bullet mold, a couple of lead bars, pipe, tobacco, rolls of leather thongs, a pouch full of small springs and screws, gun flints, several glass bottles with waxed stoppers—and the needle with its winding of thread.

He looked up, meeting Travis's sober blue eyes. "Ye can do it, Dick. I got faith in ye."

Richard wanted to throw up, to run screaming from this horrible place. "My hands are shaking."

"So're mine," Travis said with a grin. "Wal, coon, we'll be plumb scairt together. Hell of a good scrape, warn't it? That old Half Man, he's some. Sure foxed me."

"You sound like you admire him." Richard closed his eyes, and took a deep breath. He flexed his muscles, burning up the energy that pumped through him. Exhaling, he bent down, unwrapping the thread from the needle.

Travis watched him levelly, taking his measure. Richard drew strength from that cool look.

"Yep. I figgered he's a gonna raise ye, Dick. I's halfway to my feet when he took that swipe at me head. Cunning old coon. Crafty as a fox. Now, yer a gonna have ter tie a big knot in the end of that thread. That's it. Now, another. Cain't have that slipping through my hide."

Richard fumbled the knot, then got it right. The mending he'd been doing on his clothes might stand him in good stead now. But mending on a person?

"Now, I'm a gonna lay on my side. Just like this. Ye got ter take the tip of the needle and run it right through the skin, not getting so deep as ter take any gut with it. Ye follow?"

"I think so." Richard held his breath and bent over Travis's bloody side. He lowered the point of the needle. "God, I'm scared, Travis."

"I reckon ye don't need ter tell me that, Dick. It ain't fixing ter make a body feel particularly at ease."

The needle dimpled Travis's bloody skin.

The long trail was finally coming to an end. Packrat nodded with satisfaction as he studied the horse droppings. They were so close, the manure hadn't even crusted.

He glanced at Heals Like A Willow—saw the tension in her eyes. *You know the end is near, don't you?*

He raised his hands to the sun, saying, "I swear, before

the sun sets on this day, I will be *rid* of this witch woman! One way . . . or another.''

He glanced back to read how his words affected her. That mask had fallen into place again and she remained aloof, as coldly beautiful as ever.

Half Man was close. As soon as they found him, Packrat would be free of her. He could begin the long process of purification. The air would taste sweeter to his lungs. His muscles would work with greater energy. He could feel his wounded soul chafing to finally escape the darkness. He could cure his manhood, for not even in dreams had his penis stiffened since that horrible day when she'd polluted him.

And how will you ever trust yourself to lie with another woman? He drove the thought from his mind, looking back at Willow to say, ''You'd like that, wouldn't you? To think you could make me afraid forever. Well, you've made a mistake, Weasel Woman.''

She gave him the briefest hint of a smile—and that maddening, knowing look. The anger rose, barely controlled. She could see inside his soul, know what he was thinking. By the Morning Star, he had to finish this now.

He kicked his horse to a trot, dragging her along behind. He could lie with a woman again, couldn't he? And what if he tried? What if he had the chance, and his penis remained forever limp?

His skin went hot at the thought. Among the Pawnee there were no secrets. They'd laugh at him behind his back. Some day, a woman would offer herself. *I'll say no. Walk away.*

And when it came time to marry? How long could he put it off? His mother would make an alliance. And when he moved into his wife's house, into her bed, what then?

The hatred festered.

He jerked around and called, ''What if I just kill you?''

''I be with you forever,'' she told him with complete sincerity. ''Inside your soul. You can only be free when I am.''

He bit his lip, straightened, and longed for Half Man as he'd never done.

The tracks led down into a tree-filled drainage lined with

brush. As his mount stepped down the trail, he could see other horses tethered to the trees along what looked like a small stream.

"Half Man! It is Packrat! I come to bring you a gift." His heart leapt. Here, at last, was freedom from the witch. He could begin healing now. The other problems could be solved one at a time.

"Half Man?" He cocked his head, reaching for his bow as a skinny *La-chi-kut* stepped out from among the trees. He looked pale, and very scared. He held no weapon.

Packrat glanced around. Several of the horses belonged to Half Man. Better yet, the tins they carried were whiskey tins.

All the wealth I will ever need to pay for a cleansing! He slipped his bow from his back, and drew an arrow. Where was Half Man and the other *La-chi-kut*? He could sense that something was wrong, felt a dark intuition that he'd arrived in the nick of time.

The skinny White man was talking in the gobbling White man tongue. He looked terrified. So, not a warrior? Maybe one of the men who made black marks on paper?

Packrat cocked his head. "Where is Half Man? Where is the other *La-chi-kut*?"

"We here. Hurt," a second voice called from the brush in badly inflected Pawnee. "Horse kick! Give help."

Packrat glanced around, looking for any sign of ambush. The skinny White man swallowed hard. Warily, Packrat kneed his horse forward, bow ready. He could see the second *La-chi-kut* now. His shirt was bloody.

"Half Man?" Packrat asked.

"Gone fort," the wounded man croaked. "Give help."

Packrat counted the horses. Ten. Then he saw the bloody spot on the ground, the drag marks where a body had been hastily pulled into the brush.

Packrat drew his arrow, pointing it at the wounded *La-chi-kut*. "I think Half Man is dead."

The wounded man stared at him for a moment, eyes drained, then slowly nodded his head. That's when Packrat saw the scars. The sign of the bear. This man had fought the grizzly—and lived.

"Tell me," Packrat rasped, a melting sensation in his guts.

"Tried to kill us. He wanted whiskey." The Bear Man made a sign for truth. "I would not let him steal it. If you know Half Man, tell me if my words are false."

Packrat aimed for the soft spot just under the White man's ribs. *Dead? Half Man dead? This White man will die, and then the skinny one. After all of Packrat's suffering to . . .*

Willow laughed, her mockery tearing something in his soul. Gone! Every plan ruined, as ruined as his life would be!

He spun his horse, seeing the victory in her eyes. No, an arrow would be too good for her. He wanted to beat her, to hear and feel the impact of his club as he broke her skull. Lowering the bow, he snatched up his war club. *Destroy her. Kill her! Strike her down as she has stricken you with her witchery.*

As from a great distance, he heard himself shout: "You killed him! You witched him! You did this—you knew!"

In fury, he slashed downward with the war club, but she dodged enough to take a glancing blow on the back. The club, deflected, struck her mare on the kidneys. The horse bucked violently, throwing Heals Like A Willow from its back. She hit hard, bounced on her bottom, and blinked with dazed eyes.

Packrat leapt from his own shying mount. Kill her first, then the White men. She seemed stunned, unable to focus. He swung at her, hissing his rage. She barely managed to duck the blow, scrambling awkwardly backward across the shade-dappled grass.

He skipped to one side, kicked her brutally in the ribs, and raised his club high. *No escape now, Willow.* Their eyes locked, and in that instant, he exulted in her terror. "Now you *die,* witch!"

He'd just started his club on its downward arc when the concussion knocked him sideways. He staggered, dazed, the ground twisting up to hit him. He blinked, thoughts gone muzzy. A ringing sounded in his ears, and his chest felt odd, sharp with unsensed pain. He coughed, raising his hand to the wetness at his mouth, surprised by the blood. So much

... blood. He blinked again, seeking to drive the grayness from his vision.

Heals Like A Willow was watching him, drinking his soul with her eyes.

Witch, you won't win. I'll beat you ... in the end. ...

The ringing in his ears, the growing gray mist before his eyes, they seemed to fade. If he could just remember ... what he'd ...

NINETEEN

To this war of every man, against every man, this also is consequent; that nothing can be unjust. The notions of right and wrong, justice and injustice have there no place. Where there is no common power, there is no law; where no law, no injustice. Force, and fraud, are in war the two cardinal virtues. Justice, and injustice are none of the faculties of neither the body, nor mind. ... It is consequent also to the same condition that there be no propriety, no dominion, no *mine* and *thine* distinct; but only that to be every man's, that he can get; and for so long as he can keep it.

—Thomas Hobbes, *Leviathan*

Reckon that was plumb center!'' Travis called from where he lay. The musket fell from Richard's numb hands as the last echoes of the shot died away. He walked through the curling blue smoke, smelling the odor of sulfur from the burned powder. The horses snorted and stamped, panicked by the scent of blood and the sounds of human violence. Richard stared at the macabre scene.

What have I done? The young Pawnee's body—the chest torn open—dear Lord God, so much blood! How did the human body hold it all?

The young man's eyes were wide in the penny-brown

face, staring and glassy, the black pupils large. Clots of frothy red blood still leaked from his mouth, soaking into the moldy leaves beneath his cheek.

Young. So very young.

The woman moaned and moved in a slow writhe. Richard turned, backing away from the dead man, watching her uncertainly. She winced in pain.

The Indian hit her. Richard remembered that twisted fury when the young warrior turned on her. Why? Because she'd laughed. Right there in the middle of the nightmare, she'd laughed. And the warrior had gone berserk.

The war club whistling down; the woman twisting desperately away; the war club bouncing off her back to hit the horse; the animal rearing. Her body had slammed the ground like a sack of onions. Still, she'd struggled to escape as the warrior pursued on foot. But her hands were tied . . . tied. . . .

And then I grabbed up Half Man's musket. Lifted it as the war club was raised. Had he sighted down the barrel, or just pulled the cock back and triggered?

Don't remember. But the echoes of the shot remained— along with the image of the young warrior jerking from the bullet's impact. Frozen forever in Richard's mind.

He blinked at the woman. Mute misery reflected in her face, and with it, fear. A young woman, beautiful in a wild sort of way. Her glossy black hair was loose, spilling over her shoulders. Had he ever seen hair that black, that lustrous before? Her skin had a smooth radiance, a vitality he didn't understand.

She had such slender hands, the fingers long and delicate. Then he saw her wrists' red welts and the rawhide thong that had cut and chafed them.

"You're safe now," he told her gently, and tried to smile. He reached out to her, to reassure her. But his guts felt suddenly queer. The trembling in his fingers moving into the hand he'd offered her, and on to all of the muscles in his body. Shaking uncontrollably, he sat down to cradle his head in his hands.

"Oh, God, what did I do?"

"Dick?" Travis called. "Ye all right, coon?"

Richard rubbed his face with shivering hands. "I'm alive, Travis. I guess I'm . . . alive. Dear sweet Jesus. I'm alive."

"Easy, coon," Travis soothed. "It comes on a body, sometimes. It'll pass."

I killed a man. Shot him dead. He didn't need to look again. Those empty staring eyes, the blood, would be with him whenever he closed his eyes. But for the wound and blood, the young Pawnee would have looked peaceful, as in repose for a nap, his arm outstretched.

Richard glanced at the woman; she watched him intently with fathomless, dark eyes.

The trembling receded, leaving hollow weakness in its wake. He stood, again offering his hands. For an eternal moment her eyes bored into his, and then she reached out to him.

Her hands were cool, firm in his. As he pulled her to her feet, Richard saw the pain in her face. "You're tougher than I am," he told her. "After what you've been through, I'd be screaming."

He held her hands up. The knots had pulled so tightly that he couldn't undo them.

Her eyes fluttered, expression going slack. She swayed on her feet then, head lolling, and Richard caught her as she wobbled and collapsed.

"What the hell?"

Travis laughed from where he lay. "Reckon she took a hell of a wallop when she hit that ground. This child would guess she stood up a mite too quick. Pack her over hyar, lad. Let's see what ye ketched."

Richard got a good grip, and dragged more than carried her. She should have been heavier. Then he was shockingly aware of her soft breasts against his arms. He laid her down gently, awed that he'd touched her so.

Travis studied her with quizzical eyes. "Snake, by damn! What in hell's she doing clear out hyar?" Then, "Slave, by God."

"Slave? But she's Indian."

Travis gave him a disgusted glance. "And I reckon yer Roosoo don't figger 'man in nature' takes slaves?"

"It's Rousseau. And no, he didn't."

"Wal, lad, a Pawnee don't tie up his wife with bindings like this. Let's see—roll her moccasins down."

Richard tried not to touch her warm skin as he pulled the soft tops of her moccasins down to her ankles. The welts there had mostly healed.

"Slave, all right." Travis cocked his head, curious blue eyes on Richard. "Reckon she's yern."

"*What?*"

Travis scratched at his beard with blood-caked fingers. "Wal, hoss. Ye raised that Pawnee what had her. She's yers now by mountain law. Reckon she's worth keeping, too. She's right pert. Do ye a good day's work. Warm yer bed at night, if'n she don't drive a knife atwixt yer ribs while yer on her."

"*Travis!* She's—she's a human being. I *won't* own another human being. It's . . . beastly."

"Wal, fine, Dick. Reckon ye won't mind if'n I take her?"

"You take. . . . Hell, no! She's free, Travis."

The hunter chuckled. "Ye takes some, ye does, Dick. You and yer Yankee ideas."

Richard sighed wearily, absently stroking the woman's hair. How incredibly soft. He'd imagined Indian hair to be bristly. But then, he'd never touched a woman's hair like this—or a woman's breast, for that matter. She was so unlike his Laura.

Travis winced. "Now, why don't ye take my strike-a-light, and build us a fire. I reckon we ain't a-going nowhere soon."

"I don't know how to make a fire, Travis."

"Wal, coon, it appears t' be yer day fer larning."

Heals Like A Willow slept late into the night. She
blinked, coming awake slowly. The pain wasn't just part of
her dreams. She cataloged the sounds as she tried to gather
her muzzy thoughts: the distant hoot of an owl. Horses
cropped nearby, and water was trickling through the grass.
A fire popped. Someone grunted in pain.

Pain? She reached up to rub her face. Her head ached as
if she'd been clubbed half to death . . . and the memories of
the afternoon came back in vivid clarity.

White men! Packrat was dead.

Willow sat up and gasped. The ache in her head left her
sick and reeling. Agony shot up through her hips and back.

A blanket had been placed over her against the chill of
the night, and when she looked down, her wrists were free.
When had that happened? How long had she been out?

Short flames licked up periodically around a chunk of
firewood lying in a round bed of glowing coals. In the firelight, she could see one of the White men, the old one.
Those odd, pale eyes watched her with interest. His face
was drawn in pain. It looked wrong, somehow misshapen,
but she knew little of White men and how they ought to
look.

He made the sign for her people: "Snake?"

She nodded, then signed: "What are you going to do with
me?"

He smiled crookedly. "Free."

She cocked her head. A trap hid in this. But where? Why
would the White man at the fort offer two guns for her,
when these White men would turn her loose?

The man's hands continued, "The young warrior killed
the Pawnee who kept you. The young warrior says you are
free."

She glanced at the third set of blankets. The young White
man was rolled up like a papoose. He hadn't seemed much
of a warrior. She remembered the soft look in his eyes as
he'd reached out to her. Then he'd been betrayed by the

shakes. What had she seen in those brown eyes? Confusion, relief, excitement, all mixed together?

She gazed down at her hands. She'd seen that look before—in the eyes of her husband. *Was that why I took the White man's hand? Or was it the fall that addled me?*

Willow rubbed her flushed face, recalling the way she'd gone dizzy and fallen into the White man's arms.

How long ago? What did they do when I was senseless? What men did with any woman, no doubt. She reached down under her skirt, but found no indication that a man had taken her. Maybe White men didn't—but, no, that wasn't what the *Ku'chendikani* claimed. According to the people who knew Whites, they were as bad as, if not worse than, anyone when it came to coupling.

She flushed at the old White man's knowing eyes as she pulled her hands into view. "Free?"

He nodded, signing, "Free. But I would ask the Snake woman to stay for several days. I will be very sick. Fevered. The young warrior knows nothing of wounds, or fever. If you help him to help me, we will give you horses. We will take you to your people."

Take her to her people? Was this where the trap . . . ? She stifled a cry as she shifted and white-hot pain lanced through her. *Tam Apo help me, my back isn't broken, is it?* Drawing deep breaths helped, and she shifted to a different position that eased her back.

At that moment the fire flared; she got a good look at the White man's face. She'd seen scars like that before. He'd fought the white bear—and survived. A powerful warrior, White man though he might be. But why free her? Brave or not, it didn't make sense to turn a good captive loose.

She signed, "My people live many moons to the west."

"In the Shining Mountains," he returned. "I know where the Snake live. I have seen their land. We are headed close to there. We will take you home. I speak straight."

"Why?"

"Maybe trade with your people."

Ah! Now I begin to understand. "What makes you think we want trade?"

"Everyone wants trade."

Her fingers flashed angrily. "Trade not good. Trade for rifle, must trade for powder, trade for bullet. This is good?"

He watched her with thoughtful eyes. "Trade makes people wealthy and strong. Snakes need guns to fight the Blackfoot. Blackfoot enemy to Whites as well as Snake people."

"Is it not better that Whites kill Blackfeet?" She glanced at the metal tins. "Is it not better that you trade medicine water to Blackfeet? Make them crazy and weak? Then *you* can kill them."

He smiled at her, and signed: "You are too much like Young Warrior. Many questions. Answer one question and he asks two more."

She started to stand, got dizzy, and sank back.

"Hurt?" he signed.

She ignored him, heart racing, senses going blurry.

"Bad fall," he signed, then pointed to his side and added, "Bad cut. Young Warrior sew."

She made the signs: "Half Man cut you?"

He nodded. "Tried to steal whiskey."

"I heard," she grunted in Pawnee.

How free am I? She nerved herself, rising slowly to her feet. Squinting against the horrible headache, she made her way, step by step, into the brush. Holding onto a tree, she relieved herself, half expecting a cry of pursuit. When none came, she stepped carefully to the creek and scooped up water. She relished the water's cool touch on her hot skin. She drank all she could hold.

Go, now. Escape! She glanced out into the darkness, wincing at her pain and blurring vision. How far could she make it before she collapsed? Her stomach tickled with the urge to vomit. Like it or not, she needed rest.

But she would do one thing before hobbling back to her blankets. She picked her way to where Packrat lay, almost falling over him in the darkness. With questing fingers she found his war club and picked it up.

She gasped as she stood again, vision swimming. Her skull must be cracked to ache this badly. She waited out the nausea, and carefully picked her way back to the White man's camp.

The Bear Man sat as she'd left him.

"Where are you from?" she signed.

"All over."

"And Young Warrior?"

Bear Man said the word aloud: "Boston." In signs he added, "Young Warrior will tell you about Boston until you are sick of hearing it."

She grunted noncommittally. Her vision was spinning—the headache shredded her thoughts. *Rest a while.* Then, after a couple of hours' sleep, she'd slip away, find her mare, and be on her way before sunup.

"Name?" Bear Man asked.

In *Dukurika* she said, "Heals Like A Willow." Then made the signs for it.

"Travis," he said, then pointed at the Young Warrior all wrapped up in his blankets. "Dick."

She grimaced against the headache. "Trawis. Dik."

"Please," he signed. "Help the Young Warrior."

She closed her eyes, sinking back. Not even bearing her son had been this painful.

The soft light of morning bathed the land when Richard folded back his blanket. In the half-light the brush had taken on a grayish tint, the dark trees like mysterious spirits suddenly frozen while waving armlike branches.

Richard yawned, reassured by the lilting trill of the meadowlarks and the long call of the robins. Then he remembered the previous day and sat up. Travis Hartman hadn't moved a hair. Blessed God, he hadn't died in the night, had he?

Had yesterday really happened? Or was it all a dream? Across the stream, the Pawnee youth still sprawled, the blood turned black. Damnation, it wasn't a dream. *I killed him. And what does that make me?*

Richard stood, rubbed his eyes with a knuckle, and walked down to wash his face in the clear water. His reflection—little more than a dark silhouette against the morning sky—stared back at him. *What have I become?*

The dark shadow on the water returned no answers.

The fire had burned down to white ash. Richard stirred it and added the last of the branches he'd collected. Bending down, he blew the embers to life. He sat, stomach growling, staring at the flames through vacant eyes while the previous day replayed over and over again.

"Yer up?" Travis asked hoarsely.

"Yes." Was life like firelight? An instant of wavering brilliance, snuffed so quickly?

"Reckon I could use a drink, Dick."

Richard fetched Travis's tin cup and filled it at the spring before crouching at Travis's side.

"Travis, what happened yesterday? None of it makes sense. Half Man going berserk, trying to kill you because I asked questions. The two of you fought like animals. What you did to him . . . ripping his eyes out . . . beating him to death. . . ."

Travis looked ashen, eyes sunken in a drawn face. "A feller's gotta fight like a banshee out hyar. Ain't no way around it. Now, don't go a-blaming yerself for Half Man making his play. He was a-looking fer an excuse. Thought he had me off balance, and took his chance. Come right close ter working, too, Dick. Now, afore ye gets all carried away with yer philos'phy, think hard on this: Reckon he's a-laying out there, all stiff and gone under. If'n I hadn't a kilt him, we'd both be laying hyar dead. Green's whiskey'd be plumb gone, and that Pawnee coon would be one rich red son of a bitch."

"And the young man? I don't understand that. Where did he come from? What did he want?"

"I ain't figgered that meself." Travis resettled himself,

wincing as he eased his side. "But, coon, no matter what, we was dead men again. The only thing what saved us was Heals Like A Willow, the Snake woman. I was looking inta that Pawnee kid's eyes. He was gonna kill us dead with that bow, and take the whiskey. That light was a-burning in his eyes as he looked at the tins. And right then, Willow up and laughed. Saw the expression in his face, didn't ye?"

"Yes. His face screwed up like something wild. It scared me, Travis. I saw she was tied. I just couldn't watch him kill her like that."

Travis chuckled—and winced. He lifted a hand to his side. "Reckon I didn't bet wrong on ye, Dick. I saw it in yer eyes on the river that day."

"Travis, please. I'm not the kind of man you think I am. I could never be. My roots are different from yours, not of this wilderness. My only wish is to go home and take up my life again."

"With this Laura? Want ter tell me about her?"

"No."

"Wal, then, best check yer stitching, coon."

Richard lifted Travis's shirt. The sliced leather was blood-crusted now. "I've got to get this off you, wash it. Then I'll stitch it back up again."

"I'd be obliged."

Richard squinted uneasily at the curving wound in the hunter's side. It looked terrible. The skin was puckered and red; blackened blood had soaked into the thread and dried. Here and there, where the sewing was uneven, meat could be seen, and yellow crusts of pus had risen.

How on earth did I ever do this? Even now Richard felt faint.

"Is the stitches pulling?" Travis asked, looking down. "Nope? Well, that's some, it is. If'n she don't tear, I reckon I'll heal up pert."

"How do you feel?"

"How do I feel? What sort of idiot Doodle question is that? I feel like if I laugh or sneeze, my guts is gonna fall out on the ground."

"I mean, besides that."

"Hot. A little giddy and girlish. Sort of floaty. Reckon the fever's a gonna start."

"I'll get you more water."

"I'd take that right kindly." Travis closed his eyes. "Hyar's things ye need ter do. Go strip them Pawnee corpses. Half Man had powder, bullets, and makings in his possibles. Reckon we'll take that kid's bow and arrers, and any outfit he's got. Pull them moccasins, and wrap the whole keeboodle in their blankets. Ye savvy this, Dick?"

Loot the dead? Richard's stomach turned. "Yes. I'll do it, Travis."

"Roll up all the plunder—inter a pack, understand?"

"Yes."

"Keep watch, Dick. Check the priming in my rifle. If'n ye needs ter shoot, pull the cock back, pull the back trigger first, then the front one. She won't shoot like that Injun trade gun did. This one's a Hawken. Back trigger first."

"You think there will be more trouble?"

"Hell, I never counted on that second Pawnee yesterday. He caught us nigh dead to rights. Be careful, Dick. Oh, and one other thing. I asked Willow ter stay and help ye. Maybe she will, maybe she won't. Keep in mind, boy. She's Injun. Aboot as trustworthy as a buzzworm."

"She's a woman, for God's sake!"

"She ain't no *white* woman, Dick. She's Snake . . . and she picked up that Pawnee kid's war club and went ter sleep with it last night. Don't turn yer back on her."

But she was so pretty! Richard glanced over his shoulder. She lay under the blanket he'd draped over her last night. When he looked her way he could see her eyes glint, narrowed slits, watching his every move.

Even the wary vigilance of a wounded and hunted animal finally ebbs. Heals Like A Willow lay under her blanket, hurt and exhausted. The fear of the White men, despite their assurances, goaded her to watchfulness—as if she could defend herself, groggy and swimming as her senses were. Her punished flesh, however, demanded respite, no matter what the consequences.

Willow never realized when she crossed the divide from consciousness to sleep. . . .

I remain hidden beneath my blanket the way a grouse tucks herself under a log when coyote is hunting the black timber. The scent of danger lingers on the wind, something acrid, like the stench of rot mixed with smoke.

I hear a stick crack in the trees behind me. A foot crackles dry needles as weight shifts in the darkness.

Who? I peer out at the shadowed forest with new alarm, but see nothing in the dark shadows.

When I look back at the White man's camp, a giant bear now sleeps where the wounded White man was. The fierce head rests on large paws, the claws gleaming in the fragile moonlight that penetrates the dense canopy of the trees. He is an old animal, his silver-tipped hair giving him a frosted look.

Buckskin rasps against bark in the forest as the enemy creeps closer. The sound is loud enough, close enough, to stop my heart—but the giant bear doesn't hear. He sleeps on, and only now do I notice the beast's breathing is labored and weak.

He's dying. The voice repeats over and over within me. The bear couldn't protect me if he wanted to.

I tense under my blanket as stealthy feet come closer, ever closer.

Run! I throw off my blanket and dash for the timber like a frightened rabbit. I know I am hurt but fear gives my legs new power. So long as I don't think, don't accept my weakness, I can run forever.

I duck between the trees and into the dark protection of the forest. I know this place, understand how the elk trails run—well defined as they leave the clearing, but fading into nothing back in the black timber. I duck shadowy branches, leap deadfall in my desperate haste.

He is still chasing me, crashing through the forest, his steps pounding the ground, shaking the very earth. I charge ahead, heart hammering, arms pumping, full-tilt through the jumble of interlacing branches, deadfall, and duff.

Sticks snag my dress, and I have to bat branches aside as the forest closes in. Where a huge tree has fallen across the trail, I drop to my belly and squirm under, only to plunge ahead into a virtual net of splintered dead wood.

In the end I have to wiggle through the deadfall like a bull snake through a serviceberry thicket.

Upon reaching the other side and regaining my feet, I stagger into a grassy, moonlit clearing. From the trees, an owl hoots, and coyotes yip and wail in the distance. I circle, panting for breath, while my body shakes with fatigue. No matter where I turn, an impenetrable mass of forest blocks any escape.

The owl hoots again, and the coyotes sound like they are laughing.

He's coming, dry wood cracking as he pushes through the deadfall.

The moonlight shines eerily in Packrat's crazy eyes. He smiles at me, and throws his head back to scream his triumph at the stars. As the ululation echoes, the forest turns silent.

Packrat grins, moonlight sparkling on his teeth, and speaks to me from the Land of the Dead: "Your souls, Willow. This time, I want your souls . . . forever. . . ."

He opens his arms and steps forward, his moccasins sinking into the brittle grass.

How do I defeat the dead? I back away, the chill certainty of defeat shivering through my exhausted body.

So much pain, so much hurt, is it worth it? Why continue to fight when the only result is more suffering?

A voice inside me says, Give up, Willow. The world belongs to Coyote, full of tricks and pain. Drop to your knees. Let Packrat take your souls. Accept it. Misery is inevitable.

Packrat cocks his head in anticipation, his shadowed eyes like black pits in his smooth face.

At that moment, the mist white dog dances into the clearing, twisting and leaping. He cavorts like milkweed down on the wind, flitting this way and that, twirling and rising, then rushing down to skim the surface of the grass.

Packrat's expression strains with shock and disbelief. The mist white dog dances past him and blood begins to drain from Packrat's mouth. He falls, sprawling in the grass. His mouth opens and closes, making bubbles of frothy black blood.

Panic drives me thrashing through the forest. I must find a way out.

The pale mist dog dances before me, teasing, then leaps, curls in the air, and beckons. Fear burns bright within me, but I follow the spirit dog. The way leads down a winding maze of trails that crisscross through the dark forest.

At the foot of a mountain, the way turns steep and rocky. I climb with the mist dog cavorting above me like a spark from a fire. From rock to rock, grasping for purchase with fingers and toes, I lever myself up the mountain. Finally, I pull myself onto a high pinnacle.

There the mist white dog sits, his tail wagging. As if irritated, he barks. When I do nothing, he whines insistently.

"What are you?" I ask, reaching out to pet the animal.

I barely touch him when, in a flash, he strikes savagely, sinking teeth into my hand.

I cry out, tear my hand away, and stagger back. The mist dog shoots up, spinning in the air. This time, instead of barking, he howls with Coyote's keen voice. The misty hair hardens, and the pale color darkens. I cannot mistake that pointed muzzle, or the pricked triangular ears.

For one eternal instant, I stare into Coyote's blazing yellow eyes. Then, in a snap of the fingers, he turns and races off, his bushy tail bobbing behind him as he skips across the landscape.

I grind my teeth against the pain. Settling onto the rock, I tuck my bitten hand in my lap. I fight the desire to weep.

TWENTY

The passions that incline men to peace, are fear of death; desire of such things as are necessary to commodious living; and a hope by their industry to obtain them. And reason suggesteth convenient articles of peace, upon which men may be drawn to agreement. These articles, are they, which otherwise are called the Laws of Nature: whereof I speak. . . .

—Thomas Hobbes, *Leviathan*

The morning grew hot. Slanting yellow rays of sunlight penetrated the new leaves, fresh burst from the bud, to dapple the ground with shadows. Flies buzzed in·a wavering column over the two dead Pawnee. Birdsong, light and melodic, mingled with the tinkle of spring water.

Willow lay still, recruiting her strength as the Young Warrior, the one called Dik, cared for the Bear Man. He kept glancing shyly in her direction, unsure of her.

The feeling is shared, White man.

That wretched headache had dissipated to a dull throb that only bothered her when she moved too quickly. She stretched, feeling each muscle and its attendant aches. Better. But how far could she push herself? Had she healed sufficiently? Or, if something went amiss, would she leap to her feet only to topple into a pile again?

The Bear Man moaned. Willow watched Dik lay a hand on his forehead. He mumbled nervously in White tongue, and shook his head.

Willow sat up noiselessly. So far, so good. The headache still throbbed, but her senses weren't swimming. Her bones ached, but she gambled that that would go away with movement. She clutched her war club and stood, waiting for the dizziness. When it didn't come, she took a careful step. Then, to her relief, another.

Dik never heard her, but jumped aside with surprise when she crouched beside him.

She met his startled eyes and smiled innocently, saying in Shoshoni, "If I'd wanted to kill you, Dik, you'd have never known until the instant I broke your·skull."

He bobbed a happy nod and smiled his reassurance, then turned thoughtful brown eyes on Trawis.

Willow placed a hand to Trawis's cheek. "Hot. Fever."

She took a deep breath. Her fingers had looked just like that as they lay against her husband's cheek. Then, too, she'd felt the heat that had burned him to death from the inside out. *I couldn't save him. I failed.*

And this hair-faced White man?

She studied him in the daylight—especially those scars.

The bear had torn off half his face. From the scars' look, he must have been pus-fevered then, too. "Are you strong enough, Trawis? Can you beat the fever again?"

Dik was talking, the words as meaningless as wind over the rocks.

With her hands, she asked: "What medicines do you have?"

Vacant eyes watched her signs, then he slowly shook his head. In reply he spoke White babble.

She leaned back, elbows on knees, and inspected him. "So, you can't even make signs. Are all Whites ignorant of the most basic of things?"

Maybe he didn't know anything about medicine, either. *But, do I? Or am I only fooling myself?* A familiar desperation, one she hadn't felt since Packrat captured her, slipped around her guts. *What if I fail? What if my Power to heal is truly broken?*

Dik rose and walked to a bundle of cloth by his blanket. He ripped off a piece, stepped to the creek, and dipped it in water. When he returned, he used the cloth to wipe Trawis's sweaty head.

Willow lifted the leather hunting shirt to study the wound. Pus had begun to leak from some of the stitches, but other parts had scabbed over nicely. The stitching itself was rough, inexpertly done, but effective.

Dik was babbling again, and Willow ignored it. She looked around, recognizing few of the plants she needed. In her country, she could have found phlox, the first shoots of gumweed, and . . . Well, here, at least, was willow. That would help with Trawis's fever and her own headache. She pulled Trawis's steel knife from his belt.

Dik went silent, unease in his wide brown eyes.

"You think I'd take his knife to kill you? When I have the war club in my other hand?" She snorted derisively, before winding her way down to the patch of willows beyond the spring.

When she had her cuttings, she located a small metal pot in the packs, scoured it with sand, filled it with water, and put it on to boil. With the war club and a flat slab of limestone, she pounded the willow to loosen the bark. Her deft fingers stripped off the bruised bark and placed it in the water to boil.

As she worked, her stiffness eased. From the tenderness, a horrible bruise must have marked her where the war club had glanced off her back—and the rest of her trouble came from the fall from the mare. Thank *Tam Apo*, no bones had broken.

Where the earth had slumped at the edge of the caprock, she located green shoots of goosefoot. The other flowers defied her. This country produced no shooting star, no biscuit root or desert parsley. No balsam root sent up shoots to mark its location. In the soggy ground below the willows, she found mint and added that to her collection.

"Who'd live here?" she wondered. But certainly most of the plants she saw must be edible or medicinal.

By the time she returned to the camp, the willow bark had boiled down to a murky paste. With sticks Willow plucked the pot from the fire and cooled it in the spring. When she could hold the pot, she tasted the bitter contents. Some she drank for her own aches, and then walked up to where Trawis lay.

He was awake, watching her through glittering eyes. Sweat continued to bead on his forehead before slipping down his scarred face in rivulets that disappeared into his beard. She made the sign: "Drink."

Trawis choked down the bitter brew without complaint and gasped.

Dik came to kneel beside her as she lifted the shirt again. Pus not only leaked from the stitches but had begun to swell the flesh. "If only I knew the plants, knew what spirits live in this land."

She glanced sideways at the big triangular tins. "Spirit water? Medicine water? They call it many names." But would it work? What had White Hail said, that he'd seen visions?

Willow tapped Dik on the shoulder and pointed at the tins.

"Whiskey," he said.

"Whiskey," she replied. Then she reached for the tin cup

Dik used to get water for Trawis. "Whiskey," she said, pointing inside the cup.

Dik frowned, then nodded hesitantly before taking the cup. She watched, seeing how he untwisted the lid and poured the clear liquid. No doubt about it, these White men were very clever. Among her people, the best container was still a gut bag. The pottery they made was brittle, primarily for the storage of winter foodstuffs.

When Dik brought her the spirit water, she did not take it at once. She leaned forward, smelling its tang, and cautiously looked into the liquid. She didn't quite know what to expect, maybe some amorphous form swirling like fog, faces, or tiny shapes. But only clear fluid lay between the surface and the bottom of the cup.

She had been around Spirit Bundles, fetishes, and medicine before. Most could be felt—a sense of Power in the air. Now, she felt nothing, no sense of threat. Nerving herself, she took the cup and studied the wound.

"White man's spirit water," she mused. "White man's wound." Her mind made up, she poured the spirit water along the puckered cut.

Trawis grunted, eyes popping open as he tried to sit up.

"Shssh!" she told him, placing her fingers to his lips and easing him back. "Do not fight."

Dik was speaking in low tones, talking to Trawis. She caught the word "whiskey" a time or two.

Trawis blinked, then stared into Willow's eyes. He signed: "That will cure or kill me."

She nodded, then scrutinized the wound to see if anything happened. Would it smoke? Perhaps little demons would come wriggling out like worms. She'd seen some of the *Tukudeka puhagans* suck bloody feathers, bear claws, and other objects from the sick. Would such things pop out of Trawis?

The pus pockets would be a problem. She'd seen Dik digging in the leather bag that lay beside Trawis. She pulled it over, found an awl made of metal, and raised the sharp point to the light.

"What you do?" Trawis signed. Dik was looking nervous again. Did neither of them have a brain in their heads?

"Your wound must be drained." She made the signs, then bent over his stitched side. Unlike plants in strange country, when it came to draining wounds, she had plenty of practice. The metal awl worked much better than the sharpened rabbit bones she was used to. She lanced the puffy flesh, twirling the awl at the same time.

Trawis grunted and hissed as she worked. Mostly he kept his eyes closed, pale features even whiter, if that were possible.

"You'd think I was working on a ghost," she muttered to herself. Then looked up to meet Dik's eyes. She handed him the cup and pointed at the whiskey again.

He nodded hesitantly and left.

Willow lanced the last of the pockets, very gently squeezing the wound. To her satisfaction, the pus mostly ran clear. She dribbled whiskey on the oozing sections, and bent down to squint at the flesh while Trawis made suffering sounds. To her disappointment, nothing like bloody feathers or bear claws popped out.

She sighed and sat back, thankful that the willow-bark extract had killed most of her headache. To the uncomprehending Dik, she said, "I can do no more for now. Let him rest. In the meantime, I will boil the goosefoot and mint for something to eat."

Dik smiled at her then, soft lights in his brown eyes touching her soul. He took her hand, raised it, and pressed his lips to the skin on the back. In clear tones he said, "Thank you."

In return, she lifted his hand, brushing her lips on the back of the pale skin. "Thank you." Some curious custom of the Whites?

He laughed, shaking his head and jabbering away in White talk.

"Excuse me," she said. "If we are to eat, I had better do something about it. From the looks of things, you Whites would starve to death." As she bent to the task of boiling the goosefoot and mint, the thought crossed her soul: *If the Whites are so helpless, why haven't they starved to death before this?*

Travis hissed, teeth clenched, as Richard poured whiskey on the stitches in his side. It took several seconds for the sting to drain away and the world to come back into focus.

"Waugh! That's some, it is. Damn, I'd like ter give ye a dose of that!"

"You did," Richard said, bending over him. "Back on the boat, remember? When I had the scours? You were the one made me eat that gall. I think it was you who said that the worse the taste, the better the cure."

"Wal, ye better go easy on that whiskey. Tarnal Hell, whiskey's supposed ter go in a feller, not on him."

Richard shrugged. "Perhaps. The pus isn't as bad today. Fever's broken, too. I think Willow was right about pouring it on you."

Travis bit his lip as the inflamed skin on his side cooled in the air. "Spirit water," she'd signed, making a motion for Richard to pour it on the suppurative wound. And damned if it didn't seem to help. The scab was tight and dry on his side, whereas pus had leaked out of his bear cuts for weeks.

Travis looked down at the curving scar. Half Man had come damned close to killing him.

Green would be at the rendezvous today, or tomorrow at the latest. Tarnal damnation, they were a hard day's walk from the river. Time was running out.

"I been laying hyar two days now." Travis made his decision. "Real slow, Dick. Take my hand. Help me up."

"You can't get up! You'll kill yourself!"

"Dave's gonna be waiting. Worrying himself sick." Travis reached out. "Come on! Hell, child, I'm half-healed already. This hyar's a scratch."

Heals Like A Willow came up behind Richard. In her sibilant speech, she said something that Travis could tell was unkind. Richard reluctantly held out his hand and helped pull Travis upright. His weight tugged at the stitches. "Damn!" Cold sweat popped out, the pain building.

"Whew! Hang onto my hand, Dick. Reckon I'm just a hair stiffened up. Need ter move a little, warm my joints."

"Crazy damn bastard!" Richard scowled his disapproval.

"What? Ye larning ter talk like an American?" Travis blinked as he looked around the shaded bottoms. Over there, where Richard had dragged them, lay the Pawnee corpses. They'd be stinking something fierce real soon.

Willow, still muttering to herself, took Travis's other arm. He set his jaw, and took a step, hating the premonition that his guts were about to spill out on the ground.

"I'm just going to walk a little. Nothing tricky like." *And by Hob, don't let me fall down and bust open like a rotten melon.*

For several minutes, he hobbled around, and sure enough, his side seemed to soften. He dared not turn, reach, or bend, but he could walk.

"Now, Dick, I reckon ye might pack them hosses fer me."

"You *can't* travel!"

Travis looked at Willow, his hands making signs. "You would help me get to the river? Help with the horses?"

A curious respect grew in her eyes, then she nodded slowly, almost grudgingly.

"Why did you stay?" Travis asked.

She smiled crookedly while her graceful hands told him, "I did not feel good, either. Head hurt until this morning. I also said I would help Young Warrior."

"You are a good and brave woman."

She laughed cynically at that.

Travis indicated Richard, and asked, "Will you help him with the whiskey?"

After a thoughtful glance, she walked off to bring in the horses. Travis hobbled over to the two dead Pawnee. Glancing back, he saw that Hamilton and the squaw were out of sight. Gingerly, he bent his knees, easing down. The bloated corpses reeked of death. Flies had blown the wounds, and the little maggots were wiggling and feasting under the caked blood. Funny how maggots made rot smell worse.

Travis took his knife from his belt, and did what he

needed to. Placing his prizes in his possibles, he straightened, ever careful of the stitches in his side.

One slow step at a time, he walked back to the horses. Richard had learned the basics of packing, and was doing tolerable well at hoisting the tins, tying the knots, and checking the balance.

"Watch that lash cinch," Travis warned. "Yer a bit far back 'round the belly. If'n that nag were ter throw a fit, ye'd have a hellacious wreck—whiskey all over Tarnation."

When the last of the horses was packed, Travis gritted his teeth and hobbled up the winding deer trail, moving as carefully as possible. How far to the river? Six, seven miles?

And I'm racing along at maybe a mile an hour.

"Travis?" Richard asked, head down.

"Huh?"

"Those men . . . the Pawnee . . . well . . ."

"Well, what, fer God's sake?"

"We ought to give them a decent burial, don't you think?" Richard scuffed his toe on the grass.

"Tarnation! What's a coyote ever done ter ye? Anything?"

"Why, er, no. Nothing."

"Then let 'em eat, Doodle. Coyotes, wolves, buzzards, worms, hell, they all got ter make do out hyar, too, don't they?"

Richard's mouth had dropped open.

"I ain't saying no more about it." And God alone knew, he'd better save his breath for the climb out of this little valley. Those gentle slopes now looked for all the world like the highest of the Shining Mountains.

He was panting when he made it to the caprock, eased over the lip, and looked onto the flats. A sea of grass led eastward to the bluffs above the river. He stepped aside as Dick led the horses past.

"You're a fool, don't you know?" Richard called. "You'll be dead before nightfall!"

Travis squinted up at the sky. "Too much buffler meat in my blood, coon. I'll swear ye this! If'n I up and decides ter die, today, I'll do'er at the river. Hyar's fer the mountains, Dick. This child'll race ye ter the water!"

Heals Like A Willow was saying something in her tongue. Telling him how stupid he was, no doubt. "Wal, hell," he said, whether they heard or not, "Hugh Glass crawlt this country after Old Ephraim tore him up. Afore that, old John Colter outrun the Blackfoots plumb naked. He crossed half the Plains without a stitch on his hide. Me, I got, oh, maybe a hunnert or so. I reckon I'm way ahead o' Colter. And I done been bear-chewed long back. If'n that didn't kill me, well, by God, I'll make her."

An hour later, he was wondering if maybe he shouldn't have had his lips sewed shut along with his side.

Anything ter keep ye from a-spouting off like a jackass! A terrible weariness had settled on him, making each step an agony. Had he ever been this tired?

Yep. And in a hell of a fix worse'n the one I'm in now.

"Travis?" Richard asked, pacing alongside, lead rope in hand.

"Yep."

"Are you all right?"

"Hell, no! As smart as yer always claiming ter be, I'd reckon ye'd be right mindful of what old Half Man done ter this beaver with that knife of his."

"We could rest."

Travis slowed to a stop, staring around at the waving bluestem and the puffy clouds that had built to the west. How far had they gone? Maybe a mile.

Feels like I've crossed half the world. "All right, Dick. Ease me down. Reckon I could rest a bit, get my puff back."

Richard helped him down. The grass prickled against him, smelling of spring. Damn! Why did it have to be so cussed hot? *What I'd do fer a cup of water.*

Heals Like A Willow leaned down, studying him. By God, she was a smart-looking woman. Travis allowed his imagination to play as he watched her full breasts sway while she checked his wound. He'd been too long without a sits-beside woman. The whores in Saint Louis were just relief for a man's pizzle. Maybe if this trip didn't kill him . . .

But he'd had his one great love: Calf in the Moonlight. A young Crow. Her gaze, so like Willow's, haunted him from the past. She smiled at him, that dancing twinkle in her eyes. How they'd loved through that too short period. His heart twisted with the old familiar sorrow.

Hell, stop it. She's dead, damn ye. Ye damned well knows ye cain't live with no woman. Not after her.

Willow hunched down beside him, making signs. "I must find medicine. Then I will be gone"—she held her hand to the sky, making the sign—"two hands."

Two hands? Not long. The sun traveled that in a couple of hours.

He closed his eyes, head spinning. So very weary. The world had gone floaty, shimmery. Travis smiled, falling back into the dream, seeing Calf in the Moonlight. That year had been like magic. Everything had been new, heady as foam on cool ale. A man could come to like living like that, his robes warm each night. And, unlike white women, she was always willing to open herself to his need. How they'd loved, and shared, and merged two lives into one.

And to think he'd always dreamed of having a white wife. But why? White women were nothing but trouble. *Stupid coon, how come ye never understood that afore?*

"Because us fools always bought the notion that white women was fer successful men. Injun women, hell, they's fer the mountains and plains." But a white woman, she had to be cared for, a stay-at-home woman who lived in a cabin, baked bread, and raised children.

He could see Moonlight so clearly. He was walking toward her and she looked up, laughing at him. Her white teeth gleamed, that soft black hair streaming over her shoulder . . . Gone. Dead, lost in the hazy past.

Voices. He knew them, coming from the haze that had wrapped around him.

Someone leaned over him, blocking the sunlight. He frowned up at Michael Immel. Tall and lanky, and so young. Yes, that had to be Immel bending over him.

Travis chuckled hollowly. "Reckon ye had her wrong, old coon. Thought ye'd be headed back ter Saint Loowee a rich man. Figgered ye'd get yourself some fancy lady, all decked in rustling silks. Stick ter the Crows, or maybe the Sioux. If'n ye wants ter do it up right, I'd say find ye a

Cheyenne wife. She'll stick with ye through thick and thin.''

"Travis?"

"Stay away from the Yellerstone, hoss. I had me a dream that you and Jones went under. Dreamed ye were ketched by the Blackfoot and kilt.''

"Travis! Wake up!" A hand reached out of the shimmering past and shook his head.

"Huh?" He blinked and asked, "Dick? Whar'd Immel go? He's just hyar."

"Travis, listen. You're sick. Wounded. This is Richard Hamilton. Willow brought in some cactus and peeled it. She tied it onto your wound. Then she got on her horse and rode away. Travis? *Travis!* Listen to me! What do I do?"

He frowned, mouth dry. "I got a terrible dry on, Dick. Fetch me a tin of water, will ye?"

"Do you hear me?" Dick bent down, eyes wide. "Willow took her mare and left! *What do I do?*"

"Serves ye right fer setting her free, pilgrim. She's some woman, did ye know? Be a sight better fer ye than some white gal who only wants to sit around a house and live on a feller's labor. An Injun woman, Dick, she's more. Work side by side with ye, she will."

"I don't want a woman. I want you to tell me what to do. You're raving, Travis. Out of your head. You just had to push yourself, didn't you? Well, if you die out here, what am I going to do?"

"Foller the rivers, Dick. A feller cain't get lost. Clear out to the Black Hills, all the rivers run east to the Missouri. Beyond the Black Hills, the rivers run north to the Missouri. Any creek will take ye ter the Missouri. Foller the Missouri downstream to Fort Atkinson."

"What about the whiskey?"

"We gotta get that ter Davey. Reckon he'll go bust without her. We owe him, Dick. Kept us alive he did, nursed us after Old Ephraim tried ter put us under. Davey's a good man. Got grit whar it counts. That's all that matters in life— if'n a feller's got . . . grit."

Richard shook his head. "I've got to figure out a way to move you. We can't just stay here. There's nothing to tie the horses to."

"Back," Travis whispered. "She'll be back—in two hands. How long?"

"What?"

"Willow. She'll be back."

"Maybe. If she comes, it will be a miracle. I sure wouldn't."

"Reckon ye would, Dick. It's in ye. Yer not the kind ter up and quit." Damn, when did it get so hot? "Reckon I'd do fer a mite of water, Dick."

"I don't have any, Travis. The closest is back at the spring."

"Wal, I reckon I done without water afore. This child's just plumb tuckered, that's all." He swallowed hard. "Let me close my eyes. Just fer a while."

In the hot blackness he floated, hearing voices from far away. Firelight flickered, and the sparks formed into faces. Immel, Jones, Keemle, Joshua Pilcher, Manuel Lisa. They sat joking, smoking long-stemmed clay pipes. Four heavy log posts gleamed golden in the background, upright to support a square smokehole. Mandan lodge. The fire popped and sparked.

Someone was singing "Yankee Doodle," while a squeeze box wheezed and tooted the notes. Along the southeast wall, where the horses were sometimes stabled, *engagés* danced and cavorted in their heavy white canvas clothing. The red hats bobbed and swung with each merry dancer's pirouetting steps.

"She is dying, Travis," Manuel Lisa said. The long-faced Spaniard watched him through those brooding dark eyes. *"The river, she will never be the same. Perhaps the Omaha chief, Blackbird, poisoned it like he did all of his rivals. We had but a moment, a shining time. The river is going to die soon, choked in steam and smoke. But I have suspicions about the mountains beyond. They, too, will die. But for a time, the freedom will be there."*

"The mountains?" Travis asked. "We're a-headed thar. Me and Davey Green."

"Watch out fer the Blackfeet, coon," Immel warned. *"Watch yer topknot, Travis. They'll hit ye when yer not ready."*

Jones puffed at his pipe, cheeks sucking in. He lifted a lip in disgust, then broke off an inch of the stem, the white clay discolored from the smoke. He puffed again, and smiled, saying, *"Much better. She smokes a mite sweeter now."* Jones raised his eyes. *"Yer stars has always been lucky, Travis. Bug's Boys ain't whar ye expects 'em. Light out south. They'll seek ye all along the river, a-figgering ye'll double back fer the Mandans."*

"Ain't no Blackfoot down here near Fort Atkinson." He wished the fire wasn't so hot. Lord God, he was hotter than a Doodle in a sweat lodge.

"Travis?"

"Huh?"

"Travis! Wake up!"

He felt something cool—water—passing his lips in dribbles. He blinked, dazzled by the bright light of afternoon. A gut water bag was placed to his lips. He sucked down more of the refreshing liquid. Not Immel and Jones, not Lisa. He squinted up at Dick Hamilton and the Snake woman, Heals Like A Willow.

"Travis," Dick told him, "we've got to get you up. Willow made a . . . well, a thing. We can get you to the river."

Travis took a deep breath, hating the lightheaded floating. *Fever! It's still got ahold of me.*

Willow on one side, Hamilton on the other, eased him to his feet. He stood on weak legs, the wound stinging and pulling. The scrubby little mare waited, head down, a travois tied onto her withers. Travis hobbled to the woven mat of willow and hazel branches. Then he settled back, feeling the springy wood give under his weight.

Willow lifted his shirt then, and checked the split cactus on his wounds. She made the signs: "Cactus will keep the wound from drying and cracking. At the river we will poke the wound, make it flow. Then more spirit water."

"Whyn't ye just up and kill me?" Tarnal Hell, that whiskey stung like rattlesnake poison.

He winced when the mare started forward. He eased his side as best he could given the jolting and watched the trails of bent grass made by the travois legs. The sky was clear this afternoon, cloudless and wonderfully blue. The water had helped, but he felt so terribly weak.

He reached into his possibles and brought out the scalp he'd carved from the young Pawnee's head that morning. With his patch knife, he began to carefully scrape the bloody tissue from the skull side of the hardening skin. As the knife scraped, dreams of Moonlight flitted through his head like cottonwood down on warm morning breezes.

TWENTY-ONE

We must not confuse selfishness with self-love; they are two very discrete passions both in their nature and in their effects. Self-love is a natural sentiment, which inclines every animal to look to his own preservation, and which, directed in man by reason, and tempered by pity, is productive of virtue and humanity. Selfishness is nothing more than a relative and factitious sentiment, engendered in society, which disposes every individual to set a greater value upon himself than upon any other person, which inspires men to all the mischief they commit upon each other, and is the true source of what we call honor.

—Jean-Jacques Rousseau, *Discourse on the Origin and Foundation of Inequality Among Mankind*

High clouds burned with a salmon pink radiance in the peaceful dusk. Richard made a final inspection of the night's camp. Through gaps in the trees, he could see the evening-silvered waters of the Missouri flow past. The surface looked so smooth, polished pewter marred only by the shimmering columns of insects that hummed over the water.

He checked—then double-checked—the picket line that held the horses. The knots were tight on the rope that stretched between two cottonwoods. Willow had helped him with the work, surprising him with her strength as she carried the heavy tins of whiskey to the pile. She'd watched him warily as they watered the horses, and studied him with those large dark eyes when they tied the lead ropes to the picket line.

What was it about her? Why did he keep sneaking glances at her? He shook his head, irritated with himself, with the attraction he felt, and concentrated on his duties.

Everything looked sound. Even the fire that he'd made—luck riding his shoulders with this, his second-ever fire from a strike-a-light. His first smoldering spark had caught in the char-cloth and blown to flame in the dry grass he'd used for a starter.

Travis lay on his blankets beside the firepit. His eyes had cleared and his color was better. Tongue stuck out the side of his mouth, he worked on a small patch of hide with his little patch knife. Long black hair streamed from the pale leather. Horse mane? No, the hair looked finer than that.

Richard dropped to a squat. "You feeling all right?"

"Heap better, coon." Travis looked up, mild curiosity in his eyes. "Reckon I caught a tetch of fever today."

"Shouldn't have tried to leave before you were healed."

Travis waved his piece of hide toward the river. "We beat Green hyar, didn't we?"

"They might have poled past here—or been on the far bank."

"Yep, or even sailed if they got wind. But they didn't."

Richard followed Travis's gaze. Willow sat on a downed cottonwood at the water's edge. Since they'd finished chores, she'd stared in silence at the river. At this point it had to be over two hundred yards across. What thoughts were in her head?

Richard said, "I never thought she'd be back. She saved us."

"Yep. I reckon she did." Travis smoothed the glistening black hair with his callused fingers. "Hunt around in my possibles. Build us a smoke, coon."

Richard did so, lighting a twig to start the bowl. He puffed and passed the pipe to Travis.

The hunter pulled and exhaled the blue smoke through his nostrils. "I reckon tomorrow morning ye might want ter take that gnarly-looking brown gelding. I'd backtrack, oh, maybe a mile or two, then cut straight south. Follow along the flats where the bluffs break down toward the river. Yer two days' hard ride from Fort Atkinson."

"What are you talking about? You mean to go get help? Willow says you're going to be all right."

Travis fixed those hard blue eyes on him. "If'n yer not dumber than a Kentucky fence post, I don't know what is. The *fort's* two days *south*. Reckon I'd take that Injun trade gun. Being smooth bore, she ain't fer long shots, but she'll raise anything up close . . . even Pawnee."

Richard took the pipe, staring. "You mean, you want me to ride off?"

"Wal, yer game, Dick. Reckon I'll just up and tell Dave ye got the slip on me, and I kilt ye when I finally run ye down. Reckon that'll give them *engagés* something ter think about. Davey, wal, I reckon he'll weasel it outa me by the time we make the Mandan villages."

Richard drew on the pipe, staring down at the crackling fire. Free? Just like that?

He glanced at the brown gelding standing head down, eyes half closed on the picket line. The evening deepened, faint rays of light spreading amber across the sky while shadows grew among the trees. On the eastern bluffs, several miles away, the hilltops looked golden.

A mourning dove cooed out in the trees.

"What about you? What if Green's really upriver? Do you think Willow is going to stay? She could leave, too."

"Reckon I'm about healed, Dick." Travis lifted his shirt, staring down at the ugly wound. "Ye done right fine. Hell, ye otta seen the job they did on old Louis de Grotte. Looked like chickens danced on his gut."

"I was scared to death."

"I know. So's I. Don't know which of us was shaking worst."

"I was," Richard said softly and vividly recalled his tacky red fingers, the needle dimpling the blood-slick skin, and the sodden pull of Travis's flesh on the thread.

How did I ever do that? He looked down at his hands. The sun had burned them dark brown, the skin rough and callused; dirt made dark arcs under his nails. They looked like a man's hands. That thought startled him. *Are they really mine?*

Heals Like A Willow rose and walked slowly toward them, head bowed, her long glossy black hair slipping around her shoulders. Her leather dress was worn, but it clung to her in a way that accented her broad shoulders, full breasts, narrow waist, and the provocative curve of her hips. The tattered hem ended just below her knees. Richard had never seen a woman's legs before; unabashed, he kept staring. Her skin seemed so smooth and silky. The way the soft leather outlined her thighs and flat abdomen brought thoughts to Richard's mind that he'd never encountered before.

"Reckon ye'd best close yer mouth," Travis observed. "Yer like to start drooling."

Richard threw his tormentor an irritated glance, but by then Willow had arrived. She shook out her blanket, gave Travis a solicitous inspection, then settled herself. Expressionless, she stared into the fire.

"Willow, why do you look so sad?" Richard asked.

She cocked her head, listening intently to his words as she studied him. Were her lustrous eyes larger than a white woman's? Was that why they seemed to engulf him? Could they swallow a man's soul?

She made signs to Travis and he made signs back.

"She says she's sad because her husband and son are dead. They died of a fever this last winter. She was supposed to save them. She's a healer—uh, medicine woman. They died anyway. They were Meat-Eater Snakes, *Ku'-chendikani.* She's with the high mountain Snakes, the *Dukurika,* Sheepeaters. She was on her way home when Packrat—that Pawnee kid ye sent under—captured her."

"How'd she get here?"

Travis made more signs, and Willow's hands traced out the shapes of a response. "She says Packrat was Half Man's son. Packrat was bringing her to Half Man as a sort of Pawnee insult—a way to shame his father for having shamed his mother. Packrat hoped to gain power and prestige among his people.''

Richard scratched at his bristly chin. "Let me get this straight. Packrat was going to give her to his father, and by doing so, shame him?"

Travis puffed on the pipe. "Wal, the Pawnee, they got their own ways of doing things. Like clever jokes. For instance, let's say a warrior says another Pawnee is a miser, selfish when other people are in need. Such a thing can destroy a man's reputation among the Pawnee. To stop any such nonsense, the feller accused of hoarding, he up and gives everything he's got to the feller that shot off his mouth. Ye can damn well bet it would put the gabber in his place fer good."

"I see. Aesop would have liked a story like that."

"He one of yer perfessors?"

"No. He was a Greek. Wrote fables. Like the dog in the manger? Ever heard of that?"

"I reckon."

"Stories with a moral message . . . and the Pawnee put the stories into practice?"

"Reckon they do. And, when ye think about it, it makes a sight more sense than throwing a coon inta jail."

Willow's slender fingers danced.

"What did she say?" Richard longed to reach out and touch her long hair where the firelight played in it.

"Wants to know about us, coon. Yer not married, are ye?"

"No."

Travis's hands molded the response. Willow continued her inspection of Richard, then she signed again.

"She wants to know why you keep staring at her that way. She says it's a lost-puppy look."

Richard blushed and avoided her eyes. Good God, what would Laura think? "Tell her . . . Tell her I . . ."

But Willow's hands were in motion again.

Travis chuckled. "She says that I look at her with lust, but you look at her with a different eye, the soul's eye."

Richard glared hotly at Travis. "Stop looking at her that way!"

Travis laughed out loud, winced, and placed a hand tenderly to his side. Willow glanced curiously between them.

"What about this soul's eye?" Richard asked. "The soul doesn't have an eye."

Travis made his signs. Willow started a response, then made a cutoff sign. She stood, walked over to Richard, and settled herself immediately in front of him. She placed cool hands on either side of his head. Then, her face inches from his, she looked deeply into his eyes.

Richard fell into those endless pools. Brown, limpid, they expanded and engulfed the world with their soft strength. She probed, challenged, and waited for a reaction.

It's as if our souls are touching. Richard's heart leapt, rising to the challenge. He reached up, cupping her face with his own hands, meeting her challenge and searching as she did. The blood had begun to pulse in his veins.

How long were they locked like that? An eternal moment. She nodded then, lowered her hands, and backed away.

Richard sat like a statue, hands frozen in the air, still caressing the memory of her soft warm cheeks. His heart slowed its hammering beat, the blood cooling in his veins.

Her hands formed graceful signs, and Travis said: "The soul's eye."

Richard nodded and took a deep breath as the tingling surge slowly boiled out of his blood. She continued to watch him, her full lips pursed pensively.

When her hands moved again, Travis translated: "What did you see?"

Richard answered, awed, "I saw your soul, Willow."

"She wants to know if you were afraid."

"No. Not at all. Why should I be?"

Travis made signs. "She says most men fear women's Power. Men fear her in particular. She does not act as men think proper. She seeks medicine Power. With it, she destroyed Packrat."

"Willow"—Richard reached out, desperate to keep that link—"I do not fear you. I am a philosopher, a seeker of truth."

"Ain't no sign fer philos'pher," Travis growled. "Hell, I'll just make this up."

"Don't!" Richard cried. "This is important. I've been looking for her! Don't you see? She's proof!"

"Proof?" Travis screwed his face up. "Proof of what?"

"Man in nature, Travis!" Richard beamed in his excitement, Willow watching him with glowing eyes.

"Wal, hoss, if'n ye think's she's a man, yer not only an ignerant Yankee, but tarnal blind to boot!"

Richard grinned triumphantly. "Tell her I have hoped to meet someone like her. I want to . . . to talk to her. Ask her questions."

Travis translated. Willow watched curiously, then responded: "What questions?"

"About God. About perception and the nature of mankind, the epistemological basis of reality that dictates—"

"Whoa, now! Damn it, Dick! I ain't got no signs for none of that hoss crap but God!"

"Dik," she said, then her hand made a sign.

Travis translated: "Learn . . . Talk . . . White man."

"It takes a long time," Richard told her.

She gave him her challenging stare and said, "Willow learn talk White man."

"I'll be damned," Travis muttered. He put his pipe back in his possibles and retrieved the hairy piece of hide. He fingered the long black hair and studied Willow thoughtfully.

Richard grinned. "I'll teach you."

Travis lifted an eyebrow and signed.

"What's that?" Richard asked.

"I asked if she was going with us up the river."

Her fingers flew.

Travis related: "I will travel with you for a while. It would be wise to know more about the White men. You have not been what I expected." In English she ended, "I will learn. Eye of the soul."

"Eye of the soul," Richard agreed. "One day we will talk about God, and nature, and man's place within it."

Travis scraped his piece of hide. "Careful, coon. I gotta hunch she ain't just any old squaw."

"How's that?"

"I believe that bit she said about Packrat. She said she

destroyed him. Watch yer topknot, coon. See that she don't destroy yer soul whilst she's a-looking at it.''

"What do you mean?"

Travis studied Willow thoughtfully. "When she walked up and looked ye in the eyes, didn't ye feel it?"

"I did indeed."

"Power, coon. Heap big medicine. I felt it afore, at Okipa and Sundance, but never from no woman. I reckon she kilt Packrat, all right. And saved our bacon in the process. Reckon she knew what she's about the whole time."

Richard gave Travis a quizzical glance. "How could magic kill? It's irrational. Ask her, Travis. Willow, how did you kill Packrat?"

Travis made the signs, and read Willow's answer: "I drove his soul from his body and made him insane."

Why am I doing this? Heals Like A Willow walked barefoot along the muddy bank of the Missouri, as the Whites called it. The golden morning had dawned cool, with a light mist rising above the water.

Throughout the long night, she'd dreamed of Dik, of the way his soul had reached out to touch hers. She had never dreamed that a man would look at her with such fearlessness. What kind of man was Dik? She'd seen him shaking after killing Packrat, and yet he had no fear of her. Even the Bear Man now looked at her with reservation. Deep in his soul, Trawis understood what she'd done to Packrat, if not the exact way of it.

She crossed her arms, wisps of hair blowing around her like a cloak. *I used my* puha. *I didn't hesitate, didn't worry about acting correctly, or as other people expected me to. I used all of my* puha, *and Packrat is dead. If I had used all of my* puha, *instead of being so cautious, would my husband and baby be alive today?*

She drew a deep breath to counter the bitter ache in her soul. Her husband's face hovered at the edge of her thoughts—but she dared not reach out to him, fearful of what the attempt would do to his souls on their journey to the afterlife.

If only I had allowed myself to use all of my Power. . . . But she had been frightened of where that would lead, and what would happen to her. *And if there is a next time?*

She knotted her fist, refusing to consider the possibility.

The roiling water flowed past—an incredible moving sheet of brown that shaded into gleaming silver before it met the far wooded shore. Behind her, the new cottonwood leaves rattled in the breeze from the blufftops. With it came the smells of grass, wildflowers, and dry earth.

Far out in the river, a giant cottonwood rolled with the current, the branches yellow and pointed, scrubbed bare of bark. Two great blue herons flapped slowly upriver, their needle beaks and trailing feet thin against the sky.

Trawis said that a huge canoe was being pulled upriver, that it would meet them here. She tried to comprehend what he'd told her. A canoe longer than fifteen men. She couldn't form the image of such a thing in her mind.

I will ride this big canoe, and learn more. She stopped, toes in the lapping water, and looked up. An eagle soared in easy circles against the morning sky. *Is that you, husband? Are you still watching out for me?*

No answer came to the aching loneliness inside. What would he say at the sight of so much moving water?

Dry-eyed, she blinked, clearing her soul's vision of his smiling face. Killing the desire in her heart for his gentle touch.

Perhaps getting captured hadn't been such a bad thing. She'd had no time for grief. During that long ride with Packrat, her concentration had centered on endurance, and the battle of wills with her captor. Like two otters on an ice floe, they'd teetered back and forth, but in the end she'd worn him down. Right down to the moment when he drew an arrow back to kill Trawis.

The moment I laughed, I won, Packrat. She curled her toes in the muddy sand. Her only hope at the moment had been to lose him the whiskey, to thwart his little victory. But Power worked in mysterious ways, and Dik had killed Packrat. Why? Because Packrat was beating her. What Indian man would kill another because he was beating a slave?

Strange beings, these White men. Trawis, she could understand. He was just a man, possessed of all the normal things a man was possessed of, and of some things more so. Courage, for one. No one could doubt his courage, or the strength of his soul. Not only had he insisted on traveling to the river when he should have stayed flat, but he had insisted on healing on the way. *And he hasn't died.*

Dik had played a big part in keeping Bear Man alive, but Dik didn't seem to realize his Power. Had no one trained him, taught him to open his soul? What a curious man. He didn't shrink back from a woman using her medicine skills. Didn't he fear the loss of his manhood? That she would somehow weaken him?

Behind her, a rifle made a *pop-boom* as Richard practiced.

"Keep yer eye open, coon! Ye gotta keep yer aim after the flash in the pan!"

She cocked her head, trying to follow the words. "Eye," she knew, and "yer," "ye," and "keep." Dik had worked with her all evening, until she went to sleep, her souls spinning with new words.

Today Dik was learning to shoot, a fact confusing to her, since he'd shot Packrat dead.

She bent down to touch her fingertips to the water and let the crystalline drops run down her hand. *What brought me here, so far from my people? Where is Power taking me?*

A person could ask the questions, and the answers always came, but only after a long time.

She caught one of the drips of water on the tip of her tongue. The important thing was to ask the questions. Two Half Moons might have had a glimmer of that truth when she climbed up under the rim to save Willow from freezing to death.

Perhaps Slim Pole had been part of the pattern, aware of her shaken belief in her Power, and frightened of the consequences among his people.

Red Calf knew and rightly feared me. I would have destroyed her. And to what purpose? Justice? The Pawnee showed a great deal more sense than the *Ku'chendikani* when it came to settling disputes.

Pop-boom!

"Reckon that's a mite better, coon! Ye hit the tree," came Trawis's reedy cry.

"Reckon," that meant to think, but there were other words for the process. "Tree," she'd learned that word, too.

So, you will go upriver with them? Why, Willow? The smart woman you used to be would take a horse and race straight back to the Powder River Mountains. Her gaze played over the huge river. Like clouds, the water never made exactly the same pattern twice.

"And how," she asked herself, "will you act when a White man crawls into your blankets at night? You are a lone woman traveling with men. Men are no more than they are."

As women are no more than they are. But are we so different? Yes, we are. A man seeks to plant his seed in as many women as he can. The more women, the better his chances of making a child. A woman seeks a man who will keep her secure and help to raise the child. Because of this, we are always pitted against each other.

"That doesn't answer your question, Willow. What will you do when one crawls into your blankets?" She made a face at the notion of ghost white skin against hers. It would be the same as coupling with a corpse.

A *Dukurika* woman knew ways of keeping men off. Her hand slid down to the smooth handle of the war club she'd tied to the rope around her waist. With it, Packrat had subdued her. *But I will subdue any man who threatens me.* Similarly, she would claim Packrat's bow and arrows. She hadn't practiced with one since girlhood. Perhaps the time had come to grow proficient again.

Dik will protect me. The thought surfaced in her soul.

"And you are a fool, Heals Like A Willow. Only you can protect yourself. Anything else is a lie."

She entered camp and found the bow and arrows rolled in Packrat's blankets. Stringing the hardwood bow took all of her strength. Most of the arrows were headed with soft-iron trade points, the kind that cut cleanly but bent upon impact with bone. She'd seen the effect they had on a man. Those she would have to save, but the blunt-headed bird points could be used for practice.

Pop-boom! At the shot, the horses started, then relaxed.

She headed toward the shooting, testing the pull on the bow. "Are you ready, Dik? I am coming to shoot against you. You with your White man's rifle, and I with my Pawnee bow."

The Indian pony that Richard rode had the roughest gait he'd ever felt. The little animal hammered each stiff-legged step down the grassy slope, following the travois tracks. Richard held the reins in his left hand, the Pawnee trade gun in the right. To his annoyance, he wasn't a good enough rider to keep from bouncing on the animal's back like a corn kernel on a tin lid.

The horse snuffled and shook its head.

"Whoa, now. Damn you, keep your head up. Travis told me about you. If you get your head down, you're going to buck me right off."

The afternoon sun cast golden light into the hazel-skirted grove of oak and ash that lined the bluffs descending to the river; it blazed in the high tops of the cottonwoods on the floodplain. Beyond, in shadow, the river had a bluish-brown sheen broken by the sinuous lenticular shapes of sandbars on the far side.

The wiry pony picked his way down a deer trail, and onto the grass-rich cottonwood bottoms. Richard booted him, and the little horse pounded his way forward in that bone-jarring trot.

Camp was right where Richard had left it, spirals of blue smoke rising from behind the circular fortification of whiskey tins. Their feet had beaten the grass flat, and trails led down to the water's edge. The other horses whinnied from their pickets.

"Hello, Dick!" Travis called from where he was propped comfortably on the packs. "See anything?"

Richard reined the pony to a stop and gratefully slid off the animal. It took a moment for his rubbery legs to hold him. The muscles quivered like violin strings from gripping the horse's barrel. "Can't these Indians use stirrups?"

"Reckon not. They figger it's only fer white men what can't ride."

Richard led the horse down to water, Travis hobbling along behind. "I saw the *Maria*. She's coming, Travis."

The hunter sighed, then grinned. "Been a sight worried, coon. Hell, now wouldn't it just figger? We make her all the way around that cussed fort, and they catch Davey with them forged papers and confiscate the boat?"

"Well, rest assured, she's coming. I'd say she'll be here by noon tomorrow." Richard watched the horse drink. Each swallow of water could be seen as it traveled up the throat. "Willow's still around?"

"She's gone hunting. I reckon she'll be back." Travis gave him a sideways look. "Yer not sounding happy."

Richard kicked idly at the sand, then stared out over the silver sheet of river. "I guess by noon tomorrow, I'll be breaking my back on the cordelle, that or wearing a hole in my shoulder with the pole."

"Reckon so." Travis was silent for a moment. "Why didn't ye run? Ye could have kept right on going—straight south into the fort."

"It was tempting. To be honest, I thought about it. I thought about a lot of things. But I have an obligation, Travis. You were wounded on my account. I gave the Pawnee the opportunity. If I'd kept my mouth shut, he'd be alive, you would be healthy, and I wouldn't have killed a man."

"That bothers ye? That ye sent that Pawnee under?" Travis lifted a grizzled eyebrow.

"I keep thinking about his body, the way it bloated. How it was covered with flies. I have nightmares at night, shooting him over and over. All that blood . . . the look in those glassy eyes. . . . He was a young man, Travis. Barely more than a child. I still don't believe I killed—murdered him like that."

Travis scuffed his moccasined toe in the soft sand. The

horse had raised his head, muzzle dripping, ears pricked, to look out over the river.

"Thought ye was the one wanted ter be so damned rational? Wal, if'n ye'd not shot him, Willow'd be dead. I'd be dead. And, why, Tarnal Hell! Ye'd be dead, too!"

"It's not a matter of rationality. It's . . . it's how I *feel*, Travis."

The hunter said, "Wal, Dick, I ain't got the words fer it, not to palaver with a philos'pher. Maybe it's God, maybe it's plumb chance, but there's times when a body's headed fer a mess. Half Man and me, we both knew that first day on the trail that one of us would kill t'other. He figgered he'd walk away, I figgered I would. That was the only real question. What's that word? The one for when something's just bound ter happen? Ain't no way around it?"

"Inevitable."

"Inevitable. That's it, Dick. What's yer philos'phers say about that?"

"They say that human behavior can be changed by reason."

"Wal, maybe so, given enough time, and given men of like minds, but do ye reckon ye could have reasoned that kid outa killing Willow? Or Half Man outa not trying me?"

Richard fingered the lead rope. "I don't know. So many of the answers that were crystal clear are turning fuzzy and fading now."

"Reckon that happens when a man starts growing. This child suspects that any fool can write a book when he's sitting in a room in a city with folks around ter keep his arse safe, a fire in his stove, and his belly full. A feller can justify anything he wants . . . so long as it's rational, and there ain't no consequences if'n he's wrong. But out hyar, wal, it plumb ain't real."

Richard scratched his neck and said nothing, his gut churning.

Travis reached out to Richard's side and tied the piece of hide to his belt so that the long black hair hung down along his leg. "Wear that, coon. It'll bring ye luck."

"What is it? What animal did you take it off of?"

"A kind of skunk that lives out hyar."

Richard fingered the long hair. "Is it a fetish?"

"What in hell's a . . . sure, yep. Reckon so. That's what she be." Travis had a funny look in his eye. "Wal, now, Dick, I got me an idea. Seems we got us eleven hosses, twelve if'n ye counts Willow's. Ain't much above here but trouble. The Omaha country is a couple of days' journey north, but beyond there, yer not going ter find nobody but Sioux, Rees, and Cheyenne until we reach the Mandan. Ain't none of 'em but would lift them hosses plumb quick."

Richard fingered the glossy skunk hair. "What do we do?"

Travis reached for his possibles and pulled out his pipe, gesturing with it as he talked, "Wal, the way I'm thinking, a coon needs to have help a-guarding these hosses. Now, if'n ye'd be of a mind not to escape, perhaps I could use ye."

"Promise not to escape?" Richard frowned, then shook his head. "I can't, Travis. What was done to me was wrong. I have ethical values, and I must stick to them."

Travis pursed his lips, the effect pulling the scars tight across his ruined face. "Yep. A man's gotta do what he's gotta do. I keep forgetting that."

"Why do I always get the feeling that you're mocking me?"

"Mock ye? Wal now, Dick, that's about the silliest idea I've heard since flying buffler chips. Reckon ye'd never catch me a-funning ye, not with all them philos'phy ideas in yer head."

A twinkle filled Travis's eye as he turned and made his way carefully back to the fire.

Richard's horse jerked him away from the river, but he led the animal to the picket line instead of letting it crop.

After he'd tied the horse, he stopped and fingered the fetish. He lifted the long hair and sniffed. It didn't smell like skunk.

He was still studying it when he got to the fire. "You said this would bring me luck?"

"Yep." Travis seemed suddenly fascinated by his stained-leather knee. "It's a sign of respect in these parts, Dick. Reckon ye could say it's a sign of a man, one ter be listened ter, and looked up ter."

Richard frowned and sat cross-legged in front of the fire. "Respect? Why? I mean, why me?"

Travis puffed on his pipe and handed it over to Richard. "Ye done a man's job this hyar trip. Ye saved me . . . saved the whiskey. Saved Willow, fer that matter. Made us rich on hosses—and they'd have cost a heap of goods about the time we made 'er to the Mandans. Yer a man, Dick. By all the rules of this country, red and white. That thar, what did ye call her, fetish? That fetish ain't nothing more than the proof of it."

Richard glanced skeptically at Travis. "But I'm still a slave?"

"Man's a slave only so long's he allows himself ter be. Reckon that Packrat, he larned that lesson and did her the hard way."

"He was going to kill Willow."

"Of course, she'd beat him at his own game. When a man's got no choice but ter kill his slaves, he's plumb licked. At least by that particular slave. See whar my stick floats, Dick?"

"Not exactly." Richard puffed on the pipe. The tobacco was welcome—even if it wasn't up to Bostonian standards. "What good is freedom if you're dead?"

"Ye ever figger what would happen if all the slaves in the world said no ter their masters? Reckon they'd be beat the first day, whipped the second, starved from then on, maybe even all kilt. Wal, all right, so let's say all the slaves was dead all over the world. Now, do ye reckon thar'd be any more slaves?"

"Someone will always turn another person into a slave," Richard objected, pointing with the pipe stem. "Plato wrote in his—"

"Plato? Another philos'pher in a room?"

"He was. And my point still stands."

Travis pulled at the fringes on his sleeve. "I reckon so, but a slave can only stay a slave if'n he sets more store on his life than on his freedom. I got the story outa Willow. That's how she drove that Packrat coon plumb crazy. Ain't the first time I heard that story. Come upriver with a man what wouldn't be a slave."

"Life is a pretty powerful argument . . . especially when it's yours."

"Hand me my pipe back! Ye gonna smoke her dry?"

"Sorry. I'm sort of used to arguing with a pipe in my hand, but with much better tobacco."

"Life, ye say," Travis mused, taking a pull. He studied the tendrils of smoke rising from the stained bowl. "Ever hear tell of them Spartans? The ones back in Rome what fought off that Egyptian king and died fer it?"

"That's a Persian king. At Thermopylae, in Greece. No Romans were involved. What's your point?"

"They died ter save a heap of others, Dick. Reckon yer no different, not down deep. Reckon if'n it was Katy bar the door, ye'd be just as quick jumping inta the breach. Figger this"—Travis waved his pipe in emphasis—"yer house is on fire. Now, yer whole family is in thar a-screaming, and all ye've got ter do is jump inta the fire, burn yerself, and hold the door open to let 'em out. Ye'd do her, wouldn't ye?"

"Using my family for an example isn't very smart, Travis. If it was my father in there, I'd be throwing oil on the blaze by the bucketful."

Travis raised an eyebrow. "No wonder he kicked ye outa Boston. But, anyhow, ye get my meaning."

"Yes, yes, the examples are necessary. Just not sufficient."

"Huh?"

Richard grinned. "Philosophical standards—but, yes, people do risk their lives, and lose them to save others. That's not at issue here. Slavery is."

"Reckon so, coon. And my point is that no slave needs ter be a slave if'n he's willing ter give up his life ter save himself and all the others. Now, tell me, ain't it damned peculiar—illogical, in yer words—that all the slaves don't just up and quit? Take their chances just like folks do all the time to save their friends and kin, hell, even strangers! No one would have to be a slave again . . . ever.''

Richard reached for the pipe, puffing as he frowned. "Mass civil disobedience."

"Yep."

"It would never work. It is the nature of the slave to value vain hope for the future over almost certain death and potential greater good."

"Plumb irrational, wouldn't ye say?"

"I see what you're getting at. Sure, people are irrational all the time. But, don't you see, it's only through rational action that we can improve our lot."

"Uh-huh. And if'n ye was rational, ye'd give me yer word that ye'd stick her out to the mouth of the Yellerstone, and help me with the hosses."

"Why do you care so much?"

Travis stared moodily at the fire. "Just a cussed streak I got in me. I reckon the bear's outa the cage. Maybe I want ter see him become a real bear."

TWENTY-TWO

Then again, on the other hand, the unsophisticated mind takes under its guardianship, the good and the noble (that is, what retains its state of meaning in being objectively stated), and protects it in the only way possible here—that is to say, the good does not lose its value because it may be linked with what is bad, or mingled with it, for to be thus associated with badness is both its condition and necessity, and the wisdom of nature is found in this fact.

—Georg Friedrich Wilhelm Hegel,
Phenomenology of Mind

Travis grinned as he watched Willow. She stood frozen, stunned as a surprised deer, mouth ajar, eyes wide with astonishment. Her disbelief tickled him clear down to his roots. In the end, she could only shake her head and mutter softly. The *Maria* was being poled upriver, momentum carrying the boat forward against the current before the next set of the poles. The keelboat might have been some giant water insect, propelled by multitudes of legs across the roiling brown water.

Travis hitched his way down the muddy bank to stand between Willow and Richard. He raised his rifle, firing a shot into the air. Willow jumped at the concussion.

"Sorry, gal," Travis mumbled.

"All right," she whispered absently. Shots answered from the boat, puffs of blue smoke rising over the cargo box. In incredulous tones she rattled away in her Snake tongue.

Travis pressed a gentle hand to his side. Still damned tender. "Dick. Like her or not, yer on hoss duty fer a couple of days."

Richard gave him an uneasy glance. "Why me?"

Travis chewed at his lip and squinted into the midday sun. "Wal, reckon it's like this, coon. This hyar beaver's got a cut in him bigger and uglier than Hob's smile. Reckon I cain't go a-traipsing after the hosses. I plumb sure ain't gonna turn Trudeau nor any of them other French lard eaters out to guard 'em. That leaves ye, Mister Hamilton."

"I told you I'd escape."

"Hoss crap! If'n ye'd a wanted ter, ye'd be gone."

"I told you, it's ethically untenable. I had a responsibility to ensure that you made it back to the boat. That you were injured was partially my fault. Here's the boat. When they drop the plank, I will have fulfilled that obligation."

"Nope. Nothing's changed. I ain't up ter hunting and hoss keeping. Not fer another week at best. Reckon ye can do yer duty, then escape when I get all healed."

"Travis Hartman," Richard whispered, "you are a black bastard at heart."

"I reckon so."

Maria turned gracefully, coasting in toward the bank. Travis had picked this place precisely because the bottom dropped off and the river didn't carry much current. The perfect spot for onloading the whiskey.

"How do, coon!" came a familiar cry, and Travis shaded his eyes to study the brawny black man at the bow. He stood like a sassy pirate, his dark face shadowed by a large-brimmed felt hat.

"Baptiste? Tarnal Hell! What are ye doing aboard?"

"Ha! I be yor new partner, coon!" The ebony face split with a smile. "Life at the fort ... wal, 'tain't nothing but poor bull. I reckoned I'd come along and hunt down that Pawnee what kilt you, but I see yor topknot's still on!"

"Reckon so, but she was Katy bar the door! Don't ye come a flying off ter give me no bar hug, neither. Ye'll squeeze me guts clean out!"

"You hurt?" Green called from the cargo box as the *Maria* swung up against the shore. *Engagés* were craning their necks, eyes wide as they whispered back and forth.

"Sliced nigh in two! But old Dick, hyar, he done sewed me up."

"Got a squaw, too?" Green studied Willow with a cocked look. "Hell! That's the Snake woman I saw at Fort Atkinson. Where's that Pawnee kid she was running with?"

"Dick raised him. Shot him plumb center."

Green gave Hamilton a sidelong glance. "Do tell."

The plank came out and Willow backed slowly away, looking like a rabbit about to break for the tall sage. "Easy, gal." Travis made the signs. "You are safe. No one will hurt you, I promise."

She gave him an uncertain look and signed: "Yellow-haired White man tried to buy me for two guns at fort."

"Why, I'd a fetched five fer ye." Travis winked to reassure her, then in a loud voice hollered: "Hey, Dave! This hyar's Heals Like A Willow. I don't want no harm t' come ter her. She's with me." Travis narrowed an eye to glare wickedly at the *engagés* who stared down with appraising eyes. "Y'all hear that, coons? If'n she don't kill yer arse fer trying ter fool with her, I'll do it! Or maybe Dick, hyar.''

Laughter rose at that.

"The woman is to be left alone!" Green ordered.

Henri was leaning on his steering oar, and rubbed his blunt jaw as he glanced dubiously back and forth between Willow and the *engagés*. He finally muttered, *"Chercher des ennuis! Beaucoup troubles."*

Travis patted Willow on the shoulder. "Ain't nobody gonna bother ye none."

Engagés trotted down the plank, headed for the trees and the tins of whiskey. They leered at Willow with hawkish eyes, and she glared right back at them; her grip on the war club tightened.

Baptiste strode down like a lord, his long buckskin shirt swaying at mid-thigh. Leggings and high moccasins rustled with long fringe. A man might have danced on those broad, muscular shoulders. White teeth flashed in his black face as he looked Travis up and down.

Willow uttered an amazed sound as Baptiste stopped before them. She made signs, and Baptiste laughed, signing back. Timidly, Willow reached up to rub at his face, and then his hands.

"What's this?" Richard whispered, leaning toward Travis.

"Trying to see if the soot will rub off," Travis told him. "Dick, this hyar black cutthroat is my old friend, Baptiste. He goes by Baptiste because he's afraid some coon might recognize his real name."

"I reckon there's a death warrant fo' me in the United States," Baptiste said easily. He withdrew his hand from Willow's and offered it to Hamilton. The Yankee swallowed hard, but shook, the grip strong.

Good work, Dick. That'll set ye right with Baptiste.

Baptiste turned to Travis. "Yor looking a mite peaked, coon. I done warned you about that snaky Pawnee."

"Wal, I fetched him in the end." Travis cocked his head. "But I thought certain ye had more sense than to sign on ter a crazy venture like this. Ye've always had a fondness fer that topknot of yern."

Baptiste leaned his head back, the sun's rays bathing his face. "A man can't live shy all his life, *mon ami*. I smelled a possibility."

Green came bouncing down the plank issuing orders to the *engagés* as they filed out of the trees, heavy tins perched on bent shoulders. He looked at Travis, worry in that bulldog face. "How badly are you hurt, Travis?"

Travis grinned, and lifted his shirt.

Green let out a low whistle. "How long ago did this happen?"

"About three days. Dick, hyar, he done a mite of sewing on this old coon. Reckon I'd let him darn my socks now. He's plumb practiced."

Green, muttering, gave Richard another skeptical glance.

Baptiste bent down and scowled at the wound. "Stay at it, Hartman. Another five or six years on the river and you'll use up all the hide you got left."

"Huh! Wal, come the day my pizzle gets sliced up, this child's quitting!"

Baptiste gave Willow an amused inspection, adding, "Then steer clear of this'un, coon. She's pizen!"

Richard stiffened, but Travis reached back with a hand to cut him off. "Baptiste, I want ye and Dick hyar ta see ter the hosses. Reckon I'm gonna take my leisure like a booshway, and ride like a king up on the cargo box."

"Travis!" Richard cried.

Travis ignored him. "Now, Baptiste, Dick hyar, he's a mite of a greenhorn yet. Reckon I can recall when ye were of a same mind, all piss and vinegar and damn little sense. Dick's got savvy and larns right quick, but ye need ter explain things in simple words and with a lot of detail. Like I say, he's a-larning. That said, I'd take it as a favor if'n ye didn't cut his throat fer a couple of days, lessen, of course, he really riles ye."

Baptiste snorted, his dark stare pinning the sputtering Richard. "I'll see. Come on, pilgrim. Show me what you've got."

Travis gestured for Richard to follow the black man toward the picket. Willow hesitated, then trotted after them, sticking close to Richard.

Green squinted, then pointed. "Hanging on his belt . . . that's not what I think it is?"

Travis chuckled. "Reckon so. Our Boston Yankee thinks it's a . . . what in Hob, uh, 'fetish.' That's what he calls her."

"What's a fetish?"

"Beats hell outa me. But pass the word. We don't want none of the crew a-telling him he's wearing that Pawnee's topknot on his side."

"Civilized, my ass!" Green fingered his chin.

"Whar ye been?" Travis asked, turning toward the boat. "Take my hand, Dave. Reckon I cain't afford ter fall off'n the damn plank. Thanks."

Green helped him balance as they crossed to the deck. "Had no trouble at all. Seems as if the Company factor was down sick." Green slapped a hand to his leg. "That Baptiste, he's a sly one. Showed up just as we landed at the fort. He was standing on the bank cursing like a sailor. Gave me all kinds of hell for being late. Said we were due in a week ago, and how in hell could the Company expect to keep the upriver trade if the supplies were late."

"Do tell?" Travis settled himself against the corner of the cargo box and slid down onto his butt.

"You put him up to that?" Green asked.

"Nope. Reckon he figgered this was his chance ter head back upriver. Baptiste, he's a clever coon. He's figgered there's a chance fer him with us. One he ain't never gonna get with the Company. Treat him square, and he'll back ye to the hilt."

Green watched the last of the whiskey being toted aboard and stowed. Henri was shouting orders as the plank was drawn in. "After that cocky captain signed our papers and had his boys search the boat, Baptiste walked up as plucky as a strutting cock and hired on. Asked for ten percent."

"Ten?"

"Yep, and I gave it to him. He's another American— black though he might be. He'll stick . . . if you will."

The *Maria* was swinging out from the bank as the polers drove her into the current. "He'll do. Half cat scratch and all fury. But he's just looking fer the same things the rest of us is. Wants ter be treated like a man, and willing to fess up ter the consequences.''

"He's got it." Green watched the trees passing by on the bank. Through the trunks, the horses could be seen, Baptiste, Richard, and Willow riding along. "Since we weren't under suspicion, I took an extra day and signed on three more *engagés*. The gamble is they'll more than make up the time. Now, what's between you and that damned Yankee?"

Travis leaned back and told the story. When he finished, he cocked a grizzled eyebrow. "And that's the whole of it. That Packrat had us dead ter rights. Woulda kilt us all, and lifted the whiskey. Willow suckered him, and Dick kilt him. We end up with fat cow instead of poor bull."

"Is he going to run?"

"Hell, I don't know. He don't even know. He's all knotted up inside over this philos'phy. Got all these high and mighty notions of ethics and responsibility. Reckon the trouble is, folks can spout what they will, but that coon's never mixed his idears with real life. It's a-playing Hob with him. Shoulda seen him trying ter talk me inta burying them damn Pawnee."

"So, you sent him out with Baptiste?"

"Yep. Poor Dick. Fer a feller full of worries about being a slave, I reckon old Baptiste is a gonna fetch him up right smart."

TWENTY-THREE

As an unbroken courser raises its mane, paws the ground, and rages at the sight of the naked bit, while a trained horse patiently suffers both whip and spur, in a like manner the barbarian will never extend his neck into the yoke which a civilized man bears without murmuring, but prefers the most stormy liberty to a peaceful slavery.

—Jean-Jacques Rousseau, *Discourse on the Origin and Foundation of Inequality Among Mankind*

Richard studied Baptiste surreptitiously. With his swinging fringe, heavy rifle, knife, and a pistol jammed into his belt, the hunter fit every image of a swashbuckling brigand. He sat his horse as if he were a centaur. The blacks Richard had known were mostly house servants, like Jeffry, waspish, elegant, and mannered.

Baptiste rode to Richard's left, Willow to his right. For once she wasn't asking for words in her headlong charge to learn English. Rather, those beautiful eyes reflected a pensive struggle. Reprising the morning's events, no doubt.

He longed to reach out, to pat her arm reassuringly. Anything to see that warm glow in her eyes. His gaze kept slipping in her direction, fastening on the curve of cheek and nose, the fullness of her lips, those high breasts pressed against the soft leather of her dress.

"Known Travis long?" Baptiste asked. He rode with his polished rifle held easily across the horse's withers.

"No. Only since they dumped me on the deck one night."

"Reckon yor not gonna find a better coon nowhere."

"Indeed?"

Baptiste examined him with veiled eyes before returning his attention to the countryside. Richard had noted the same habit in Travis: constant vigilance.

Richard cleared his throat. "Look. I'm not here of my free will. I was robbed, tied up, and sold to Green. I'm a man, not a chattel!"

Baptiste used a finger to push his hat up on his head. "Then why're you heah? I'd a run by now, hoss."

Richard slumped, wishing he had stirrups. "It's a little complicated. It's partly my fault that Travis got hurt. You heard him. I'll stick it out until he's well. Then I'll do what I have to to gain my freedom."

Baptiste laughed sourly. "Freedom, coon? Look around. Where on God's green earth is you gonna be more free than heah?"

"Boston."

"Shit!"

"Have you ever been there?"

"City, ain't it?"

"Perhaps the grandest in the world."

"They got slaves there?"

"There are . . . some." *Like Jeffry, God forbid.*

"Ain't no freedom in no city, coon." Baptiste's smile rode crookedly on his face. "Ain't no freedom nowhere there's men. Freedom only comes of a wilderness."

"Then you don't know the meaning of freedom. Freedom is born in the mind, in the ability to think and question. It is reason that raises man above the beasts."

"Do tell."

"Indeed I do! Can there be any vocation greater than the search for absolute truth? I think not. And how, the question is asked, can we, as mere mortals, search for the ineffable and sublime? Our only course is through reason, Baptiste. Absolute truth is attainable, and our minds are the levers by which we shall lift ourselves to that lofty goal. There, sir, is the only meaningful freedom."

Baptiste was looking at him as if he were some kind of unusual new insect. "What did you just say?"

"We agree that rationality, the ability to reason, is what sets us apart from the rest of the animals, don't we?"

"The ability to figger."

"Exactly."

Baptiste scanned their surroundings, then frowned. "Reckon so. And yor saying that the ability to figger is what makes men free?"

"Absolutely."

"That's a passel of nonsense, Dick."

"My name is Richard. And if you don't think reason sets us free, what does?"

"Wal, Richard from Boston, fo' me, it was a double-bitted ax."

"I don't understand."

Baptiste made a slicing gesture with his hand. "Whacked off my massa's head. Cut her right clean, I did. Shoulda seen his eyes a-blinking when his head bounced on the ground. A feller don't die right off when his head's cut off, you see. It takes a couple of seconds afo' the blood drains out."

Richard grimaced. "I thought we were talking about freedom, not murder."

Baptiste chuckled. "Reckon it can be the same thing."

"Why'd you kill him?"

"I wanted to be free, boy. I runned off twice. Got ketched both times—and whupped like a damned dog both times. Reckoned I warn't gonna live like that. No, suh. So, I whacked the planter son of a bitch what owned me, and I runned again." Baptiste gave Richard a hard glance. "Now, yor not a slaveowner, are you?"

"N—No, I'm not. I don't believe in it. One human being shouldn't own another human being."

Baptiste jerked a nod. "Reckon I'll tolerate you."

They passed the next minutes in silence. Rather than contemplate the fact that he rode beside an ax murderer, Richard turned his attention to the country. The plants seemed greener in the bright sunlight. Three buzzards spiraled in the hot air. Wildflowers of all colors swayed at the passage of the horses' feet through the tall grass. Birdsong rose and fell.

Richard finally nerved himself and asked, "Is that why you're out here? You can't go back because of, uh, having dispatched your owner?"

Baptiste tilted his head, making another inspection of Richard. "Aw, that's right, I forgit you ain't got no idea of freedom. I'm out heah to be free, coon. It ain't like yor Boston. Ain't no folks out heah to be shackling a man's legs in iron." He jerked a thumb back toward the river where the *Maria* now moved under sail, the wind finally having turned to the north. "I got ten percent share. Why? 'Cause I can be who I is. It don't matter if'n I be a nigger. Dave Green sees a man when he looks at Baptiste. He don't see no runned-away slave. So, tell me, what's all this head-shit about reason and freedom?"

Richard frowned. *God in Heaven, what do I say to that?*

Baptiste went on, "Reckon fo' this coon, I done found all the freedom I can stand. Tarnal Hell, I hated that fort. All them so'jers looking at me like I was some kind of animal instead of a man. Listen well, Mister Dick. So long's you can stay ahead o' them folks from back East, you'll be a free man. It's only when they shows up with their army, and churches, and solid folk that a man's got to bow his head 'cause he's a nigger.''

"That isn't what—"

"Now, I reckon you can chaw on that fo' a while. It ain't no easy thing to larn, and old Travis, he said you needed a mite of larning. So, I'm larning ye, Doodle.''

Richard sighed. "All right, I'll think about it. I'm not a boy.'' He glanced at Willow, but she'd obviously been unable to follow the conversation. *Good! She doesn't know I'm sounding like an idiot.*

"Huh, wal, that's notional.''

"You don't talk like I'd expect a man raised in slavery to talk.''

"How so, massa? Sho 'nuff, I's a-gwine talk like dis from now on? Make yo all feels right at home now, chile?'' Baptiste threw his head back and laughed. "Tarnal Hell, coon. Folks judge a man by how he talks. Old Travis, he done larned me that right off. Told me, 'Now, ye needs ter talk like a white man. Do her, hoss, and ain't no sheriff a gonna figger yer no 'scaped slave.' So I larnt it.''

"How long have you known Travis?''

"Since the day he saved my sorry hide down to New Orleans. Reckon that's back in eighteen and eleven. They plumb near had me, hounds closing in, folks swarming the country with rifles, shotguns, and knives a-looking fo' me. I's about as dangerous a nigger as had been loose in them parts in years. That's when I run acrost old Travis. He skins me up an old live oak and I hides up there in the moss. Meantime, Travis scrapes this gouge in the mud next to the bayou. When that posse shows up, he's a cussing and stamping, swearing some buck nigger just done stole his pirogue.

"Me, I lays up there on that limb, still as an old gray squirrel. That posse, they ask some questions, and finally turn right around and head back south. Travis, why, he scouts around, sees thar ain't nobody watching, and waves me down. From there, we lit a shuck north. Follered the river right up.''

As Baptiste talked, Richard measured those powerful shoulders and swelling biceps. Dear God. Richard absently fingered his neck. How soft and fragile it felt.

"Why did you kill your master?"

"Man can beat another man," Baptiste said simply. "Reckon that ain't so much. Reckon it was justice, Dick. That planter, he's just plumb cruel. Now, I run, and I got beat fo' it. Fair's fair. But he beat hosses, and wimmen, and every slave he had, good, bad, or innocent. I's running again. I knew he knew it. He's waiting, see? Gonna beat me to death in front of my woman and childrens. Make me an example. Shouldn't otta drive a man to desperation. I's desperate, and one day he turned his back when he shouldn't."

"Is cruelty worth a man's life?"

"Ask yerself, Dick. Way I hear it, you done kilt that Pawnee what was beating Willow."

Richard exhaled slowly. *How do I judge him when I'm no better?*

"Then I suppose you understand better than anyone why I have to get away."

Baptiste's hard brown eyes displayed no emotion. "Travis beating on you? Green?"

"No. But they took advantage of me. I was robbed—tied up! They made me sign that contract. Held a knife to my throat!"

"Who did?"

"François and August."

Baptiste betrayed the first surprise Richard had seen. "And yor still alive?"

"If that's what you call this."

Baptiste shook his head. "Waugh! That's some, it is. That François, he's as mean a snake as you'll find. Pilgrim, yor just plumb lucky. Be right happy to see each sunrise. François don't let many of his victims live."

"But they've turned me into a slave here!"

Baptiste turned his head long enough to give Richard a narrow-eyed stare. "Reckon I'm scouting ahead, boy."

Richard licked his lips as Baptiste trotted his horse ahead, the long fringes waving with each step the animal made.

"What that?" Willow asked, breaking her silence and gesturing at Baptiste.

Richard rubbed the back of his neck. "I guess I just made a fool of myself."

" 'Guess'? 'Fool'? Dik?" Her eyes probed his, questioning. Dear Lord God, how did a woman get to be so beautiful?

"Yes, you could say that. Dik a fool."

What kind of people are these? The question hung in Willow's souls like thin blue smoke on a cold day. She walked through the evening encampment, winding between the fires. Men sprawled about the crackling blazes, staying close to sparks and heat in an effort to avoid the humming columns of mosquitoes.

As she passed, the *engagés* looked up at her with lust gleaming in their eyes—just like yellow-eyed bobcats when they inspected a covey of sage grouse. *I am not prey for the likes of you,* she mocked from within. *Not unless you want your head split.*

She'd heard White men called "dog-faces," and how true it was. They all had hair growing out of their faces. At first, she'd been startled. Men shouldn't grow hair on their faces. It made them look peculiar. But then, the Pawnee, Oto, and Omaha shaved their heads, and that looked just as peculiar to her as hair on the face.

Wolf-men. Even to the light-colored eyes. Wolf-men who traveled on a floating lodge bigger than any council lodge she'd ever seen. Their spirit water had healed the wound in Trawis's side. She'd seen her reflection, so clear, in one of their mirrors. Their metal pots could be dropped without shattering the way ceramic ones did. Their heavy rifles killed the small whitetail deer at distances that defied a bow.

Perhaps, like Wolf, they really were powerful.

But what do I think of them? That question lurked in her thoughts and dreams. She'd searched for evil, and found none. Nor had she found anything other than the ways of men. Laughter, lust, hunger, kindness, and cruelty.

When they watched her, it was as men watch a woman; not with suspicion like *Dukurika* would watch a Crow woman, even if she came among them as a friend and not a captive.

Baptiste had become oddly protective when he learned that she'd been a captive. His skin was not painted, but naturally black. He'd patiently allowed her to feel his soft kinky hair so like a buffalo's.

The White men ranked themselves in an interesting way. The booshway was chief. Trawis and Baptiste were like war leaders, and the patroon was in charge of the boat. Finally came the *engagés,* French, a different tribe of White men who spoke a separate language. She still hadn't placed Dik in the system of rank. He seemed high, yet low. He could speak to Trawis or Green at any time. The *engagés,* however, despised him.

Did no one understand his Power? Didn't they see that he was a seeker of visions?

"Willow!" Trawis called from Green's curious cloth lodge. "Reckon we could use ye."

She'd picked up most of the easy phrases. Now she crossed to Green's lodge. She stepped through the flap to see Trawis being settled on a blanket. Two small fires wavered on the wax sticks they called candles. Dik was shifting nervously while Green saw to Trawis's comfort.

"What happens?" Willow asked.

"Stitches have to come out," Dik told her. He looked nervous, licking his lips, and paler than usual.

"Wal, come on, coon," Trawis muttered.

"Travis, don't you think someone with a little more—"

"Hell, ye sewed 'em in, ye can yank 'em out!"

Dik made a face, then leaned down. Green was saying something Willow couldn't understand. Dik lifted a small metal tool from a wooden box. She watched with interest as he inserted his fingers in the little loops opposite the points.

"What?" she asked, pointing.

"Scissors," Dik muttered. Then he grunted uneasily and dropped to his knees.

"Easy, hoss," Trawis said. "Snip, and then ye gots ter jerk."

Willow craned her neck to watch. Dik slipped the sharp tip under a puckered thread and the scissors clicked and cut it as cleanly as an obsidian flake.

"Losing yer nerve?" Trawis asked.

"Be quiet," Dik growled back. He said some other things Willow couldn't understand.

When Dik finally finished, Trawis was blotting at little beads of blood where Dik had pulled the threads out. Dik wiped sweat from his forehead and took a deep breath. What a curious man, so fragile, but at the same time so incredibly strong. Of all the men she'd ever known, only her husband had ever engaged so much of her souls.

Willow signed to Trawis. "Why is Dik so worried?"

"He's never pulled strings out before." Then Trawis barked a laugh. Green slapped Trawis on the shoulder and ducked outside.

Willow seated herself and inspected Trawis's scar before signing, "It will heal fine."

Dik slumped, head down, hands on his knees. Willow took that opportunity to examine the scissors.

"Careful," Trawis signed. "Sharp. Don't cut yourself."

She plucked up one of the bloody stitches from the floor and experimentally snipped it in two. What a marvelous thing this was.

She signed, "White men are very clever with things."

"Clever any way you look at us," Trawis responded, talking in time to his signs.

"People can be clever with things, but not with God or spirits." She snapped the scissors open and shut.

"How so?" Dik asked after Trawis translated.

"When do you talk to spirits? When do you take *Tam Apo* into your heart?"

"God must be examined by the mind, by thought." A strange gleam had come to Dik's eyes. "How do Shoshoni think of God?"

She shook her head, signing and filling in the White words she knew. "This is too hard for us now. I must learn more talk to discuss this."

What an odd idea, that *Tam Apo* could be known by thoughts. Didn't these White men understand that Our Father could only be felt in the soul? *Later. You must learn their tongue; then you will understand.*

She settled herself and studied Dik from the corner of her eye. Did he have a woman waiting for him? And if so, what was she like? To Trawis, she signed: "Where are the White women? Or are there only men?"

Trawis chuckled. "White women are all back East. They do not come here."

"Why don't they come?"

Trawis pulled at his beard. "It wouldn't be right. Not out hyar. This country is too hard on them. Too dangerous. They couldn't stand the hardships."

Willow glanced around at the snug tent—warm, light, and waterproof. Then she thought about the huge boat with all of its space and goods. Too hard on their women? These men traveled in unheard-of luxury! No packs to carry. No lodges to pack on a travois and then unpack. What sort of women were these?

She said, "I do not understand."

Trawis and Dik talked for a moment, then Trawis replied, "It would not be proper to have white women here. It ain't their place."

"And what is their place?"

Trawis glanced uneasily at Dik and the two of them muttered back and forth. Willow caught the word "lady" several times and asked, "What is 'lady'?"

"A woman. No, I mean, well, special woman."

"And what is her place?"

"Uh . . . in a house."

"What is house?"

"Wal . . . like a lodge."

"Ah!" Willow nodded. "Lady's place is in lodge." But that didn't make any sense, either. By words and signs, she noted the tent. "This is lodge. Very fine lodge. Warm, dry, easy to move. Why is this not lady place?"

"Aw, hell!" Trawis threw his hands up.

Dik said, "Lady is gentle. To be . . . to be prized. Very special. Do you understand?"

"Who works?" Willow wondered. "Men?"

"Yes, men." Dik nodded happily.

"White women keep the lodge," Trawis signed. "Take care of children for men. Cook, clean, make clothing."

"But not travel," Willow mused. "Why?"

"Too dangerous," Trawis asserted. "Woman might get killed."

Willow snorted irritation, fingers flying. "Indian women get killed all the time. That is part of life. Part of war, of bad luck—lightning, snow, starvation. Anything can kill. Why are White women not to be killed?"

Trawis signed, "White men do not think white women should be killed by these things. White women are too precious."

"A man protects a lady," Dik said solemnly. "Very precious. A lady is delicate. Understand? Like a flower, to be cherished."

Willow's eyes narrowed. "You mean weak?"

Trawis shot a wary glance at Dik, but signed, "It's not the same."

Willow's lips twitched. "Is that why you come here? You seek strong women? Like horse breeders, you wish to strengthen your blood?"

Trawis made a face, lowering his voice as he talked to Dik. Dik's expression betrayed mystification.

"No," Trawis muttered. "I know." His hands made the signs, "White women are prized. Very special."

Willow considered. Both men had begun to fidget. She asked: "Lady does what man tells, yes?"

"Yes."

She didn't have all the words, so she signed, "White woman is very special to White man. She is to be taken, then kept safe in the lodge to have children. Man works to take food to her, because man works and White woman doesn't. She is a prize, not to be risked. I understand this."

Trawis translated, and Dik grinned.

Willow continued. "I understand this because *Ku'-chendikani* do the same. They treat special buffalo horses this way. They take food to them in the winter and always guard them. So, White men treat women like horses.''

. Trawis's face fell.

Willow puzzled on the idea. What kind of woman would a White woman be? Like some helpless child? Who'd want a woman like that? Worse, what would it be like to *be* a woman like that? Locked in a lodge, fed by someone else, and doing nothing but bearing children?

"No, no," Trawis was muttering. "White women are . . ."

"Weak," Willow muttered.

"No."

"Like coup? Won from other men?"

"Yes!" Dik cried.

"Shut up, coon," Trawis muttered. "It ain't the same. Courting ain't winning."

"Courting?" Willow asked.

Trawis made the sign, and added, "We don't fight over our . . . Hell, that's a tarnal lie!"

"Prize," Willow supplied. What was that other word? "Trophy?"

Trawis stared at Dik. Neither looked happy.

Willow clapped her hands. "You come here, find Indian women. Not prize. What is the word? 'Partner'?" She lifted an eyebrow.

Trawis finally shrugged and grinned. "Reckon so."

Willow gave them a sly smile and signed, "But where are you going to find an Indian woman who would want to lie with a man with such white skin? She'd shiver so hard at the idea of that ghost skin against hers that she'd clamp too tight to enter. And if she did, when she looked up at you—saw all that hair on your face, she'd think she was coupling with her dog!" And at that, she squealed with laughter.

After Trawis translated, Dik's face turned a violent red and he slipped silently out into the night.

Willow gazed thoughtfully at the swaying tent flap, then asked, "Dik have woman?"

"Nope." Travis raised an eyebrow. "Ye interested?"

"No," she said much too quickly.

Travis nodded solicitously, but she could see the twinkle in his eye.

TWENTY-FOUR

◆

Savage man and civilized man differ so greatly in the depths of their hearts and in their inclinations, that what constitutes the supreme happiness of the one would reduce the other to despair. The first longs for nothing more than repose and liberty; he desires only to live, and to be immune from labor; nay, the ataraxy of the most confirmed Stoic falls short of his deep indifference to every other object. Civilized man, on the other hand, is always in action, perpetually sweating and toiling, and racking his brains to discover occupations still more laborious; he continues a drudge to the last minute; nay, he courts death in order to live, or renounces life to obtain immortality.

—Jean-Jacques Rousseau, *Discourse on the Origin and Foundation of Inequality Among Mankind*

Richard, Baptiste, and Willow were driving the horses along the west bank. They followed dim trails through groves of ash, elm, and oak that gave way to grassy meadows. A hot wind blew from the prairie to the west and added to the bright sun's heat.

Richard tried to concentrate on Laura, but he couldn't stop glancing at Willow, catching that speculative look in her brown eyes. In the sunlight her copper skin seemed to glow with a new radiance. In spite of himself, he kept smiling at her, almost wishing that Baptiste were somewhere else. But what would he say to her?

She's a savage, Richard. Not your kind of woman. If you

must think of a woman, think of Laura. He concentrated on Laura's blue eyes, her golden hair, and charming smile. Yes, that was it. Think about her thin waist, and the way her skirts rustled when . . .

"That tall bluff," Baptiste's voice intruded, "yonder, with the mound of dirt. That's the Blackbird's grave." Baptiste pointed, the long fringes hanging down from his arm.

"The Blackbird?" Richard studied the high point. Laura Templeton had vanished into nothingness.

"Heap big Omaha chief. Some years back the Mahas controlled the river. And Blackbird controlled the Mahas. Nothing passed this part of the river 'thout old Blackbird's approval."

The wind switched to gust down from the north, thrashing tree branches and bending grass in rippling waves. Willow tucked her hair back where the wind had pulled long strands loose. She gave Richard a shy smile, attentive to Baptiste's words and the hand signs he used as he spoke.

The high bluff to the north dominated the skyline, piercing the tree-crowned heights. Beyond, the clouds raced southward in puffy mounds of white.

Richard peered at Baptiste. "Tell me about this Blackbird." Anything to take his mind off Willow.

"Traders give him arsenic, hoss. He was a canny one, old Blackbird was. Anybody challenged his power, sho' 'nuff, he'd slip poison into their food, then foretell their deaths. Got so that nobody among the Mahas would cross him. Smallpox finally kilt him. His last wish was to be buried up on that hill, a-sitting on his warhorse. The old coon said he wanted to be up thar high so he could see the white traders coming up the river."

As he spoke, Baptiste's dark hands made signs for Willow. She stared up at the knob. "I heard of him," she said. "Strong chief."

Richard ground his teeth, forcing his gaze away. The wind had pressed her dress against her like a second skin, outlining her perfect breasts and thin waist. Damn it, he was a gentleman, and a gentleman didn't look at a woman that way.

"Reckon," Baptiste agreed. "Story is that once he had a trader brought up to the main village. Had all the trader's plunder—all his goods—brought in. Old Blackbird, he took half, called it a gift. Now, that trader figgered he was just about to go bust, when Blackbird up and says, 'My friend, you may trade the rest to my people . . . fo' whatever price you wants.' That coon made his fortune, 'cause t'warnt a one of Blackbird's people would say no to the trader."

"That's piracy!" Richard manfully fastened his gaze on the high point. "Blackbird. Now, there's a man my father would really like."

Baptiste gave Richard a thoughtful inspection as the horses wound through the trees. "Travis done told this child a mite of that story. Yer pap, now, he done sent you out heah?"

"Yes, he did. But for him I'd still be studying philosophy in Boston." Richard ducked a low branch. "He cut me off. From my studies, that is. I was supposed to deliver money to a booshway, to outfit a Santa Fe expedition. So, what happens? François steals the money. That French brigand is headed back to civilization to live rich all the rest of his life, and I'm on a fur expedition. What kind of justice is that?"

"Beats being dead, Dick."

"My name is Richard."

"Rhitshard," Willow said softly, her soft brown eyes meeting his for one glorious moment.

"Richard."

"Ritshard."

"Willer, yor a quick one." Baptiste made a smacking sound with his lips. "Never knew an Injun to pick up talk as fast as she's a-doing." Baptiste gave the country another of his careful scrutinies. "Wal, Dick, I reckon yor pap figgered to make a man of you."

"Maybe. Looks like he made me a slave, instead."

"Boy." Baptiste's voice hardened. "You don't know shit. Yor no more than a damned planter's boy. They's times you makes me want to puke with yor whining. A slave? Shit! You don' know the fust thing 'bout it."

Richard returned hot glare for glare.

Baptiste lifted a lip in disgust. "Do tell, what's this? You reckon you can kill me with a mean look like that? Care to back her up, coon? Want to try and whip it outa this sassy nigger?"

For a second Richard held that gaze; then cold shivers wound through his guts. He dropped his eyes and reddened in humiliation. The worst was, he couldn't hold his own in Willow's presence.

"Good. Last man what tried to whip me's a-laying dead in the grave."

"Perhaps slavery was a bad analogy."

"Reckon so, coon." Baptiste turned his gaze ahead. "If'n yer keen to larn, I'll be happy to show you what a slave's life is all about."

"I can guess."

Baptiste's expression sharpened. "Do tell?"

"Maybe I can't. Oh, I don't know. I don't seem to know much of anything anymore."

For the first time that day, Baptiste smiled. "Wal, coon, I reckon that's when yor ready to larn. Cain't larn a damn thing when you knows all the answers already."

"You sound like Travis now."

"Yep." Baptiste resettled his rifle. "I come outa Louisiana ready to whip old Hob hisself. I's mad, boy. Plumb clean killer mad. They done took my pap and sold him off ter Tennessee. Had me a woman. They wanted a strong buck like me to make young 'uns. So I had me a woman. Sold her off to Cuba after I run the fust time."

Baptiste spit off the side of his horse. "Shit. Lost everything I had. Old friends wouldn't even talk to me. 'Fraid they'd be beat, too. So I's mad." He grinned. "Hell, even tried to slice up old Travis just afo' we made Memphis. That coon, he's some, he is. Took my knife away and boxed my ears till I couldn't stand up fo' the ringing. And, hell, I figgered I knowed how to fight right fierce."

"You tried to knife Travis?"

"I done told you, Doodle. I's a rough nigger in them days. Had the fight on. Wal, old Travis he done taken it right outa me. That's when he set me down, all bunged up and bleeding, and we had us a parley. That coon talked sense inta me. Understand? He told me just what I's doing, and why, and asked this child when I's gonna straighten out, 'cause he wasn't about to waste his time on no nigger bound ta get hisself hung fo' being a stupid ass!''

Baptiste slapped his leg. ''Hell, Dick. I didn't know shit neither.''

''What if they'd caught you?''

''A murdering slave? And a runaway to boot?'' Baptiste lifted an eyebrow. ''They'd a kilt me. Reckon Travis, too. It don't do fo' no white man to go ferrying 'scaped niggers north.''

''Why do you think he did it?''

''No telling. Not with Travis Hartman. Says he saw something in my eyes that day I run inta his camp. Hell, he mighta done her fo' the hell of it. Why, catch that coon in the right mood, he'd spit in old Hob's right eye.''

''You like him, don't you?''

''Reckon so. Now, he asked me ta larn you, so scrape the wax outa yor ears, Dick, 'cause old Baptiste's a gonna do just that.'' He held up a black finger. ''Don't never go agin' yer pap. Don't matter what's ahind you, I reckon it can be patched. If'n not, I reckon I'll trade you, 'cause you got a pap and I don't.''

At Baptiste's cutthroat glare, Richard kept his peace. Willow was listening intently, struggling for the words.

''I mean 'er, Dick. If'n ye lives, make peace with yer pap. T'aint a small thing, having a pap. White folk think everybody's got one, just like a right hand. Black folk can tell y'all different.''

Richard chewed at his lip, remembering Phillip's hard face, the fleshy nose and pinched-on glasses. *How can there be any reconciliation? We might as well live in different worlds.*

Richard asked, ''What do you think my chances of living through this are?''

''Depends, coon. How bad you want to live? If'n yor of a mind to go under, I figger you'll be maggot meat afore the Yellerstone.''

''Thanks for the confidence.''

Baptiste turned to Willow, ebony hands flying. For a long

moment she studied Richard with those large dark eyes, then made signs in return.

"What's all that?" Richard demanded.

Baptiste sucked at his lips, dark eyes burning under the wide brim of his hat. "I asked her if'n she thought you'd live. She says she thinks so. She says yor a medicine man, but you don't know it yet. She says that none of us knows yor Power. That such medicine is a gift not many people have. She says you carry the answer down inside. If'n you wants to live, you'll do her, but the only one can call it up is you. She says she don't understand why the spirits would give such Power to a young white man."

"Medicine? Power?" He let his gaze follow the smooth curve of her cheek, remembering the soaring sense when they'd looked into each other's eyes that day in camp. Was that what had touched his soul?

Willow's fingers were moving again, dancing gracefully.

Baptiste continued, "She says that you need to sweat, to purify yourself. That yor confused. Power's pulling you lots of different ways. To larn yor Power, you gotta be cleansed of the White man's confusion. Become pure, and seek yor vision."

"Vision? My only vision is of Boston."

At that, Willow laughed and said, "Ritshard not think his way to God." She tapped her chest. "God hyar. Souls know *Tam Apo,* not thoughts."

Power? Spirits? It was nothing more than the superstitious nonsense of the savage mind. No matter how he might be attracted to Willow, that gulf between the savage and the civilized would always separate them.

So, Richard, think of something else. He cleared his mind and turned his eyes back to Blackbird's grave. A river pirate. Red instead of white. *You weren't any different from my father. Maximize your investment, even if it took poisoning your competition.* And what did that imply about the state of man in nature?

I just haven't found it yet. I need to look a little further, beyond the influence of the traders.

But that meant going farther upriver. Ever farther from Boston, and civilized society.

Remember, I'm only stuck here until Travis is well. Then, I'm off for those pleasant streets. Pick a goal? Why, Boston, of course, and Laura, and the life we'll have together. That's it. My spirit quest.

And when he returned, there would be no compromise with Phillip Hamilton. Some things, like shattered crystal goblets, could never be put back together again.

"Got an answer fo' Willow?" Baptiste asked. "About God?"

"Whose answer do you want? Hegel's? Anselm's? Augustine's? Voltaire's? How about Montaignè's observation that while men create gods by the dozen, they can't breathe life into a lowly worm?"

"Want truth, Dik," Willow said simply.

"Truth flies like a bird," Richard whispered, staring up at the windy point.

"Like eagle," Willow said softly. "Or hummingbird who brings the thunder. Or Magic Owl. Truth flies high."

Richard ignored her, lost in thought. What if he went beyond the reach of the traders and still found men willing to pay any price for goods?

Blackbird, just how different were *you from my father?*

And if men should all prove to be the same, no matter what their origins or circumstance?

No, that thought was too grisly to entertain.

Just make it home . . . to Boston, Richard. Nothing else matters.

His fingers absently caressed the long silken hair on the fetish Travis had tied to his belt.

Morning bathed the land with new light; mist drifted across the smooth river and through the trees lining the bank. Smoke hung in blue smudges over the fires as the men in the messes finished their corn and venison. Overhead, the heart-shaped cottonwood leaves hung silently, waiting for the dawn. Occasional coughs and the metallic clank of pots and tin cups accented the *engagés'* low voices.

Richard sipped at his steaming coffee as he sat on a weather-silvered cottonwood log. He glanced across the fire at Willow, then quickly averted his eyes. She and Laura were like night and day.

Dreams of Willow had tortured him all night long, of her smile and the straightforward way she looked at him with those incredible eyes.

That knowledge plagued him, as if he'd been somehow disloyal to Laura's faith in him. *It's not that I'm in love with Willow, just fascinated. As a scholar. It's my business to investigate her thoughts, to learn about her and her ways.*

But Willow kept creeping into his thoughts in the most unscholarly ways. With the exception of Laura, he'd never bothered with women. They frightened him even more than they fascinated him. Those he'd met in Boston—gentle ladies, every last one—either stared right through him as if he weren't there, or they gave him a gushy, airy-eyed look of false worship. And in no instance had he carried on a conversation of importance with a woman. They just dithered on about the weather, or was the coffee prepared correctly? Always trite.

And now Willow fills my imagination—an Indian woman, who barely speaks English, has never held a book, and carries a war club, bow, and arrows. Yet they'd conversed about God, and souls, and he'd barely touched the rind of her knowledge about life. And that slight touch had enthralled him.

She's an illiterate savage! But what fed the glow that filled her eyes when she looked at him? He shook his head, biting his lip.

His coffee was bitter, watery, laced with the now familiar taste of riverwater. Dear God, what he'd give to be in a coffee shop in Boston, tasting the rich brews—dark and steaming. The aroma filled the nose. He'd add a dollop of cream and fine Jamaica sugar. Just right . . . *Someday.*

He glanced at Willow. What would she make of Boston? He could imagine her laughing, eyes shining as she raised a porcelain teacup to her lips. No, impossible! The vision burst like a ruptured bladder.

His blankets were rolled and tied, ready to be packed.

Across the fire from him, Willow was working the snarls out of her raven hair with a comb Travis had given her, the teeth sliding through that glossy wealth.

Travis ducked out of Green's tent and walked through the camp to hunker down beside Richard. Through squinted eyes, the hunter watched Willow. "Purty, ain't she?"

"Indeed she is," Richard admitted. To his embarrassment, Willow glanced at him from the corner of her eye. "And I think she's learning English much too quickly."

"Do tell, coon?" she asked. "I reckon I don't know shit yet."

Richard took a deep breath. "Willow, that's . . ." But, what? She was learning the speech of these frontiersmen, not the cultured language of the civilized East. "I mean, well, there are different ways of speaking. Some are proper, and some aren't. Ladies don't say words like that."

"Like what?"

He colored. "Like . . . 'shit.' It isn't polite for a lady to use."

She lifted the corner of her lip, then said, "White lady is no better than horse to White man. Willow is no trophy, Ritshard."

Travis laughed, reached across, and took Richard's coffee. He sipped, swished the liquid around his mouth, and swallowed. "That's some, it is. Gonna philos'phy her to death?"

Richard ignored him, concentrating on Willow. "Do you want to learn the proper way?"

"Hell!" Travis growled, giving the tin cup back. "She ain't never a-going to no Boston. Leave the child be."

"Proper?" Willow studied him thoughtfully, her long fingers caressing the comb.

"Formal. Like the way I speak. You've been learning the way Travis and Baptiste talk, that's fine for here, on the river, but not for civilized places."

Travis snorted disgust.

"I learn," Willow told him, and gave Travis a challenging glance.

"Good!" Richard cried. "We'll begin at once."

"Reckon not, coon," Travis interrupted. "Daylight's a-wasting. Fetch up the hosses, Dick. I'm a-riding today. Old Baptiste, he done snuck off with his rifle a couple of hours afore daylight. Now that we're past the Omahas, we otta cut buffler sign.''

Richard looked the hunter up and down. ''Do you really think you're fit?''

''Hell! I been a-loafing on that damn boat.'' He pulled up his shirt to expose the wound. Scabs had fallen off to leave shiny red scars on Travis's white hide. ''If'n that ain't healed, I'm a sorry pilgrim.''

Willow glanced at the wound, nodded, and rose to her feet. She walked off toward the river, long hair swaying. As she passed through the camp, the *engagés* went silent. Heads turned; gleaming eyes followed her.

Richard stiffened unaccountably.

''Finally started ter notice, have ye?''

''Notice what?''

Travis lowered his voice. ''Ye seen Trudeau?''

Richard glanced around. ''No. But then, I haven't been looking for him.''

''Uh-huh. Wal, I run up on his sorry carcass last night. Caught him slipping through the brush ahind Willow.'' Travis paused. ''Thought fer a second that French varmint was a gonna try me.''

''Following Willow? Try you? I don't understand.''

Travis gave him a disgusted look. ''Dick, why's a man foller a woman inta the brush? What's he after? Now, ye don't see a whole lot of wimmen fer these coons ter go a-bedding, do ye? Trudeau's gonna be a mite of trouble fer Willow. He's pulled his horns in fer now, but ye mind that coon close, hear?''

Richard's gut tickled. ''Is that why they've started looking at her that way?''

''Reckon so, coon. Man gets ter missing woman flesh against his own. She's a heap of woman. Reckon they'll be trouble over her.''

''Trudeau?''

''He's the ringleader. And he's got the glint in his eye. Heard tell he signed on because a feller from Kaskaskia was a-looking fer him. Something about a daughter. Trudeau's supposed ter have lifted her skirts against her will.''

"You mean rape?"

"I warn't thar, coon. Reckon in this country, a feller don't just up and point a finger. Ain't got no proof, Dick. 'Sides, we got a boat ter get upriver."

"That justifies anything, doesn't it?" Richard threw out the last of his coffee, picked up his bedroll, and tramped to the boat. He tossed his gear onto the deck and headed through the tall grass for the horses.

Lugging the *Maria* northward outweighed any morality these human beasts had. *The time has come. I've got to run, escape. Find a way back to Saint Louis . . . and then to Boston.* At least there he could find a decent cup of coffee. And conversation worthy of a man of letters. In Boston, Laura's mere presence would drive away plaguing thoughts about Willow.

Travis slumped in the saddle as he rode into the clearing. Not much had changed since the last time he'd camped here. How many years ago had that been? Nigh to five, now. Old Manuel Lisa was still head of the Fur Company. That was back when . . .

He pulled his horse up and tightened his grip on his rifle. That little tickle of wrongness was playing with his guts. The wily Pawnee gelding he rode pricked its ears, attentive on a thicket of hazel across the clearing. Overhead, the cottonwood and ash leaves rustled with the breeze.

"What is it?" Richard asked from behind.

"Hush!" Travis kneed his horse forward, half-raising his rifle. Nervous as a cat on a floating log, he eared the hammer on the Hawken back, the click loud in the still clearing. There, behind that thicket. "Come on out!"

"I don't . . . who's there?" Richard asked from behind. The horses snorted and stamped, aware of the sudden tension.

Travis raised his rifle, sighting toward the hazel, ready for a snap shot.

Willow had ridden her horse off to one side, hurriedly stringing her bow and nocking an arrow.

The evening sun slanted through the leaves to dapple the clearing. Off to the right, fifty yards away, high grass screened the Missouri's muddy bank.

A man stood up behind the brush—a whip-thin Indian. His hair was worn loose except for a long braided scalp lock rising from the center of his head. Two wary black eyes stared out from a flat face with a straight nose. Despite the heat, he was dressed in tight skins that covered most of his body. Behind him, a woman half-crouched in the brush with a little boy at her side.

"Omaha," Travis muttered to himself. Then, in a louder voice, he added, "Banished, by God."

"Banished?" Richard asked.

"Yep. That's the only reason an Omaha buck would wear a full set of skins in this weather. And he's Omaha, all right. It's in the cut of his clothes and that scalp lock. Where his hair is parted, it's painted red. A mite faded, but red it is."

The Omaha stepped out of the hazel and spread his hands wide. He walked forward, smiled, and waited nervously.

Travis signed: "What do you want?"

In return the Omaha signed: "We friends. Hungry. Make trade."

"Trade for what?" Travis asked in signs.

"Whiskey."

"What's he saying?" Richard asked.

"Wants ter trade." Travis squinted. "Keep yer eyes peeled, coon. He might be banished, but there could be others."

In signs, Travis asked, "What would a banished man have to trade with?"

The Omaha turned and called out. The woman walked forward, leaving the child partially hidden. No expression betrayed itself on her round face. A dirty stroud dress hung on her like an old tent. She'd parted her hair in the middle, two braids falling down her back.

The Omaha glanced uneasily at Willow, and then asked in signs, "You have woman?"

Travis nodded. "We have woman."

The Omaha sagged, then signed. ''I can only trade woman. I am poor. White men are powerful and rich. They will take pity on me.''

Willow exhaled her disgust. The faint calls of the *engagés* could be heard as they pulled for the meadow and the night's camp.

''Boat come?'' the Omaha signed.

''Yep. Boat come.''

''Have whiskey?'' The Omaha's eyes lit with a crazy anticipation.

''What's he want?'' Richard asked again.

''Wants to use his woman for trade.''

''He . . . what?'' Richard sounded genuinely puzzled.

''Wal, coon, yer about ter come face to face with that philos'phy of yern.'' Travis cut off any further questions with a slashing of his hand. Eyeing the Omaha, he signed: ''You are banished for murder. Tell me the story.''

The Omaha's eyes dulled and reluctantly he began to make signs.

Travis could barely make out Richard's shadow. The lad had done exactly as Travis had instructed: He hunkered in the darker shadows of the cottonwood trunks, a thick tree to his back so that no one could sneak up on him from behind.

Travis cocked his head to listen: distant coyotes, leaves whispering with the breeze; crickets and night insects.

''Dick? It's me, Travis.'' He started forward. ''Seen anything?''

Richard straightened, the Pawnee trade gun in his hand. ''Nothing here, Travis. Just horses farting and chomping grass.''

Travis checked the picket line, found it tight, and leaned against one of the cottonwoods. His eyes and ears probed the night. ''Seems quiet.''

''Yes.''

''Yer sounding a tad sour, Dick.''

"You should have chased him away."

"Uh-huh, and he'd be out in the dark somewhars with all kind of idears about our hosses. As it is, he's nigh ter stumbling drunk and fit ter fall flat on his face and snore the rest of the night away."

"We're no better than he is. We're accomplices."

Travis plucked a stem of grass and chewed the sweet end. "Immoral as all Hell, ain't we? Plumb gone ta Hob hisself with sin the likes of which ain't been seen since Sodom and Gomorrah. Wal, I'll tell ye, it ain't up ter Green and me ter tell the men they can't dally with no squaw. Not when she's been offered right fair."

Richard snorted derisively. "It's pure prostitution! What kind of people are these Omaha?"

"Folks like most other folks, only a sight more virtuous than a lot of 'em out hyar."

"Virtuous? That . . . that *beast* is using his wife for a whore, Travis. That's hardly what I call moral rectitude!"

Travis squatted next to the fuming Richard. "Tell me, why is it that you figger that every man otta be measured by yer plumb line and level? One book of laws fits 'em all? Hell, it don't matter, white, red, or black, every man's gotta live up ter Dick Hamilton's ten commandments of philos'phy, or by God, he ain't even dirt! Must make life pure hell, such a damn set of notions ter live up ter."

"There are universal criteria of proper behavior, Mr. Hartman. Ethical rules by which men in society mutually govern their behavior. It's not just my beliefs that are—"

"Wal, good. I'm glad ye thinks so. So do most other folks."

"Evidently not the Omaha or they wouldn't—"

"Damn right they would! Tarnal Hell, Dick, ye drives me ter the point of cutting my own throat so I don't gotta listen to yer jaw flap! Now, shut up, or I'll fetch ye one."

"You don't have to get mad." Richard scowled into the night, both hands gripping the trade rifle.

"Don't I? Yer more bullheaded than Adam's off ox! Since ye got all the answers already, tell me about the Omaha. Go on, do her."

"Well, I . . ."

"Uh-huh. I'm waiting."

"Travis, I don't need to know about the Omaha to know that what he's doing—"

"Is plumb wrong! Son of a bitch! Imagine that. Now, listen up, coon. Hyar's the way of it. Omaha is about the strictest Injuns out hyar, except maybe fer the Cheyenne. They got their ways, and most is plumb persnickety 'bout who flirts with who. They take pride in giving their word. A man don't lay with another man's wife. He don't steal from his people. They take friendship all the way to death . . . a heap further than most white men I know. Ye wants ter talk morals, wal, Omaha have got 'em by the barrelful."

"What about Blackbird?"

"What about him?"

"He was a despot, a tyrant. He used poison to make himself rich."

"So'd King George. So'd Napoleon. Hell, he's a chief, and a black-hearted one ter boot. And that makes my point. Folks always got one or two bad apples in their barrel." Travis paused. "If'n I was ye, I'd wonder what in hell this Omaha's doing out hyar when all the rest of his people are out hunting buffalo."

"All right, what's he doing here?"

"Banished for murder. That's why he's all dressed up in them hides. It's punishment. He's been cast out fer four years. Seems he got drunk and killed his father-in-law when the old boy caught him beating his wife."

"And she went into exile with him?"

"Hell, no, she divorced his sorry arse. No, this woman that's with him, she run away fer committing adultery. Her husband caught her with a feller and she took to the brush before they could beat her. The way the Omaha tells it, it ain't the first time, so her family was like to whup her good and she didn't want no part of it."

"Good God." Richard cocked his head as a nighthawk's wings buzzed in the night.

"Yep, wal, I figgered ye'd need the whole story lest ye get in a foaming philos'phy mood and start preaching Roosoo or something."

"But how do people get to be like them?"

"Oh, just 'cause they's people, I suspect. Why, I reckon thar be folks ye wouldn't be right proud of in Boston, neither." Travis stood, patting him on the shoulder. "Now, keep yer eyes skinned, Dick."

"Who . . . who's he been trading her to?"

"Trudeau mostly. Right after the boat tied off, he started swapping fer whiskey. I reckon Trudeau's promised his daily ration fer two months by now."

"It just makes me sick," Richard said miserably. "A human being should be worth more."

"Should be. But most ain't, son. And that's just the way the wind blows and the water flows."

"I think we got trouble," Travis told Green as he ducked out of the evening shadows and through the hatch into the cargo box.

They'd crossed the Niobrara earlier that day, and a freak wind from the south had allowed them to make fifteen miles up the twisting Missouri. Now, after having satisfied himself with the establishment of the camp, posted guard, and lined out the messes, Travis had the opportunity to talk with Dave Green.

Green hunched over the flour barrels, a candle in his burly right hand. The oaken-plank roof wavered in the candlelight, flickers chasing shadows behind the bales, packs, and tins.

Green had been squinting in the dimness, inspecting his goods, searching for any water that might have pooled in the bilge. Seepage could turn trade goods into disaster.

Green turned his eyes to Travis. "Trouble how?"

"Trudeau's getting ideas about Willow."

"Tell him to leave her alone. What's the matter? Didn't he get his fill of that Maha squaw?"

Travis pulled on his beard, tugging the scars tight. "Some men just got themselves a passion, Dave. Fer some it's the bottle, fer others a game of monte. Reckon fer Trudeau it's wimmen."

Green gazed at him thoughtfully. "You know, I'm counting on that girl. She's a Snake. Seeing her home safely might make for real good trade with her tribe.''

"Reckon so.'' Travis lowered himself to sit on the steps. "I warned Trudeau off. Don't know that it'll take. Might have ter kill him.''

"I suppose.'' Green leaned over stacked kegs of gunpowder and reached out with the candle to stare down into the blackness beyond. "And how'd your day's ride treat you?''

"I'm a mite stove up yet. A couple more days and I'll have vigor back in my blood again.''

"Enough to take Trudeau down?''

"Him and four others.''

Green turned his head, his face sallow in the candlelight. "You getting killed won't do me any good.''

"He ain't gonna do nothing yet.'' Travis braced his elbows on his knees. "I'm just a-warning ye, it's coming. 'Sides, I reckon Trudeau'll tie into Hamilton first. They had words this morning. The kid was grousing about the Omaha selling his woman, and Trudeau, he was a bragging about how good she was. Sort of prickled old Dick's hide, I tell ye.''

"And Trudeau didn't kill him?''

"I was too close. And, wal, I reckon Willow would'a drove an arrow through old Trudeau if'n he hurt Dick. She's plumb smart with that bow, you know. But, yep, it's a-coming between Dick and Trudeau. Matter of time.''

"Well, it won't be much trouble burying Hamilton.''

Travis cocked his head. "Trudeau sent a shiver down Dick's back, all right. That Yankee pilgrim looked fer all the world like he's a headed straight ter Hell.''

"How come he hasn't jumped ship yet? He's still figuring on that, isn't he?''

Travis chuckled. "So he claims. Just as soon's I'm all healed. Reckon it'll be one thing after another. He ain't going, Dave. He just don't know it yet.''

Green set his candle on a crate before dropping down to feel about under the plank decking. "*Sonuvabitch!*'' Green jerked back, banging his head on a whiskey tin in the process. Something scampered in the darkness.

"What the hell?'' Travis demanded.

Green shivered, rolled back, and stared owlishly into the dark hole he'd just pulled his hand from. "Grabbed a damn rat in there!" In the candlelight, he studied his hand and then rubbed the side of his head. "I *hate* rats. Did I ever tell you that?"

"Time or two. Find any leaks?"

"Nope. We're still tight, Travis. After we grounded so many times the last couple of weeks, I was getting worried. Damn rats! I hate 'em."

"Comes with the country, coon." Travis fingered the worn oak steps. "We've done right fine, Davey. No serious trouble."

Green retrieved his candle and picked his way carefully through the cargo. "I don't call you getting gutted no trouble."

"Ain't nobody dead yet. Nobody drowned. No holes in the boat. Nobody arrested at Fort Atkinson. We're plumb chipper."

"We're just reaching the frontier, Travis." Green blew out his candle, and Travis rose and climbed out onto the deck.

"You find anything?" Henri asked as he stepped around the *passe avant.*

"She's dry." Green thrust thumbs into his belt, staring out at the river. For a time the three of them stood there, watching the gathering darkness over the water.

The evening was cool, the air still, and the river had taken on a silvered sheen in the sky's fading glow. As the current tugged at it, the long steering oar canted to the starboard. Travis slapped a mosquito that had been humming around his left ear. Swallows swooped low over the water to skim a drink.

"Think we'll make it?" Green asked as he watched the dark river swirl below them.

Travis shrugged. "Sioux country is up ahead. Never can tell about Sioux. Since Leavenworth made such a fool outa himself, it's hard ter say how they'll react. Then we got the Rees up near the Mandans now. Probably still madder than hell. Tarnation, Dave, we're on the upper river now. Who knows? The game changes past Blackbird's grave and the

Mahas. Downriver, yer more likely to drown. Upriver, yer more likely to get shot, scalped, starved, or froze. If'n 'tain't water, it's fire.''

"I take water every time," Henri said as he flexed his powerful hands. "If there is one law on the river, it is that God lets no man die old, *non*?"

Green nodded thoughtfully. "Makes you wonder what sort of fools we are, doesn't it? So many things could go wrong. A sawyer could rip the bottom out of the *Maria*. We could run into a band of Sioux with the prod on. The Rees could figure us for a lone boat and ambush us.''

"And I might get ate by a bear. Reckon there ain't no gain if'n a body don't take no risk. What the hell, Henri is right. This coon's done figgered he'll lose his hair afore he dies of old age. Life's fer living, Dave. It's fer taking a gamble and seeing where yer stick floats. Hell, yer not figgering on dying in a bed in Saint Loowee, are ye?''

"No, I suppose not."

"Then stop yer cussed worrying. Each day takes care of itself.''

They could hear the *engagés* singing softly as their supper cooked on the bank. Travis batted futilely at a swarm of mosquitoes humming above him in a wavering column.

"These mosquitoes," Henri growled. "Like the plague, they come to a man most just when he wants to rest. *Nusibles!* Ah, well, I got to check the painter before I see you at ze tent, *bourgeois*.'' The patroon slapped at the humming air and disappeared around the corner of the cargo box.

"He's a good man," Green noted. "I got lucky."

"Yep. And we'd best hope that luck holds, coon."

"I hope all night and most of the day. Come on, I'm half starved." Green started for the *passe avant*. "Baptiste cut any buffalo sign today?''

"Yep. Old, but still sign." Travis followed Green down the bouncing plank.

"River's up." Green pointed to where the water had risen. "Must be a flood somewhere upriver." He hesitated. "Travis?''

"Huh?"

"Thanks.''

"What fer?"

"For being here."

Travis patted Green on the back. "C'mon. Let's fill our bellies and get shy of these skeeters afore they suck a man dry."

Heals Like A Willow sat at the fire, a blanket over her head as protection from the mosquitoes. This night, camp had been pitched on a high bank, the keelboat tied off to gnarled old cottonwoods. She'd placed their fire off to one side, away from the other *engagés*. These White men ate and camped in little groups called "messes." She shared hers with Trawis, Dik, and Baptiste. Dave Green and Henri camped right in the center of the messes, the two of them generally eating alone before the square-walled tent.

The flames danced happily around the wood. Unlike the White men who chopped logs in two with their axes, she'd used the tried-and-true Indian method of breaking them into lengths, often wedging them between two tree trunks to get the leverage. She didn't need as much fire as the Whites who built bonfires and sat back away from them. Her people built small fires and sat right on top of them.

Baptiste lounged on the flattened grass, idly slapping at mosquitoes and scratching itches. In her country, she would have used a mixture of larkspur and fir sap to keep the bugs off. Here, among these strange plants, she didn't know what to use except smoke and the blanket.

From the protection of her blanket, she watched Ritshard—seeing past his blank face to the unease he tried to hide within. From across the camp, she could sense Trudeau's hungry interest.

And when the two finally faced off over her? It didn't take much imagination to visualize Trudeau beating Ritshard into unconsciousness.

And when he does, I'll split the Frenchman's skull with my war club. The deadly maternal urge to protect rose within her until her eyes slitted, and she briefly considered rising, stalking across the camp, and killing Trudeau before he had the chance to cause real trouble.

No. Doing so would shame Ritshard. And from that, he might never recover. But why did she even care? A smart woman would let them sort it out between themselves.

Why Ritshard? She ground her teeth, knowing full well what attracted her. Power hovered around his soul like mist around a warm pond, and it drew her relentlessly toward him.

And do you really think he could follow in the place of your husband? He doesn't know the simplest of things. Do you think he's a warrior? He nearly threw up after facing Trudeau!

No, it would be impossible. He couldn't speak a word of the People's tongue. The *Dukurika* would eventually laugh him out of camp. And worst of all, what would her father say? It had been bad enough when she married a *Ku'chendikani*.

The gentle strains of a song rose on the night air as the men finished their suppers and lit pipes full of fragrant tobacco. So peaceful now, but Trudeau would be trouble—as inevitable as winter on the heels of a late fall wind. Up to now, she'd been able to avoid him, using her skills to slip away when he prowled after her.

From the corner of her eye, she watched Ritshard. *I should leave. Take the trouble away before I get him killed.*

But she stayed, watching, seeking to find that link of understanding within herself. Who were these ghost-skinned men from so far away? Their talk of giant villages, of boats larger than *Maria* that crossed oceans, the fascinating things they manufactured from metal, wood, and cloth, all drew her to know more.

And to think I ridiculed White Hail for wanting White man's things.

The Whites took wealth so casually. The day before, Travis had given her a looking glass, one that portrayed her with such clarity that she might have been seeing another world rather than a reflection of this one. Among the *Dukurika* the looking glass would have been a source of awe for the entire band, passed from hand to hand with cries of

amazement. Trawis had handed the magical glass to her with no more ceremony than he might have used to give her a rabbit-bone bead.

The fire popped, and sparks twined into the night sky. In the trees, an owl hooted, the mournful note interwoven with the voices of coyotes out in the bluffs.

Rich in things, yes. That was the White man's way. But of their souls she could detect little if anything. Some of the *engagés* knelt in the morning, mumbling to themselves, eyes closed, and finished with a motion of the hand, touching forehead, stomach, and each breast. Praying, Ritshard had said. Sending a message to God, as they called *Tam Apo.*

But on their knees like children? And with their eyes closed? How could a man find God with his eyes closed? And if he mumbled, how could God hear? Among her people, praying was done standing or dancing, arms upraised, eyes open to allow the soul to embrace Creation. When calling out to God, one sang, rejoicing and raising one's voice so that *Tam Apo* or the spirit helpers could hear clearly.

And perhaps that is the key. The White men keep Tam Apo *locked up like a little thing inside them.* If so, how did God feel, to be treated thus?

When she questioned Ritshard about it, he used words far beyond her. Trawis would make signs, but they, too, ran out of meaning. Talking in signs was for trade and the interactions of peoples having different languages, not for such things as the nature of God.

Ritshard had told her that Whites kept a special ''lodge''

for God. A place called "church." Was it the nature of Whites to enclose things? That they did so with their women was understandable if one thought of a woman like a good horse—but the idea that anyone would try such a thing with God confounded her.

Trawis stepped out of Green's tent. His pipe was in hand, and he puffed at it as he walked over to the fire and settled himself cross-legged beside Ritshard.

"How do, coon?"

"I'm fine," Ritshard responded.

Baptiste spoke up, "Reckon tomorrow I'll scout northwest, see if I cut buffler sign."

"Ought to. We're close." Trawis stared at the end of his pipe stem. "This child's froze fer buffler."

Willow kept her head down as Trudeau walked past, then beyond into the darkness. She could hear him urinating just beyond the halo of firelight.

When he returned, he stopped long enough to nod at Trawis and give her that toothy leer she'd come to dislike.

After he'd left, Trawis said quietly, "Willow, you stay close ter me, hear? Reckon ye'd best not be walking off by yerself."

Baptiste nodded as he reached for his belt knife and began fingering the shining blade. "Reckon that's a heap of sense. Old Trudeau, he's on the prod."

"I avoid him," Willow replied. A small ache touched her soul at Ritshard's expression—strained, shamefaced.

"Yep, well, that's good," Trawis added. "He's some at moving a boat. Be a shame ter have to send him under."

"Always the boat," Richard muttered wearily.

"Boat's all we got," Trawis answered in that lazy voice he used sometimes.

Ritshard slapped a mosquito, but remained silent, his eyes on the fire. What did he see that was so far away? What did he long for with such yearning in his eyes?

"Ritshard? You have woman in Boston?" Willow asked.

"No."

"Family?"

He laughed sharply. "Yes, but none who would miss me."

"What is in Boston?"

He closed his eyes and whispered softly, "*Everything.*"

TWENTY-FIVE

◇

Thus the distinct boundaries and offices of *reason* and of *taste* are easily ascertained. The former conveys the knowledge of truth and falsehood: the latter gives the sentiment of beauty and deformity, vice and virtue. The one discovers objects as they really stand in nature, without addition or diminution: the other has a productive faculty, and gilding or staining all the natural objects with colours, borrowed from internal sentiment, raises in a manner, new creation. Reason being cool and disengaged, is no motive to action, and directs only the impulse received from an appetite or inclination, by showing us the means of attaining happiness or avoiding misery. Taste, as it gives pleasure or pain, and thereby constitutes happiness or misery, becomes a motive to action, and is the first spring or impulse to desire and volition.

—David Hume, *An Enquiry Concerning the Principles of Morals*

E asy, coon," Travis whispered as they crept along a brush-choked drainage. Richard paid careful attention to his feet, making sure that each step was placed so as to avoid rustling the green grass. His heart was pounding with excitement. This was the hunt!

The drainage cut like a twisting wound through the flats. Buffaloberry, currants, and spears of cedar lined the slopes, while a trickle of water fed rushes and cattails in the bottom. Sunflowers and daisies sprinkled color through the grass.

Overhead, the sun's white intensity flushed water from every pore in Richard's body.

"Close," Willow whispered behind him. "Wind is right. Waugh!"

Travis throttled a chuckle.

"Waugh is not proper English," Richard reminded Willow, but he grinned and winked at her. To his delight, she winked back and gave him a smile that melted his heart.

"Shhh!" Travis raised a finger to his lips. The hunter dropped to his belly and snaked into a dry gulch that branched off from the cut. Richard dropped to follow, the green smell of crushed vegetation filling his nostrils. His blood began to quicken.

Digging in with his elbows, he followed Travis's moccasined feet. A hole had worn into the grass-polished right heel.

Travis slipped sideways past a patch of grass-bound prickly pear.

In a matter of moments, Richard's muscles started to protest from the awkward position. This mode of travel was ordained for snakes and salamanders—not human beings. He bit his lip and squirmed along in Travis's wake, aware of skittering insects, blades of grass, and the sun's heat boring into his back.

How far were they going? He tried to lift his head to see, but Willow slapped his foot. When he shot a glance over his shoulder, she shook her head emphatically.

He grumbled under his breath and dragged himself onward.

Travis had wriggled up to a patch of thorn-bristling rosebushes that clung to the side of the now shallow depression. Heedless of the vicious stems, the hunter eased up to the edge of the draw, parting the plants carefully to slide the long Hawken through the leaves.

Richard winced as he scratched himself and eased into place beside the hunter.

"Careful, coon," Travis whispered. "Buffler don't see worth a damn, but it shore ain't no sin to be extra careful."

Richard peered through the screen of small serrated leaves and thorns. Blooms had already opened in puffs of pink that delighted the nose. But where had . . . ? Yes, there!

The shaggy hump of the animal was no more than fifty paces away. Willow appeared as immune to thorns as Travis as she crawled up beside Richard.

The metallic click of the hammer might have sundered the world, but the buffalo remained oblivious. Time passed interminably.

"So, why don't you shoot?" Richard barely mouthed the words.

"Poor bull," Travis hissed. "We'll wait. Fat cow'll step up in a minute."

The minute turned into an hour under the relentless sun. The first fly was almost bearable as it buzzed around Richard's head. The rest who came—no doubt at some inaudible fly call from the first—drove him to distraction. The best he could do was flip his head to discourage the beasts, but all that earned him was a disgusted look from Travis, whom the flies seemed to ignore.

The bull had moved away, but a second animal, smaller, almost tan in color, was grazing closer with an agonizing slowness.

"Fat cow," Travis said under his breath, slowly lifting the heavy rifle.

The long wait continued.

Step by step, the buffalo moved into range. Rosebushes and grass screened most of the animal. All Richard could see was the humped back nearly seventy paces away. The stubby tail flipped and swished with a manic passion.

"We'll die of starvation," he muttered as he twitched to unseat the flies.

"Hold still, coon," Travis warned. "Ye'll have every critter from hyar ter the Yellerstone a-running."

Richard barely noticed when the cow turned sideways.

Pffft-boom! At the report, blue smoke obscured everything ahead.

"Hit her in the lights," Travis chortled.

Richard started to rise, only to have a strong hand pull him down.

"Yer a damned Yankee pilgrim, Dick. Hold tarnal still and listen."

Richard glared in hot reply, but cocked his head. "I don't hear anything."

"Uh-huh." Travis slipped the rifle down beside him and rolled onto his back as he fiddled for his powder horn. The sunlight accented the white lines of scar tissue crisscrossing his face. As he poured powder into his measure horn, he gave Richard a sideways glance. "And if'n they's a-running, ye'd hear 'em, eh?"

Richard grabbed fruitlessly at the fly. "You mean you shot one . . . and the rest are just standing there?"

"What's a buffler ter be a-feared of? Maybe a griz, but no bear's a gonna take a full-grown buff on fer the fun of it. Nope, men's about the onliest thing they's a-feared of. We don't stand up, they'll figger it's just thunder or some such. Buffler don't savvy gun shots."

Richard swiped at the flies and ran his dry tongue around his mouth. "They'll just stand there and let us shoot them?"

"Reckon so." Travis extracted a ball from his bullet pouch and placed it on a patch. He short-seated the bullet and used the keen blade of his patch knife to trim the cloth. With careful motions, he pulled the ramrod and sent the load home before priming the pan and snapping the frisson shut.

"Hyar now, coon," he handed the heavy rifle to Richard. "Crawl up aside me. Slowly, now. Oh, don't mind the damn rosebushes, them little scratches will heal. Hell, look at my face and tell me about scratches!"

Nevertheless, Richard winced as the tiny thorns scored his skin. He inched forward until he could see more humped backs. The buffalo remained unconcerned.

Travis continued to whisper in his ear, "Slow, pilgrim. Now, pull yer rifle up. That's it. Get a good brace and set the stock in yer shoulder. Thar ye be. Now, put yer hand under the forestock; that's it. Ye want solid bone under the gun. Don't wobble that way."

Richard settled in and nestled his cheek against the stock so he could squint down the sights.

"Hold up, now. We'll wait her out."

Richard waited, his left arm slowly going numb under the weight of the rifle. He blinked to clear his right eye.

"Don't sight all the time, coon. Keep both yer eyes open

till yer ready to shoot. What damn fool larned ye to close yer eye?''

"You did."

"Eh? Oh well, guess we never got this far."

"Shoot good," Willow whispered from behind.

Shoot good? Richard took a deep breath. What if he missed? This was his first buffalo, his first hunt. *Don't bungle it, Richard.* He could imagine the disgusted look in Travis's eye. Worse, Willow would think he was a complete doof. Anything but that.

"Cow's coming up," Travis hissed. "On yer right. Now, don't shift. She'll come ter ye."

Richard swiveled his head, seeing the animal through the masking grass. Close . . . so close. What? Forty paces?

If I miss from forty paces. . . . He'd never survive Willow's disdain. *Please, God. Just this once, let me do it right!*

And then his heart began to pound with a terrible vengeance; excited blood boiled bright in his veins. Never in his life had he experienced this heady rush. Each nerve tingled, breaths coming in quick succession.

"Easy, coon. That's the fever a-coming on ye. Breathe easy, now. That's it, slow and careful. Relax, hoss. Take yer time and think."

Richard swallowed hard and watched the buffalo. His electric heart refused to still its pounding. The cow took a step, lowered her head, and continued grazing. Richard could hear the grass tearing, the grinding of her jaws, and the puffing of her breath.

Another step, and another, and he could see most of her above the mat of grass and flowers.

"Cock the hammer," Travis whispered.

The click should have deafened God.

"Take aim," Travis continued. "Set yer sights right ahind the shoulder joint. Low down . . . way down. Buffler hearts sit low in the body."

Sweat trickled down Richard's flushed face. The heavy rifle seemed to waver like a snake in his grasp.

"Shoot!"

Richard flinched and jerked the trigger.

Nothing happened.

"Figgered that," Travis grunted. "Now that ye got all the foolishness outa ye, pull the back trigger to set the front one. And remember, when ye gets yer shot, she'll flash in yer face. Don't move a breath. Recoil ain't gonna hurt ye, and it all comes after the bullet's been shot."

Richard settled himself, watching the front sight blade in the V of the rear. It settled behind the cow's shoulder. There, right there . . .

Pffft! Fire erupted in his face. *Boom!* The Hawken butted his shoulder. *Spat!* He heard the bullet hit home.

"Don't move!" Travis growled, his heavy hand already on Richard's shoulder.

"Are they running?"

"Nope. But ye hit her high, Dick. Lung shot."

"Lung shot?"

Travis reached out and slipped the Hawken back from Richard's grasp, then slowly raised himself, heedless of the vicious prairie rose.

Richard eased up, barely aware of the needling thorns tracing angry patterns across his flesh. Travis was reloading, a crooked grin on his face. Several calves who were close grunted and turned to look at them. Willow reached out to pat Richard's leg, the action more rewarding than a chorus of huzzahs.

The buffalo cow trotted off a few paces and stopped, head down, the short tail up.

"I didn't kill her?" Richard asked frantically.

"Reckon ye did, coon. But listen close, Dick. Larn this. If'n ye shoots a critter and she don't drop dead, ye settles down fer a second shot. The last thing ye do is go a-charging down there like a runaway stallion, 'cause if'n that animal gets its blood up, it'll run halfway to Mexico afore it falls over."

"So you wait?"

"Yep. Let the critter lay down and stiffen up. Hell, I seen a feller chase a gut-shot antelope nigh onto five miles once. And if'n he'd just set tight for a short spell, that prairie goat would a been dead in minutes."

"So we're waiting?"

"Yep. Not long, Dick. Ye hit her plumb solid."

The other buffalo switched their tails and watched the wounded cow for several minutes before dropping their heads to graze. From where he sat, Richard could see bright red blood draining from the cow's nose. She grunted, took another wobbling step, and dropped to her knees before sinking onto the grass.

"Good shot," Willow whispered happily, and took Richard's hand. "First buffalo?"

"The first." And Richard watched, torn with remorse and an unquenchable pride. "But, Travis, shouldn't we shoot her again?"

"What? And waste the powder? Dick, she's dead. Ye gotta larn, thar ain't no store around hyar no place. Use only as much as ye needs ter get the job done. There's times a mite of powder has to last a coon fer a long spell."

The cow lifted her head, then dropped it.

"She's nigh gone under, Dick. Ye done made meat."

The fever had drained away to leave him oddly empty.

The cow's last hoarse gasp carried to his ears; then she was still.

Travis rose to his feet, and as Richard and Willow stood, the other buffalo turned to stare, some raising their tails and defecating.

"That's a warning," Travis said. "Watch their tails. The more nervous a buffalo gets, the higher it puts its tail. Like a warning flag that there's trouble."

As Travis spoke, the animals whirled, charging away with a pounding of hooves. How many were there? Seventy? A hundred?

Richard followed Travis forward. To one side lay the mounded shape of Travis's buffalo. It had pitched forward and fallen on its side.

Reverently, he walked up to his cow.

"Careful, coon," Travis warned. "Foller me. Cain't never tell when a critter's dead. I remember old Jonas Farb. Why, he walked up and grabbed ahold of a bull's head that he'd shot. That bull come to, flipped his head, and old Jonas, he had no place to go so he jumped right a-straddle that bull's back. Let me tell ye, that bull stood up and took off lickety-split fer parts unknown . . . and there was old Jonas, a-hanging on that hump fer all he's worth. By the time he got shut of that bull, he's five days' walk from camp."

Richard nodded soberly, failing to see the twinkle in Travis's eyes.

The cow lay dead, eyes wide, her nose planted in a pool of foamy blood.

"My God, look how *big* she is!" Richard spread his arms and gaped.

"Reckon yer a gonna find out just how big she is, all right. Now the work starts." Travis poked the cow in the side with his rifle. "Let's get her guts out. Hump roast and boudins fer dinner tonight!"

Willow placed a caressing hand on the buffalo's back, then raised her arms to the sky and sang softly, the Shoshoni words lilting in the air. When she finished, she walked over to Travis's animal and repeated the gesture.

"What's she doing?" Richard asked.

"Praying fer the buff, or this child don't know sign. Injuns figger that critters got souls. They thank 'em for the gift of meat."

"I guess there's something to that."

Travis gave him a sidelong look. "Rational, huh?"

Richard grinned and looked away. But inside, he, too, said a prayer for the animal.

"Now what?"

Travis handed Richard his knife. "Slit her around the neck just back of the ears and horns. Then cut her right down the back to the tail. No, not that way. Yer just a-cutting hair. The edge has to be under the skin, that, or ye'll dull yer blade till it won't cut a dry fart."

Willow had already begun work on the cow Travis had shot. Glancing over, Richard couldn't help but admire the way she used a knife, so practiced and efficient. Bent like that, her buckskin dress emphasized the roundness of her hips and the slender lines of her back.

"Uh, reckon ye wouldn't mind watching what yer a-doing? She's a right smart woman, I'll agree, but I'd rather ye kept yer eyes on what yer cutting . . . my fingers being so close to that blade, Dick." Travis pulled the thick hide down while Richard blushed and severed the tissue.

"Easy, coon. Cut along the hide, not into the meat like a Yankee would."

"I've never done this before." The exposed flesh was hot against his skin, the muscles still quivering. White patterns of fat contrasted to the warm red of the meat.

When they had peeled the hide down, Travis took the knife and began slicing cuts of meat. These he placed on the grass until only strips of meat hung on the bloody bones.

"I'm gonna fetch the hosses and a hatchet," Travis said before he turned and trotted away.

Richard picked at the clotted blood drying on his hands. The flies buzzed in excitement around the carcass. How ephemeral life was, the scavengers drawn so quickly to the dead.

He walked over to Willow, who still labored on the other cow.

She gave him a radiant smile, and he noticed blood on her lips. "Meat!" she cried. "You are a hunter now, Ritshard. You have killed a buffalo. Today is a special day for you."

"Special?"

"Special among my people." She sliced another thin strip of meat and handed it to him.

He shook his head and she shrugged before popping the treat into her mouth. He watched her jaw muscles working under smooth brown skin. The sparkle in her eyes, the happiness reflected in the set of her mouth, made his soul sing. "You don't cook it?"

"Of course." With a dainty pink tongue, she licked a bloody morsel from her finger. "But for now, it is food."

He bent down to help her. Unlike Travis, who cut across the grain, she severed each muscle individually, cutting it loose from the bone. Her deft abilities had already stripped the backstrap, hump, and ribs.

She glanced at him, a curious smile playing along her lips. "Do you always help women butcher?"

"No . . . I mean, this is the first time."

"Why?"

"Why not? I like to help you." He fidgeted, oddly uneasy. "You prayed for the animals. Sang to their souls."

The wind teased her long black hair. "White men do not?"

"Most don't. But, well—I did."

She paused, the bloody knife hanging. "I do not understand. White men do not thank the animals who die to give them life? Ritshard, are White men without respect? Do they not understand that everything is related?" She shook her head. "I think your people are rich in many things . . . like knives and guns and pots. But in your souls, I think you are all empty."

He took a deep breath, meeting her dark eyes and the certainty expressed there. The memory of the woman on the steamboat surfaced, her voice shrill as she smacked her child. "Many are, I guess. But not all. Some men spend their entire lives seeking to understand the soul."

"Some men?"

"Anselm, Augustine, Meister Eckhardt. We have many men in our history who have sought God and the soul. It's an old quest in our society."

"What is quest?"

"The search."

"Men again? Women do not seek?"

"Not very many. Some do. It has been suggested that women do not have the same capacity for understanding the infinite that men do."

She lifted an eyebrow, then bent to her work. "In some ways, White men and Snake people may not be so different."

"For every Heloïse there are twenty Abelards."

"I don't understand."

"No, you wouldn't. But it's—"

"I quest," she told him as she sliced another thick slab of muscle from the buffalo. "Does that bother you?"

He reached down, pulling on a rubbery muscle as she severed it from the bone. "What do you hope to find?"

She glanced up at him. "In your words—understanding. Of everything. You did not answer. Does that bother you?"

Richard glanced up at the sky, aware of the spiraling wings of a hawk far overhead. "No. I mean, after all, that's what I've spent my life studying."

"Studying?"

"Uh . . . larning."

· She nodded, that secret smile on her lips. "Isn't that all anyone can do? Try to larn?"

He looked into her gorgeous eyes and his soul floated. Her lips parted, and he reached for her, barely conscious of taking her hand. At the sound of approaching hooves she lowered her eyes, the connection severed.

Richard turned away, self-conscious, as Travis rode up out of the drainage, sitting his horse like a lord. On a lead rope, the tail-hitched cavvy followed with heads up and manes flying. At the smell of blood, the horses snorted, backing and pawing. Travis handled his animal with a firm hand until the mare settled down. He landed lightly on his feet, soothing the horses.

The hunter dragged the mare forward, tying her off on the last of the man-sized cedars at the edge of the gully. He pulled a hatchet from his possibles and stalked across the grass. Richard pushed to his feet, ears burning redly, but Travis seemed oblivious.

"Now, what's left?" Travis asked absently before using the hatchet to separate the ribs from the gut cavity. Richard dodged flying chips of bone and stared at the organs as Travis and Willow cut the last of the muscles loose and lifted the ribs off.

Travis chortled as he reached into the wet mass to tug out the heavy liver. From this he sliced long strips and handed them around. Willow immediately sank white teeth into the bloody stuff. Richard stared as Travis asked, "Ye gonna eat? First meat, coon."

"It's not cooked."

"Yer a Yankee Doodle if'n I ever saw one. Eat'er, child, or I'll whack ye one."

A quest? A search for understanding? Richard made a face and bit into the rich, hot liver. He tried to ignore the hot blood dripping down his chin.

◈

Travis hunched over his horse's neck as the toiling line of men leaned into the cordelle. Like some curious caterpillar, they splashed through the rippling shallows in the river below him. Willow sat placidly on her horse, fingers tracing the handle of the Pawnee war club. The horses stamped at the few flies brave enough to dare the weather.

Gray clouds had settled in; drizzle fell in fits and spits, coupled with gusts of cold wind. Thunder growled out of a mass of black clouds rolling in from the western plains.

The river had a sullen look, as if resentful of the progress the line of men made as they pulled the *Maria* into the strengthening current. Travis picked out Richard Hamilton as he struggled along, sloshing and wet, the heavy cordelle over his shoulder. Farther up the line, Baptiste bent his powerful body to the thick rope, his black skin contrasting with that of the white *engagés*.

This particular passage was deadly, the worst they'd encountered yet. Richard hadn't wanted to go back to the cordelle, but here they needed every hand to pull the boat through the fast water.

"So much work," Willow said. "In all the world, only White men and ants work like that."

"Reckon so," Travis agreed. "It's a bad spot, Willow." He pointed to the embarras of twisted logs and splintered branches that had dammed half the river. Water spilled around the end of the obstacle, but against that rush *Maria* was hauled inexorably forward, whitewater foaming at her bow, the cordelle pulled tight enough to bead droplets. Under that weight, the mast bowed perilously. On the cargo box, Green raced back and forth like a desperate mouse, shouting orders, watching fearfully as disaster loomed. Face twisted, Henri braced his feet and leaned against the protesting steering oar to keep *Maria* out of the tangled wood.

"If anything goes wrong, there'll be hell ter pay," Travis said softly. "Painter crap, I otta be down there with 'em."

Maria gained a few feet against the rush of the water, each inch made at the expense of tearing muscles and straining joints.

"Ritshard did not want to pull the boat."

Travis grinned. "Reckon he still figgers he's a gentleman."

"Jentl . . . What is that?"

"Gentleman, uh, like a sort of chief. Not like a worker. Whites have these differences among them."

"So do Pawnee." A frown marred her brow. "Ritshard is a chief?"

Travis reached into his possibles and found what remained of his tobacco twist. He cut a length and chewed it until it juiced. After spitting a brown streak, he said, "Not a chief, exactly, but I'd guess you'd say a respected man. One looked up to by most people."

"But not the *engagés*."

"Now, Willow, ye got ter understand, Dick's got ter earn his way." He waved his hand. "This hyar ain't Boston. It's the river, and rules is different wharever ye goes. Dick ain't larned that yet."

"Tell me of this Boston."

"It's a city. Cold in winter. Good taverns . . . but a mite hard on coons deep in their cups. Not the kind of place a feller wants ter go a-sleeping in the street, that's plumb certain."

"Ritshard wishes for a place like this?"

"Wal, ye see, he figgers it a bit different than this child. 'Course, every feller's got the right ter his own brand of hydrophobia."

"Hydro . . . ?"

"Foaming mouth—like the critters get. White bubbly spit leaking from the mouth? Won't get near water. Crazy mean—bites everything in sight. You know the sickness I mean?"

"I know it. You think Ritshard wanting Boston is a sickness? Crazy?"

"Yep."

"Why do you not let him go, Trawis?"

He reached up and scratched his ear. "In the beginning we needed men, Willow. Just like ye see down there, each one pulling as hard as he can. Times is, just one body can make the difference atwixt living and dying."

"Green took on men at Fort Atkinson."

"Yep."

At that moment, Richard stumbled on the cordelle, dragging two more men down after him. Another fell, and then another. Shouts carried up to them as the men floundered, battling the rippling brown current and the weight of the cordelle. The river's grip pulled *Maria* back, and the scrambling men with her. Some were dragged through the water, floundering as they sought their feet.

"Come on. Come *on.*" Travis knotted his fists, moved his quid from cheek to cheek, and prayed fervently.

Baptiste let out a bellow, bracing himself and gripping the cordelle. Trudeau cursed and shouted, plunging along the thick rope. The men who'd fallen had scrambled for a hold, slowing the retreat, stopping it just as the *Maria* swung like a pendulum toward the end of the embarras with its foaming whitewater and pointed logs.

"*Pull!*" Green's scream carried from the river. "One more slip and we're dead!"

Henri battled the steering oar while *Maria* slipped closer to death on the jutting logs. If she hit, they'd tear through her like teeth.

The *engagés* bellowed and pulled, Trudeau motioning them onward. *Maria* edged ahead.

"Come on," Travis prayed. "Hold her, boys."

For long minutes they watched silently as the misty rain picked up. The boat inched forward against the surging water.

Willow pulled her blanket over her head, and Travis noted the strain in her face. Richard had been dragged through the mud. He coughed, soaked and bedraggled, as he leaned into the cordelle.

Maria edged away from destruction.

"Close one." Travis rubbed his face. "Mighty close."

Maria pulled clear of the current. The weary *engagés* toiled toward the sandbar. At the lead, Lalemont staggered out onto the land, feet pocking the muddy sand.

Henri steered wide of the shallows to keep draft. Green was rocking from foot to foot, still tense with fear.

"What if the boat sank?" Willow glanced at Travis.

"We'd be in a mess. If'n we lose that boat, she's a long

walk ter Saint Loowee. Green would have lost everything he's worked for. All them years . . . gone.''

"You White men are hydro . . . hydro—''

"Hydrophobied.''

"Crazy.''

"Reckon so, gal. Ain't no worse than some, I'd say.''

"Some?''

"Folks. Guess we're all a little crazy. Maybe yer *Tam Apo* made us that way.''

"Not in the beginning, Trawis. But after the Creation, when Coyote was making trouble, that's when the world got crazy.''

The *engagés* had all reached the thin spit of sand. They lined out now, holding their places on the cordelle, catching their breath.

Trudeau walked down the line to Richard, waving his arms, shouting angrily. Richard stood stoop-shouldered, chest heaving as water trickled down his face.

Travis couldn't hear the words over the distance, but Trudeau balled a fist and drove it deep into Richard's gut. The Yankee doubled under the impact and dropped flat onto the mud.

"Son of a bitch,'' Travis growled, eyes narrowing. "The kid couldn't help falling.''

Baptiste had left his place, running down to pull Trudeau off. The other *engagés* watched silently. Trudeau and Baptiste stood toe-to-toe, and finally Trudeau shook his head with disgust and tramped off to take up the cordelle again.

Baptiste had bent over Richard, then pulled him to his feet.

"*Levez!*'' came Trudeau's cry. And the *engagés* threw themselves into the endless pulling.

Richard stood bent over, head hanging as the *engagés* pulled past him, none daring to look him in the eye.

Willow sat in stony silence, a hardness in her delicate face.

"Wal, I'd reckon thar's more coming from Trudeau.''

"Ritshard should kill him,'' Willow said woodenly.

Travis allowed himself to slump in the saddle again. "Ye care fer that Yankee, don't ye?''

She glanced at Travis with smoldering eyes. "Power . . . how do you say? The medicine is strong in Ritshard. He has a fire in his soul, one that he does not know yet. Green has his boat. The *engagés* their work. Ritshard looks for more. I understand that quest."

"Quest?"

"The search, Trawis. One day, Ritshard will find it, and when he does, he will be a great man."

Travis ground on his quid for a moment, spat the juice, and crossed his arms. "Maybe. 'Course, we gotta keep him alive long enough."

TWENTY-SIX

———————— ◇ ————————

It may seem strange to some man, that has not well weighed these things; that nature should thus dissociate, and render men apt to invade, and destroy one another: and he may therefore, not trusting to this inference, made from the passions, desire perhaps to have the same confirmed by experience. Let him therefore consider with himself when taking a journey, he arms himself, and seeks to go well accompanied; when going to sleep, he locks his doors; when even in his house he locks his chests; and this is when he knows there be laws, and public officers, armed, to revenge all injuries shall be done him; what opinion has he of his fellow-subjects, when he rides armed; of his fellow citizens, when he locks his doors; and of his children, and servants, when he locks his chests. Does he not there as much as accuse mankind by his actions, as I do by my words?

—Thomas Hobbes, *Leviathan*

Sheets of rain slanted down from the night sky to spatter steam from the smoking remains of Richard's fire. He shivered in his blanket, wet to the bone. Water dripped through the soaked tarp he'd tied overhead.

His belly hurt where Trudeau had hit him. Dear Lord God, how low could a man sink? To be abused by brutes, tormented and cold, and somehow ashamed that he'd only been able to lie in the sand while Baptiste rescued him.

Trudeau wants to kill me.

Numb from the cold, Richard fingered the soggy fetish on his belt. Lightning flashed whitely in the sky, illuminating the slanted blanket shelters, shiny-wet against the backdrop of the dripping cottonwoods. Several seconds later, the bang of thunder hammered the air.

Richard closed his eyes. *Why haven't I run? I could have been back to Fort Atkinson by now. Or on my way to Saint Louis by pirogue or bateau.*

But he hadn't taken any of the opportunities. Instead, he'd promised himself it would be the next day, or the next, when he made his break, stole a horse, and galloped south.

"I'm a coward," he whispered, and wrung water from a twist of his blanket. Perhaps Laura did deserve Thomas Hanson more than him.

Trudeau. Damn Trudeau! If only he could have blocked that blow, given the boatman back measure for measure.

And degenerate into what? Another human beast like Trudeau?

"Coon?" Like some hunched night creature, Travis ducked out of the dark into the shelter. He grunted, pulling off his hat and wringing it out. "I reckon they's frogs what will drown in this."

"Go away."

"Ain't much of anywhere to go. Hell, even the hosses won't get stole in weather like this. River'll be up another couple of feet in the morning. Creeks is all flooded."

"Then maybe we'll be lucky and all drown."

"Yer not sounding so pert, coon. This beaver figgered ye'd be keen ter philos'phy me half ter death with yer Roos-soo."

"He can drown, too—except he's already dead."

"How's yer gut?"

"Sore."

"It warn't yer fault. Fellers slip in the mud. Could'a been Trudeau as likely as ye."

"But it wasn't, Travis. Let's face it, I'm not fit for this. It's not my place. I should be back in Boston, working on the docks if nothing else. I had that chance once . . . Patrick Bonnisen was hiring." *Damn you, Father. Maybe I should have taken him up. You'd appreciate that, wouldn't you? A son who worked as a dockhand?*

Travis had seated himself cross-legged. A flash of lightning illuminated his terrible face, the scars water-slick. "I worked docks before. Men there is the same as Trudeau."

"How cheery. Something to look forward to when I get back to Boston."

"Don't have to be that way."

"Indeed? Perhaps you know something about my father that I don't? I'm a failure, Travis. All I wanted was to continue my studies, stay at the university. I lost my father's money, was kidnapped to this Hell, killed a boy . . . almost wrecked everything today. All I'll ever be is a failure."

Travis's face twisted. "Ye ain't no failure—lessen ye wants ter be."

"Oh?"

"Hell, coon, ye knows a sight more than old Travis. All them fellers ye talk about. Roossoo, Haggle, Kant. And a passel more I been hearing ye tell of."

"A great deal of good it does me here."

"Yep, wal, yer not seeing things with a skinned eye, coon. Willow's free of that rascal Packrat. I ain't wolfmeat 'cause ye sewed me up."

Richard pushed his wet hair back. "I didn't have any choice."

"Reckon ye did. What of all that free will yer so fond of spouting up?"

"Do I look free, Travis?"

"Yep."

Richard stared silently at the fire's steaming ashes. Rain pattered in the darkness, accented by louder spats of water falling from the trees. The smell of smoke carried from the half-drowned fires to mingle with the wet scents of trees, grass, and ground.

"Dick, a feller's only as free as he makes hisself. Ask

Baptiste. Hell, ask me. I done been in a sight worse mess than yer in. On a brig in the middle of the ocean, ye can only dance the jig while the fiddler plays the tune."

"I'm not convinced."

"Lord God A'mighty, Dick, yer problem is that ye've got to thinking ye've all this high and mighty truth tucked away inside, but ye don't. I ain't read all them books. I don't know what them fellers said, but I know about living, and freedom, and going whar my stick floats. And that, coon, is why I'm a heap smarter than ye—and all yer book larning to boot."

"Aristotle would be pleased to hear that."

"I'll tell him next time I see his sorry arse. But tell me this: If'n a philos'pher's got all this truth, it sure otta stand up ter living, ottn't it? I don't know what's in them books, but I do know this: If'n ye've got all the larning in the world, it's poor bull ter fat cow if'n yer not willing ter be wrong. Ye might as well be a turtle as a man."

Richard studied Travis's dark silhouette. "What are you saying?"

"I'm saying yer right. Yer a failure. And ye'll always be one unless yer a-willing ter look life straight in the eye. The way I figgers it, ye've growed up thinking it's all easy. Even yer philos'phy. Read a couple of books, and ye knows it all. No sweat and blood, no pain and misery. Wal, coon, philos'pher or not, yer gonna be a failure lessen ye stands up like a man. Maybe ye'll get shot straight through the lights ... and maybe ye won't. But ye'll know yerself. And die like a man instead of a boy."

Lightning arced in the sky, flashing weird shadows over the sodden camp.

"Yer pretty damn silent fer once."

"I was just thinking of Socrates," Richard said uneasily.

"I knew a slave by that name once. On a plantation in South Carolina."

"A slave ... no, Travis. This is the real Socrates. A Greek philosopher who lived two thousand years ago."

"And he wrote one of these books?"

"No. But he taught the men who did. Any student of

philosophy has heard his immortal teaching: 'The unexamined life is not worth living.'"

"Did he get that out of a book?"

"No. As you would say, he stood up and looked life straight in the eye. He was an orator, and a soldier. When Athens went to war, he picked up his shield and sword and fought. When he encountered a wise man, he questioned him, regardless of the consequences. In the end, it cost him his life." Richard stroked the fetish. "You'd have liked him."

"Real cat-scratch scrapper, huh?"

"Yes." Richard took a deep breath. "So, what do I do?"

"Take life as she comes. Why, ye've an opportunity most men'd kill fer. Yer on the river, Dick. Headed fer the Shining Mountains. Stop trying ter see everything from outside, and see it from inside fer once."

What was it about Travis Hartman? Where did that fearless self-assurance come from?

The same place as Socrates', the internal voice told him. *From having tested the truths in the crucible of life.*

"I've been a fool, Travis." He rubbed his stomach. "The lesson's a little painful, is all."

"Them's the best ones."

"I guess Trudeau was right to hit me."

"Nope. Warn't yer fault. Reckon that Frenchie's gonna be a thorn in everybody's butt lessen I take him down."

"Why you?"

"Running the men is my job."

"It's me he's after . . . and Willow."

"Yer not up ter Trudeau. He'll make wolfmeat outa ye."

"I could learn, couldn't I?"

"Might mean taking a couple of lumps, Dick."

Richard stared out into the night rain and swallowed hard as he made his decision. "Trade you."

"How's that."

"You teach me how to whip Trudeau, and I'll teach you how to read and write."

"I cain't larn that!"

"Painter crap, as you would say. Or . . . are you afraid of failing?"

Thunder blasted the night.

"I . . . uh . . . *Me?* Larning ter read?" Travis snorted in final defeat, then smiled. "Yer a damned Yankee bastard, Dick."

Yes, but then, when it comes to being a damn bastard, I've had good teachers.

The experience was magical. Heals Like A Willow sat on the front of the cargo box and looked down over the bow of the boat. In the lee of the storm, the wind blew strongly from the south, and *Maria*'s bulging sail drove her upriver.

Muddy water sparkled in the sunlight as the boat raced the waves upriver. The sensation of such movement lifted Willow's soul as if born on the wings of a mighty eagle. She couldn't see enough of the bank passing, of the wake left behind, or the current sliding under the pointed prow— and without muscles to do it! The boat seemed alive, a sentient being instead of a human creation.

And in that lay another puzzle. Did White men have the ability to create beings?

High overhead the last of the delicate clouds raced them northward, contrasting to the deep blue of the rain-fresh sky and the aching green of the trees and grass. So clean compared to the muddy river with its flotsam.

Dave Green came to sit beside her, resplendent in a jade shirt and fawn-colored pants. His blond hair caught glints of golden sunlight, and his blue eyes sparkled. Eyes she still hadn't grown used to seeing; they simply shouldn't be that pale and curious-looking.

"A good day," Green told her, clasping his hands in his lap. "After yesterday, I can use a day like this. Sailing, by God. What a relief. But help me watch for floating logs. The banks will be washing out and toppling trees."

"The boat moves," she said. "Strong medicine."

"You've seen the wind push a leaf across a pond? Same thing, but bigger. I've come upriver many times, and the wind is always a chancy thing. I was starting to believe it had deserted us altogether."

Willow tucked a long strand of black hair behind her ear. "I never would have figgered such a thing."

Green's expression betrayed his delight with the day. "If we could have a couple of weeks of this, we could ride up to the Yellowstone in complete comfort."

She glanced up at the curving sail. "Canvas," they called it. Such an incredibly strong and light fabric. Even the finest scraped buffalo hide could not match it for strength.

"You have many marvels, Green. I had heard the stories told by some of my people. I did not believe them." She touched the looking glass she wore on a thong around her neck.

"I hope all of your people share your enthusiasm." Green rubbed his hands together. "I've been thinking, Willow. This first year we'll set up at the mouth of the Big Horn. Trade with the Crows. If that goes well, maybe we'll move up the Big Horn, put a post in Snake country. Maybe around the Hot Spring."

She knew the place of which he spoke: *Pa'goshowener,* Hot Water Stand. The huge hot springs where the Big River ran through the canyon in the Owl River Mountains.

"Why would you go there?"

"Your people could come to trade. They would have their own post, Willow. As it is, the Snakes must travel a great distance, through many enemies, to trade hides for white goods."

She shook her head slowly. "You call these things 'goods.' I am not sure they are good. Marvelous, yes. Good? That is a word I worry about. Ritshard and Trawis have taught me the word 'medicine.' " She made the hand sign for "Power." "Among my people, medicine can be good or bad. It depends on how people use it. A healer can use medicine for good. A sorcerer can use it to kill. These things you Whites would trade, they, too, have medicine. Tell me, Green, are they really all good?"

His blue eyes probed hers. "Travis told me you were a smart squaw, and that I'd best not underestimate you. Well, Willow, I'll tell you the truth as far as I know it, all right?"

"All right."

"I don't know if all the things White men make are good for them, or not. I guess it depends on how you use them. A gun kills more efficiently than a bow. A man can defend his home better with a bullet than an arrow."

"But you must trade for powder and bullets. And if your gun breaks, you must get a White Man to fix it."

"That's true. But in the meantime, an Indian can make him a new bow and arrows until he runs into a trader with gun parts."

"A gun is heavy thing to pack around while looking for a trader."

"Not if you have a post at the Hot Springs. The parts would be there whenever you needed them."

"And if this trader wants as much for the gun—what did you say? Parts? Those are the pieces?"

"That's right. A gun is made of parts."

"But if one part breaks, the gun is worth as much as the broken part. What then, Green? I heard the story about Blackbird. He let the trader charge what he wanted. And the people had to pay."

The booshway frowned. "Happens. On my honor, Willow, if I am your trader, I will never charge as much for the part as I would for the whole gun."

"But you might charge a lot."

He gestured at the boat and the *engagés* riding along the *passe avant*. "This costs a great deal, Willow. I had to pay a heap for the boat, and the men don't work for free. You understand about money?"

"Yes. Trawis explained. Like trading plews. So many for a certain thing."

"Well, it's a bit more complicated than that, but yes. I still have to make more on trade than I give out. You understand that? I must make enough more so that I can get the things I want for myself."

She lifted an inquisitive eyebrow. "And what do you want, Green? I think you would be a hard man to satisfy. You remind me of my . . ." *How do I say brother-in-law? What is their word?* "Of a man I know. He always wants more, and will risk himself to get it. One day it will kill him. You are such a man, Green. I can see your soul. It will never be full.''

Green stared out at the river, the waves breaking in white-caps. ''You can see my soul?''

''Medicine has given me certain ways of seeing. Your soul is a lot like Ritshard's. He is driven to know. You are driven to have things. Neither one of you will ever have enough of what you want, but Ritshard will try to share what he seeks. Will you try to share your things, Green?''

He took a deep breath and laughed. ''Damn, woman, do you always ask so many questions?''

''Ever since I was a little girl. It is said that I'm nothing but trouble. Better for you that Ritshard shot Packrat and freed me. Think how you would have felt if you'd traded two rifles for me back at the fort. You'd want your rifles back.''

A twinkle filled Green's eyes. ''I doubt it, Willow.''

''We have not solved the problem of your 'goods.' They can be bad, can't they? Like the whiskey you carry. People will want more and more of them.''

''If they didn't, I couldn't trade for very long. Willow, many things the whites have make life easier. A metal pot lasts forever. An iron ax is sharper than one made of stone. It takes less labor to chop down a tree.''

''Gunpowder runs out. Whiskey is all drunk up.''

''Iron needles are better than bone ones. Blankets are lighter than buffalo hides—and just as warm.''

She placed her palms together, rubbing her hands. ''The *Ku'chendikani* believe that horses are good for them, too. Now they move camp all winter long looking for grass for the horses. I think they work harder for the horses than the horses work for the people. Would trade be this way? If all the bands want White things, will they be working all winter to hunt enough beaver to pay for gunpowder, needles, pots, and whiskey? Are these things you bring just something else to take my people away from their old life? From the familiar ways of doing things?''

Green made a face. ''Hell, Willow, I don't . . . I mean . . . Look, I can't *make* them trade for things. It's up to them, isn't it? You've got to understand how trade works. I've got to bring things people want. If I haul a boatload of blankets all the way upriver and no one wants a single one, I'm broke. I sure can't make a man trade for a blanket he don't *want*. Follow my stick?"

She nodded. "Plumb center, Green. My people *wanted* horses. They still do. More than anything else in the world. I fear they will want the White man's goods with the same—is the word 'passion'?"

"It is."

"Then your goods may be very bad, Green."

He fingered his chin. "Blackfeet and Crow will have these things. Guns give warriors a big advantage in a fight."

"The *A'ni* and *Pa'kiani* seek out the *Ku'chendikani* just to take their horses. The *Dukurika* high in the mountains are mostly left alone. The *A'ni* and *Pa'kiani* don't like to ride their horses up the mountains. And the *Dukurika* have nothing they want to steal."

"Sheepeater," Green said, understanding in his eyes. "You're not a Snake? Which tribe do you belong to?"

She shrugged. "We are just the People. Some live far to the west and call themselves the *Agaidika*, the Fish-eaters. Some are the *Po'hogan'hite*, the Sage-people. It depends on where the People are and what they do."

Green ran his thick fingers through his hair. "Willow, it's going to happen. If I don't set up a post and trade, someone else will. You and your people have to understand. The white traders will go any place they must to find hides. They'll fight for trade just as hard as the Blackfeet and Crows fight with each other. If the river can be made safe, many traders will race for your country. Take my word, they'll come. Just as winter follows summer."

Just as winter follows summer? The words settled in her soul. She couldn't help but stiffen at the thought.

"This place you will make, it will be like Fort Atkinson?"

"No, not that big. Just a small post. A couple of houses, a storehouse, and the trading house."

"And what if it isn't good for us, for my people, Green?"

"You've seen the things we have. Wouldn't life be easier with them? A copper pot doesn't wear out like a buffalo gut. Glass beads are brighter than porcupine quills. A good steel knife works a heap better than a stone one. That can't be bad.''

Water slapped at the bow, splashing whitely against the brown water. Despite the magic of a huge boat that moved with the wind, she couldn't shake the sense of worry.

Someday my people will regret the coming of the White men. And she couldn't help but think of Coyote, who promised wonderful things—and brought disaster.

"That wasn't fair!" Richard picked himself up off the grass and wiped his bloody nose. Every muscle ached, and his nose stung. The only saving grace was that Willow was on the boat and didn't have to see him look a simple fool.

They stood out in the open on the bluffs west of the river. The horses watched them with pricked ears, then lowered their heads to crop at the fresh grass and challenge the limits of their ground picket. A brisk south wind tugged at Richard's shirt and ruffled his sweaty hair. Out in the grass a meadowlark trilled the most peaceful of songs. Beyond wave after wave of grassy hills, the horizon lost itself in the distance. Patches of white fluffy cloud contrasted to the crystal blue heavens.

Travis stood with feet planted, thumbs in his belt. The insolent wind teased the long fringes of his tawny hunting jacket. "Dick, the thing about fighting is that yer supposed to win."

Baptiste laughed and added, "Boy, you gotta figger that Trudeau ain't a gonna worry about fair, neither. He ain't no gentleman. And, Dick, you gotta savvy this: Out heah, winning means living."

Richard stared at the bright blood on his fingers. "So what am I doing wrong?"

"Yer holding back. Now, try her again. Give her all ye've got. Fight with yer heart. C'mon. Try me." Travis gestured him onward.

Richard tasted blood and spit. "This is just practice. Do I have to bleed?"

"Hell, yes! Fighting ain't painless, coon. That nose ain't shit ter what Trudeau'll do ter ye. Here I come."

Richard squared his shoulders, knotted his fists, and Travis closed. This time, Richard blocked two of Travis's blows before a third landed in his gut. Richard doubled, thumped into the ground, and wheezed fer breath.

"C'mon, ye silly girl!" Travis cried, bounding from foot to foot. "Get up, ye stinking Yankee. Yer dog shit, boy! Farting philos'pher! Ye've got the guts of a buzzard!"

The mocking tone goaded him. The humiliation of that last blow, the indignity of his dripping nose, all broke loose at once, and he threw himself at Travis, a red rage burning free inside.

Clawing and scratching, Richard kicked and gouged, heedless of the blows that rained down on him. But Travis slipped inside, backheeled him, and dropped him to the ground.

"That's it!" Travis leapt back, a grin on his ruined face. "Ye turned yerself loose!"

"You son of a bitch!" Richard staggered to his feet.

"Them's fighting words!" Baptiste crowed.

"Whoa, now!" Travis held his hands wide. "That's just the first step. When yer a-fighting, rage is half of it. T'other half is in yer head. That's what we gotta work on next."

Richard glared, fists knotted.

"All right, coon. Come over hyar. Now, grab a-holt of me. What I just did was wrap my leg around ahind yers and push. Give her a try."

Richard did, while Baptiste pointed out the proper place to put his feet.

"Gonna have you all fit to whup Old Ephraim hisself," Baptiste declared. "Ain't nobody on the river knows knuckle and skull like ol' Travis Hartman."

Richard threw the hunter, surprised at what he'd done.

"Now, coon," Travis told him from flat on his back. "Jump plumb in the middle of my lights, and I'll show ye how ter gouge a man's eye out. Ain't gonna do her fer real, mind. I got lots ter see afore I goes under."

"Gouge a man's—"

"When ye fights, coon, ye fights fer yer life."

"But, Travis, a man's *eyes*? My God, that's—"

Baptiste stepped close, his black face grim. "Make yor choice now, white boy. Life ain't fair. It ain't just. Fighting ain't nothing more than two animals going at it to see who wins. Ain't no rules out heah. You win, yor alive. You lose . . ." Baptiste ran a suggestive finger across Richard's throat.

Reluctantly, Richard nodded. "All right, Travis, how do I gouge a man's eye out?"

Hours later, Richard picked at his blood-crusted nose as they waited by the side of the river for the *Maria*.

Travis sat cross-legged, peering intently at the ABCs scratched into the dirt. Baptiste lounged on his side, watching with amused interest. Laboriously Travis scratched out: T-R-A-V-I-S. Then wiped it out and started again.

"Gives a coon a curious feeling, a-wiping out his name like that. Injuns, they figger words got power, heap of medicine in 'em. Most like a-stepping on a grave."

Richard winced as he shifted his abused body. "Well, think of it this way. As long as you can write it again, you're still alive. And unlike the spoken word, the written one can last forever. Like those of Socrates, who spoke two thousand years ago. Were it not for writing, his thoughts would be long gone. All that wisdom, vanished forever."

"Tee. Are. Ay. Uh—"

"Vee."

"Yep. Vee. Eye. Snake. That's what it is."

"Ess."

"Wal, she looks like a snake ter me, coon. Them letter sign, wal, it's some harder ter cipher than this poor child ever figgered on."

Baptiste chimed in. "Where I comes from, it's agin' the law fo' niggers to larn to read."

"It's an immoral law," Richard replied. "They're afraid of what slaves would learn if they started to read. You might pick up a copy of Rousseau, or Hegel, and get ideas that might cause dissent."

"What?"

"Unrest. Rebellion. As long as the slaves are ignorant, they can be oppressed. In Boston, there are abolitionist factions who would change that."

Baptiste gave him a blank look.

"Abolitionists," Richard repeated. "People who want to abolish, do away with, slavery. It's quite fashionable among the intellectuals."

Baptiste picked a twig from the ground, cocked his jaw, and one by one, began to trace out the letters Richard had drawn. "Reckon I could larn, too. If'n it's agin' the law, this coon's fo' it."

Richard moved his sore arm, watching both men make letters in the sand. *Here I am, a prime candidate to die by violence, learning to fight like a ruffian, and teaching an escaped slave to read.*

But the memory of Trudeau, of the triumphant look in his eyes, had burned into Richard's soul. *One day, Trudeau, you're going to regret that punch to the belly. So help me, God.*

The anger of that promise sobered him enough to wonder, *What am I becoming?*

Richard climbed slowly to his feet, walking out into the trees. One nostril was still plugged with blood. Had that been him, clawing and kicking in red fury?

I was a wild man. The antithesis of everything I've ever believed. He stopped to watch a squirrel dashing through the cottonwood branches overhead. Beyond the belt of trees lining the river, the plains stretched endlessly toward the western horizon. A man stood alone out there, naked to the eye of God. And from what Travis had told him, the plains stretched on for weeks, months—endless grass, caressed by the sun and wind, home of the buffalo and the Indian.

"You can't lock Tam Apo *into a lodge, Ritshard. He is everywhere . . . and can only be known here."* And Willow had pointed to her heart. For the first time he fully understood the truth she'd taught.

The Power of raw God overwhelmed him; his sense of smallness crushed him. "How do we know what we know?" Professor Ames had asked as an introduction to the works of David Hume. "How does the mind perceive?"

In far-off England, safe amid the tame and fertile fields, and the cozy, brick-paved streets, Hume could ponder such weighty questions. Here, in the wilderness, perception was pressed on a man. It wasn't to be examined, but experienced.

And where was Richard Hamilton to find rationality so close to raw God? He gazed out at the ocean of grass, and remembered waves marching endlessly across Boston Harbor.

So far away.

For long moments, he lost himself in the distance, seeking . . . what?

He walked on, struggling to fit together the changes within himself. In breaks through the trees, he could see the river, brown water chapped by the wind. In defiance of rationality, he'd come to sense the river's soul. Power, Willow would have told him. All things having a soul. An idea discarded millennia ago by Western civilization.

Or have we just disassociated ourself from the natural world?

That strange awareness of land and water, wind, storm, and sun, had fingered his soul, heedless of his rational mind. Yes, Power, a sort of spiritual essence, uncaring of men or their concerns. A force to be accepted, but never denied. This face of God cared not for the desires, prayers, and wants of men.

How silly to think God was only an internal experience. No wonder Willow dismissed the idea that God could be encompassed by a cathedral. What a silly thing a man was, how insignificant when abandoned in such a wilderness. Was that the revelation experienced by Moses in the desert? Had such a forge tempered Augustine's soul in the isolated caves of Egypt?

Richard took a deep breath, trying to sort through his confusion. *I am learning to fight, to kill. Where is my purpose in this land of quick death?*

Did God even care?

Richard stared down at his hands, those hands that had held the fusee that blew Packrat's life out of his body. No divine wrath had descended from the heavens. The Pawnee youth's red blood had drained out of his body, and the birds had continued to sing. Richard Hamilton had continued to breathe, eat, see, and feel. Only the flies had taken note of the fact that a life had been terminated—with little more effort than Travis wiping out his name.

"What kind of world is this?" Richard threw his head back, eyes closed, listening to the cottonwood leaves rattling overhead. The air moved against his skin. Nothing changed with death. Life was only meaningful for the living.

He shook his head, and when he opened his eyes, it took several seconds for the sight to sink in. The men walking slowly toward him carried half-lifted rifles and bows. They wore breechcloths, leather leggings, and feathers stuck into their gleaming black hair. No expression crossed their hard faces. Keen black eyes watched him warily as they spread out to surround him.

Richard filled his lungs and shouted: *"Travis!"*

TWENTY-SEVEN

As everything is useful for man, so, too, is man himself useful, and his singular characteristic function consists in making himself a member of the human herd, to be utilized for the common good, and serviceable to all. The extent to which he looks after his own interests is the measure to which he must also serve the interests of others, and so far as he serves their needs, he is taking care of himself: the one hand washes the other.

—Georg Friedrich Wilhelm Hegel,
Phenomenology of Mind

Travis dodged from tree to tree, his Hawken in hand. There! He caught sight of movement, signaled Baptiste, and ducked low as he scuttled behind one of the thick cottonwoods.

Hamilton stood surrounded by six warriors. They'd cornered the Yankee fair, and the leader was fingering Richard's clothing, paying particular attention to the coup at his belt.

Travis filled his lungs and bellowed, *"Waugh!"*

At the call, the Sioux whirled, weapons ready.

To the side, Baptiste had wriggled up behind a log, slipping his Hawken over the scaling bark.

"Dakota!" Travis cried, walking out and making the hand sign for good. *"Wash-te!"*

Richard threw him a terrified but grateful glance. Travis chuckled, and called out, "Dick, if'n ye gets any more scairt, yer eyes is gonna pop plumb outa yer body and ye'll be blinder than a cussed gopher!"

The Sioux shuffled uncertainly, staring about, worried that there might be more Whites.

"Stand up, Baptiste," Travis called. "Let 'em know they got a shooter on them."

Baptiste raised himself to a sitting position, his Hawken braced for a shot.

In signs, Travis gestured, "We are friends. Traders. A boat is just downriver with many men. You have something to trade?"

This was the part that puckered a man's string. The Sioux glanced back and forth, evaluating their chances. Travis held his breath; then the leader smiled, signing, "It is good to see our White brothers. Traders are always welcome among the Water Spirit's people."

Water Spirit, *Wah-Menitu;* so that's who the tall coon was. A Teton Sioux chief, Water Spirit could go either way depending on how his medicine played out. Maybe he'd lift hair, or maybe he'd be a man's best friend.

"Wah-Menitu," Travis called out loud. *"Wash-te!* It is good."

At a command from Wah-Menitu, the other Sioux lowered their weapons.

"C'mon out, Baptiste, but keep yer iron ready."

"Got that right," Baptiste agreed, rising slowly.

Wah-Menitu made the sign for "It is good." He was a

lodgepole of a man, thin of frame and tall. Scars puckered the skin on his breasts. When he smiled, his projecting upper lip exposed worn yellow teeth. The aquiline nose hooked like a bird of prey's. Copper bracelets, tarnished as dark as the flesh beneath, decorated his sinewy arms. Tin cones held the horsehair tassels on his moccasins.

He pointed to the coup on Richard's belt. "Whose?" he signed.

"Pawnee," Travis signed back. "A warrior named Pack-rat."

At that, the Sioux yipped and began to leap about in enthusiastic joy. Richard had begun to sweat, his balled fists pressed desperately to his side. If he stood any stiffer, his joints were going to snap like dry sassafras sticks.

"Easy, Dick. Ye ain't dead yet. Stay calm, coon. They's just glad ter see ye."

Wah-Menitu touched the scalp reverently, then threw his arms around Richard in a bear hug that nigh to squeezed the grease out of the Yankee. The rest of the Sioux continued to leap and yip their shrill calls.

"What . . . what's happening?" Richard gasped.

"Made friends, coon." Travis laughed in spite of himself. *And if'n old Dick ever figgers out what that "fetish" is, he's gonna come plumb unstuck.* "Now, Dick. Whoop and holler a little yerself. C'mon, coon. Dance and shout! Join 'em. Or, yer wolfmeat!"

His back rigid as a keel, Richard jerked into step. Had his voice not been cracking, the whoops would have sounded a little more enthusiastic. The way Richard pirouetted reminded Travis of a stick figure on a string. The Sioux didn't seem to mind. They leapt and shrieked, nimble as hunting cats.

"What am I doing, Travis?" Richard shot him a frightened glance.

"Why, making friends, Dick."

"Am I gonna die?"

"Reckon. But if'n ye'll dance a little harder, it won't be hyar and now."

Richard jumped and bucked like a spring foal.

Baptiste sidled up to Travis, whispering, "Now, don't that beat all?"

"Reckon so. If'n his perfessers could just see him."

Travis stepped forward, grinning, and as the dance wore down, offered his hand around, smiling and shaking. Baptiste did the same, one hand still gripping his rifle.

"Smoke," Wah-Menitu said in English.

"Waugh!" Travis made a gesture and seated himself, digging his pipe and fixings out of his possibles. With flint and steel, one of the young warriors conjured a fire, and Travis used a twig to light his pipe.

Travis glanced up at the nervous Hamilton. "Sit down, Dick. Right hyar next ter me. That's right. We's gonna have us a palaver." Travis puffed his pipe to seat the fire, offered it to the four directions, and handed it to Wah-Menitu. The Sioux made his offering to the four sacred ways, to sky and earth, then puffed before handing the pipe to the next man. In silence, it made the rounds to Dick.

"Do like they done," Travis coached. "Follow the directions sunwise, then up and down. In the beginning, White Buffalo Cow Woman taught the Sioux how to use the pipe. Tobacco's sacred. Takes prayers to *Wakantanka*, to God. All words spoken here will be spoken truthfully."

Richard did as he was told, but his fingers shook as he offered the pipe and took a puff.

In signs, Travis said, "You gave my young friend a start. He thought you might have been Pawnee."

The Sioux laughed uproariously.

"You have boat?" Wah-Menitu asked.

"Downriver a mite. Be hyar soon."

"Our village is one day's travel upriver."

"He talks," Richard whispered in surprise.

"Hell, he got a tongue and talker like everybody else," Travis chided. To Wah-Menitu, Travis said and signed, "I am Travis Hartman, this is Dick Hamilton, and hyar's Baptiste. We will come to your village." He lifted his foot to show the hole in his moccasin. "Reckon I'm right keen ter trade, hoss."

The Sioux laughed again.

Wah-Menitu was studying Travis with hard black eyes. He said, "I know of you, Trawis Hartman. It is said yer a great warrior and a man of yer word. You have wintered with the Dakota before. Helped with the hunt. Shared our lodges and fires."

"Time or two, I reckon."

Wah-Menitu gestured to indicate the scars on Travis's face. "The bear left his sign. Only a strong man would keep his hair . . . and the bear lifted some of yers."

"Yep, wal, I reckon I got a sight more of his than he got of mine."

Wah-Menitu smiled. "It will be good to have you. Shining times for you, booshway. *Beaucoup* vittles." Wah-Menitu reached over to touch the coup on Hamilton's belt. "The Teton Dakota always have a welcome for warriors. We will dance . . . honor Dick for his courage and victory. Not all White coons are strong and brave."

"Damn that cussed Leavenworth anyway. Ye fought the Ree two years back?"

"Yer Leavenworth, and his soldiers, have water for blood."

Travis snorted. "Some do. Not all."

"But you, friends, are some. You are warriors. You come with yer boat, Trawis Hartman. Dance. Eat. *Wash-te*."

Richard leaned close. "What's *wash-te*? They keep saying that."

"Means good."

They stood, everyone smiling, shaking hands, and Wah-Menitu called out, "*Hooka'hay!*"

The Sioux let out blood-curdling screams again, and danced away through the trees.

Travis replaced his pipe, and said, "C'mon. We'd best hustle and make sure we still got hosses. Be just like them red varmints ter have lifted 'em while we was a-palavering."

"But they said they were friends," Richard cried.

"Whar ye been all yer life, Yankee?" Baptiste muttered. "Among Injuns, even friends steal each other's hosses."

"I was someplace sane," Richard muttered as they trotted back toward the horses.

Travis grinned again. If the pilgrim thought today was a scare, he'd be plumb twisted come tomorrow night.

"Sioux." At mention of the word the assembled *engagés* peered fearfully out at trees turned so suddenly ominous in the twilight.

Heals Like A Willow shifted nervously as she too stared into the woods. She knew the Sioux as *Bambiji'mina,* the Cuts-Off-A-Head People. And their sign was the cut-throat sign. Among her people, only the *Pa'kiani* were more hated.

The entire attitude of the party had changed. The *engagés,* normally of cheerful countenance come the evening camp, now fidgeted. An unbidden shiver ran down her back.

Trawis, Ritshard, and Baptiste stood at the center of the knot of men. Behind them, *Maria* lay snugged tight to the bank by her painter. Green stood halfway up the plank, thumb thrust in his belt.

"All right," Green called out. "Before we eat, I want trees drug up. Let's fort up. Horses inside, and double guard tonight. Baptiste, take first watch. Dick, you're in charge of second, and Travis third. I don't want anybody wandering out into the dark, hear?"

As Willow studied the men's faces, she decided any such order was needless.

"How many Sioux?" Trudeau asked.

"Handful," Trawis stated. "But we ain't taking no chances, not with Sioux. Hell, after Dick hyar got ter dancing with 'em, I figger he wore them varmints plumb out."

"Dancing?" Green asked. Trudeau scowled his disbelief.

"Hell, yes! Jumping and screaming like a young buck back from his first hoss raid," Trawis cried. "Why, ye should have seen 'em! Dick had 'em bunched up in a circle by the time we got there. If'n they'd had a fight on, all Baptiste and me woulda had ter do would be plug them coons from the trees."

Green lifted an eyebrow. Ritshard looked sheepish. Trudeau snorted and stomped off in disgust.

"You heard me, now. Let's get forted up! Nobody eats until I'm satisfied." Green waved them away. "And I don't want nobody out there alone gathering logs! Groups of three, and sing out the second you see anything."

The *engagés* muttered among themselves as they started for the trees. Trudeau kept glancing back over his shoulder and swearing sourly.

Green turned. "Travis? What's your opinion?"

Trawis pulled thoughtfully at his beard as he walked up to the plank. "Reckon they won't try anything. That's just a hunch, Dave. The way I figger, they's been starved fer trade last few years. Might have a couple of kids sneak out just fer a try at the hosses. One of them 'Just ter show ye we could do her' raids. Mostly, I'd guess that Wah-Menitu would want 'em ter leave us alone."

Green glanced at Baptiste, who said, "I'd say the same, Booshway. Way I read it, Wah-Menitu's savvy enough to know he'll get more from happy traders than mad ones."

"And Dick had 'em circled up?"

Ritshard flushed red, glancing down at the toes of his moccasins.

"Just the way I told ye," Trawis said with a twinkle.

"Shore 'nuff," Baptiste added, straight-faced.

"Uh-huh." Green looked at Willow. "I want you on the boat. No sense in baiting the Sioux with a Snake woman. You'll be a heap safer aboard."

Willow reached down to the war club tied at her waist. "I am no *White* woman, Green."

"Oh, I know that, Willow. But I want you out of harm's way, hear?"

She glanced at Trawis, who nodded, fixing her with those

knowing blue eyes. "It ain't a' gonna hurt nothing to stay on the boat fer a couple of days. These Sioux, they're a sneaky bunch."

Ritshard looked up. "Please, Willow?"

One by one, she read their souls. Green wanted her safe for his trade. Trawis worried that a friend might come to harm. And Ritshard? That look betrayed the ache in his heart should anything happen to her.

"I will do this. But if there is fighting, I will take my bow and arrows and fight like a *Dukurika*."

"It'd be a help," Trawis replied.

Ritshard kicked hesitantly at the dirt, then looked up with resignation. "Mr. Green? Just a moment." Ritshard walked up to the plank. He clenched his fists, face strained. "I . . . I'd like a rifle. Not that Pawnee's trade gun, but a Hawken. One like Travis's. And powder and ball."

Green glanced at Trawis and saw his scarred eyebrow raise. "You want a rifle?"

Ritshard shrugged. "Yes, sir. I do."

"Why?" Green cocked his head. "I thought you were going to run the first chance you got. Why should I take a risk on a rifle?"

Ritshard took a breath. "On my word as a gentleman, I won't run off with your rifle."

"But you might still run off."

Ritshard swallowed, struggling with himself. "I . . . I won't run off—at least, not yet. Not with the Sioux so close."

Willow noticed the barely suppressed smirk on Trawis's face. Baptiste's black eyes glinted as he leaned on his rifle.

Green cast another glance at Trawis, who nodded. "All right, Hamilton. It'll go against your wages. You understand?"

Ritshard now stood lodgepole-straight. "Yes, sir. I understand."

Green shrugged. "Come on, then. I'll fetch you a rifle. I just hope to God you're better at shooting Indians than you are at dancing with them."

As Ritshard walked past, Willow could see the gleam in

his eyes, as if he'd just proven something to the world, and himself.

She turned to Trawis. "He did well today?"

Trawis grinned outright now. "Wal, now, I reckon with a little work, he'll come around. He's a-fixing ter be more than he figgers he can. Just you be careful the next couple of days, Willow. Them Sioux, they might go fer the hosses, but they'd sure as hell make a try fer ye. If'n they do, it'll mean a fight to get ye back, understand?"

"Why fight for me?"

Trawis patted her shoulder. " 'Cause yer one of us." Then he walked out to supervise the forting up.

Baptiste touched a finger to the brim of his hat before he followed the hunter.

One of them? She sighed as she began collecting wood, careful to stay within the bounds of the camp. Trudeau was watching her as he worked, stripping her with his eyes. She glared back at him, and spat contemptuously.

"No, Trawis. I am *Dukurika*. I can never be anything else." The day would come when she would leave them. She hoped that it would not hurt Ritshard or Trawis. But they would forget. Such was the nature of men: red or white.

In the meantime, she would stay on the boat. Given a choice, she'd take thieving Pawnee over cut-throat Sioux any day.

When the night skies finally darkened, and ominous silence settled on the camp, Ritshard walked over to her fire, his new rifle in hand. He seated himself on a blanket, staring wearily at the flames before inspecting the stew she'd set to boil over the coals.

"Long day," he said, a faint smile playing on his lips. He turned brown eyes on her. The intimate inquisitiveness of his look brought a tingle to her heart.

"You are lucky the Sioux didn't kill you and cut yer head off." Then she smiled, and for a long moment their eyes held.

"But they didn't. It's so different, Willow. Not Boston at all."

"Boston. Always Boston. Tell me of this place."

He rubbed his face, the tenuous intimacy gone. "Willow,

sometimes things must be lived to be understood.'' He gestured around. ''This is your country. Boston, well, it's like a completely different world. So many people, endless buildings and paved streets. Those words don't mean anything to you, do they? I can't explain it any more than you could have explained this to me a year ago.''

She stirred the stew, glancing at him from the corner of her eye. ''This is *not* my country. My land is high, what is the word—mountains? The trees are different, and air is clear and cool. The colors are brighter, even the dirt. From the mountains, I can see forever, the way *Tam Apo* and eagle see.''

He rolled onto his stomach, gazing up at her. ''What was it like, growing up in a place like that?''

She tasted the rich stew and laid the ladle to one side. ''My father, High Wolf, he let me do things the other children couldn't. I like to think he saw something special in me, but it was probably just because I was his favorite. He let me hold his sacred things, and listen to their voices, even though I was a girl. Since he was a great *puhagan,* no one said anything.''

''He wanted you to be a medicine man, too?''

''No. At least, he didn't really encourage me. But I wasn't strange, or anything.''

''What do you mean, strange?''

''Sometimes, when Power lives in a person, he acts strangely. You can see it. A hollow look in the eyes. The head cocked, listening to spirit things other people can't hear. As a child, I was like the other children. I played among the rocks and trees, seeking out brother marmot and hunting rabbits. As children, we would build little mountain-sheep traps. The littlest children got to be the mountain sheep and the older children drove them into the trap and threw blankets over them. I was always hard to catch.'' She grinned at him, the memories fresh in her soul.

His eyes twinkled, as if imagining her as a child. ''It sounds like fun.'' He idly twisted the grass into knots. ''I never played much. I didn't have many friends.''

''Boston is not full of children?''

''Oh, yes, full of them. I just didn't get out to play much.

Father was always so busy. Jeffry and the other slaves took care of me. Mostly I read books. They were my friends.''

She wondered just what a book was, Ritshard talked of them so much. "This way you lived, it doesn't sound good, Ritshard."

He shrugged. "It was all I knew. How about you? Did you see your father often?"

"Every night." She looked up at the trees, the branches lit by firelight. "After we ate, Father would play with us. Sometimes he was Coyote, and chased us around trying to eat us. But when he caught us, he just tickled us until our bellies hurt. He told us the stories about the beginning of the world, and how *Tam Apo* made things. Mother would nod at all of the important places. Then, when I started to fall asleep, Father would carry me to the robes and tuck me in."

"How lucky you were." He frowned, still toying with the grass. Finally he asked, "What did you want out of life?"

She lifted an eyebrow. "Want out of life?"

"What did you think you'd be doing? I mean, what did you dream of being?"

She paused. She'd only told High Wolf, and then, only once. A woman did not speak of such things. But Ritshard was different, and the honest interest in his eyes overcame her reserve. "I wanted to be a *puhagan*, just like my father. I wanted to know all the things he knew. To cure, to sing, and to seek *Tam Apo*." She hesitated, unsure of herself. "I do not talk of these things, Ritshard. They are between us and no one else."

"Why?" He cocked his head. "Your people wouldn't approve?"

She looked around, then bent down close to meet his eyes. "Among my people, women do not seek *puha*. It is said to be dangerous, that a woman might not be strong enough, that she would damage the Power and use it for evil."

"Like a witch?"

"What is this word?"

"A woman who uses magic—uh, power—for evil. To kill and inflict disease."

"Witch." She sounded out the White word.

"Did your husband know you wanted power?"

"A little." She backed away then, averting her eyes.

"Did . . . did you love him?"

"Yes." The memory stung her. *And I couldn't save him in the end.* To avoid more hurt, she asked, "Did you ever love, Ritshard?"

He shrugged, lips parting as if to speak, hesitated, and said, "I didn't do well with girls. They just didn't . . . I couldn't talk to them. Do you understand? They weren't interested in philosophy, in ideas. They just wanted to be pretty and admired."

"White women," she said sourly.

He chuckled uneasily. "Yes, white women." Then his brow lined. "Oh, someday I'll have to marry, I suppose. Father always expected it of me. Later, you understand, after I'd proven myself, I'd be quite a catch, rich, capable of providing a good home. A friend of mine has a sister. A very attractive young lady."

"And this *lady* will be pretty . . . in her house . . . and admired?"

"Yes. Just that." He studied her pensively. "I could do a lot worse. Laura is a very charming girl."

Willow watched him. "Is that what you want, Ritshard? Charming? Or do you want Power, and truth, and all the pain it brings?"

He shrugged, looking away into the night so that she couldn't read his expression.

Willow dished out a bowl of stew and handed it to Ritshard before filling her own. She was becoming proficient in the use of the little metal spoon. Why did her fingers suddenly seem so clumsy?

She said, "My father was disappointed that I married a *Ku'chendikani.* I think he wanted me to stay with the *Dukurika.* But when I made my choice, he smiled and wished me well."

"How lucky you were." Richard blew to cool the stew. "By the time I return, Laura will no doubt be married to that irritating Tom Hanson, and I'll probably end up with some blithering shrew who faints all the time."

"I don't know all those words."

He waved it away as inconsequential.

"I think you have been lonely all of your life, Ritshard. It should not always be so."

"Maybe not, but in Boston there aren't many women like . . ." He glanced away, swallowing hard.

"Like me?" Her souls began to stir uneasily, like snakes twining around each other.

He started to nod, then shook himself. "Some things, Willow . . ."

She waited. "What is it, Ritshard?"

"Oh, life, the way people are. God, what a sorry mess we are! I think your people are a lot smarter than mine."

"People should be who they are."

He kept sneaking glances at her.

"Ritshard, your eyes have changed. Now, you look at me as a man looks at a woman."

He glanced down at his empty bowl. "I'm sorry."

"You do not have to be sorry."

"A gentleman does not look at a lady that way."

She bent down, staring into his eyes again. "I am not White, Ritshard. I am Heals Like A Willow, a *Dukurika* woman. I am not a lady."

His lips parted as he reached up to touch the side of her face. "Lord God, what you just said. If you only knew how I . . ." Then he shook his head. Rising to his feet, he said, "Thank you for supper, Willow. Travis needs me. I . . . I've got to go." And he hurried away into the darkness.

Willow took a deep breath to settle her writhing souls, and exhaled wearily. In silence, she watched the fire burn down to glowing red coals.

"You been quiet all day," Baptiste noted. "Got the Injun shivers?"

"No." Richard shook his head as he led the string of horses. He'd had an odd dream the night before, as if he'd floated over the land, draped in a misty white. He'd been

seeking something, unable to find it in the mist. And there at the end, he'd felt someone watching, eyes staring at him out of the mist.

The whole day had been eerie. Walking along with Baptiste, he couldn't shake the uneasy feeling. Maybe Baptiste was right, and it was nothing more than a case of Sioux-induced nerves.

The abandoned Arikara village they'd passed that morning hadn't helped matters, either. The place consisted of nothing but big round depressions, as if God's finger had dimpled the flats. Timbers stuck out here and there, most of them charred and splintered. A thick carpet of grass had already reclaimed the town, but an occasional broken piece of clay pot, a scattering of burned bone and beads, could be found. Open storage pits were a hazard for man and beast.

Something about the old Ree town depressed the spirit and dampened any optimism the morning might have had. Who had those people been? Once, children had played and chased among the domed houses. Men and women had smiled at each other, and built bright futures out of dreams.

The most unsettling sight for Richard had been the skull. Baptiste pointed out where a coyote had dug out a den in the side of a low earthen mound. Just inside the hole, half lodged in the soil, the skull had lain watching with dirt-filled eye sockets.

To avoid his thoughts, he pointed at the *engagés*. "I can't believe the change in them."

The men struggled along the bank, dodging around cottonwoods that hung out over the water. Instead of gay songs, jokes, and good humor, they labored in silence, as if doom hung over their bobbing heads instead of the bright late-spring sky.

"They's worried 'bout Sioux," Baptiste told him. They walked along, feet swishing the new grass. The horses followed reluctantly on their lead ropes; they wound their way around the gray boles of cottonwoods, and paused only long enough to crop a mouthful of grass.

Richard and Baptiste paralleled the bank, staying close to the sweating men on the cordelle. Baptiste's gaze never rested as he scanned the grassy bottoms, the branches overhead, the tangles of deadfall and driftwood.

But what an odd dream. Not in his wildest imagination had he ever been a cloud before. And what had he been looking for?

What have I always been looking for? Truth, ultimate reality, an understanding of myself and the world around me.

"Want to talk about it?" Baptiste asked suddenly. "If'n you got a sense of something, you tell ol' Baptiste. In this country, a feller best heed his hunches."

"It's nothing. Honest. Just a dream I had last night."

"You wasn't scalped and dead, was you?"

"No. Nothing like that." And Richard laughed to relax. "Oh, all right. I dreamed I was a cloud."

Baptiste grunted, and renewed his wary inspection of the quiet trees around them.

Richard tightened his grip on the Hawken, reassured by the slim rifle's weight. He'd loaded it the night before, careful not to spill a single grain of powder. He could still feel the ramrod pushing the half-inch ball down the smooth rifling, seating it against the powder. Knowing his life might depend on it, he'd taken special care with that load.

He cast another glance at the *engagés*. "It doesn't make sense. I've seen them skip from log to log across a flooded *embarras*. I mean, the slightest misstep, and they'd fall into the torrent, be swept away before anyone could lend a hand. And they do it *singing*!"

"French is curious coons," Baptiste said with a shrug. "Way I figgers it, men got different fears. These French . . . maybe it's something Catholic, about being scalped and cut up. Killed in blood. I ain't Catholic, so I don't know. But a boatman, he don't scare a hair over bad water that shivers my bones. Hunt up Injun sign, though, and he plum turns to quivers."

"They didn't seem so nervous when we crossed Osage, Kansa, and Maha country."

"Them's tame Injuns." Baptiste pulled his big black hat off and wiped a sleeve across his sweaty forehead.

"Tame?"

"I tell ye, Dick, I been out heah nigh onta fourteen years now. River's changing, and it's white men what's doing it. Tame means broke, hear?"

"How's that?"

"Missouri, Oto, Omaha . . . they used to rule the river. Remember Blackbird? That Omaha chief buried up on the mountain? Why, he's like most was. These Injuns, they get their time with the coming of the whites. But it don't last. Think back. How many Injuns did you see on the way up-river? Reckon not more than a handful—and them in rags. Just like that drunk Omaha selling his squaw. The rest was all out fo' the spring buffler hunt. Used to be they'd hunt buffler within a couple of days' ride of the village. Now they be gone fo' months. Buffler's plumb scarce on the lower river, hoss. But so's the Injuns. I heard tales of the Kansa—the Wind People, they called themselves. Them and the Missouri, they controlled the lower river a while back. They's just a handful now."

"Why? The constant war?"

Baptiste squinted, a bitter twist on his lips. "Maybe. But I figger it's more. It's white men. They's like a plague rolling slow across the land. Like them locusts in Egypt. Look back, Dick. Ain't nothing atwixt us and the frontier but a dead zone—just like that village we passed this morning— and it's filling with whites. Farmers, you know. The great tribes, the Oto, Ioway, the Big Osages, the Mahas . . . hell, they ain't shit now. Disease kilt most of 'em. Why, I seen piles of bodies after that pox come through. Whole villages left standing empty—and nothing but dead bodies a-laying where they fell. Biblical, I tell ye. Plumb biblical.''

"You make it sound like the Apocalypse.''

"Reckon you and I, we got different ideas about white folks.''

"How's that?''

"You ain't never been no slave.''

Richard considered as he scanned the country for lurking Sioux thieves. "Not all white people are bad. I told you about the abolitionists. Some of us believe that all men have the same potential.''

"In Boston.''

"Yes.''

"Wal, Dick, I tell ye, that ain't normal fo' white folks. Most of 'em take, and take some more. Them farmers down to Saint Loowee? I don't go there. They look at me and they sees a nigger, a man what otta be a slave. Hell, them coons live in them dinky log huts, scratching in the dirt, living in it. They don't know nothing but what's in their Bibles— if'n they can even read at all. And they looks down on me. *Me*, what's seen the Shining Mountains, taken a plew, and sat side by side with warriors. Them's yor white folks, Dick.''

"But here you are, partnered up with white folks.''

"Yep, but this is the wilderness. That's a heap different. Men be free heah. Larn this, Dick. Out heah, it's what you do, how you act, that gets you judged. Ain't no color of yor skin that counts a damn when the Rees come a-fogging down on you, or the cordelle breaks. Yes, sir, it's what's in a man's soul that makes him poor bull or fat beaver out heah.''

Baptiste threw his head back, broad nostrils flared as if scenting the winds of freedom. "Won't last, though. Them farmers, they gonna come and kill all this land. You'll see. But afore that, this coon's gonna be gone under. That's some, it is. I reckon I'll go as a warrior. Proud. This child's gonna die like a man.''

Richard walked wide around a pile of debris left by a long-past flood. He peered intently into the tangle of logs, branches, and old brush, seeking any sign of a lurking Sioux.

"Yor a-larning," Baptiste said with a smile. "Come cat scratch, a feller can hole up in a pile of junk like that. Old John Colter, he hid under a mess of embarras that time the Blackfoot cornered him. Always look to the holes come tough times. They can shore 'nuff save yor life."

Richard licked his lips. "But getting back to what you were saying. Whites don't ruin everything."

"Huh! Yor a white man what can go where you wants, do what you wants. Try 'er as a black man, or an Injun. White folk make things plumb shining fo' other white folk. But they sure as hell ruin everything fo' everyone else."

"That's not so. They bring civilization—" The words stuck in his throat.

"You was saying?"

Everything he'd said to Charles Eckhart on the journey down the Ohio came back to haunt him. Those bitter fights with his father about commerce defeating the higher callings of man, were they just words? The silly ideas of a spoiled young man living in the land of plenty? "I was about to argue against everything I've come to believe about civilization."

Baptiste seemed not to hear as he continued, "I'll tell you about yor civilization. It's built on the ruin of others. I had me a squaw one winter. Shawnee, she was. Died of fever that next spring. She's the last of her family—a cousin to Tecumseh and the Prophet. Rest of her kin was killed of smallpox, or shot dead by white soldiers."

Baptiste gripped his rifle in emphasis. "The Shawnee, they owned that whole Ohio country, boy. And now, they ain't but memories. I tell you, it'll be the same heah real soon. Nothing but memories of the Injuns . . . and farms as far as the eye can see. Nothing free then, not even the birds in the sky."

"And the Sioux? You think we'll destroy them, too?"

"Yep. And the Rees, Arapaho, and Blackfeet. Them and all the rest. Even the Mandan. Hell, probably the Mandan first. They likes white men. White man always ruins his friends fust."

"What do Travis and Green say when you talk like that?"

"Travis, he agrees. Reckon Green does, too. They just figger a feller's gotta make what he can. You come cross country from yor Boston, what did you see? White folks everywhere. How're you gonna stop 'em, Dick? Spout a little philos'phy to them farmers? Whar they gonna go? Back to Virginia, maybe back to yor Boston? Ain't no room fo' 'em all.

"Naw, Dick, it's just the way things is. That said, all a coon can do is make his way whilst he can. That's what this beaver's a-doing. Anything else is like trying to stop the wind."

They'd reached a place where the Missouri curved out in a wide loop. *Maria* had pulled over to the shore, the *engagés* hauling in the long cordelle and coiling it on the deck before breaking out the poles. Richard could see Willow sitting cross-legged on the cargo box. She held her bow in one hand. Even from here she looked regal. Perhaps it was the way she held her head, proud and high.

"We'll slip across this neck"—Baptiste pointed—"and meet 'em when they comes around t'other side."

"You know, it would be a lot shorter trip if the river ran straight."

Baptiste gave him a grin. "Yep, but like I told ye, it's just the way things is."

"Do you think we'll make Wah-Menitu's village by dark?"

"Reckon. Old Travis, he'll have scouted the whole way."

"Think he's all right? Going up ahead like he did?"

"That coon could sneak up on old Hob hisself. If'n thar be an ambush up ahead, Travis'll sniff her out. He's hell on Injun sign, that coon is."

"What if it comes to a fight? What do I do?"

"Don't shoot till the last." Baptiste plodded ahead after making sure the horses were following. "You got one shot in that Hawken. Injuns generally don't charge lessen they knows they can take you. Why, I've seen one man hold off thirty Injuns with a loaded rifle. A band of warriors knows that whoever makes the first play, he's gonna get shot. I tell you, it settles a man's blood to stare down a rifle barrel."

Remembering the gaping maw of Green's pistol, Richard could agree.

"That's the secret—and it ain't no sure thing. Keep that shot till you needs 'er. That's the only thing a man's got going fo' him when he's outnumbered. The Injuns might know they can kill you, but yor taking more of them rascals with you than they're getting. If Injuns figger they'll get one scalp to the loss of three, most times they'll back off."

What would Kant or Hegel make of that? Richard shook his head. "I hope I never have to find out."

As the sun slanted into the western sky, the *Maria* rounded yet another of the river's oxbows, and Travis walked out onto the riverbank to watch them approach. A number of Sioux warriors stepped out of the trees to stand behind him.

Richard and Baptiste checked the lead ropes one last time to ensure that none of the stock were loose. The horses approached the waiting men with pricked ears.

Richard swallowed hard, sweaty hand tightening on the rifle. Nothing in the world could have reassured him like the feel of that hard wood and steel. He yearned for his father's pistol—the one he'd so foolishly left behind in that other world. What a reassurance it would be. In that instance, at least, his father had been right.

Travis leaned on his rifle, a huge smile twisting the scars on his face. "About time ye coons made her this far. Right up round the bend hyar, thar be a good place ter camp. Little creek runs out along a grassy flat. Dick, reckon you and Baptiste can make a picket fer the hosses."

"How far to Wah-Menitu's village?" Baptiste asked before striding forward to shake hands with the grinning warriors.

" 'Bout a half mile. They's camped up on the bench above the river where the breeze keeps the skeeters off."

Richard forced a smile and ceremoniously shook hands with each of the warriors. They looked fierce enough— keen-eyed, with faces that could have been carved of dark walnut. Streaks of yellow, red, and black paint decorated cheeks and foreheads. Several had feathers stuck lopsided in greased hair. A small leather pouch—sometimes beaded or covered with quillwork—was suspended from each neck. Brightly painted bags with long fringe and beadwork hung from breechclouts. Fringed moccasins and colored blankets made up the rest of their apparel. Each carried a bow, a war club, or a trade gun. The latter exhibited polished brass tacks driven into the stocks in geometric patterns.

Maria had come into sight, the *engagés* poling her nervously onward. Trudeau shouted at those on cordelle to keep them moving. Green waved from his place on the cargo box beside Henri. Willow was conspicuously absent. Inside the boat, no doubt.

Travis led the way toward the campsite, walking in the midst of the warriors. He talked with the Sioux, hands making signs despite the rifle he carried. To Richard's eyes, it looked like the reunion of long-lost friends.

Richard started at a rustling in the grass to his left. There, hidden so carefully, lay two young boys, big-eyed and excited at having sneaked so close to the White men.

Richard nodded at them. One gasped, while the other leapt to his feet and charged off, only to be outrun by his frightened companion.

"Kids is kids anywhere," Baptiste noted with a shake of the head.

More Sioux, Wah-Menitu in the forefront, waited silently in the clearing Travis had chosen for their camp. What thoughts were passing behind those black eyes? Richard could see women standing behind the men at the edge of the fringe of trees.

Travis stopped and spread his hands wide, shouting in Sioux. Wah-Menitu barked out an answer, and lifted his pipe. The Sioux surged forward.

"What do I do now?" Richard whispered. His nerves tightened.

"Smile and act glad ta see 'em." Baptiste grinned like it was a birthday.

Richard met grin with grin, bobbing his head, enduring the hugs and cries of amazement as fingers felt his fetish. The horses stamped and shied until it was all Richard could do to hold his string.

The camp Travis had located proved perfect. Four trees

stood in a small clearing beside the slow stream. The river lay no more than a hundred yards away.

"Throw yer picket around them trees." Travis pointed out the four. "We'll pen the hosses thar. Reckon we can pitch the camps round the outside." He raised a grizzled eyebrow. "Get my drift, thar, Dick?"

"I do." Surrounded, the horses would be much harder to steal.

As *Maria* pulled up, the Sioux rushed down to watch, babbling in excitement as the wary *engagés* lowered the plank and tied off the painter. Even as he watched, more Indians appeared out of the trees, clustering around the boat.

"Green'll be needing help," Travis said softly. "I got ter go down and keep them red coons from swarming the boat. See ter yer hosses, Dick. Then come give me a hand. Baptiste?"

Together the two stalked off toward the growing crowd of Sioux. Richard hurried to stretch his pickets and crowd the horses into the enclosure. As he pulled hobbles and halters from the packs, Sioux women were picking their way toward the boat, backs bent under doubled hides. Squealing children and yapping dogs followed in their wake.

Richard checked and double-checked the picket, making sure each horse was secure.

Toussaint and Louis de Clerk trotted up, packing blankets and a rifle. To Richard, Toussaint said, "We take care of the horses. The booshway wants you at the boat."

Richard grabbed up his rifle and headed for the knot of Sioux crowded around the *Maria*.

He shouldered through the throng, surprised by the smoky smell of the Indians. The women watched him with wary black eyes while suddenly-quiet children clung to their leather skirts.

At the plank, Green had set up his table and taken a chair. A pile of buffalo hides was already laid out for inspection while Wah-Menitu stood with arms crossed, talking in mixed Sioux and English with Green. Travis and Baptiste stood to either side, guarding the plank that led to the boat.

Richard sidled up next to Travis. "What's happening?"

"Trade. Reckon it'll go on till about midnight. After that, we'll mosey up ter the village fer a feast."

Richard scanned the growing crowd of Sioux. "They'll clean us out."

"Yep, if'n they could." A gleam came to Travis's eye. "That's the art of trade, Dick: Give as little as ye can fer as much as ye can get—but don't rile the Sioux in the process. That's whar Davey shines. He's got the savvy fer it. This child don't."

Baptiste added, "That's why he's Booshway and I ain't."

At the same time, Henri was carrying out blankets, hanks of beads, gun flints, mirrors, knives, lead, and other items. He spread several blankets on the ground and laid out the articles atop them.

"Injuns want ter see it all, make up their minds about what they want ter trade fer," Travis explained. Even as he spoke the Sioux crowded around, fingering needles, kettles, and iron arrowpoints. Bolts of colored cloth passed from hand to hand amidst muttering and some little shoving.

"Is that wise?" Richard asked, indicating a warrior who picked up an ax and walked away.

"He ain't a gonna steal it. See that mean-looking rascal yonder with the black strip painted across his eyes? He's a soldier, like camp police. He's a-watching. Wah-Menitu don't want no trouble over this."

"But they'd take the horses."

"That ain't trade, that's stealing."

Richard scratched the back of his neck. "So, why steal a horse, but not the ax?"

"'Cause it's the rules, Dick. And if'n that coon did walk off with the ax, that soldier yonder would make him bring it back."

"Honor among thieves?"

"Listen up, Dick. Ye camps in a Sioux village, ye can leave yer possibles whar ye will. Nobody'll touch 'em. Or, if'n they do, they'll bring 'em right back after they done used 'em fer whatever. Ree and Crow, now, that's a sight different. They'll steal ye plumb blind given half a chance. Most folks, they don't steal from their own kind. It'd be . . . wal, it just don't happen."

"And if someone does?"

"They cast his arse out in the snow and let him freeze. Sort of like that Omaha. That, or the thief's relatives whack him in the back of the head some night rather than have the culprit bring down shame on the family."

"Some sense of justice."

"Yep. Wal, I reckon it works a sight better'n ours." Travis studied Richard from the corner of his eye. "Now, when we get up ter the village, ye be on yer uppers. Anything I asks ye ter do, ye do. And Tarnation, lad, do 'er with a smile. Ye don't know the rules, and they can kill ye dead. Savvy?"

Richard nodded. The warrior returned with the ax and muttered something to a woman who followed him with a bundle of furs on her back. Then he took the ax to Green, and commenced haggling.

Richard began practicing his smile.

TWENTY-EIGHT

All men in the state of nature have a desire and will to hurt, but not proceeding from the same cause, neither equally tobe condemned. For one man, according to that natural equality which is among us, permits as much to others as he assumes to himself; which is an argument of the temperate man, and one that rightly values his power. Another, supposing himself above others, will have a license to do what he lists, and challenges respect and honor, as due him before others; which is an argument of a fiery spirit.

—Thomas Hobbes, *Leviathan*

As Richard followed the dark trail over the rim of the bench, Wah-Menitu's village greeted his eyes. It was a sight that he would never forget. The village covered the flat—a series of conical skin lodges, each three times the height of a man. Bonfires cast wavering light over the tipis. The rows of illuminated lodges against the star-filled night sky took his breath away.

Men and women stood around talking and laughing, some highlighted by the fires, others mere silhouettes. Camp dogs barked and growled while the trilling shrieks of happy children created a benign chaos.

"Let's do her up!" Travis chortled, a salt-glazed jug of whiskey riding on his shoulder.

Richard steeled himself, nodding resolutely, and strode forward across the trampled grass. He'd expected nothing like this, figuring the Sioux would be dour and stoic as Scotsmen. As he walked past the fires, looking into the faces, he couldn't shake the notion that they looked a great deal like ordinary people but for their barbaric dress. No

one failed to call a greeting, and flash them a smile.

"Wah-Menitu's lodge is up hyar." Travis bulled his way forward, heedless of whether Green, Baptiste, or Richard followed.

A roaring fire in the open space before the chief's lodge crackled and sent sparks wheeling up into the starry night. Around it were seated several rows of Sioux men, all older, all dignified. Wah-Menitu himself rose from where he sat in front of his large tipi. The hide walls had been painted with rude images of buffalo and horses, and with round dots. Several hand shadows decorated the doorway. For ventilation, the lodge skirts had been rolled up and tied on the poles. Richard caught glimpses of buffalo robes, blankets, and hard leather cases on the inside, as well as what appeared to be a backrest. A painted war shield stood on a tripod behind Wah-Menitu, along with a bow, quiver, and rifle.

"Greetings, coons!" Wah-Menitu cried, raising his hands. "Come, sit. We will smoke and say the blessings. Then ye can share the hospitality of Wah-Menitu!"

"Where'd he learn to talk like that?" Richard asked.

"Traders, Dick," Baptiste answered. "Ain't nobody else out heah."

Richard followed Travis and Green to a blanket spread beside Wah-Menitu. With great ceremony, the pipe was brought forth by a young warrior. In the meantime, Richard studied the faces of the Indians, who in turn studied him. Each man wore an elaborate headdress, finely worked buckskins with dangling fringe, and bead-covered moccasins. Some held fans in their hands, many made from the entire wing of an eagle. Others carried painted sticks, and still others sat before long poles from which feathers and bits of hair dangled in the wind.

They did indeed look noble, all except for one who'd lost an eye and left the gaping socket uncovered. That one fierce eye fixed on Richard with an unwavering intensity and filled his soul with ice and horror.

Richard jerked his gaze away, heart hammering. *But why? I've never seen him before. Who is he?*

Wah-Menitu was holding a beautiful pipe up to the sky and had begun a singing chant. The others nodded their heads, as if in approbation.

"What's he saying?" Richard asked.

Travis leaned over to whisper, "Telling the story of White Buffalo Cow Woman, and how she gave the sacred pipe to old Standing Hollow Horn back in the beginning of time."

At last the pipe was offered to the east, south, west, and north, then to earth and sky. After Wah-Menitu puffed and exhaled, he passed the pipe to Green, who repeated the ritual.

Richard took his turn, surprised by the pipe's weight. As long as his arm, the bowl had been carved from some red stone and fitted to a wooden stem. Feathers hung from the carved and painted wood. Warily, Richard puffed, and exhaled. He could taste tobacco, but the other odors defied him.

Person by person, the pipe was passed around. When at last it had been returned to Wah-Menitu, he placed the pipe on its beaded bag before him, and smiled at Green. "We have missed our White brothers. Waugh, it is good to see you again. The trading was good, no?"

"Good, yes," Green replied, fingers dancing in signs as he spoke. "I am pleased to have made such good trades."

Wah-Menitu politely translated to the others as Green spoke. At the same time, women appeared bearing horns of stew, steaming joints of meat, and platters of roasted vegetables of a sort Richard had never seen. He smiled up at the young woman who laid a bark platter in front of him.

"What is this?" Richard poked at the small animal on

the platter. The pink flesh had been cooked until it slipped from the bone, but what sort of . . .

"Just eat it," Travis growled.

"But what . . . ?"

"Eat!"

Richard twitched his nose and pulled a piece of the hot meat loose, blowing on his fingers to cool them. The tender meat melted in his mouth, curiously sweet and satisfying. "I've never had anything like it."

"Reckon not. Sioux delicacy, cooked just fer us. Eat 'er all, Dick. Then suck the bones clean. Make like it's real doings."

Following such instructions wasn't hard. His stomach had been growling for hours. When he sucked the last of the juice from the little bones, he sighed. "Excellent."

"Good, coon. Ye done ate yer first dog."

"I . . . *what?*"

"Dog. Puppy. Just special fer us. Good, ain't it?"

Richard's gut cramped and he started to stand, only to have Travis fasten a hand like an iron shackle to his arm.

"Now, try this hyar," Travis insisted, handing Richard a horn of stew. "She's buffler tongue chopped ter bits and biled with onions and mint."

"Travis, I don't think I'd better eat any—" The grip on his arm tightened.

"Eat 'er, Dick. They done this special fer us."

Under Travis's hard eye, Richard sipped at the stew, pronounced it tasty, and gulped down a swallow. The ugly one-eyed man watched, his good eye half-slitted. Richard did his best to avoid that vulture's gaze. Even the other Sioux seemed to shy from the old buzzard.

Green uncorked the whiskey jug, pouring the clear contents into another of the buffalo-horn bowls and passing it around. "For my friends, the Dakota!" Green cried.

Shouts of "*Wash-te*" raised from all sides. The horn bowl was passed around as yet another was filled.

"Time ter shine!" Travis whooped, and took a swig of the horn that passed his way. Richard sipped, made a face, and passed it on. Bad whiskey on top of dogmeat was too much to contemplate.

"Good friends!" Wah-Menitu cried, leaping to his feet. "Times is shining! The traders have come back!"

"Death ter the Rees!" Travis bellowed, jumping to his feet and hopping from foot to foot.

Raised whoops and screams erupted from all sides, men leaping up to cavort and whirl about.

"Get up!" Travis gestured to Richard, who was finishing his stew.

Richard clambered up and Travis shoved him, half stumbling, into the space before the fire. "Hyar's a coon what raised a Pawnee warrior! Hyar's ter Dick!"

A nervous hand at his stomach, Richard stared at the faces surrounding him. Wolfish eyes gleamed back at him in the firelight.

"Ter Dick!" Wah-Menitu cried, shaking a fist and ululating the most horrible of war cries. Then he barked out words in Sioux, and the others whooped and screamed ecstatically.

"Dance!" Travis hissed in Richard's ear. "And hold up that fetish."

Richard fumbled at his belt, only to find Travis's quick fingers had beaten him to it. The skunk hair was thrust into his hand as Travis shoved him forward. "Dance, coon. Dance smart, now!"

Richard started roughly, jumping and twirling as Travis began chanting, "*Hey-a hey-a-hey-hey.*" The Sioux joined him.

"Hold 'er up!" Travis prompted. "So's everybody can see!"

Richard raised the fetish and skipped in the milling circle of warriors. A song rose on the lips of the Sioux, and a drum began a rhythmic beat. The excitement of it built in

Richard's breast, a kind of exhilaration he'd never experienced before. His feet found the rhythm of the music, and he mimicked those around him: step-shuffle, step-shuffle, leap.

He leapt and ducked, pirouetted and jerked in time to the warriors around him. Electric energy seemed to pulse within him, flowing up from the ground, down from the sky, and through him so that his feet grew light. Time vanished in the exertion and wheeling bodies.

Free! I feel free! An ecstasy bright as the Sioux fires burned in his breast. His feet skipped and leapt with the airy buoyancy of the sparks that flickered upward.

He wrapped himself in the singing of the Sioux, weaving himself within it. He let the music carry him, like moss in a gentle current. Men, women, and children had come to watch, all swaying with the chant. They were stepping and clapping in time with the lilting song.

As if we were all one, together, relatives instead of strangers from different worlds. Richard threw his head back, whirling in time with the dance. His spirit soared, buoyed by the dance until his body had become remote, a leaf on the wind.

In the end, all that remained was a pure, shining bliss the likes of which he'd never experienced. Power rose within him, stretching, opening itself to the night and the rising harmony of Sioux voices.

How long did he dance? Winded, sweating, he slipped from the circle, in time for Travis to hand him a hornful of alcohol. This time he choked a burning draught down his throat.

"Shining times," Travis cried, then crowed like a rooster.

"Shining times," Richard agreed, wiping his sweat-shiny face. "What next? God, for a drink of water!"

"That gut bag hanging yonder. That's water, coon. Haw! Lookit old Baptiste! He's a-prancing like a buck antelope come fall! And thar be Green. Lookee there! Reckon he'd outjump a buck mule deer in high sage!"

Richard grinned, watching the others cavort with the Sioux.

"Hell, Doodle, ye ain't done, are ye? Night's young!

Fetch yer water and go gallivanting! I'd be a-dancing with 'em ... specially afore they notice yer not out thar!''

Richard drank his fill from the musty-tasting gut, then charged back into the gyrating bodies.

When he staggered back to Wah-Menitu's lodge, sweating and grinning, the ugly old man still sat in his place, single eye gleaming in that ruined face. Richard hesitated; the old man raised an age-callused finger, beckoning.

Willow lay in the darkness, aware of the rustling rodents scurrying behind the cargo. She'd lived most of her life with mice sneaking into the lodges. Mice were a necessary evil, the little creatures doing as *Tam Apo* willed, seeking to fill their bellies and raise their pups. Rats, too, had their place. The kind she knew best were the bushy-tailed packrats of the mountains: the ones who'd leave a rock in place of a shiny bead. Packrats chewed anything leather, or even the sweaty wooden handle of a hammer or the middle of a good bow. They raided food caches, and generally made life miserable for humans.

The old conflict favored neither side, for when times got hard and starvation rubbed a person's belly raw, the *Dukurika* set fire to packrat nests, ambushed the fleeing rodents, and roasted their little carcasses for their soft pink meat.

These dark gray rats, however, were different, with glinting eyes and naked scaly tails that gave her the shivers.

She resettled herself in the bedding Green and Henri had laid on the packs of blankets. Over the furtive scuttling of the rats, and the water slapping the hull, the faint beat of a pot drum, and the yip-yaiing snatches of song carried down from the Sioux village. The edges of her souls frayed with each distant scream.

Here I am, hidden away in a White man's boat, while he trades with the Cuts-Off-A-Head People. And what if the cut-throat Sioux turned on their guests? Murdered them all?

She could imagine Ritshard's headless body, white and naked in the sunlight, flies thick in the blood pooled beneath and severed neck. Those soft brown eyes would never sparkle again. He would never have the chance to seek the answers that lay just beyond the fingertips of his soul.

Trawis wouldn't go down without a fight. He'd shared his soul and blood with the white bear—the greater the honor for the Sioux who finally killed him.

This is ridiculous. I'm only doing this to torture myself. Trawis and Green know what they are doing. Or did they? She tightened her grip on the war club that lay between her breasts. *I should leave as soon as I can. Sneak away into the night and find my way home.*

It couldn't be that hard. Follow the rivers west. Eventually they'd rise to the mountains, and as a girl she'd walked most of them, or heard the stories about which rivers ran where.

So why don't I go? The lie she had told herself, about learning more about White men, had worn as thin as last year's moccasins. She'd learned enough about the Whites.

She blinked at the dark roof over her head, images of Ritshard growing in her soul. What was it about him that drew her so? Had he cast some spell on her that day she'd looked into the eye of his soul?

That was it, wasn't it? He'd done what no man of the *Dukurika* would dare to do. And he'd done it without fear, without anything except curiosity.

And does that bother you, Heals Like A Willow? Is that what draws you to Ritshard? Is it because he didn't see you as a woman—or did he see you as a complete *woman?*

She shifted uneasily. The sounds from the Sioux camp grew louder.

"You're being an idiot," she told herself. "*Tam Apo* alone knows who these White fools will find next. Maybe the next people will just kill them . . . and you, too! You should run while you still can."

She nodded to herself. Yes, run. Now . . . tonight. Before anything else horrible happened to her.

Just as she'd made up her mind, the soft scuff of leather on wood reached her ear. Every muscle stiffened. Her soul pictured a wily Sioux creeping along the *passe avant,* intent on murder and theft.

A shadow darkened the doorway, but Willow had already lowered herself into a gap between two flour barrels. She clutched the war club in one hand, her knife in the other.

Step after careful step, the intruder eased down the stair slats. Cloth rasped ever so softly, and a big man slipped over to her bedding.

Willow's skin crawled. He reached out cautiously to finger her blankets.

One of the rats scampered away, and the man jerked, stifling a curse.

Couldn't he hear the pounding of her heart, the fear pumping in her blood?

He grabbed at her bed now, searching frantically, then whirled to peer around the black interior of the cargo box.

If he reached into her hiding place, she'd strike with all her strength. Thrust up from below with the knife so that he had little chance to block it. Then she'd rise, braced against the barrels, and hammer him with the war club.

"Willow?" he whispered softly.

She strangled the cry within, recognizing the French accent. Not a Sioux—an *engagé*. Why?

Ritshard, Trawis, and Green were gone. Only Henri slept atop the cargo box.

Who? Trudeau, most likely, but it could have been any of the others. In the charcoal black, she couldn't be sure.

He stood in silence for what seemed an eternity, then carefully turned, easing back the way he'd come.

Only after the shadowy form ghosted back up through the doorway did she take a deep breath and wipe at the fear-sweat that had beaded on her upper lip.

The one-eyed Sioux continued to beckon with his crooked finger. In his other hand he clutched an eagle-feather fan as long as his withered arm. In desperation, Richard looked around for Travis, Baptiste, or Green, but only Wah-Menitu remained seated, his pipe resting on the ground before him. Now the chief's feral eyes narrowed as he studied Richard.

The beating of the drum, the eerie singing of the Sioux, and the tramping shuffle of feet filled the night, but the music had changed, turned ominous.

"Sit." Wah-Menitu pointed to a spot on a blanket in front of the old one-eyed demon.

Richard swallowed hard, and sank to his knees. His entire body was trembling from exertion and the sudden sense that something had gone very wrong.

"Who are you?" Wah-Menitu asked. "The *wechasha-wakan* wants to know."

Richard glanced at the one-eyed man, and fear chilled his guts. That single burning eye pinned him like a lance. "Richard. Richard Hamilton."

The old man spoke, his voice rising and falling, saying lots of *wh* and *che* and *sh* sounds. The gaping wound where his eye had been seemed to study Richard with a red-wealed, scar-tissue intensity that looked through Richard: saw all that he was, and was not.

Blessed God, where's Travis? The panic rose to pump as brightly as Richard's blood.

"He says he saw you," Wah-Menitu said. "He says that you came to him last night in a dream. You came as a cloud white dog, but when you looked at the *wechashawakan*, your eyes were those of a wolf, or maybe it was a coyote. Because of that, he has come to see you tonight. He wants to find out what you are."

Richard's throat had gone dry. "I . . . I'm Richard Hamilton. From Boston. That's all. I didn't have any choice when I came here. I was forced to. Honestly. I just haven't had a chance to escape yet."

Wah-Menitu drank some of his whiskey, then translated. The old man's eye gleamed, and he sucked his thin lips over peglike brown teeth. Richard's stomach turned as he realized that the dark patches in the eye socket weren't shadows, but crusted dirt lodged in the scar tissue.

The old man was talking again, his horn-dusky hands moving to form shapes and signs. Then he reached out and grasped Richard's hands in his. His skin was warm and dry, the grip powerful.

What should he do? Pull back? Shout for help? What was it Travis had said? Do as he was asked, or they might kill him?

The old man leaned forward and spat on the backs of Richard's hands. Richard flinched as the spittle cooled in the night air. Then the old man took his finger and rubbed the saliva on each hand around in circles. He closed his good eye, and bent down to inspect the damp spots with his gaping socket.

Richard fought the urge to vomit.

The old man straightened, opened his eye, and spoke again, his voice a low growl.

"He wants to know if your stomach hurts," Wah-Menitu translated.

"Yes."

One-Eye grinned evilly, and laughed before he chattered in Sioux. Wah-Menitu said: "He says the cannibal's stomach always hurts. It is hard to eat yer own kind."

"Cannibal? Eat my *what*?"

But the old man leaned so close that his single baleful eye filled the world. Richard couldn't break that sudden connection. From some corner of his mind, the words "eye of the soul" floated, then slipped away. One-Eye reached out with the eagle-wing fan. He used the tips of the feathers to trace the outline of Richard's head, chanting softly. Then he touched the feathers to Richard's forehead. A sensation like chilled mint extract flowed through Richard's head, and the world seemed to shimmer and fade.

What are you? The words came soundlessly. Richard shuddered as his insides went greasy with fear. *You called to me, came floating through the sky as I spread my wings in the night.*

"I did what?"

"You came here, looking, searching. What do you want?"

"To go home."

The horrible gaping socket was so close now, he could see the rippling folds of scar tissue, and what looked like eroded bone in the back. At the same time his soul stood naked, transparent as window glass.

Wowash'ake fills you, White Cloud Dog, burning like a slow fire.

From a great distance, Wah-Menitu's voice told him, "He says you are *wah'e'yuzepe*, confused. You have been fooled. Like *Inktomi*, the Spider Trickster, you have fooled yourself. Now, you must choose."

"What are my choices?"

Paralyzed, Richard gazed into the depths of that terrible empty eye, seeing flames reflected there. But as he watched, the flickers of firelight began to dance and shift, spiraling, falling, metamorphosing into snowflakes. The cold stole through him, driven by winter winds. His bones might have become ice, snow crystallized in his lungs.

Wah-Menitu's drunken voice said, "The *wechashawakan* says this is your future that you feel. This awaits you up-river. Snow, hunger, and cold. A dog curls up and freezes under the snow. He dies there without man to feed him.

"The *wechashawakan* says that four paths lie before you. You can take the red way, up the river. There, if you live, you will become a wolf . . . or maybe a coyote. Or, you can take the black way, and go east. There, you will always be a white dog—all hollow inside.

"What will you do, *Washichun*?"

Richard clutched himself, shivering in the reflected winter in the old man's eye. It seemed like an eternity before the old man backed away, and Richard gasped, breathless, at the warmth of the summer night that seeped into his frozen body. He panted for breath, exhaling air cold enough that he swore it frosted in the air.

"And if I go home, to Boston—I'll be hollow inside? Forever?"

The old man grunted then, and ran weathered fingers over his eagle fan. He spoke in a breathy voice, hesitating every now and then, nodding and gesturing with his hands. Then he stood, joints crackling, and walked off into the night.

"What did he say?" Richard asked. He rubbed his shaking hands on his leather pants.

Wah-Menitu made a face, as if the whiskey was bothering him. "He said he does not know if you will survive the snow on the red way. He does not see that far, so it is uncertain what will become of you. He only sees you starving in the snow, and no more. But truth lies there. An end to the confusion.

"If you take the black way, he said he saw you in a *Washichun* place where lodges are stacked on lodges and the streets are made of stones. He saw you there, lonely and sad—and your soul was empty, like a buffalo-gut bag with all the water drained out."

Richard shook his head, shivering from more than the chill in his bones. "But why did he spit on my hands?"

Wah-Menitu drank more of his whiskey and grinned foolishly. "When he spit, he tried to wash off your outside to see in. He wanted to know what kind of creature you were . . . if you were human at all, or some kind of monster who had come to harm the people. If you were a monster, he would have to kill you before you could do harm. When he looked inside you, he saw the white cloud dog looking back, terribly afraid. If you do not remain a dog, you can become a coyote, or a wolf. That's why you came here. Not to bring trouble to the *wechashawakan* or our people, but to choose what you will be—and how you will live."

"That's crazy. I didn't *come* here at all. Not of my . . ."

"The *wechashawakan* says you did." Wah-Menitu shrugged and belched, having trouble focusing his eyes. "Here. Drink this, White fool. I didn't want to waste whiskey on a man who might be dead soon." And he handed Richard the drinking horn.

Richard lifted it in shaking hands, drank deeply, and let the horrible stuff burn away the last of the bone-deep chill inside him. *They're drunk, that's all.*

But what had that terrible cold been? Where had it come from? The old man thought he was a white dog? And he was supposed to choose to become a coyote or a wolf? Richard shook his head. "Superstitious nonsense."

Wah-Menitu was watching him though half-lidded eyes, looking very drunk. "I think ye'll stay a dog, *Washichun*. White men are naturally dogs. They do not have the Power inside them. Inside here"—he thumped his chest with a fist—"to become wolf."

"I don't think I understand."

Wah-Menitu grinned, his mouth falling crookedly open. "I speak of Power, of looking inside yourself . . . and seeing through what ye are." He wiped at a dribble of saliva that escaped his lips. "And I think yer a coward, White Cloud Dog. Go home. Die empty." At that, he laughed uproariously.

Travis let out a whoop and came stumbling into sight, a young woman under each arm.

Willow jerked awake at the sound of booted feet on the steps that led down into the cargo box. Slivers of pain lanced her cramped back. She sat crouched in her hiding hole, propped by the rounded sides of rough oak barrels. *Tam Apo,* when had she fallen asleep?

"Willow?" Henri called, squinting at the rumpled bedding on the blankets. "Morning is here. Willow?" He stepped forward to prod the empty blankets. *"Sacré! Non! Les Sioux diaboliques!"*

"Henri?" she called.

He whirled, a hand to his heart. A slow smile crossed his mustached lips. "Ah, *mon papillon*, you are safe. But what are you doing down there?"

Willow placed her war club atop one of the barrels and groaned as she pulled herself up. A gasp escaped her as blood ran into her numb legs. "A man came in the night." She indicated the narrow space. "He did not find me."

"Sioux?" Henri glanced warily about.

"Engagé." Prickles like a thousand nibbling ants coursed down her legs, and she made a face.

"Who?"

Willow shook her head. "I do not know. It was dark."

Henri growled under his breath, then sighed. "This is not good, *ma petite femme*." He paused, an eyebrow rising. "And this happens when the Sioux are near . . . and the booshway is gone? I do not like this. *Très mal!*"

Willow took a hesitant step, and had to lock her knee to keep from falling. Henri, breaking from his dark musing, reached out and offered his arm. The surprising slabs of muscle in the patroon's arm felt like a thick, gnarled root.

Together they climbed out into the gray of the false dawn. The *engagés* were swarming around like bees. Normally, they lingered like lazy dogs over their coffee, waiting until the last moment to take up the cordelle.

As if he read her thoughts, Henri said, "The Sioux have put a fire in their hearts, eh? Today, *mon papillon,* we will make many miles, *prêter serment.*"

Having found her legs again, Willow made her way to the privacy on the other side of the boat to relieve herself. Below her, the restless waters roiled and stirred as if alive. A thin mist hung over the surface like a faint silver skein of spiderweb.

You must leave, Willow. Trouble is coming, and you are bringing it upon yourself. She stood at the sound of feet on the deck. The *engagés* were filing onto *Maria* and pulling their poles from the top of the cargo box. She could hear the cordelle buzzing as it was pulled over the bow to the cordellers.

This day, too, she would ride inside the cargo box lest some Sioux see her. She nodded to Henri, who had taken his place at the steering oar on the cargo box. Then, reluctantly, she climbed down into the musty darkness.

Only for today, she insisted. But how many more hostile tribes lay ahead? Did they expect her, a *Dukurika,* to ride the whole way inside this black box like a rabbit in a sack?

She ran her fingers over the line of rifles in the rack by the door. The wood was so smooth, the iron cool and remote to the touch. They had a menacing power all their own. Not the warm familiarity of a bow and good arrows, but a darker presence that might be understood only through time and familiarity.

There is nothing for me here. She straightened, the decision made. She would leave, but not in a panic, like Coyote fulfilling some whim of the moment. No, instead, she would go like Wolf in his wisdom. From this day onward, she would prepare for the long journey home.

Henri barked out orders. She settled herself on the blankets and stretched her back to release the kinks from her cramped sleep. She would need food, extra moccasins, a good pack, netting, a stout thong for a snare, new arrows.

As she planned, she couldn't shake the memory of the shadowy hand reaching out of the darkness for her bedding.

Travis waved a final farewell as Wah-Menitu's warriors lifted lances and rifles. The Sioux wheeled their mounts with mechanical precision and raced away across the plains, southward, toward their village.

Travis ran a hand over his face and groaned aloud. The bright sunlight and warmth of the day did little to ease the splitting ache of his whiskey-head. God, he'd drunk half the river that morning to cure the terrible thirst.

Baptiste and Dick sat their horses, slumped over like the newly dead. Of the two, Richard certainly looked the worst off. His face was pasty, his mousy brown hair sticking out at all angles. Grease had matted his wispy beard on one cheek.

"I swear that coyote piss is running in my veins," Baptiste muttered, squinting after the disappearing riders.

"Nice of them boys ter see us this far," Travis mumbled, his gut trying to heave again. He fought it down.

"Yep," Baptiste agreed. "How in Tarnal Hell is we gonna mount a guard on these hosses tonight?"

"Just do 'er," Travis grunted. "Reckon one night of fun ain't gonna kill us . . . but I sure feel it might. How 'bout ye, Dick? Can ye stand guard all night?"

Hamilton, face green, gave him a bleary-eyed glare.

"C'mon," Travis heeled his horse around. "Let's make

tracks. Them boatman'll probably make fifteen miles to-day.''

As the horses plodded along, Hamilton asked dully, ''What's a *wechashawakan?*''

''Ye mean old One-Eye?'' Travis asked. At Richard's slight nod, he added, ''*Wechashawakan* means holy man, a medicine man. And old One-Eye, he's a heap powerful medicine. The story is that he can see the future, turn hisself into an owl and fly around—and Sioux ain't too keen on owls.'' Travis struggled to keep from belching, fearing what might come up with it. ''Why? He talk ter ye last night?''

''Yes.'' Richard's body swayed like a grain sack with each step his horse took. ''Said I had to choose, that I was a white cloud dog.''

''He didn't up and hex you, now?'' Baptiste gave Richard a sidelong glance. ''I ain't ridin' with no hexed man. No, suh, not this child. Why, hell, you could have lightning and all sorts of grief called down on you. And, if'n that's the way of things, I ain't gonna be no part of it.''

Richard croaked, ''Said I had to choose. Die like a dog, or turn into a coyote or wolf. Then he almost froze me.''

''Huh?'' Travis closed his eyes tight to make the spots go away. ''Froze ye? That why ye drunk all that whiskey? Hell, I figgered ye fer a frog fer a while. Drinking and dancing.''

''I was trying to forget,'' Richard declared.

''Old One-Eye put the scare into you, boy?'' Baptiste asked.

Richard nodded his head carefully, as if afraid it might fall off. ''Damn right, he did.'' Then a pause, as if to change the subject. ''I can't believe I drank that much . . . and danced all night. And you, Travis, I can't believe you slipped away with that squaw.''

Travis ran his tongue around his mouth and grimaced at the taste. The spots had come back. ''Worked well for both of us . . . I think.''

''You cain't remember?'' Baptiste chided.

''Wal, of course I remember, ye damned fool! What in Tarnal Hell do ye think?'' Travis lied, forcing his eyes to search the surroundings with their usual wariness.

"Then ye'll remember how cussed ugly she was. Older than Abraham's boot. Hell, couldn't ye dicker fer a pretty young one?"

Travis flipped up the pan on his Hawken, checking the priming. "Ye know, I could blow ye right off that Pawnee nag yer riding—'cept the sound of the shot might kill me."

Richard made a strangling sound, cheeks and eyeballs protruding. Then he belched, and groaned. "Thank the dear Lord God, I thought I was gonna throw up again."

Travis tried to grin, but it hurt too much. And damn it, his own stomach was none too easy.

They rode for a while longer, angling down into the bottoms with their lush cottonwoods. An eagle cut lazy circles in the hot sky, and puffy white clouds scuttled across the northern horizon far beyond the tree-banded river.

Richard was mumbling under his breath, saying, "Choose? Choose what? Die like a dog? I heard him . . . talking in my head. How'd he *do* that?"

A fly kept buzzing around Travis's sweaty face. Oh, to be able to kill the miserable creature. To crush the life right out of that tiny black buzzing . . .

"Fort Recovery," Baptiste pointed. "I thought this country looked familiar."

Richard perked up, staring across the meadow to the abandoned building, little more than ruins. "That's a fort?"

"Used ter be," Travis said. "Missouri Fur Company gave up on her last year. Forts in this country, they come and go. Reckon that'll change one of these days. Once ye get a real fort, most everything just up and dies."

Baptiste swatted a deerfly that lit on his arm, and said, "We're a day shy of Fort Kiowa."

"Another fort?" Richard gestured at the fallen timbers. "Like that one?"

"Yep." Travis rubbed his chin. "Pratte and Chouteau, that's the French Fur Company. Rivals of Josh Pilcher's. Let's see, old Joseph Brazeau built it. He's a cuss if ever they was one."

"Is he a friend of yours?" Richard asked.

Travis made a face. "Sort of."

"He went under last year," Baptiste said.

"The hell ye say! He did, huh?"

"Yep. Just up and died." Baptiste slouched in the saddle.

Travis spat off the side of his horse. "I'll miss that old coon. Just up and died? With his hair on? Reckon that's a wonder fit fer the second coming."

"Hell of a country," Baptiste said dryly. "People keep dying everywhere."

"Reckon it's the same all over." Travis glanced at Richard. "Even Boston. I hear tell folks die there, of occasion, too."

Richard seemed curiously attentive, a gleam fighting to establish itself in his glassy eyes.

Travis picked the most likely reason. "Figgering on slipping away come Fort Kiowa?"

Richard scowled and looked away.

"Maybe we'd best put the Doodle on the cordelle tomorrow," Baptiste offered.

"How 'bout it, Dick?"

"I ain't going nowhere." He sounded uncertain.

Travis patted his horse and squinted against the pain in his head. "Wouldn't do ye no good. The trader at Fort Kiowa ain't gonna give a care if'n ye's indentured or not."

Richard bit his lip and stared at the collapsed timbers across the meadow. "If that's the only kind of fort they've got up here. . . ."

"Reckon so." Travis made the "It is finished" sign with his hand. "Dick, I figgered after last night, ye'd come ter enjoy our company."

"Maybe we don't dance nigh enough," Baptiste said. "Tarnal Hell, Dick, I'll dance with yor sorry arse. Reckon you gots to tie a rag on yor arm first, but I'll shake a leg with you."

"Why a rag?"

"Well, these coons up heah, when they ain't got no women to dance with, they up and ties a rag on. The ones with rags is the women."

"Charming," Richard growled.

"Maybe we should a traded foofawraw fer a woman fer Dick last night?" Baptiste offered. "Yes, sir, we needs to get his pizzle squeezed by some pert young squaw. That'd take some of the rough off him."

Travis rubbed his sore eyes, then blinked hard before squinting at a mirage to see if it were real. Or had his vision gone blurry again? It wasn't real. "Naw, he's a-saving hisself fer Willow."

"Travis!" Richard warned, glaring.

"Got a rise outa the coon, shore 'nuff," Baptiste observed, grinning.

Richard quickly asked, "Will the Sioux really come steal the horses? I mean, after last night. We shared their hearth, ate their food. Danced with them."

"Toss a coin," Travis growled. "Like as not they will."

"But it wouldn't be fair. We're their friends."

"Yesterday, Dick. Today's a different day. Hell, hosses is hosses, white or red. Them what can take 'em, takes 'em."

"But you said they wouldn't steal from people that had been in their village."

"Nope. I told ye they wouldn't steal from ye while ye was *in* their village."

"Then, correct me if I'm wrong, but I get the feeling that out here all ethics are situational."

"What'd he say?" Baptiste wondered.

"Cuss me if I know." Travis blinked his eyes to clear the bleary image. "But if'n words could kill, Dick'd be right deadly."

"My name is Richard."

"He keeps saying that," Baptiste remarked.

"Coon's gotta flap his lips about something. I reckon Dick figgers that's as good as anything around us ignoramuses that don't savvy philos'phy."

"Ignoramuses?" Baptiste asked. "I don't know no word like that."

Travis pulled at his beard. "Wal, by God, Baptiste, yer hellacious living proof of that. Ain't that so, Dick? . . . Dick?"

Sounds of retching came from behind.

They wound down to the river, letting the horses drink. Richard slid off his mare and doused his head in the murky water. Travis noted that the *engagés* had stippled the shore here. The boat was upstream.

Richard stayed on all fours, his hands in the water, head down. "The one-eyed *wechashawakan* . . . do you think he really knows anything? I mean, do you believe any of this power talk?"

Travis squinted up at the hot sun. "Reckon so. I seen some things, Dick. Old One-Eye, the Sioux call him *Wah-Kinyahdonwonpe Konhe,* the Lightning Raven. They say he can see things other folks can't. Chase souls into the Happy Hunting Grounds. It sort of surprised me ter see his lights around a whiskey doings. He don't hold with drinking whiskey."

"What happened to his eye?" Dick sloshed a little farther out into the water and drank deeply.

"Story is that he fought a monster once—like a big rattlesnake, and it bit him in the eye. To kill the critter, Lightning Raven plucked out his own eye and fed it ter the monster, and why, sure 'nuff, it died on its own pizen."

"Damn!" Richard cried suddenly, smacking the water with a fist.

"What's wrong, coon?" Travis immediately went wary, eyes on the peaceful trees around them.

"I don't believe it!"

"Believe what?" Baptiste had also stiffened, thumb going to the cock on his gun.

"There I was, right in the middle of a Sioux camp! Surrounded by them!"

Travis shot Baptiste a wary glance. "Yep. So?"

"I didn't ask a single one about how they perceive the world! About their concept of good and evil, about God, or principle, or the nature of reality!"

Travis took a deep breath.

Baptiste slumped in the saddle. "Tarnal Hell, fo' a minute I thought we's dead. And it's 'cause of what? What didn't you do, Dick?"

"He didn't drive them coons half mad trying ter figger out why the world's the world." Travis yawned.

"And I ate dog!"

"And liked it."

"Don't remind me."

Travis grinned to himself. *And ye'd go a mite crazy if'n ye knew ye done a scalp dance last night.*

"Then they called me a dog!"

"A what?"

"Oh, they were drunk, Travis. I just forgot about it until now. Cannibals, dogs, coyotes, wolves—and I could have asked about God, and truth, and reality."

"Life's like that." Travis glanced suspiciously at Baptiste. "That squaw, she *warn't* bad-looking."

"Wal, fer being nigh onta sixty years old, and fer as few teeth as she had left, I'd say she's right pert, Travis."

From the lift of Baptiste's eyebrow, Travis could tell he might even be saying that kindly.

Go home. Die empty.

Richard sat in the thick green grass on a low bluff overlooking the river. In the twilight, the water gleamed silver. Birds filled the trees with their lilting evening songs. Around him, the grass waved beneath the breeze blowing in from the west. Grasshoppers hung on gossamer wings. He could hear occasional voices and the periodic clank of metal as the *engagés* set up camp in the trees below.

What are you? the voice whispered inside.

Surely, not a monster. *When he looked inside me, he saw a frightened white cloud dog looking back.*

Confused, tricked by myself. Am I a dog or a wolf? What the hell did that mean?

No matter what he'd told himself, Lightning Raven's empty eye socket and his haunting words remained sharp as splintered glass in Richard's memory. That eerie voice whispered in his mind; the terrible chill lingered in his bones.

Richard rubbed his arm, stiff from where Travis had thrown him in one of their "larning ter fight" sessions. The pain jarred in contrast to a mourning dove cooing in the trees.

How peaceful this was, the sun setting behind him, its

light burning yellow on the bluffs across the river. Just to the north, he could see what they called the Grand Detour. A loop of the river twenty-five miles around that would leave *Maria* within a half mile of her starting place.

Richard caught movement to his right, and watched as a pair of buffalo wolves—disturbed by the arrival of the humans—headed up out of the trees and trotted westward toward the setting sun and a night's hunt.

So, why didn't I slip away to Fort Kiowa? He could have just sneaked off and ridden hell-for-leather back to the log post. A French Fur Company boat would have been along in a couple of weeks. Any boat would take a strong back in this country.

And to think, I now have a trade with which I can sell myself. He smiled, remembering the twinkle in Will Templeton's eyes. He'd find the joke a grand one, indeed.

Boston, and Laura, seemed farther away than ever—and each step took him ever more distant from the lodestone of his dreams. Already they were well into June, the days long and hot.

Were it not for François, he'd be home now. Back in Boston, safely investigating the intricacies of Hegel and Kant. *I'd be spending my evenings with you, Laura, instead of learning how to break an assailant's hold and cut his throat in the process.*

But fate and perfidy had brought him here, to this low bluff above a silver ribbon of winding river and beneath an eternal dome of gold-lashed sky. To a place where all he could do was remember Boston, and ask himself why he hadn't escaped when every opportunity in the world had presented itself.

The wechashawakan *said that I'd be empty, like a buffalo-gut bag with all the water poured out.*

It's because you don't have any of the answers anymore. Nothing works the way you thought it did.

Maybe it didn't, not here in the wilderness. But in Boston, that was a different story. There, he could stroll into Samuel Armstrong's bookshop on Bullfinch Street to search for the latest volumes from Europe. Armstrong kept all the new titles as well as the translations of older works. From there, he could cross to John Putney's fine clothes emporium at 51 Newbury, or the even finer clothes at Henry Lienow's over at 3 Roe-buck Passage. A far cry from the worn and stained moccasins and the already tattered leather coat he now wore.

And afterward, decked in new finery, what a delight it would be to step into John Atkins's tobacco shop on Cross Street for a tin of his latest find and a bit of polite conversation while he smoked a good bowl.

You could leave any time you wanted. Just take a horse and ride south.

But here he sat, staring out at the smoothly deceptive river. He took a deep breath, allowing tranquillity to soak into his churning soul. To the river, he said, "Perhaps I'm afraid."

Was that it? Fear of the look in his father's eyes when he reported the theft of more than a year's profit? Thirty thousand dollars: more money than most people saw in a lifetime. Lost.

Until the river, he hadn't understood the real value of that incredible sum. Money had simply been an abstract. *Engagés,* solid men like Toussaint, would labor for two years, their lives in peril, for a total of two or three hundred dollars. To them, thirty thousand dollars was a fantasy.

And I lost it through stupidity. He winced, rubbing his bruised knees. *How could I ever have been that naive?*

On one thing Lightning Raven had been correct. The time had come to choose. Richard smacked a mosquito and asked himself: "So, what are you going to do, Richard? Head upriver to freeze to death, or slip away and ride off to Fort Kiowa and wait for a boat?"

At that moment, Travis and Willow stepped out of the trees and began climbing the steep slope. From Travis's posture, something was wrong.

Willow had a hard look on her face, too. But, now that he thought about it, she'd been looking a bit grim ever since the night they'd camped with Wah-Menitu's Sioux.

"Seen any Injun sign, coon?" Travis called up. "Ain't no ambush atop the hill?"

"Just ten thousand cussed Blackfeet waiting to lift yer hair, pilgrim."

Travis and Willow continued their climb.

When they crested the bluff and walked over, Richard asked, "What's the trouble?"

Travis settled on his haunches. "That night we were with the Sioux? Wal, Green hid Willow in the cargo box. I'd sort of figgered she's been a mite tight-jawed the last couple of days, and I finally got it out of her. Some coon snuck in in the middle of the night."

"What?" Richard shot an uneasy look at Willow.

"An *engagé,*" she said, face expressionless. "I heard him coming. I hid between the . . . how you say?"

"Barrels," Travis supplied.

"Barrels. I hid there, in a small place. Very dark. He couldn't see me—or the knife and war club that would have killed him when he found me."

"Why didn't you scream?" Richard asked.

"Why scream? He'd find me sure." She continued to watch him with those probing dark eyes.

"Well, because it's . . ." He shrugged. "Someone would have done something about it."

"And give myself away to Sioux?"

Richard frowned and turned to Travis. "Who'd sneak after Willow?"

"Reckon any of 'em. Willow's a pretty woman." Travis shook his head. "I didn't hire no saints fer this trip, Dick. I took men, no questions asked. Hell, I'd a taken François and August given half the chance. Even if'n I had ter kill 'em afore Fort Osage, that would a been that much farther they pulled the boat."

"The boat, the boat . . . yes, I know." Richard sighed. "So, what now?"

"We keep Willow close."

"I take care of myself," she said firmly, and patted the war club. "I come close that night."

"But ye shouldn't have ter," Travis said softly. "Not on our boat, as our guest."

A faint smile curled her lip. "Trawis, the time has come. I should go back to my people. I have been hyar too long."

"Don't." Richard laid a hand on her arm. "We haven't even had the time to talk. I—I don't . . ." He lowered his head, surprised at his sudden panic.

"You don't? Don't what?"

"Want you to go," he finished lamely. In his mind's eye he could see Laura's eyes narrowing, her lips hardening.

Travis pulled a grass stem from its sheath. "Wal, I reckon that's some fer elocution. Couldn't a done better meself, and me without a lick of philos'phy."

Richard felt himself redden and growled, "I'll bet it was Trudeau. Was it him, Willow?"

"Don't know. Couldn't see. Very dark." She shrugged.

Richard fingered the wood on his rifle, glancing down at the camp hidden in the trees. "If this happens again, I'll beat the hell out of whoever's doing it."

She gave him that enigmatic smile, dimples forming in her sleek bronzed skin. "So, Ritshard is a warrior now? And a seeker as well?"

He shrugged. And to think he'd just been drowning in memories of Boston, and gentler days when men didn't sneak around in the dark after women.

From the very beginning, Trudeau had tormented him, right up to the moment he drove that fist into Richard's gut. A lot of payback was owed to Trudeau. *But, if it comes down to it, can I take him? Or will he just kill me like swatting a fly?*

TWENTY-NINE

Man's initial feeling was of his very existence, his first care that of preserving it. The earth's produce yielded him all the necessities he required, instinct prompted him to make use of them. Hunger, and other appetites, made him at different times experience different manners of existence; one of these excited him to perpetuate his species; and this blind propensity, quite void of anything like pure love or affection, produced an act that was nothing but animalistic. Once they had gratified their needs, the sexes took no further notice of each other. . . .

—Jean-Jacques Rousseau, *Discourse on the Origin and Foundation of Inequality Among Mankind*

Heals Like A Willow planted her moccasined feet carefully on the trail, alert to the sights and sounds of the hot afternoon. A woman couldn't be too careful in uncertain country like this. Cuts-Off-A-Head warriors might be lurking, ready to take an unwary captive. Ritshard's tracks had already imprinted the soft deer trail she followed down from the flat ridge that made the narrow neck of the Grand Detour. The way led through the green plum, hazel, and raspberry bushes to the sandy shore below. Lazy cottonwoods stood just up from the sand, the leaves waxy in the heat.

The day was stifling, cloudless, and perfect for a bath. The *Maria* was far away, struggling around the far bend of the Grand Detour. On the narrow neck of land above, Travis and Baptiste were processing buffalo meat. She had left them telling stories, waving lazily at flies, and feeding wood to drying fires as the smoke and sun cured long bloody strips of buffalo. They'd shot a young cow that morning.

Birds sang in the cottonwoods, and she caught the gentle musk of the river on the breeze.

Willow stepped out of the rushes and onto the packed sand, seeing the pile of Ritshard's clothes. His rifle, bullet pouch, and powder horn lay propped on a piece of driftwood. He floated in a riffle of current, no more than twenty paces out, lost in his thoughts, looking downstream.

A crystal brook emptied into the river here. The whims of current had left a sand spit separating the Missouri's muddy water from the clear mouth of the creek. The pure water looked so inviting. For the first time in days, she could really feel clean.

Willow unlaced her moccasins and slipped her dress over her head before taking one last look around. Placing her war club on the folded leather, she waded slowly out into the water. She was within a body length before he looked up, stunned. His mouth dropped open, but no words formed.

"What a good day," she said by way of greeting, stepping off into the deeper water and seating herself on the gravelly bottom. She splashed water over her hot skin, then used sand to scrub under her arms.

"What . . . What . . ." Ritshard had huddled into a protective ball. His tanned neck and hands contrasted with the stark white of the rest of him. How could skin be that glaringly pale? Ritshard's chest wasn't covered by the dense mat of black hair she'd seen on some of the *engagés*, but rather with a mist of brown curls that gleamed in the sunlight.

"Bath," she told him. "Doesn't it feel good?" She used a thumbnail to chisel dried buffalo blood from her cuticles.

His agonized expression betrayed growing horror. What could possibly be causing him to panic so?

Willow dipped her head in the water to wet her hair before she lifted her face to the sun and wrung the water out. *Tam Apo!* He hadn't been bitten by something poisonous, had he? "Are you all right?"

"You . . . you're naked!"

"Naked. I don't know this word."

"B—Bare! No clothes!"

Her brown knees bobbed up as she lay back in the water

and gave him a curious glance. "Yes. Take off clothes for bath. You did."

"But—I mean—you're a *woman*!"

She thought for a moment. "Ah! I see. White women take bath with clothes on?. How do they do that? I think it would be hard to wash all over through clothes."

He swallowed hard. "Willow. Men and women . . . they don't bathe together!"

She used a wet finger to clean out her ear, then splashed her face, rubbing it vigorously. "They bath with clothes on?"

He closed his eyes, took a deep breath, and said, "Among whites, it is considered inappropriate to see each other without clothes on."

"I'm not White."

His gaze kept straying to where her breasts floated in the chest-deep water. In the end, he looked away, whispering, "This isn't proper."

"I could go away." Willow began scrubbing her long legs, then rinsed the sand from her muscular thighs and calves. The current carried her closer to where he squatted, his feet solidly planted under his tightly tucked body.

He rubbed his face with a wet hand and gave her a worried smile. "No, it's all right. It's me. Not you."

"Ritshard, easy, coon." She gave him an annoyed look. "Why do Whites not bath together? They have separate rivers?"

"No, it's done inside. In a building. It's just not proper, that's all."

"Why?"

"You're not supposed to see another person's brea . . . body!"

"I did not know this. Among my people, we bath together all the time. Why do Whites think this is bad? Are they all ashamed of being so . . . white?"

He gave her a miserable look and shook his head, still crouched, arms crossed tightly in his lap. "It's just not proper, Willow. Because . . . because that's the way it is."

"You saw Trawis's body when you sewed it up."

"That's different, I didn't see his . . . uh . . . man part."

"Are man parts not all the same? You know . . ." She made a fist with her left hand, dangling the index finger of her right over the top in a semblance of a penis over a scrotum.

"I suppose."

"Then why are you so afraid I might see you?"

"Because it makes a man think of things he shouldn't." He squeezed his eyes shut. "And I'm *not* thinking the things I'm thinking right now. I'm not. I'm really not thinking them—not even a little bit."

A slow smile curled her lips. "Ah." This time she wrapped the fingers of her left hand around the index finger of the right and made suggestive sliding motions. "How silly." Willow splashed him with water and shook her head. "I will never understand Whites."

"Well, don't try this with the *engagés*. At least, I'm a gentleman. And right now, I'm concentrating on Saint Jerome, on Anselm, Aquinas, and thinking about what happened to Peter Abelard when he let his carnal desires lead him astray."

"Ritshard," she said wearily, "I am Willow, clothes on or off. Do Whites think a person changes with the clothes they wear? Where does this come from?"

"From two thousand years of Christian thought, from the Bible, from our scholars and teachers."

"I don't know these words."

"I'm starting to wish I didn't either." This time when she looked his way, he was watching her with unabashed interest. His expression of wonder grew as his gaze traveled her body. He wet his lips, taking a deep breath. Her heart skipped, her own interest suddenly perked by his fascination. Not even her husband had ever looked at her with such adoration and longing.

"I understand," she whispered, staring down at her firm breasts. Crystal beads of water caught the sun, contrasting with her smooth brown skin. "What the White man thinks is forbidden, he desires most."

"We have stories about that. Adam and Eve." He raised his hands. "And here I am in the Garden. I guess it's pretty hard for you to understand." He slapped at the water with a cupped palm. "Thinking about it now, I guess I don't understand, either." He paused. "Don't *Dukurika* men want women more when they see them naked?"

She settled back in the water, excited by his desire. "I don't think so, Ritshard. When a man desires a woman, he makes signs that he's interested. She either agrees or not, as is her wish."

"Do your people—when they bathe—do they stare at each other?"

"We grow up seeing each other at the river. It isn't anything strange to us. Not like it is to you. I wouldn't have come here if I'd known."

"But you've been on the boat. You don't . . ."

"The *engagés* are not my friends. I don't trust them. When they look at me, I see lust in their eyes. That is the word—lust?"

"But you trust me?"

She reached out, touching his arm, smiling. "The eye of my soul has seen into yours, Ritshard."

"And what do you see now?"

"That you want me. In the way that a man wants a woman." She felt him tense, the corners of his eyes tightening.

His voice turned husky. "How does that make you feel?"

Willow, if you tell him, you'll be committing yourself. Are you sure? Instead, she said, "You're so—white."

"It would be like lying with a corpse? Like mating with your dog?" They were her words from the night they'd removed Travis's stitches.

She traced patterns in the water with a slim brown finger. "My husband died six moons ago. He filled my heart so full that I wonder if another could ever find a place in it again. I think about you—as a woman does when she is interested in a man—but I don't know if I want to join with you."

The tension had eased from his shoulders. "That makes me feel better." But she could see that it didn't.

"What would become of us, Ritshard? What I think is all right, you think is wrong. You are not *Dukurika*. You don't know our ways. How could you come and live among my people? What would you do? The men would laugh at you, make you miserable."

He pursed his lips, then said, "I can't be an Indian, Willow."

"Besides, Ritshard, you are going back to Boston. I have listened when you and Trawis have talked about Boston. I don't think I want to go there."

He gave her a weary smile. "I'll admit, I dream about you, Willow, about the way you walk, how I'd love to touch your hair, how I'd love to hold you. And then I think about Boston, about you in Boston. I might be starting to love you, but you're right. I'm not Shoshoni, and you're not white. People would never let us forget that."

She watched a flight of ducks flash past in a pounding of wings. A honeyed sadness filled her. *Why, Willow? This is just the way it is, isn't it?*

"God, how I've changed," he mumbled. "Look at me! Laying naked in a river, talking to a naked woman."

She lifted an eyebrow.

His soft brown eyes had begun to twinkle with amusement. "When I look back at the sort of man I was, and compare that to who I am now, I can't help but wonder." He paused, frowning. "How long were you married?"

"Four years."

"Children?"

"A son. He died when my husband did."

Ritshard frowned, resettling himself. "I never think of you like that. Married, I mean."

"He was a good man. My soul still aches. It always will."

"Obviously you're not a virgin," he whispered.

"I don't know that word."

He gave her an irritated glance. "A woman who's never laid with a man."

"Wirgin." Why did she have such trouble with the V sound? "V-v-v-virgin."

Ritshard tilted his head back. "Well, another dream slips away like mist in the morning."

"I don't understand."

"Oh, nothing," he growled.

She studied him from the corner of her eye, aware that he'd settled back in the water, braced on his elbows, white knees poking up. She could see him now, white like a fish belly except for the black mat of his pubic hair. With skin that pale, she'd halfway thought his pubic hair would be white, too.

"Among my people, we have stories of *Pachee Goyo*, the Bald One. He's an irritating young man who wants everything—and rarely listens to his elders. He sets out on a journey, and never seems to realize how he changes as he travels. It isn't until his escape from the great Cannibal Owl that he realizes he's become a man."

Ritshard watched the water flowing over his hand. "A cannibal owl?"

"Cannibal Owl catches *Pachee Goyo* beside the lake where the Underwater Buffalo live, and carries him far to the north, to an island in the middle of a big lake. There, among the bones of the dead, *Pachee Goyo* makes an arrow of obsidian, and kills Cannibal Owl before it can eat him. To escape the island, he makes a boat from the owl's huge wing and sails for days until he makes shore and can find his way home."

She kicked her legs out to float and studied her toes where they stuck out of the water. "Until I saw *Maria*, I never would have believed anything could float so far."

"Your husband," he asked halfheartedly. "What was his name?"

She fixed her eyes on the sky. "Among my people, we do not say the name of the dead. It can affect the *mugwa*."

"Mugwa?"

"The life-soul, the spirit. It leaves the body when death comes."

"Ghosts," he muttered, still irritated with himself, or her. She wasn't sure which. "Do you believe in ghosts?"

She flicked water with her toes. "I don't know, Ritshard. The souls must go someplace when we die. I buried my husband and my son according to *Ku'chendikani* ritual. It was what he wanted. I have to believe it is so for him. By believing, his *mugwa* will find its way to where he wanted to go."

"That isn't a very sound philosophical framework."

"Framework?"

"Uh, basis, foundation, support."

She nodded. "I believe for him, so that it can be true for his souls. I can do that because I still love him."

"But what about for you?"

She laughed, kicking hard enough to splash water in a silver sheet. "For me, Ritshard, I question. I don't know what my *mugwa* will do when I die. If it comes free of my body, fine. If it travels to the Land of the Dead, fine. If it stays in my body and rots with the rest of me, fine." She lifted her hand. "But I hope it goes free of my body and I can find my way to *Tam Apo*."

"God? Why?"

"I want to know why He made the world the way He did. Don't you wonder why winter has to come? Why does the world have to freeze? Why do men have to die? Why can't we live forever?"

He leaned forward, brown eyes gleaming, a hunter closing on prey. "What's the Shoshoni reason?"

"In the beginning, *Tam Apo* created the world and all things in it, including Coyote. Some say *Tam Apo* took the form of Wolf to do this. At that time, men and animals looked the same. How they came to be different is another story."

"Wolf and Coyote," he whispered, gaze unfocused. "Go on, Willow. Tell me about Wolf and Coyote."

"Coyote and Wolf constantly argued about the world *Tam Apo* had created. Coyote looked around and saw people everywhere. In those days, when a person died, he could be brought back to life by shooting an arrow into the ground underneath him. Coyote told Wolf, 'We should let some of these people die. The *mugwa* can float away in the breeze and the rest can turn into bones.'

"Wolf was tired of hearing Coyote complain, so he agreed, but Wolf made sure that Coyote's son was the first to die. Coyote, of course, was very upset, and immediately shot an arrow into the ground underneath his dead son. When the boy didn't come back to life, Coyote ran to Wolf, complaining, 'My son has not come back to life.'

"Wolf told him: 'It was you, Coyote, who complained that too many people were in the world, who asked that when people died, their *mugwa* would drift away on the wind, and they would rot into piles of bones. This I have granted you.'

"And so, death is forever."

Ritshard gave her a skeptical glance. "You don't believe that, do you?"

"Perhaps. I would ask *Tam Apo* about it." She fished a rock from under her bottom and threw it out past the sand spit to splash in the muddy water of the main current. "Why do we have to suffer grief and sorrow because Wolf and Coyote had an argument just after the world was created?"

"The sins of the father. . . ." Ritshard made a face and rolled over to stare at her. His white buttocks bobbed like pale stones. "It sounds like you worry about the problem of God's justice with the same passion that whites do."

She narrowed her eyes. "It makes my people very uneasy when I ask questions like that. That's why I left the *Ku'chendikani*. I was afraid my husband's brother's wife would accuse me of being a . . . what was the word? Witch?"

"Witch," he agreed.

"That's it. I was on my way back to the *Dukurika* mountains when Packrat caught me."

Ritshard stared into her eyes with that look that betrayed the Power in his soul.

You will dream of him tonight, Heals Like A Willow. You will stare into those eyes, and wish to feel the warmth of his body, the strength of his soul twining with yours. Her blood quickened. Unbidden, her hand reached out to his, their fingers lacing together.

"So," he mused, "you're an outcast, too. I know how that feels, Willow. To ask questions that make others nervous. I, too, would question God, for if He is all-powerful, all good, and all-knowing the way my people believe, why does He allow suffering to exist? He *must* hear the sobs of a mother weeping over the body of her child . . . like you over your husband and son."

At his words, the grief tightened in her chest. "I would

have given anything to save them. I begged and cried to the Spirit World. I offered anything to save them." *If only I had had the courage to send my soul into the Land of the Dead to bring their souls back.*

"But they died. I know." Ritshard tightened his grip on her hand. "God is either a bastard, or He isn't what we believe Him to be. There's always a flaw in the stories we're taught. At least, there is in the Christian dogma. From what you say about the Shoshoni, it's probably the same, right? Always a problem when you really think about what the story means?"

"Yes!" she cried happily. "I was always told to fear the dead. That their ghosts would be angry if they weren't cared for properly and sent across the sky to the Land of the Dead. Why, Ritshard? My husband, he was a good man. His *mugwa* was good, because I saw it reflected in his eyes. Why would it change because of death?" She flicked a fly away.

"Do all Indians have these beliefs? Or are some different?"

"The Pawnee think the world was created by *Tirawahat*, 'The-Expanse-of-Heaven,' and Morning Star had to fight a war to mate with Evening Star. And from that mating, the first woman was born. The *Pa'kiani* believe the world was created by *Napi*. In the beginning it was all water, and an animal had to dive to the bottom to bring up mud for the Flat Pipe to rest on. Everyone has a different story. Can they all be true?"

A twinkle glowed in Ritshard's eye. "I don't think any of them are true."

"Why?"

He took her other hand and floated closer to her in the warm water. "Because none of the stories I've heard tell of a purpose."

"A purpose?"

"Why did *Tam Apo*, or *Napi*, or *Wakantanka* create the world, Willow? Think about all the stories you know. Wolf and Coyote and death. What is the meaning of all this?" He gestured to the world around him. "Why did God do it? Why does it work the way it does? But the most important question is: What is the *reason* for the world? Does it have a purpose? That's what I want to know.''

She matched his smile with her own. "That is why I would seek *Tam Apo*! I'm tired of believing things because the people tell you that's the way it is.''

Her spirit felt ready to burst. She had never dared speak these questions aloud. Now, here, so far from her mountains, she'd found a man who understood. They floated closer together, the hot sun beating down to sparkle off the water.

Perhaps he read the glow in her eyes, for his muscles tightened as he held her hands. Honeyed sensations began to stir deep within her, born through her blood by each beat of her heart. The parting of his lips, the pulsing veins in his neck, betrayed his growing want.

His hand rose to stroke the side of her face, his touch gentle. She closed her eyes, images shifting and whirling within her.

Her arms went around him as they drifted together.

"Willow?'' he whispered as their bodies touched.

She savored the sensations as her breasts pressed against his chest. She traced the muscles of his back and felt him shudder. His hardened penis slipped along the curve of her hip as his hand slid over her buttock.

"We've got to stop,'' he whispered, as if in pain.

"Yes.'' But she held him for a moment, savoring his male hardness before she turned him loose. She climbed to her feet and splashed the sand from her skin. She raised her face to the sun, letting the sexual tension drain away like the water running down her skin.

When he stood, he staggered like a wounded man, taut penis bobbing.

"It would be very easy, Ritshard.'' She tilted her head, twisting her hair into a rope to wring the water out.

Large-eyed, he nodded. "I guess now you know why men and women shouldn't take baths together.''

Her laughter bubbled up. "It might have happened anyway, Ritshard. I spend too much time dreaming of you as it is.'' And the dreams would haunt her with greater intensity now, fulfilling in fantasy what they had so narrowly avoided in fact.

"And I you," he replied sadly, reluctant gaze tracing the curve of her breasts, the flat lines of her belly, and the length of her legs. "God in Heaven, Willow, you're beautiful."

"You have your ways, Ritshard . . . and I have mine." She glanced at him from the corner of her eye. "And I am going away soon. It is better that we do not join in that way."

He nodded distantly, staring at something invisible in the water.

She turned then, wading through the shallows to her dress. On the sand, she used her hands to wipe the last droplets from her skin, and reached for her dress. As she washed it, she glanced at him.

He stood motionless, calf-deep in the clear eddies of the stream. His hands were clenched at his sides, and the long muscles in his arms flexed. Water had slicked the brown hair on his white legs and chest and beaded like dewdrops in the kinky hair around his softening penis.

Don't even think' it, Willow. Coupling with Ritshard would only bring you heartbreak. Resolute, she pulled on her damp dress and moccasins before picking up her war club and beginning the climb back to camp.

"Reckon I seen whipped puppies what looked a heap more pert than ye do, Dick." Travis gave Richard a sidelong glance as they rode their splashing horses across the gravel-bottomed Cheyenne River.

Everything had come undone. *Laura, oh Laura, what have I done?* All those vows of chastity, the promises he'd made himself and her had come so close to disaster that day at the Grand Detour. He'd been torturing himself ever since, trying to find his way—but nothing rational remained to him.

Blessed God, I'm totally lost. Nothing makes sense anymore. That magnificent clarity with which he'd once viewed the world was gone, and a maelstrom of confusion was unleashed in its place.

Richard concentrated on not losing his seat as his white mare climbed the steep bank in buck jumps. Shouldering through the brush, the mare trotted out onto the cottonwood flats beyond. A series of sculptured bluffs—weathered, scalloped, and grass-covered—rose in the distance. Here, the Missouri had cut deeply into the plains, and the valley slopes were speckled with oak, cedar, and patches of buffaloberry.

Richard watched Travis lead the horses alongside, and gave the scar-faced hunter a sour glare.

"Wal?" Travis asked mildly. "Ye gonna tell this coon why Willow and ye are looking so sad? Hell, fer the past three days, the both of ye've been so damned careful to keep from saying anything, or looking at each other, that Baptiste and me, we're getting a mite fidgety."

Richard snorted as he tried to slouch in the saddle the way Travis did. "I should have gone ahead and jabbed you in the eyes during our fighting session this morning. Maybe it would have kept you from seeing more than what's there."

He kicked his mare into the lead, trotting the animal across the flats. For a while they rode in silence.

"Thar's another old Ree village over yonder," Travis said, pointing. "Sioux massacred a big bunch of 'em about twenty years back. Chopped the dead into pieces and scattered 'em. Even the wimmen and kids. The stories say the survivors were too horrified to return. They just left the corpses for the coyotes and the Sioux."

"Why women and children?" Richard shook his head.

"Wanted ter teach the Rees a lesson."

"A lesson? They call butchery like that a lesson?"

"Ye ever read yer Bible? They's butchery akin ter that all through the Bible. And God's work, too. I reckon Sioux just ain't civilized like them Hebrew folks." Travis paused. "I'm kinda surprised we ain't run into more of them coons. This hyar's the middle of their country now."

"And the Rees? Will they be around?"

"Reckon they sneak through here when they have the notion. All this country used to belong to them. Funny peo-

ple, the Rees. Related to Pawnee, but twice as cussed un-
predictable.''

"Indeed. Well, we've had enough trouble with Pawnee,"
Richard muttered.. Before the whiskey trip with Half Man,
life had been so simple. He could just hate, fume, and plot
his escape.

Travis continued to watch him with eyes that sliced past
all Richard's defenses. *Just like Willow, he can read my
soul.*

"I reckon if'n I's ye, I'd tie up with that gal, Dick."

Richard tightened his grip on the wrist of the Hawken.
"I don't know what you're talking about."

" 'Course ye do. We're talking about Willow and ye."

"There's nothing to talk about."

"Uh-huh."

"There isn't!" Richard glared at his tormentor.

Travis Hartman had an unnatural eloquence of facial expression. Just a slight lift of a ruined eyebrow, the quirk of
the lips, and a tightening of the eyes that declared, "Yer a
miserable damned liar."

Richard surrendered. "It won't work, Travis. I know it,
and she knows it."

"Knows what, fer God's sake? Hell, coon, if'n she's
a-looking at me with them fawn-warm eyes, I'd slip her
straight off inta the bushes. Then I'd be right tempted to
hightail my cussed butt off ter the Snake lands and never
look back."

"You would." Richard shook his head. "And then into
another Sioux woman's bed, and then a Ree's, and Crow's,
and whoever's next would be next."

"Something wrong with that?" Travis's voice lowered
menacingly.

Richard cocked his head. "No. It's your way is all,
Travis. It's not mine. I want more."

"Like a nice wife? One of them white 'ladies'? The ones
that talk about tea, and Mrs. Snootbutt's cookies, and lace?
Hell, I been a fool fer years dreaming about finding me a
white wife, of being all them things a man's supposed ter
be. It's shit, Dick. Can ye see this coon living on a farm
someplace back in the settlements? Gee-hawing a damn

mule on a plow line? Smoking up a cabin and shucking corn? Naw, coon, that don't shine, not to this hyar child. But nigh onto twenty years now, I been a-believing it.''

At that moment a small band of whitetailed deer broke from a thatch of brush. They dashed away in zigzags, white tails flagged high. ''I'm trying to decide if I believe you.''

''I don't give a damn if'n ye do or not.''

''I guess I do. You told me all this when you were delirious.''

''Ye mean raving? When I's fevered?''

''Yes.''

Travis worked his jaws, squinting into the distance of his mind. ''Reckon I remember.'' A pause, then he gave Richard a slit-eyed look. ''So, why not Willow and ye?''

''Dear God, Travis! I couldn't take her to Boston. She's a savage. She eats with her fingers! She's . . . she's an *Indian*!''

''That's it, ain't it?''

''No, that's *not* it. I made a promise, that's why. A promise to myself and Laura.''

''Who the hell's Laura?''

''A woman . . . the one I want to marry.''

''A rich Boston lady?''

''What if she is?''

''Wal, she ain't hyar, for one thing. But Willow is. And don't give me no shit about yer not in love with her, neither.''

Richard's desperation goaded him. ''She's been *married*, Travis. Another man's wife. How could I marry a widow? It's not proper. Don't you understand?''

Travis nodded, face suddenly expressionless. ''She ain't a virgin.''

''That's right!''

''Packrat took her, too.''

Richard lost his train of thought. ''What?''

Travis continued to give him that cold stare. ''Why'n hell did she hate him so much? Come on, coon. She's a slave to that Pawnee kid fer nigh on three months. What in hell do ye think? He lay in his robes each night choking his chicken? She's been used. And that just makes it worse,

don't it? A pure man like ye, a plumb dainty Yankee Doodle, wouldn't dare stick hisself where some other coon
pumped his come, would he?''

"It's not that! I tell you I—''

"Ain't it?'' Travis barked harshly. "Yer a stinking hypocrite, Dick. A damn liar! Fer all yer fancy talk about life
and justice and morality, yer nothing more than a Doodle
Dandy, as stuffed full of shit as the rest of 'em. Ye makes
me sick. And sure as hell, ye ain't worth Willow's spit.''

The tone in Travis's voice was too much. "Get off that
damn horse!''

Travis kicked a leg over and dropped lightly to his feet.

Richard leapt from the mare, facing the hunter. "You
don't *ever* use that tone of voice with me again, you hear?''

"Yer a two-faced, double-tongued hypocrite, Dick. And
Willow—and maybe this Laura, fer all I know—deserves
more than a crawling worm like ye.''

The rage broke loose. Richard struck, whipping a balled
fist at Travis's head. The hunter blocked it, and jabbed at
Richard. Knuckles glanced off Richard's cheek, but he was
already kicking out, letting loose of the Hawken to gouge
those angry blue eyes.

He never got his grip; a knee jacked into his crotch. The
force of it lifted him into the air. He was doubled up with
agony by the time he slammed the ground. For long moments he could only writhe in the grass, tears leaking from
his eyes and breath stuck halfway down his throat.

Travis stood over him, fists knotted, a soul-deep sadness
in his eyes.

Richard managed to gasp a breath. The cool air only relieved the paralysis of his sick stomach. He vomited weakly,
then lay in limp misery.

"Sorry, Dick.'' Travis bent down. "Tarnal Hell, coon, I
figgered ye's ready ter kill me.''

"I was,'' Richard squeaked. "Damn, Travis, what did
you do that for?''

"Stopped ye cold, didn't I?''

Richard rolled onto his back, hands probing his genitals,
feeling for blood or . . . well, who knew what.

"Reckon yer gonna be a mite tender fer a couple of days. Is yer sack swelling full of blood?"

"No."

"Wal, that's a relief. I'd hate ter doctor ye. I seen fellers hit hard down there and the sack fills up with blood. Sometimes the only thing ye can do is take a knifepoint, or a steel awl, and drain it out. Sort of like popping a big tick."

"Please, God, *no!*" Richard probed again, then dragged a sleeve across his tear-blurred eyes.

Travis walked over to catch up the horses and tied them off while Richard stifled grunts of pain, wiped his mouth, and rocked tenderly.

When Travis returned, he offered a thin tin flask from his possibles. "Hyar, coon. Reckon a sip'll cure ye."

Richard took the tin in trembling fingers, lifted it, and almost threw up again at the sticky pungent odor. Seeing Travis's scowl, he took a taste, gulped it down, and tried to keep his eyes from crossing.

"What in the name of God is this?"

"Castoreum, coon. It'll fix yer *cojones* and pizzle if'n they's mashed."

"Where on earth do you get something that tastes that vile?"

"Off'n a beaver's balls, pilgrim."

Richard suffered a heaving of his gut, but kept it down through sheer force of will. God alone knew, the stuff was bad enough the first time; the second might kill him.

Travis offered a hand and pulled Richard to his feet. Step by wobbly step they made their way across the knee-deep grass to a gnarly old cottonwood. There, beneath the spreading branches, Travis helped Richard to settle, then dropped down so they both sat with backs to the thick bark.

Butterflies fluttered across the grass, the sound of grasshoppers and bees filling the air with life. In the branches above, robins and a grosbeak fluttered to nests hidden in the deltoid leaves. A fox squirrel leapt nimbly from branch to branch, pausing crosswise to stare down at them with uneasy black eyes.

"Set ye off, didn't I?"

"You did," Richard said wearily.

"Good, 'cause yer being plumb stupid. Now, what's this shit about marrying a virgin?"

To kill the cloying aftertaste of castoreum, Richard pulled a grass stem from its sheath and chewed the sweet pith before saying, "Laura Templeton is my best friend's sister. She's just seventeen and the most beautiful woman in the world."

"Yer promised? Arrangements made?"

"Well, no, not exactly. She said she'd wait for me. That I could pay court to her when I got back from Saint Louis."

"An what if ye go home ter Boston and find she didn't wait? Hell, ye'll be nigh to two years gone, Dick. Reckon she'll wait that long?"

"I don't know."

"Wal, I don't figger this'll come as a surprise, but yer not the same Doodle lad that left Boston. Ye've become a man, and a heap different one than she knew. Even if'n ye went back, do ye reckon ye'll see her the same way? Folks change, grow, turn into something different.

"Meantime, what about Willow? I seen that look in yer eyes. Ye got a hard case, coon. Why in hell cain't ye love her when she's loving ye back?"

"I made a promise to myself, to Laura, that I would keep myself for her." At the skeptical look in Travis's eye, he added, "It's just the way I am. In this sullied world, is it so terrible to keep yourself for your true love?"

"And this Laura, she's yer true love? Yer sure of that?"

"I am. And it's about my children, Travis. About who their mother is. What sort of person. It's . . . Oh, God, I'm not sure I really understand, but, I tell you, it's important."

"Why?"

"Because it is, that's why. I don't want *my* child growing up the way I . . ."

"Go on."

Richard's heart had begun to hammer, and he closed his eyes, shaking his head.

"Is it about yer mother?" Travis asked gently.

Richard wiped his face and sighed. "She was a wonderful lady, Travis. From the finest Boston family. She died giving birth—to me. I never knew her. And all those years, my father would leave, late at night. It was only when I was older that I found out he had a mistress.''

"Ain't nothing wrong with that."

"I guess not," Richard lied.

"Ye guess not. Shit, tell me straight, boy, why did it bother ye that yer father let hisself be a man every now and then?''

Richard's jaw tensed. *Dear God, why?* "Because . . ."

"Ah, he wasn't being loyal to the dead, huh?'' An eyebrow raised, rearranging the scars on Travis's face. "And ye don't think Willow had a covenant with her husband? Or is it that he's an Injun?''

Richard twirled the grass stem between his fingers. "I don't know."

"Reckon ye do.''

"Do you know what she did? Back at the Grand Detour, she came down to the beach. She took off all her clothes, Travis, and waded into the water. She said that Shoshoni do it that way all the time." He pitched the grass away. "And I wanted her. I wanted her so badly that I almost gave in to what I knew was wrong.''

"Ye were gonna take her against her will?''

"No. She was willing, Travis. I'd never force myself on a woman. But it's just impossible. She knows it, I know it, and I think you know it.''

"Because a fancy Boston nob like yerself can't lower hisself to marrying an Injun?''

Richard nodded slowly. "My father—imagine the expression on his face. It would only be worse if I married a Negro.''

"It ain't yer father, Dick. It's you.''

"It's me," Richard whispered. "It's about the kind of life I want. Laura is that kind of wife, one suitable to a professor of philosophy. When I get back, I *will* marry her. Travis, you know me. How can I hold her, love her, knowing that when I was with her I'd be thinking about an Indian woman? And if Laura ever found out . . .''

Travis tapped at his knee with thoughtful fingers. "Ye don't have to go back, hoss.''

"I have to, Travis. My life is back there. That's who I

am." Richard dropped his hand down to massage his tender testicles. "If *anyone* ever found out. Travis, you've got to understand. I'm a *gentleman*."

"Is that another word fer silly idiot?"

"You know what I mean."

"Yer being a fool." Travis stared down at his sun-browned hands. "Ye come from the top and I come from the bottom of what's back there. Lookit, hyar we are, jawing up a storm, and back thar in Boston, ye wouldn't give me a nod in the street. And Baptiste, ye'd figger him worse than shit on yer heel. Nothing but a nigger, free or not. Tell me, coon, with all yer savvy about mankind and culture and morality, which way's best? The top on the top like back there, or all mixed up like out hyar? Who's free, coon?"

"Is it freedom, Travis? Or a lack of responsibility?" Richard winced as he straightened his legs.

"Huh! I figger it's freedom. Life don't let nobody skip outa responsibility. Take me and Green. It don't matter that I owed him, I'd a took this trip on account of he's my friend. If'n the play was turned around, if'n it was my boat, Davey Green would be thar. Baptiste is stringing along looking fer fun, and ten percent, sure. But if'n I wasn't with this company, nine outa ten says he wouldn't be hyar. Don't matter where ye are, ye gotta be responsible ter yerself and yer companions. That, or ye ain't a man."

"All right, accepting that argument, I must be responsible enough to say no to the temptation Willow offers. In the end it would only hurt us both."

Travis sighed in defeat. "All right, I can accept that if'n that's how ye reads sign. That's a man making a choice to keep a friend from trouble. Willow would savvy that"—Travis's eyes hardened—"so long's it ain't that she's spoilt goods, and a damn Injun in yer eyes."

Is that it? Was that why I wanted to kill Travis? Because he spoke the truth, and I really am a hypocrite?

Travis grabbed futilely at a big black fly that buzzed around his head. "White men have got some tarnal strange ideas about what's what, and right, and proper ways fer folks ter act. Same fer Injuns; just ask that Packrat. Hell, maybe ye can't make it work without breaking each other's hearts. On the other hand, coon, maybe yer gonna throw away the best woman ye'll ever meet.''

"What will people say, Travis? A white man . . . married to an Indian.''

Travis waved toward the west. "Ain't nobody out there gonna care. Baptiste figgered that out long ago. Yer only in trouble if'n ye goes back ter America.''

"But I *must,* Travis.''

"Wal, ain't no man can walk yer road fer ye. How're ye feeling? Reckon we otta drop back toward the river, see if'n the sneaking Sioux's wiped out the *engagés*. Can ye walk?''

Richard stood slowly and made a face, legs bowed. "I'll say this, Travis, I sure won't have to worry if Willow catches me in the river again. You took care of any concerns in that regard.''

"Sorry, coon. I figgered I'd take ye out afore ye fooled around and hurt me.''

"It's going to be a long afternoon on the back of that bony mare.''

Travis's face had resumed that flinty look. "Yep. Ain't nothing come free, hoss. Trail's never easy ter follow, and being a mite uncomfortable of an occasion makes a coon think a little clearer.''

"I'll remember that,'' Richard growled, as he eased himself onto the mare's back. But all he could remember was the look in Willow's soft eyes as she walked away that day.

THIRTY

Man being born, as has been proved, with a title to perfect freedom and uncontrolled enjoyment of all the rights and privileges of the law of nature, equally with any other man or number of men in the world, hath by nature a power, not only to preserve his property, that is, his life, liberty, and estate, against injuries and attempts of other men, but to judge of and punish the breaches of that law in others, as he is persuaded the offence deserves, even with death itself.

—John Locke, *Liberalism in Politics*

Baptiste led the way, trotting his horse ahead, rifle butt propped on his saddle. On the right, Travis rode with his Hawken across the saddle bows. With each movement of the horses, their long fringe swayed, beadwork glinted, and long hair danced in the wind. To Richard's eyes, they looked like barbarians crossing the flat floodplain.

This was Ree country. From the time they'd crossed the Grand River, about five miles back, Travis and Baptiste had been increasingly worried. They'd ridden warily through the scrubby bur oak, green ash, and elms that fringed the base of the cedar-studded bluff that rose like a wall to the west.

What a hot, sweltering day. The sun stood straight overhead, and through a faint tracery of high clouds, burned the sky white. Silvery mirages shimmered as heat waves played across the hot ground. Insects buzzed and the horses' feet swished through the brittle grass.

"Ain't no telling about these hyar Rees," Travis warned. "Best check yer load."

Richard did so, making sure the priming powder still filled the pan on his Hawken. Then asked, "Maybe you'd better tell me about the Arikara? Related to the Pawnee, correct?"

"Uh-huh." Travis barely nodded. "Baptiste, hyar, he lived with 'em fer longer than this child. Hell, he talks their talk, knows most of 'em fer the thieving souls they is."

Baptiste shrugged, squinting around from under the brim of his black hat. "I don't cotton to them being thieves. Hell, they just been pushed too far, coon."

"Pushed?" Richard asked.

"They been on the river fer years." Baptiste waved back toward the south. "Remember all them old villages we seen? The houses has caved in and weeds has growed up, but you'll see them big round holes in the ground. Time was, they had more'n thirty villages stretching up from the Platte clear to the Mandans. Then the Missouri and Osage come. The Omaha and Sioux and Iowa. Sickness come, too. One by one, the Rees quit their villages, moved in with kin fer protection."

"Why were the other Indians so mad at them?" Richard glanced around at the foreboding flats.

"Injuns don't need ary a reason," Travis muttered. "They enjoy killing each other just fer the fun of it."

Baptiste snorted irritably. "Man can't live without the itch to whack another man and take what's his'n. Don't make no matter. That's just the way men are. So the Rees come heah, to this part of the river . . . mostly 'cause the Omaha and Blackbird didn't want it. Look around. Not much wood grows here. Not like back south on the Platte, or up north in the Mandan lands. But the Rees hung on, fighting fer their lives against the Sioux and the others. Then the smallpox come. Blackbird died, and the Omaha didn't control the trade no more. The Sioux beat Hob outa the downriver tribes and the Rees figgered their day'd come."

"Tell him about the chiefs." Travis tightened his grip on his sweat-stained Hawken.

"Rees is different," Baptiste said as he scanned the brush. "They set right store by chiefs. Descended from *Nesanu . . .*"

"Who?"

"*Nesanu.* That's the Ree name fer God. Some Injuns out heah, Sioux, Cheyenne, Omaha, they picks a chief by what he says and does. Not the Rees or the Pawnee. If'n yer daddy be a chief, you'll be a chief, and yer son after that. Nobles, that's the word Lisa called 'em. It's passed through the family, and each village had a chief. Like a son from God. So they call their chiefs *Nesanu,* after God."

"That doesn't sound so odd. People have been doing that in Europe for centuries." Richard wiped at the sweat that trickled over old mosquito bites. His horse shied and side-stepped nervously as a coiled rattlesnake buzzed at them.

"Wal, coon, imagine thirty villages mixed inter just two. And each chief plumb equal with every other one. It's like having fifteen different captains in one boat. All they do is fight with each other. Hell, give a Ree chief a chance ter lift hair on a Sioux or another Ree chief, and sure as sun in the morning, he'll take that Ree's hair."

"That's lunacy!" Richard swatted at a fly that persisted in buzzing around.

"Ter yer way of thinking," Travis agreed, "but it's plumb normal fer Rees."

"Why did they attack Ashley?" Richard watched three buzzards spiraling on the hot air. A sign? Since his encounter with the *wechashawakan,* he'd begun to wonder about such things—much to the disgust of his rational side.

"Trade. What else?" Baptiste cocked his head to glance at Richard. "In the beginning, Lewis and Clark come through and told 'em that the Americans was a-coming to trade. The Rees figgered it was their chance. Then the Americans started passing right on by, headed fer the Mandans and Hidatsas. Rees watched all them goods going upriver, and no letup in the Sioux attacks, and all that was left was being poor and dirty. Hell, the Sioux call the Rees their 'women,' 'cause the Rees plant the corn, tan the hides, and the Sioux come take 'em whenever they wants."

"Don't matter," Travis replied. "Rees is cutthroats and thieves. A Ree brave will sell ye his woman, and cut yer throat as soon as yer pizzle's pumped dry."

"So do Sioux," Baptiste shot back. "And Mandan, and Hidatsa, and Crow, and all the rest. So don't ye go on about—"

"They don't cut yer throat the next instant!" Travis retorted hotly. His horse tossed its head and pranced wide around a patch of brush.

"Wal, coon," Baptiste growled, "we'd best not be fighting over it. You've yor way of thinking, I's got mine. I reckon we just ain't never gonna see eye to eye on Rees."

"Reckon not," Travis groused, then gave Baptiste a sly grin. The two rode close enough to playfully box each other's shoulders.

"Travis, why don't you like the Rees?" Richard asked.

"Rees have wiped out too many good friends over the years. I reckon it fogs a feller's thinking about them red bastards."

"Thar she be." Baptiste pointed across the flats.

Through the glassy heat waves, Richard could see the village: several rounded houses on the dusty bluff that overlooked the river. The palisade still stood in places, charred black, and gaping like broken teeth.

"Someone's thar!" Baptiste cried, pulling up his horse.

Travis slowed his animal and slumped in the saddle, inspecting the flats with uneasy eyes before squinting at the distant remains of the Ree village.

"Tarnation and brimstone," Travis growled. "I never did figger all them coons had hightailed after Leavenworth shot 'em up."

Richard swallowed hard, realizing that these weed-filled flats had once been small cornfields. The ruined village, the desolate fields, the heat, all seemed nothing more than a pale reflection of Hell.

"What now?" Richard asked. "Will they attack us?"

Travis licked his lips, his gnarled thumb curling around the cock on his rifle. "Wal, coons, we got ter foller the river. The *Maria*'s gonna make camp right about hyar, tonight. If'n there's ter be Ree trouble, we'd best find out."

"You mean ride in there?" Richard glanced back and forth between the men.

Baptiste flashed white teeth in a wide smile. "You figger since I lived with 'em, they might not shoot us right off?"

"Crossed my mind, coon. What's in yer noodle?"

"Oh, I reckon they won't shoot *me* right off—leastways, not till they shoots you and Dick fust."

"Yer sure sassy fer a black beaver." Travis slapped his leg. "All right, let's ride easy. First sign of trouble, we break and run like Hell's jackrabbits fer the boat. Dave'll need all the warning he can get."

Travis dropped back beside Richard, pointing at the ruined village. "During the Leavenworth fight, the chief hyar was called Little Soldier. About the time it looked like they was nigh ter getting wiped out, he come out under a flag of truce to talk. Told old Leavenworth that if the army'd hide him from the Sioux, he'd help destroy the village. Ye can't trust a Ree, Dick. Never fergit that."

"He was trying to save his kin," Baptiste called back. "White folks don't always understand what kin can mean to a man."

Travis said nothing in reply, but narrowed an eye.

"The place looks deserted," Richard noted as they rode closer to the remains of the charred palisade.

"Yep," Baptiste said, clipped. "But I make it out to be right around ten lodges rebuilt."

Richard studied the brown mounds Baptiste indicated. Looking closely, he could see a thin strand of blue smoke rising from within the village. Here and there, small plots of corn, beans, and squash were growing—but not very well. Dogs began to bark.

"It ain't the whole tribe." Travis scowled. "I'd guess about fifty people."

A bead of sweat crept down the side of Richard's head. A sinking feeling hollowed his gut, and his muscles tightened. His rifle's wrist was damp where he clutched it.

One shot. Make it count. Remember, Travis says you can always bluff with a loaded rifle. He nodded to himself, mouth gone dry as dust.

"Hold up!" Baptiste raised a hand. "Somebody's a-coming."

Through a gap in the palisade, a lone Indian man appeared. He wore nothing but a loincloth and short moccasins. In one hand he carried a pipe, in the other a rifle. Behind him, Richard could see heads bobbing as other Arikara took positions in the ditch behind the shattered palisade. Was that sunlight glinting off a rifle?

The warrior walked bravely forward, head high, the sun shining on his blunt brown features. Wide-set eyes seemed to pop out from his face, giving him a frog look. His hair had been pulled into two long braids intertwined with buffalo hair and his forelocks curled back over his forehead. Stopping short, he called in passable English, "Who comes to the villages of the Arikara?"

Baptiste smiled, urging his horse forward. "Big Yellow, by God! It's Baptiste, coon. With me's Travis Hartman and Dick Hamilton. Dave Green's coming up behind us with a boat."

Big Yellow cocked his head, but no smile of greeting turned those hard lips. "Baptiste. Good to see you." And a string of Arikara talk followed, helped along by flourishes of the pipe in his right hand.

"What did he say?" Richard demanded. Damn it all, he felt like a target sitting out here in the open. His skin crawled, as if waiting for the impact of a bullet.

"Says he figured someone would come after the army come through hyar a couple of weeks back," Travis said from the side of his mouth. "Say's whites and Arikara are at peace, and he's got a paper from General Atkinson ter prove it."

Baptiste had slipped off the side of his horse, walking forward to hug Big Yellow like a long-lost brother.

Richard ran a nervous tongue along the edge of his front teeth. "You believe that?"

Travis pulled at his beard, eyes squinted. "Yep. So long's Atkinson's upriver . . . and we're armed. Won't be no trouble, Dick. Not with Dave coming up ahind us. Reckon we're gonna be treated like kings whilst we're hyar."

"Food's cooking," Baptiste called as he turned away from Big Yellow. "What do you think, Travis?"

Hartman glanced warily at the heads watching from the broken and scorched palisade. "Reckon we'll palaver out hyar."

Big Yellow shrugged, a weary expression on his broad

face. "If you wish, Bear Man. Rees are at peace. I am *Nesanu*. I have given my word."

"And if they's another chief in thar?" Travis jerked his head toward the village. "He give his word, too?"

"I am the only *Nesanu* at this place." Big Yellow offered up the pipe. "Ten lodges. All my people, Bear Man. No one will harm you." His smile seemed forced and weary. "Some of us have learned that no good will come of harming a White man. Some of us know that Leavenworth was foolish—but soldier-chief Atkinson is not."

Travis pulled at his beard, and jerked a nod. "All right, hoss, but if'n something goes wrong, I'll kill ye."

Baptiste climbed into the saddle and rode toward the gap in the palisade. Travis lingered long enough to ask, "Want ter philos'phy him fer a while?"

Richard shook his head.

"Best slip that fetish inside yer britches, coon," Travis warned. "And if'n anybody asks about it, ye bought it down ter Saint Loowee, understand?"

Richard turned the fetish on his belt and tucked it into his britches. "But, Travis, what do these people care about skunk hide?"

Fat's in the fire now, Travis thought as he passed through the palisade gap.

The Ree village lay in shambles. Here and there, Travis could see the scars left by Leavenworth's cannon. As the army retreated, two of Pilcher's men—or maybe it was the Sioux—had sneaked back and set fire to the village. Big Yellow and his people had salvaged some timbers, and snagged others from the river to rebuild a few of the large round houses. Each measured about forty feet across and perhaps ten feet high at the top of the earthen dome. Around them lay the collapsed wreckage of much larger houses, some sixty feet across.

In silence, men, women, and children watched them pass—and their simmering anger carried to him like a carrion breeze. He could see it in their hard brown eyes, the hands clenching bows, old trade rifles, and war clubs. In their wake, people closed in behind them. Unlike the old days, the Rees wore tattered clothing: frayed, sun-bleached fabric; leather worn full of holes and missing fringe; and scanty hanks of beads. The pitiful garments seemed to hang on their bony flesh. But the hollow-eyed look of the children bored into his very soul.

No way out but to shoot our way. Travis's gut churned as he glanced back at the Arikara, who followed like a silent army. *This was a damn fool idea.* But up ahead, Baptiste rode unconcerned, talking easily with Big Yellow.

The place smelled. Old curled hides—once the coverings for bull boats—had hardened in the sun. Broken pots lay scattered about, including cracked iron and copper kettles. Scaffolding for meat racks had been rebuilt, but from driftwood that looked rickety. Piles of horse manure were drying in the sun, no doubt to be scooped up and thrown into the ever hungry cookfires as soon as they cured. Old storage pits lay open, sides crumbled, ready to trap the unwary passer-by in their yawning depths.

"This place is huge," Richard cried, staring at a big house that had somehow remained standing. The long doorway gaped like a black socket.

"This is the little village. Big one is a rifle shot up ahead." Travis tried to calm his horse as a pack of village dogs charged out to nip at the hocks.

"It looks pretty dismal," Richard said sadly. "My God, how dirty they are."

"Comes of making war on whites, coon."

"Travis, what Baptiste said? Is that true? That they were just trying to save themselves?"

"Depends on how ye read sign. They's other ways of saving yerself than killing traders."

They'd pulled up before one of the lodges and Travis reluctantly dismounted. A sunshade of poles and woven cattail matting cast a little square of shade. Big Yellow gestured, shouting orders, and a gaunt woman hustled from the throng, ducked into the long entry, and emerged a moment later carrying a buffalo hide. This she spread on the ground under the sunshade.

Travis slapped at a fly that buzzed around his nose. The whole place was curiously silent. How different from the days when Lisa's boats had arrived here. Then the crowds had thronged about the boats; feasting, dancing, and laying in the robes had followed. In those days, like kings of old, the traders had been carried up from the river in buffalo robes born by muscular warriors.

Travis kept his reins in his hand, noting that Richard had learned his lesson—he kept his animal between him and the gathered Rees.

At a gesture from Big Yellow, three boys came to claim the horses. "Don't take them out of sight," Travis told them in Arikara.

The skin on his back was crawling as he motioned to Richard, and took a place on the buffalo robe in the shade. Tarnal Hell, a coon could be shot in the back so easily. All a warrior had to do was sneak around the side of the lodge, level his rifle, and she'd be Katy bar the door.

Cattail leaves rattled in the hot breeze, the sound like dry bones clacking. At the same time the rest of the Rees closed in, seating themselves in the hot sun. For all the expression they showed, those brown faces could have been modeled of clay.

Big Yellow filled his pipe, lit it with an ember brought by a young man, and chanted the blessing to *Nesanu*; to *Atna*, the Corn Mother; and finally to Grandfather Stone. The pipe was offered to the northeast, southeast, southwest, and northwest, the four sacred directions of the Arikara.

Baptiste puffed, and offered the pipe to the directions. His brown eyes had softened as he stared out at the crowd. Then Travis took the pipe, drawing the bittersweet tobacco into his lungs. To his satisfaction, Richard copied every move correctly.

"It is good," Big Yellow began, "to have traders in my village again. Our two peoples have had bad times. Let us have no more." He made a wiping-out gesture with the flat of his hand. "The time for war between us is past."

"There has been trouble," Baptiste agreed. "Big Yellow

speaks the truth. We have come upriver with peace in our hearts. We wish nothing more than to pass in peace.''

Big Yellow sat thoughtfully, pulling on one of his braids. He looked around at the people squatting in the sun, their empty brown eyes fixed on him. ''My people need many of the things the White traders carry. We have no powder for our guns. No bullets to shoot. We are few now. The village Medicine Bundles have been carried away to the four winds. The Doctors' societies are all scattered everywhere. The White man has come like a great wind, one that has broken Mother Corn, who we also know as the sacred cedar— snapped her off clean. On every side, my people are surrounded by enemies. The Sioux come and take what they wish. If we raise a hand in protest, they kill us. We cannot stop them.''

Big Yellow indicated his silent people. ''My friends can see my children. Their arms and legs are thin, their bellies hang out. Look at the hunger in their eyes. Look at my women. They wear only what the Sioux have left us. Their dresses are worn thin. The milk in their breasts will not feed their children.''

Big Yellow fixed Travis with level eyes. ''Is this what the White men wished? To see us so?''

''Reckon not,'' Travis said carefully. ''They's hard times ter go around fer everybody.''

Big Yellow betrayed no expression. ''We have not seen hunger or want in the eyes of the Sioux.''

''Them coons take what they want. It ain't just the Rees that they've been raiding and stealing from.''

''I do not worry about others,'' Big Yellow stated. ''I worry about *my* people, Bear Man.''

''You know the trade,'' Travis countered. ''We got ter go where the beaver is. How many beaver can ye trade?''

The weary smile creased Big Yellow's lips. ''The time for easy talk is past, Bear Man. I will tell you how the Rees think about trade. We trade among ourselves, but it is to make things balance. Some do not have what they need, so we trade that all may share. In the beginning, we thought the White men were like *Nesanu*, powerful, surrounded by wonderful things inside and outside their bodies. We did not understand how you could live in our houses, eat our food, and not share everything you had with us, as we share with each other. *Nesanu* taught us to give something to everyone. But you White men keep as much as you can for yourselves. We have never understood how you could be so selfish. Until I met a White man, I did not know the word 'profit.' "

"That's the way of trade." Travis pulled at his beard. "A trader has to take all he can get. If'n he don't, he can't trade fer more knives, guns, and powder. Ree ways and white ways is different. Killing traders ain't gonna fix it. Why'd ye pick a fight?"

Big Yellow rubbed a callused hand on his bare arm. "It was because we thought you were our friends. It was because we offered you everything, and then you left us to be killed by the Sioux. In the beginning, when *Nesanu* made the world, he made it so that people would share with their friends. How does the White man act when a friend stabs him in the back? Does he not pick up his rifle and make war? Is that not what you did when the British came to trade on the river?"

Travis rolled his jaw from side to side. Hell, that's what they'd told the damn Injuns. Lisa had set in this very village and explained the war that way.

"You do not need to answer, Bear Man." Big Yellow straightened his back. "This chief understands now that your ways are different, that you do not have *Nesanu*'s words in your heart. Some of my people have told me I am a fool for coming back here to the river. They have said that I will die here, killed by the Sioux, or by the Whites." He pointed across the heads of the watchers to a low dirt mound. "My ancestors lay there, in that earth. I can feel their *sishu,* their souls. That is why I am here. If we are to die, it will be on our land, among our ancestors. So many of them are dead because of the wickedness in your souls, my life would only be one more."

"Cain't nobody keep disease away." Travis took a deep breath, his nerves tight as fiddle strings.

"Perhaps, Bear Man." Big Yellow's bug-eyed stare drilled into Travis. "We are poor now. You see what we have. When Green's boat comes, will you trade? Big Yellow understands that you are taking most of your wonderful things to our enemies, but we will offer what we can.''

Travis chewed his lip, considering. A dirty, moon-faced child watched him with round eyes. The kid's hair was matted, and he sucked on muddy fingers.

"Reckon we'll trade some," Travis admitted. "Ain't much, but it will help."

Big Yellow nodded slowly. "It will help. Your men will have been long time without women. Once, we thought it curious that you had no women of your own. It was believed that a man could give his woman to you, and afterward, he could gain some of your Power by lying with her. I think now that it was a lie. No man ever gained White Power through his woman that way. If we had, we would not be like we are today."

"Boat will be up by dark," Travis said. "Reckon we'll trade what we can. But, Big Yellow, yer a wise old coon. It wouldn't do fer some warrior ter get outa sorts. Let's keep folks separate fer the most part. Less likely ter be an accident that way."

"Reckon so, coon," Big Yellow agreed.

"So, what's happening?" Richard wondered as they walked toward their horses.

"We're gonna trade," Travis answered. "Hell, they ain't got squat but women to offer. Only thing we're getting is free passage and a lighter load."

"But it beats a fight," Baptiste replied, eyes half-lidded.

"Women?" Richard sighed.

"It's about all they got," Travis reminded.

"I'd call that whoring."

"Not according ter their lights, and it'll fill a couple of these kids' bellies."

Maria lay tied off on the bank below the Arikara village. Laughter carried on the warm night breeze. A half moon hung low over the dissected buttes east of the river, and stars dusted the sky. Far to the south, flickers of lightning danced, but no sound of thunder reached them.

This is an awful place. Willow sat on the cargo box beside Travis. She rubbed her smooth shins and watched the firelit bank. Unease, like a subtle undercurrent, twined with her *puha.* She could sense the spirits here, troubled and crying. *It would be better to leave this place of sorrows.*

Green stood just below them, a rifle in his hands. Richard sat at the bow, his Hawken across his lap while Henri stood guard at the stern. Baptiste was ashore with Big Yellow, keeping a wary eye on the *engagés* who dallied with the Arikara women.

Bonfires illuminated the ruined village in a ghostly glow; human shadows wavered against the palisade and earth lodges.

"Looks a mite more peaceful than the last time I was hyar," Travis said. "Reckon we'll get nigh away without trouble. Green and me, we done decided, about an hour afore dawn, we're heading out. Reckon them coons best wet their pizzles, 'cause we'll be humping backs upriver hard. Leastways, until we make a distance atwixt us and the Rees."

Willow filled her lungs with the musky scent of the river and slapped a mosquito that landed on her arm. "Can you feel them, Trawis?"

"Huh? Feel what?"

"The spirits. Some angry, others so sad."

He cocked his head, concentrating. "Don't know, gal. I been on edge ever since we got hyar. Reckon this place has done gone sour. It's them kids. The way they was looking at me. I never give much thought to kids afore. That's the saddest part."

"Green did not like giving them flour and so much food."

"Nope. Might make things a tad tight come winter on the Big Horn. We'd best hope we make a good fall hunt and the buffs is down in the valleys this winter. Bellies might be a shade gaunted up otherwise."

She reached out, laying a hand on his arm. "If you are worthy, *Tam Apo* will provide."

Travis sucked his lip for a moment, then shrugged. "I had me a dream back when ye made that travois. Saw old Manuel Lisa and his coons. They told me the river was dying."

"Baptiste says it is because of the White men. I think he is right. The water may continue to run, but the river's soul will wither."

"Yer a different sort, Willow. Ye see more than most folks."

"I have always been different." She rubbed her hands together. "At times it has made my life hard. I have been told I ask too many questions."

Richard shifted, and Willow couldn't help but watch him. If only . . .

Travis, ever keen, noticed and studied her from the corner of his eye. "He's a good man. Reckon the two of ye'd do right nice together."

She shifted on the hard deck. "We follow two different trails. He to the east and his people, and I to the west." But her soul was haunted by the warmth in his brown eyes, and the tender way he touched things. If she closed her eyes, she could imagine the sensation of his fingers on her skin, the warmth of his body against hers.

"Different worlds can join, gal. It ain't always a gonna fall apart."

"The White world touched the Arikara. What do they have left? Begging for food? Selling their women? I have heard the talk. The cut-throat Sioux say Arikara are like women to them. They make things just so the Sioux can come and take them away."

"Sioux is tough coons. Trouble is, they's so many of them."

"They have strong medicine."

"Reckon." Travis rubbed his ruined nose and mashed a mosquito that had settled from the humming hoard. "To my way of thinking, it makes Baptiste's notions wrong. If'n whites destroy everything in their path, the Sioux otta be about wrecked, too. But they ain't. Seems to this child that they just get stronger and stronger."

"Perhaps."

They shared a long silence.

Travis asked, "Something happened back at the Grand Detour. Dick and ye, ye ain't been the same since. Each of ye is sad way down deep in the heart."

"We saw truth in each other's eyes, Trawis." She batted at the cloud of mosquitoes. "I cannot go to Boston. I am told it isn't my place. He would not like life among the *Dukurika*. What more needs to be said?"

"He don't know that." Travis resettled his rifle. "He figgered he'd hate the river. Hell, he still thinks he hates it, but ye've seen the shine come ter his eyes. He's becoming a man, Willow. He just ain't got his sights set straight yet. A feller don't know what he's got until he can see forward and backward. I reckon Dick's still looking back so hard, he can't cotton ter what's right afore his nose."

"I do not understand."

"He's fixed on Boston, and some gal named Laura."

"Who is this Laura?" What was her Power, that she could hold Ritshard from so far away?

Travis shifted nervously. "Wal, she's little sister to a friend of his. Said she'd let him come court if'n he come back. It ain't final, ye understand, just an agreement to pay court. Them Boston folks do things that way."

"And she is a lady?" Willow's stomach soured at the thought. "Is that what he wants? A lady in a box? To be taken care of?"

Travis plucked absently at the fringe hanging from his sleeve. "He ain't figgered out that his soul's been changed. It'll happen, but he's a bullheaded son of a bitch. Might take a spell yet . . . and maybe a good whack on the side of the head, but he'll see. He's a right savvy Doodle."

She stilled the whirlwind that churned inside. *What a fool I have been.* "I cannot wait that long, Trawis. I have decisions of my own that must be made. His heart cannot rest until he has gone back to his Boston." *And he can have his White lady, in her house, with her children.* "Mine cannot find peace unless I can smell the trees, hear the birds, and enjoy a warm fire on a cold night."

"Ye sure?"

"Could you live in his Boston?"

"Nope."

She returned her attention to the Ree village, fists clenched at her side. "I think of good things, and they are all in my land. I want to see my father again, laugh with my mother. I want to hunt the mountain sheep again. We trap them in pens on the side of the mountain. My best memories are of cold mornings after a good kill. When you cut the animal open, the bodies smoke in the cold."

"Steam. That's the word, gal."

"Yes, steam. You know the smell, don't you? Of blood, and the insides of the animal. Sweet—and all the while, your soul knows that meat will be roasting, and your belly will be full. People will laugh and tell stories around the fires that night. They do not do these things in Boston?"

"Nope. Folks buy meat all cut up."

"That sweet smell, Trawis, that is the smell of life, of the animal's soul that will join with yours. At that moment, I know I'm part of *Tam Apo*'s world. I think these people in Boston do not know these things."

Travis exhaled wearily.

"What will happen when the White men come to my country? Will they take that sharing of life away?"

"I don't know."

"I think they will. They put their women in houses. They put their God in a house. I have heard Green tell me that other Injuns, Shawnee, Cherokee, Iroquois, have all been put in places. Is that what White men do? Will they try to put the *Dukurika* in a place, like flour in a barrel?"

"Yer Snakes are a long way away from whites."

After an uncomfortable pause, she asked, "What about you, Trawis? Why don't you go back? You are a great warrior, a hunter, a powerful man. The Whites should make you a gentleman."

He laughed at that, but she could hear the bitterness.

Again the silence stretched.

Finally he said, "Willow, I ain't sure the whites are gonna go clear ter the Snake lands. Traders, sure. But not the farmers. It'd take some doing ter make a living in the mountains. Hell, there ain't nothing there. I seen the Snake country. It's too damn dry fer growing corn. Only thing a body can do is hunt. And I ain't seen a damn thing can be done with sagebrush but burn it in a fire—and hardwood's the beat of sagebrush any old day.''

"I think they will come, Trawis." She rubbed her legs harder, as if to scrub the thought away. "I think the White man wants everything he can get—even if it is only sage-brush to burn in the fires.''

"Ye make it sound like poor bull, gal."

She pointed at the village. "Is that fat cow?''

Travis pulled at his beard. "The Rees went to war with the whites. That's what comes of killing white men." He paused. "There's other ways, gal. Snakes could join the whites, help fight the Blackfeet. It wouldn't have ter be grief. Yer warriors know the country. And ain't the Black-feet more trouble fer ye than the whites would be?''

"My people would kill a man like Trudeau. This would not make other White men mad?''

"Hell, I'd like ter kill him, too." But again she heard hesitation in his voice.

"You have answered my question, Trawis. Now do you see why Ritshard and I must go our different ways?''

And I must go mine, at the first chance. If she didn't, the sadness within would slowly consume her soul. Laura? What kind of a name was that?

Beside her, Travis stared glumly into the night.

THIRTY-ONE

But the most frequent reason why men desire to hurt each other ariseth hence, that many men at the same time have an appetite to the same thing; which yet often they can neither enjoy in common, nor yet divide it; whence it follows that the strongest must have it, and who is strongest must be de-cided by the sword.

—Thomas Hobbes, *Leviathan*

The four days they'd spent alternately towing and poling the *Maria* away from the Ree village had drained everyone's gumption. Green had finally called a halt, here, on a grassy bluff that looked out over an oxbow of the sun-silvered river.

Richard lay propped on his elbows, chewing the sweet stalk of a bluestem. The western breeze had carried the earliest of mosquitoes away. Every muscle ached from the time he'd spent on the cordelle, adding his strength to the work.

A wasp landed on his thigh. With a thumb and forefinger, he flicked the beast away and squinted up at the triangular cottonwood leaves. His soul squirmed between his growing desire for Willow and his commitment to Laura.

Across from him, Baptiste skinned a monstrous rattlesnake, peeling the scaly green hide from pink meat.

Travis lay flat on his back in the shade, his worn felt hat pulled low to shield his eyes. The hunter had fallen into a deep sleep, chest rising and falling slowly. The up-tipped face visible beneath the sagging hat brim exposed the crisscross tracery of white scars and bush of beard.

For the moment, Richard envied Travis his lack of responsibility. How pleasant it would be to flit about, never making a commitment to any woman. But how hollow would he feel in the end, when he finally realized that he'd never fully shared his life with a woman?

I hereby resolve I will not make that mistake, Richard decided.

Green and Henri, as usual, sat before the booshway's tent, their talk perpetually on the river and whether the water was rising or falling.

The other *engagés* lay like logs, with only the unlucky mess captains seeing to fires and cookpots. Grasshoppers chirred in the lazy air, while magpies and robins flitted through the bur oak ringing the meadow.

Richard stretched and winced at his cramped limbs. He turned his head, wondering what had happened to Willow— and from the corner of his eye, caught sight of Trudeau.

Something about the man focused Richard's attention.

Usually, the boatman swaggered, but now he walked furtively, a slight crouch suggested by his steps as he eased into the fringe of bur oaks.

I'm too damned tired to worry about him. Richard took a deep breath and lay back on his saddle, happy to let the afternoon sun warm his face. The world was filled with too many troubles as it was. Laura, Willow, his father; he'd begun to fret about all of them.

Furtive? . . . Trudeau?

He sat up with a grunt, and threw the grass stem away. Trudeau had vanished into the trees.

Richard growled at himself and stood. He massaged the stiffness in his legs with equally stiff hands, and picked up his rifle. He turned his steps in the direction Trudeau had taken, unconsciously adopting the wary hunter's stalk that had become so familiar.

The most likely path was a deer trail that wound westward, away from the river and toward the bluffs. Several of the pale leaves on a buffaloberry had been bruised where Trudeau had passed.

On moccasined feet, Richard followed silently, employing all the skills Travis and Baptiste had tried so hard to beat into him.

The trail wound uphill into the bluffs, past chokecherry and wild grape. It opened into a grassy cove lined with brush. Richard slowed as he spotted his prey. Trudeau crouched several steps ahead, screened from the clearing by a mass of oblate chokecherry leaves.

On the far side of the clearing, Willow plucked the first ripened chokecherries off their stems. She dropped them one by one into a leather sack. Each night, she'd been collecting such foodstuffs, carefully drying them, and refusing to allow anyone to partake of her growing cache.

Travel food for her journey home. Richard's heart ached all the harder. The thought of her leaving drove him half mad, but what other alternative was there?

Travis had watched her with a curious frown, but she'd only smiled and artfully deflected his attempts to persuade her to stay.

And now, here was Trudeau, sneaking after her. Richard swallowed hard as he studied the boatman's thick shoulders, the muscles bunched under a sun-bleached and frayed shirt. Black hair, like matted wire, covered the *engagé*'s powerful forearms. Trudeau moved with a cat's quick agility, and, like the cat, had little mercy in his callous soul for victims.

What do I do? Run back for Travis? At that moment, Trudeau edged forward, crossing the clearing in carefully placed steps.

Willow remained oblivious, back turned to the *engagé*.

Richard straightened, heart pounding as he gripped his Hawken. "Trudeau!" He stepped out into the clearing, scared half to death, and part of him suddenly sick from the realization that he'd just committed himself to a beating.

The *engagé* stopped as Willow turned like a startled fawn, chokecherries falling from her container.

"Who?" Trudeau's eyes slitted, shoulders bunched. "It is you, Yankee. Go away. Now! Or I will hit you hard in the stomach again, eh?"

"Leave her alone." Richard pointed at Willow, hoping his arm didn't tremble.

"Willow and I, we have a talk, eh? It is not for you, weak little American. Leave now, and Trudeau will say nothing."

Willow had plucked the war club from her belt, dark eyes narrowing as she gripped it for a blow.

"She'll break your head," Richard warned.

"She will?" Trudeau threw his head back and laughed. "Why do you worry? This woman, she is squaw, *non*?"

"She's a guest. Travis told you. And Green, too."

"Bah! She's running away. What do you think, eh? She makes dried food for the journey. Very well, but before she go, Trudeau will say good-bye! And so will you, Yankee."

"I'll tell Travis."

Trudeau started toward him, hands outstretched. "You'll tell no one anything, Yankee. I think you will not leave here, eh?"

Richard looked past him, shouting, "Run, Willow!" and lifted the Hawken. The cock clicked loudly as Richard thumbed it back. "Not another step."

Trudeau's dark eyes smoldered. "You do not have the courage to shoot me . . . no matter what hangs from your belt, *crasseux chien*."

The set trigger clicked under Richard's finger. "Believe what you want."

Willow had cut around to one side, her war club ready. Trudeau sneaked a glance at her, aware of the dark glint in her eyes.

"*Lâchement, bâtard!*" Trudeau raised his hands, backing slowly away. "Perhaps you should shoot now, *oui*? If you do not, Trudeau will make you pay."

"You talk a lot."

"You will not always have the rifle!" Trudeau pointed an angry finger. And with that, he spun on his heel and crashed off into the chokecherries.

Richard took a deep breath and lowered the hammer to half-cock. A fine film of sweat had dampened his face and neck; now the cooling breeze wicked it away.

Willow lowered her Pawnee war club and chuckled, a twinkle in her eyes.

How can she do that? I'm almost trembling! He hung his head for a moment, and looked up from lowered eyes.

"Thank you, Ritshard." She stepped close and laid a hand on his shoulder.

"I thought I was going to have to shoot him."

She shrugged. "Sometimes a man does not know when to quit. *Tam Apo* has little patience for fools."

"He doesn't?"

"How many old fools do you know?"

"Quite a few—but they're all back in the United States." He studied her thoughtfully. "You're leaving very soon, aren't you?"

She kicked at the grass with a dainty foot. "My people are far to the west. I must go." Her dark brown eyes bored into his. "My husband and child are dead. I want to mourn them. You have made a place in my heart, but I cannot have you. You will go back to Boston . . . and Laura."

"Willow, I—"

"And there is more. I have listened to Green and Trawis talk about the Whites, and what will come. I need to think about this. Until I do, my soul will be like a twig on the river, bobbing, spinning, and never resting, never knowing where it is headed. Do you understand?''

''I . . . I do.'' *But, oh, God, I don't want you to go.* He reached up, touching the corner of her cheek with the tip of his finger. She closed her eyes as he traced gentle fingers along her skin.

She took his hand, pressing it to her cheek. ''Ritshard, you must promise me, after I am gone, tell Green I will send someone to him at the mouth of the river they call Big Horn. Will you do this for me?''

Her touch stoked a hollow tickle under his heart and he drew her to him. Her arms went around him and she buried her face against his neck. How perfectly she fit against his body, as if molded for him alone. Inhaling, he savored her aroma, sweet scent spiced by leather and woodsmoke. He ran his hands down her slim back and let them settle in the curve of her thin waist. He could feel her breasts pressing against his chest, and closed his eyes to savor the sensations conjured within.

Memories haunted him of that day at the river: her lithe body in the sun, and water like diamonds beading on her firm thighs. Dark nipples on rounded breasts, her flat belly accenting the curve of hip and the mystery hidden beneath glistening pubic hair. How proud she'd looked, broad-shouldered, midnight hair shining blue in the sunlight.·

She tightened her grip, surprising him with her strength. Her body's heat burned into him, into his soul, and triggered a hammering of his heart. He wanted her, the need building with each pulsing rush of blood in his veins.

She felt him hardening and pushed away, slim hands on his heaving chest. She searched his eyes with hers, seeking desperately . . .

''Dear Lord God, I . . . I can't, Willow.'' He shook his head, panting, dropping his eyes so she wouldn't see the shame, lust, and need all mixed together.

From the corner of his eye, he could see her nod and turn away, walking toward her basket of chokecherries. He knotted his muscles against the ache in his chest and let the fever ebb from his blood. *I must think of Laura, of the promise I made to her. If I can't keep that simple promise, how will I ever look myself in the eye again and still call myself a man?*

They walked back toward camp in silence, casting furtive glances at each other. Everything seemed dreary and confused. So much piled on him: Trudeau at the precipice of a killing; Willow leaving; and the horrible emptiness inside—like rot hollowing out an old log.

Travis sat in the shadows with his back against a rolled blanket and watched Richard and Willow. Both were seated cross-legged, the fire separating them as surely as the invisible barrier they had erected. Travis braced his left arm on his knee, hand hanging limp but for snatching at an occasional mosquito. In his right, he cradled his pipe, puffing absently now and then to keep the tobacco smoldering.

Dick and Willow had placed themselves to be as far from each other as possible, but so they could watch each other in the least obtrusive manner.

Never known two people as happy ter torment each other as them two.

Once again, something had happened to upset the delicate balance they'd achieved. From across the camp, Trudeau cursed and jumped to his feet, fists balled, head bulled forward.

Just as quickly, Toussaint was up, his deep voice calming.

"Gonna be trouble with that French coon," Baptiste noted amiably as he appeared out of the darkness with a tin cup in his hand. He squatted at Travis's side, eyes gleaming from under the wide brim of his hat.

"Reckon." Travis caught the tightening of Richard's expression as he watched Trudeau. A curl of disgust bent Richard's lips. *Wal, now there's part of it. Them coons has got each other so stiff-legged they's about ter fall over.* And sure as God made sunsets, Willow was in the middle of it.

"You want I should go knock some sense inta his lights?" Baptiste indicated Trudeau with his cup. "A feller can catch a whole heap of sense with a good hard whack to the side of the head.''

Travis studied Richard from the corner of his eye. ''Let him be fer now.''

Baptiste stuck his jaw out sideways, caught the drift of Travis's thoughts, and grunted. ''He'll get kilt.''

''Yep. Reckon the fat's a-boiling fit ter spatter.''

Richard had clenched his fists, a hard-eyed squint fastened on Trudeau. Willow had turned to watch, then regarded Richard with sober eyes.

Whatever was said by Toussaint, Trudeau hadn't wanted any part of it, for he stalked away from the *engagés*' fire. He'd headed for the edge of camp, then, as if on a notion, he changed directions to pass the fringe of Richard's fire.

''Coming ter a head now,'' Travis murmured to Baptiste. ''Let her play out as she will.''

Richard had hunched up, jaw set in his thin face. Travis had seen that crazy shine in men's eyes before; the twitchy set of the lips that betrayed a man pushed too far. Willow appeared unconcerned, but her fingers had tightened around the handle of the war club.

Trudeau hesitated as he approached, started to veer off, but couldn't resist, ''You 'ave your rifle, *mon ami*? Is that what you stick in your hot Snake bitch? The only thing you own hard enough to make her moan?''

Richard's reaction even caught Travis by surprise. He leapt like a coiled spring, taking Trudeau around the waist. Richard bulled him back, pummeling with his fists. Instinctively, Trudeau clenched, lifting Richard off the ground as he tightened his grip in an attempt to snap the spine.

Richard kicked frantically and slammed an elbow into Trudeau's head before poking a thumb into his eye.

Trudeau howled, planted his hands in Richard's chest, and shoved him off. Richard tumbled backward as Trudeau rubbed at his eye, roared, and leapt in an attempt to stomp Richard's chest in. From flat on his back, Richard kicked Trudeau's legs out from under him.

With a newfound agility, Richard twisted away from Trudeau's falling body. Both scrambled to their feet in a flurry of dust to circle like bulls.

Engagés had come at a run, and now their shouts and whistles added to the din as they cheered Trudeau on.

Richard feinted and grabbed for one of Trudeau's arms. The frantic fingers slipped as Trudeau planted a foot and lashed out with a fist to graze the side of Richard's head. Before the kid could recover, Trudeau was on him.

Travis put a hand on Baptiste's arm as the black hunter started forward.

When Trudeau hammered Richard into the ground, it drove the air from his lungs. Instinctively, Richard tucked his legs up—just in time to block the knee that jabbed for his crotch. Trudeau arched, pulling back a cocked fist. Richard took the opportunity and used the muscles of his gut and neck to butt his head into Trudeau's face. The smacking impact brought a howl from Trudeau.

The *engagés* were dancing gleefully, swinging their fists in mock combat, clapping and shouting. Willow had backed away, lips parted, a gleam in her wide eyes as she clawed for the war club on her belt.

Trudeau was squealing his rage now, slamming his fist into the side of Richard's head. The Yankee gave a gasp, and the pain spurred something down inside him. His expression twisted, demonic, half mad with panic and desperation.

Travis finally moved, stepping up behind Willow as she tore her war club from her belt and started forward. "Leave 'em be," he warned, placing a hand on her shoulder. "Dick's got ter fight her out, gal."

Willow tensed, trembling, but lowered the Pawnee club.

Travis looked down at the thrashing bodies to see that Trudeau was clawing at Richard's face with hooked fingers.

Come on, coon. If'n he blinds ye, she's all over.

Dick was flopping like a fish in the boatman's grip, avoiding the gouging fingers. Sweat trickled, mixed with blood on Richard's face. As the inexorable fingers closed, Richard snapped like a turtle for a worm.

Trudeau shrieked, two of his fingers clamped between Richard's teeth. The Yankee bit down savagely, shaking his head like a terrier on a rat. At the same time, he got a hand back of Trudeau's head, and did a little clawing of his own.

Insane with pain, Trudeau bucked like a fresh colt, broke Richard's grip, and pounded a hard-boned left to the side of Richard's head to loosen those terrible jaws.

Trudeau rolled free, scrambling away.

"Dick! Get up!" Travis bellowed as Trudeau stumbled to his feet, careened off the surrounding boatmen, and leapt. Richard saw, rolled to the side, and Trudeau's hard heels slipped off his ribs instead of crushing them. As he sprawled, Richard curled and grabbed up one of the rocks from the fire ring. He grunted with effort as he bounced it off the side of Trudeau's head.

"God damn it!" Dave Green bellowed, elbowing through the circle. "Stop this at once!"

"Let 'em go, Dave!" Travis shouted, waving to get the booshway's attention. "They gotta finish it!"

Richard had used the moment to hammer the half-stunned Trudeau in the head again, but the heat from the rock was too much. He dropped it, balled a fist, and round-housed Trudeau in the face. Travis heard the bones in the Frenchman's nose snap. Richard sprawled on Trudeau's chest, hands clamping around the boatman's throat in a stranglehold.

Travis gauged the glaze in Trudeau's blinking eyes, and stepped forward as Trudeau managed to get a grip on Richard's wrists. To keep from being pulled free, Richard sank his teeth into Trudeau's ear. His neck and back strained as he tried to rip it off Trudeau's head.

"Whoa, now, hoss," Travis soothed, bending down. "Ye've got him, hear? Let him up, coon. Ye ain't ready ter kill him. It ain't what I'd figger a feller from Boston wants told in all them fancy houses on Beacon Hill."

Richard froze, muscles still straining, Trudeau's ear stretched tight in blood-stained teeth.

"Dick, damn it! Turn him loose!" Travis snapped. "That, or I'll whack ye a good one!"

Richard turned loose, rolled back on his haunches, then flopped onto his back to spit blood and saliva. He wiped his mouth and lay there, panting. Trudeau shuddered for breath, his mangled right hand going to his bruised throat, the left to his bloody ear.

"*Sacré enfant du grâce!*" whispered one of the *engagés.* "If I did not see, I would not believe!"

"Break it up!" Green ordered, waving his hands like shooing geese. "Go on! Morning comes early. Fun's over for tonight."

Willow had dropped down to one knee and dabbed at the blood running from Richard's nose. He winced at her touch, his half-burned hand cradled on his lap. His eyes had an oddly drained look as he stared at something far, far away, and mumbled, "I'm not a dog . . . not anymore."

Toussaint remained, head cocked, hands on his hips as he studied Trudeau, who lay curled on his side, gasping.

Baptiste gestured. "Come on, Toussaint. Let's get Trudeau down to the river. Reckon a dunking ain't a gonna hurt him none."

They bent down, pulling the blood-spattered boatman to his feet. As they walked off with Trudeau staggering between them, Travis heard Toussaint say, "When did zee little chick learn to fight like zee rooster?"

"Travis?" Green asked, finger flicking back and forth like a blind man's cane. "I take it this is all over?"

"Reckon so, Dave." And Travis couldn't help but smile as if it would break his face in two.

As Green walked off for his tent, he could be heard to mutter, "Massachusetts gentleman? My ass!"

Willow lay in her blankets and stared up into the cloud-black night sky. They'd crossed the Cannonball River the morning before. The French called it *Le Bulet*, for the round stones that littered the bottom of the channel. From what Green told her, the Whites had giant guns that could shoot such huge bullets for as far as a man could see. By now, she knew better than to be skeptical of such fantastic stories.

The first of the birds were chirping in the trees, a sure sign that the morning call of "*Levez! Levez!*" was near. She could hear someone stirring a fire and the sound of metal scraped on metal as the pots were laid out.

Willow turned her head to see Richard. His ghostly face was calm now, but in the night his muted cries had awakened her. Only after she'd reached out and taken his unburned hand had his sleep deepened. She rubbed her thumb over the back of his hand, comforted by the touch.

What dreams had haunted him? Boston, with its lighted windows and all the people dressed in fine cloth? She'd listened to his descriptions, trying to place building after building, some with floors on top of other floors like a human beehive. Did the image conjured in her mind even come close to the way Boston really looked?

All of those women, drowning in layers of fabric until they can barely move. What do they think of, so weighted with cloth, living their whole lives in wooden and rock boxes? Easier to imagine Cannibal Owl swooping over the peaks, looking for anyone who slept in the open, than to imagine living all of one's life inside a box.

She tightened her grip on Richard's hand as she remembered the aftermath of the fight with Trudeau. Like crossing a mountain, it marked a divide that she recognized but could not fully understand. He had fought for more than himself. He had fought for her, and that changed everything.

"I can't believe that was me," Richard kept repeating over and over as she wiped the blood from his face and daubed poultice on his burned hand.

It was you, warrior. Your courage is rising to match the puha *hidden in your souls.*

Someone coughed, one of the *engagés,* and the faint burr of snoring carried on the cool morning. At the river, ducks quacked back in the reeds.

I only wish I could stay to see you find all of yourself.

She shifted onto her hip to see him better. Only here, in the secret gloom of predawn, could she allow the longing in her souls to show. Only now, when no one might witness, could she allow herself to want him until the ache within her finally brought tears.

And that is a lesson for you, Heals Like A Willow. Coyote's lesson. The time to leave has come. For, if you don't, you will slip into his robes some night.

She'd imagined that enough times to know how it would

unfold. His eyes would go wide as her fingers stilled the question on his lips. In the beginning he'd fight weakly, trying to protest as she loosened his clothing with her other hand.

She understood him thoroughly, knew that his protests would drop to a murmured "No" that he'd repeat over and over as she pressed herself against him.

He'd gasp when her fingertips traced around his testicles, and found that sensitive place on the underside of the penis.

Lying here now, separated in the predawn darkness, she could see the expression in his eyes as they joined, the question within his soul struggling against the need of his manhood. Such a vision, as clear as if it had happened moments ago. A trick of the soul's longing. A perfect memory of what would never be, despite the warm aching in her loins.

If only you had asked me to stay, Ritshard.

At that moment, he smiled in his sleep, and mumbled. Mostly it sounded like gibberish, and then he said, "Laura . . . Laura . . ."

The effect was like ice water dashed on a warm body. But then, the world was not a perfect place. Coyote had ensured that just after the Creation.

She said, "I can't be a fool any longer," and gently untangled her fingers from his. She slipped from her blankets and rolled them. Her packs lay where she'd left them, ready for the long journey ahead. One by one, she shouldered them for the short walk to the horses.

At the edge of the trees, she stopped, closed her eyes against the pain, and whispered, "Some canyons are too deep to cross, Ritshard. If our differences are too great even for us, how will your people and mine ever find peace?

"*Tam Apo* bless and keep you safe. May the spirits guide you on your journey back to your Laura, and this Boston."

Then she slipped into the trees, following the trail that led to the horse picket. Her mountains lay many days' ride to the west. Dangers would lurk on all sides, but she would manage to find her way. With any luck the way of the land would prove more kind than the way of the heart.

Like Ritshard, she was going home, to her native land and people. Once there, she would weave the loose strands of her life back together, the way the old stories taught.

She had reached out, and the misty white spirit dog had bitten her. He'd been Coyote after all. And perhaps, somewhere in her distant mountains, she would discover a way to heal this newest wound. After all, she was *Dukurika,* and, for a woman of the People, anything was possible.

In the distance, she could hear a chorus of coyotes as their wailing song rose and fell in the still morning air.

This time, she promised, they weren't singing for her.

SELECTED BIBLIOGRAPHY

Baldwin, Leland D.
  The Keelboat Age on Western Waters. 1941. Reprint. Pittsburgh, PA: University of Pittsburgh Press, 1980.
Billon, Fredric L.
  Annals of Saint Louis in Its Territorial Days from 1804 to 1821. 1888. Reprint. New York: Arno Press and The New York Times, 1971.
Bowers, Alfred W.
  Mandan Social and Ceremonial Organization. Chicago: University of Chicago Press, 1950.
Bradbury, John
  Travels in the Interior of America in the Years 1809, 1810, and 1811. 1819. Reprint of the 1904 Thwaits edition. Lincoln, NE: Bison Books, University of Nebraska Press, 1986.
Brown, Joseph Epes
  The Sacred Pipe: Black Elk's Account of the Seven Rites of the Oglala Sioux. Norman, OK: University of Oklahoma Press, 1953.
Clokey, Richard M.
  William H. Ashley: Enterprise and Politics in the Trans-Mississippi West. Norman, OK: University of Oklahoma Press, 1980.
Denig, Edwin Thompson
  Five Indian Tribes of the Upper Missouri. Norman, OK: University of Oklahoma Press, 1961.
Dominguez, Steve
  "Tukudeka Subsistence: Observations for a Preliminary Model." Unpublished manuscript, 1981.

Dorsey, George A.
   The Mythology of the Wichita. Norman, OK: University of Oklahoma Press, 1995.
Frazer, Robert W.
   Forts of the West. Norman, OK: University of Oklahoma Press, 1965.
Frey, Rodney
   The World of the Crow: As Driftwood Lodges. Norman, OK: University of Oklahoma Press, 1987.
Gale, John
   The Missouri Expedition 1818–1820: The Journal of Surgeon John Gale. Norman, OK: University of Oklahoma Press, 1960.
Garrard, Lewis H.
   Wah-to-yah and the Taos Trail. Norman, OK: University of Oklahoma Press, 1955.
Gilmore, Melvin R.
   Uses of Plants by the Indians of the Missouri River Region. Lincoln, NE: University of Nebraska Press, 1977.
Gowans, Fred R.
   Rocky Mountain Rendezvous. Provo, UT: Brigham Young University Press, 1975.
Fletcher, Alice C., and Francis La Flesche
   The Omaha Tribe. Vols. I and II. Reprint of 1906 Bureau of American Ethnology Report. Lincoln, NE: Bison Books, University of Nebraska Press, 1992.
Hafen, Leory, R.
   Broken Hand: The Life of Thomas Fitzpatrick. 1931. Reprint. Lincoln, NE: Bison Books, University of Nebraska Press, 1973.
Hultkrantz, Ake
   The Religions of the American Indians, trans. Monica Setterwall. Berkeley, CA: University of California Press, 1967.
—— *Native Religions of North America*. San Francisco: Harper & Row, 1987.
—— *Shamanic Healing and Ritual Drama*. New York: Crossroad Publishing Company, 1992.
Hunt, David C., et al.
   Karl Bodmer's America. Lincoln, NE: The Josyln Art Museum and University of Nebraska Press, 1984.

Hyde, George E.
   The Pawnee Indians. Norman, OK: University of Oklahoma Press, 1951.
Klein, Laura F., and Lillian A. Ackerman, eds.
   Women and Power in Native North America. Norman, OK: University of Oklahoma Press, 1995.
Larson, Mary Lou, and Marcel Kornfeld
   "Betwixt and Between the Basin and the Plains: The Limits of Numic Expansion," in *Across the West*, David B. Madson, and David Rhode, eds. Salt Lake City: University of Utah Press, 1994.
Lauer, Quentin
   Phenomenology: Its Genesis and Prospect. 1958. Reprint. New York: Harper Torchbooks, 1965.
Lowie, Robert H.
   The Crow Indians. 1935. Reprint. Lincoln, NE: Bison Books, University of Nebraska Press, 1963.
Luttig, John C.
   Journal of a Fur Trading Expedition on the Upper Missouri. 1920. Reprint. New York: Argosy-Antiquarian, Ltd., 1964.
Meyer, Roy W.
   The Village Indians of the Upper Missouri. Lincoln, NE: University of Nebraska Press, 1977.
Miller, Wick R.
   Newe Natekwinappeh: Shoshoni Stories and Dictionary, Salt Lake City: University of Utah Anthropological Papers, No. 94, University of Utah Press, 1972.
Moore, Michael
   Medicinal Plants of the Mountain West. Sante Fe, NM: Museum of New Mexico Press, 1979.
Morgan, Dale L.
   Jedediah Smith and the Opening of the West. Lincoln, NE: University of Nebraska Press, 1953.
Moulton, Gary E., ed.
   The Journals of the Lewis and Clark Expedition. Vols. II and III. Lincoln, NE: University of Nebraska Press, 1986.
Nute, Grace Lee
   The Voyageur. 1931. Reprint. St. Paul, MN: Minnesota Historical Society, 1955.

Oglesby, Richard Edward
  Manuel Lisa and the Opening of the Missouri Fur Trade.
  Norman, OK: University of Oklahoma Press, 1963.
Powers, William K.
  *Sacred Language: The Nature of Supernatural Discourse
  in Lakota.* Norman, OK: University of Oklahoma Press,
  1986.
Primm, James Neal
  Lion of the Valley: St. Louis, Missouri. Boulder, CO:
  Pruett Press, 1981.
Rogers, Daniel J.
  *Objects of Change, the Archaeology and History of Ari-
  kara Contact with Europeans.* Washington, DC: Smith-
  sonian Institute Press, 1990.
Ruxton, George F.
  *Life in the Far West Among the Indians and the Mountain
  Men. 1846–1847.* 1849. Reprint. Glorietta, NM: Rio
  Grande Press, 1972.
Schlesier, Karl H.
  Plains Indians, A.D. 500–1500. Norman, OK: University
  of Oklahoma Press, 1994.
Shimkin, Dimitri B.
  Wind River Shoshone Ethnogeography. Berkeley, CA:
  University of California Anthropological Records, No. 5
  (4), 1949.
Smith, Anne M.
  Shoshone Tales. Salt Lake City: University of Utah Press,
  1993.
Steffen, Jerome O.
  William Clark, Jeffersonian Man on the Frontier. Nor-
  man, OK: University of Oklahoma Press, 1977.
Stimson, Charles Jr. and J.H.A. Frost
  Boston Directory. 1820. Boston: John H.A. Frost and
  Charles Stimson Publishers.
Thomas, David, and Karin Ronnefeldt, eds.
  People of the First Man. New York: E. P. Dutton, 1976.
Trenholm, Virginia Cole, and Maurine Carley
  The Shoshonis: Sentinels of the Rockies. Norman, OK:
  University of Oklahoma Press, 1964.

WarCloud, Paul
   Sioux Indian Dictionary. Sissiton, SD: Paul WarCloud, 1971.
Weeks, Rupert
   Pachee Goyo: History and Legends from the Shoshone. Laramie, WY: Jelm Mountain Press, 1981.
Weltfish, Gene
   The Lost Universe: Pawnee Life and Culture. 1965. Reprint. Lincoln, NE: Bison Books, University of Nebraska Press, 1977.

Available by mail from

TOR FORGE

1812 • David Nevin
The War of 1812 would either make America a global power sweeping to the pacific or break it into small pieces bound to mighty England. Only the courage of James Madison, Andrew Jackson, and their wives could determine the nation's fate.

PRIDE OF LIONS • Morgan Llywelyn
Pride of Lions, the sequel to the immensely popular *Lion of Ireland*, is a stunningly realistic novel of the dreams and bloodshed, passion and treachery, of eleventh-century Ireland and its lusty people.

WALTZING IN RAGTIME • Eileen Charbonneau
The daughter of a lumber baron is struggling to make it as a journalist in turn-of-the-century San Francisco when she meets ranger Matthew Hart, whose passion for nature challenges her deepest held beliefs.

BUFFALO SOLDIERS • Tom Willard
Former slaves had proven they could fight valiantly for their freedom, but in the West they were to fight for the freedom and security of the white settlers who often despised them.

THIN MOON AND COLD MIST • Kathleen O'Neal Gear
Robin Heatherton, a spy for the Confederacy, flees with her son to the Colorado Territory, hoping to escape from Union Army Major Corley, obsessed with her ever since her espionage work led to the death of his brother.

SEMINOLE SONG • Vella Munn
"As the U.S. Army surrounds their reservation in the Florida Everglades, a Seminole warrior chief clings to the slave girl who once saved his life after fleeing from her master, a wife-murderer who is out for blood." —*Hot Picks*

THE OVERLAND TRAIL • Wendi Lee
Based on the authentic diaries of the women who crossed the country in the late 1840s. America, a widowed pioneer, and Dancing Feather, a young Paiute, set out to recover America's kidnapped infant daughter—and to forge a bridge between their two worlds.

Call toll-free 1-800-288-2131 to use your major credit card or clip and send this form below to order by mail

- ✂

Send to: Publishers Book and Audio Mailing Service
PO Box 120159, Staten Island, NY 10312-0004

☐ 52471-3	**1812** .... $6.99/$8.99	☐ 53657-6	**Thin Moon and Cold Mist** .... $6.99/$8.99
☐ 53650-9	**Pride of Lions** .... $6.99/$8.99	☐ 53883-8	**Seminole Song** .... $5.99/$7.99
☐ 54468-4	**Waltzing In Ragtime** .... $6.99/$8.99	☐ 55528-7	**The Overland Trail** .... $5.99/$7.99
☐ 55105-2	**Buffalo Soldiers** .... $5.99/$7.99		

Please send me the following books checked above. I am enclosing $_____ . (Please add $1.50 for the first book, and 50¢ for each additional book to cover postage and handling. Send check or money order only—no CODs).

Name _____

Address _____ City _____ State _____ Zip _____

Available by mail from

TOR • FORGE

THIN MOON AND COLD MIST • Kathleen O'Neal Gear
Robin Heatherton, a spy for the Confederacy, flees with her son to the Colorado Territory, hoping to escape from Union Army Major Corley, obsessed with her ever since her espionage work led to the death of his brother.

SOFIA • Ann Chamberlin
Sofia, the daughter of a Venetian nobleman, is kidnapped and sold into captivity of the great Ottoman Empire. Manipulative and ambitious, Sofia vows that her future will hold more than sexual slavery in the Sultan's harem. A novel rich in passion, history, humor, and human experience, *Sofia* transports the reader to sixteenth-century Turkish harem life.

MIRAGE • Soheir Khashoggi
"A riveting first novel.... Exotic settings, glamorous characters, and a fast-moving plot. Like a modern Scheherazade, Khashoggi spins an irresistible tale.... An intelligent page-turner." —*Kirkus Reviews*

DEATH COMES AS EPIPHANY • Sharan Newman
In medieval Paris, amid stolen gems, mad monks, and dead bodies, Catherine LeVendeur will strive to unlock a puzzle that threatens all she holds dear. "Breathtakingly exciting." —*Los Angeles Times*

SHARDS OF EMPIRE • Susan Shwartz
A rich tale of madness and magic—"*Shards of Empire* is a beautifully written historical.... An original and witty delight!" —*Locus*

SCANDAL • Joanna Elm
When former talk show diva Marina Dee Haley is found dead, TV tabloid reporter Kitty Fitzgerald is compelled to break open the "Murder of the Century," even if it means exposing her own dubious past.

BILLY THE KID • Elizabeth Fackler
Billy's story, epic in scope, echoes the vast grandeur of the magnificent country in which he lived. It traces the chain of events that inexorably shaped this legendary outlaw and pitted him against a treacherous society that threatened those he loved."
